A Copper Mountain
Christmas

Jane Porter
Katherine Garbera
Melissa McClone

Contents

Christmas At Copper Mountain
a copper mountain christmas novella

Jane Porter

Dedication

For my incredible readers and the wonderful women on the Jane Porter and Montana Born Street Teams. You all make writing a joy. This story is for you!

Contents

Chapter One

Harley Diekerhoff looked up from peeling potatoes to glance out the kitchen window.

It was still snowing... even harder than it had been this morning.

So much white, it dazzled.

Hands still, breath catching, she watched the thick, white flakes blow past the ranch house at a dizzying pace, enthralled by the flurry of the lacy snowflakes.

So beautiful. Magical A mysterious silent ballet in all white, the snow swirling, twirling just like it did in her favorite scene from the Nutcracker—the one with the Snow Queen and her breathtaking corps in their white tutus with their precision and speed—and then that dazzling snow at the end, the delicate flakes powdering the stage.

Harley's chest ached. She gripped the peeler more tightly, and focused on her breathing.

She didn't want to remember.

She wasn't going to remember.

Wasn't going to go there, not now, not today. Not when she had six hungry men to feed in a little over two hours. She picked up a potato, started peeling.

She'd come to Montana to work. She'd taken the temporary job at Copper Mountain Ranch to get some distance from her family this Christmas, and working on the Paradise Valley cattle ranch would give her new memories.

Like the snow piling up outside the window.

She'd never lived in a place that snowed like this. Where she came from in Central California, they didn't have snow, they had fog. Thick soupy Tule fog that blanketed the entire valley, socking in airports, making driving nearly impossible. And on the nights when the fog lifted and temperatures dropped beneath the cold clear sky, the citrus growers rushed to light smudge pots to protect their valuable, vulnerable orange crops.

11

Her family didn't grow oranges. Her family were Dutch dairy people. Harley had been raised on a big dairy farm in Visalia, and she'd marry a dairyman in college, and they'd had their own dairy, too.

But that's the part she needed to forget.

That's why she'd come to Montana, with its jagged mountains and rugged river valleys and long cold winters.

She'd arrived here the Sunday following Thanksgiving and would work through mid-January, when Brock Sheenan's housekeeper returned from a personal leave of absence.

In January, Harley would either return to California or look for another job in Crawford County. Harley was tempted to stay, as the Bozeman employment agency assured her they'd have no problem finding her a permanent position if she wanted one. So far she liked everything about her job on the isolated ranch, from the icy, biting wind that howled beyond the ranch's thick log cabin walls, to the cooking, cleaning, and laundry required.

The physicality of the work was exactly what her mind and body needed. It was good to lift, bend, carry, mop, sweep, dust, fold. The harder she worked, the better she felt, and today, for the first time in years, she actually felt almost....

Happy.

Harley paused, brows knitting in surprise.

Almost happy.

Wow.

That was huge. Almost happy was significant. Almost happy gave her hope that one day she would feel more again, and be more again, and life wouldn't be so bleak and cold.

Because it had been bleak.

It'd been....

She shook her head, brushed off the little peel clinging to her thumb and grabbed the last potato, swiftly peeling it, clearing her mind of everything but the task at hand, concentrating on the texture of the wet potato, the cool water in the sink, the quick motion of the peeler, the dazzling white flurries at the window, and the crackle of the fire behind her.

She liked being here. It was good being here. This wasn't her house and yet in just one week it felt like home.

She enjoyed this kitchen with its golden, hand-planed

pine cabinets, wide-planked hardwood floor, and the corner fireplace rimmed in local rock from the Yellowstone River. She loved how the rustic exterior of the sprawling two-story cabin hid the large, comfortable, efficient kitchen and the adjacent over-sized laundry room with its two sets of washers and dryers... to handle feeding and looking after, not just Brock Sheenan, owner of Copper Mountain Ranch, but the hired hands who worked for Brock and lived in the bunk house behind the barn.

In winter the ranch hands didn't leave the property much during the week. The work was too grueling, the nights fell early, and driving at night could be treacherous on the windy, icy mountain road, so Monday through Friday Brock provided dinners for his five men, and clean, dry clothes, too. Come weekend, they were on their own, but Harley wouldn't have minded cooking for extra mouths seven days a week.

The isolation of Copper Mountain Ranch, tucked back in the Absarokas, higher than the typical Paradise Valley ranch, might have scared off other job applicants, but not her. She didn't mind the severe weather or Brock Sheenan's brusqueness—and she'd been warned about that in advance—but she was okay with a silent, gruff boss. She didn't come to Marietta, Montana looking for friendship. Like Brock himself, she didn't need conversation and company. She was here to work, and she preferred being left alone.

The employment agency liked her attitude. They said she was perfect for the temp job and filled her in on the Sheenans, one of the bigger, more prominent families that had settled in Paradise Valley around the turn of the century. She'd be working for Brock Sheenan, the oldest of the five Sheenan sons. Brock had bought Copper Mountain Ranch to get away from his dad, which had caused some bad blood within the family, but he'd wanted his own place, and had designed the two-story log cabin himself, helping build it as a wedding present for his bride.

But tragedy struck a year and a half into their marriage, when Brock's wife Amy was killed in a horrific car crash on one of the twisting mountain roads. Devastated, Brock disappeared into his ranch, becoming almost reclusive after that.

The employment agency had shared the details with her, asking for her confidence. But they thought it was important she understand that Brock Sheenan had a... reputation... for being eccentric. He didn't need people the way others did, and he'd been quite specific in his desire for a tidy, professional, and disciplined housekeeper. He wouldn't tolerate lazy and he couldn't abide chatty. He needed a quiet, orderly house, and he liked things done his way.

Harley didn't have a problem with that. She was quiet too, and this year she'd been determined to avoid the holidays, and had deliberately chosen to go away for December, needing to escape her big California family that celebrated Christmas with endless activity, festivities, and fuss.

She loved all her nieces and nephews but this Christmas she didn't want to be around kids. Because this year she wasn't celebrating Christmas. This year there wasn't going to be a tree or trimmings, no stockings, or brightly wrapped toys.

Eyes hot, chest burning, she scooped up the mountain of wet potato scraps, when a deep, rough male voice startled her.

"You okay, Miss Diekerhoff?"

Turning quickly, potato skins still dripping, Harley blinked back tears as she spotted Brock Sheenan standing by the fireplace, warming his hands.

Brock was a big man. He was tall—six one or two—with broad shoulders, a wide muscular chest, and shaggy black hair.

Harley's late husband, David, was Portuguese and darkly handsome, but David was always groomed and polished while the Montana rancher seemed disinclined to comb his hair, or bother with a morning shave.

The truth was, Brock Sheenan looked like a pirate, and never more so than now, with tiny snowflakes clinging to his wild hair and shadowed jaw.

"I'm fine," she said breathlessly, embarrassed. "I didn't hear you come in."

"The faucet was on." He rubbed his hands together, the skin red and raw. "You're not... crying... are you?"

She heard the uncomfortable note in his voice and cringed a little. "No," she said quickly, straightening and squaring her shoulders as she dumped the potato peels into the garbage. "Everything's wonderful."

"So you're not crying?"

"No," she repeated crisply, drying her hands. "Just peeling potatoes for dinner."

Her gaze swept his big frame, seeing the powdered snow still clinging to the hem of his Wrangler jeans that peeked beneath leather chaps and white glitter dusting his black brows. His supple leather chaps weren't for show. It was frigid outside and he'd spent the week in the saddle, driving the last herds of cattle from the back country to the valley below so they could take shelter beneath trees. "Can I get you something?"

"You don't happen to have any coffee left from this morning that you could heat up?"

"I can make a fresh pot," she said, grabbing the glass carafe to fill it with water. "Want regular or decaf?"

He glanced at the clock mounted on the wall above the door and then out the window where the snow flurries were thickening, making it almost impossible to see the tall pine trees marking one corner of the yard. "Leaded," he said. "Make it strong, too. It's going to be a late night for me."

She added the coffee grounds, and then hit the brew button. "You're heading back out?"

"I'm going to ride back up as soon as I get something warm in me. Thought I'd take some of the breakfast coffee cake with me. If there was anything left."

"There is." She'd already wrapped the remaining slices in foil. He wasn't one to linger over meals, and he didn't like asking for snacks between meals, either. If he wanted something now, it meant he wouldn't be back anytime soon. But it was already after four. It'd be dark within the hour. "It's snowing hard."

"I won't be able to sleep tonight if I don't do a last check. The boys said we've got them all but I keep thinking we're missing one or two of the young ones. Have to be sure before I call it a night."

Harley reached into a cupboard for one of the thermoses she sent with Brock on his early mornings. "What time will you want dinner?"

"Don't know when I'll be back. Could be fairly late, so

just leave a plate in the oven for me. No need for you to stay up." He bundled his big arms across his even bigger chest, a lock of thick black hair falling down over his forehead to shadow an equally dark eye.

There was nothing friendly or approachable about Brock when he stood like that. His wild black hair, square jaw, and dark piercing gaze that gave him a slightly threatening air, but Harley knew better. Men, even the most dangerous men, were still mortal. They had goals, dreams, needs. They tried, they failed. They made mistakes. Fatal mistakes.

"Any of the boys going with you?" she asked, trying to sound casual as she wrapped a generous wedge of cheddar cheese in foil, and a hunk of the summer sausage he liked, so he'd have something more substantial than coffee cake for his ride.

He shook his head, then dragged a large calloused hand through the glossy black strands in a half-hearted attempt to comb the tangled strands smooth. "No."

She gave him a swift, troubled look.

He shrugged. "No point in putting the others in harm's way."

Her frown deepened. "What if you get into trouble?"

"I won't."

She arched her brows.

He gave her a quelling look.

She ought to be intimidated by this shaggy beast of a man, but she wasn't. She'd had a husband—a daring, risk-taking husband of her own—and his lapse in judgment had cost them all. Dearly.

"It's dangerous out there," she said quietly. "You shouldn't go alone. They invented the buddy system for a reason."

One of Brock's black eyebrows shot up. "The buddy system."

She ignored the mockery in his dark, deep voice. His voice always surprised her, in part because it was so deep and husky that it vibrated in his chest, making her think of strong, potent drink and shadowy attics and moonlit bedrooms, but also because until now, he'd never said more than a couple of sentences to her.

16

He wasn't a big talker. But then, he wasn't in the house much. Brock spent most of his time outdoors working, and when he was inside, he sat at his desk, poring over accounting books and papers, or by the fire in the family room reading.

Maybe that's what made her so comfortable here. The silence.

The dearth of conversation. The lack of argument. The absence of tension.

She needed the solitude of the Copper Mountain Ranch. She needed the quiet. The quiet was a balm to her soul. It sounded dreadful put like that. Corny as well as pathetic, but the loss of everything she knew, and everything she was, had changed her. Broken her. All she could do now was continue to mend. Eventually she'd be able to cope with noise and chaos and families again, but not yet. Not for a long, long time.

"I'm sure you've heard of the buddy system," she said flatly. "It's practiced by virtually everyone... including the Boy Scouts."

He gave her another long look, his dark gaze resting on her as if she were a bit peculiar.

Right now, she felt a bit peculiar.

It would help if he stopped staring at her so hard. His intense scrutiny was making her overly warm, and a little bit dizzy.

"I was never a Boy Scout," he rasped.

Looking at his long shaggy black hair and shadowed jaw, she could believe it. "You're missing the point."

"I get your point." He stalked toward her, his dark gazing holding hers, his jaw hard.

Panicked, she stepped back, and again, as he stepped close, his big body brushing hers as he reached into the cabinet for a mug. "But I'm not a little boy," he added, glancing at her from beneath his thick black lashes, a warning in his dark eyes, "and don't need coddling."

Energy surged through Harley, a hot sharp electric current that made her heart race and her stomach fall. Legs weak, she took another step sideways, increasing the distance between them. "Obviously you're not a child."

He grabbed the pot of coffee, interrupting the brewing cycle to fill his cup. "Then don't treat me like one."

Her heart continued to pound. She wasn't scared but she definitely was... bothered.

Harley bit down on the inside of her cheek, holding back her first angry retort, aware that the kitchen, peaceful until just minutes ago, now crackled with tension.

"You don't think I should worry about you?" she asked, arms folding across her chest so he couldn't see that her hands were trembling.

"It's not your job to worry about me."

"No, I'm just to worry about your boxers and your stomach," she retorted.

He arched an eyebrow. "Is that appropriate, Miss Diekerhoff?"

His scathing tone made her flush and look away. She bit down on her cheek again, appalled that she was losing her cool now, and counted to ten. She rarely lost her temper but she was mad. Somehow he'd struck a nerve in her... had gotten under her skin.

When she was sure she could speak calmly she managed a terse apology. "I'm sorry. That wasn't appropriate." Then she set the thermos down on the counter—hard, harder than she intended, and the crack of metal against granite sent a loud echo through the kitchen "And you are right. What you do is none of my concern, so go out in the storm, in the dark, all by yourself. As long as I'm getting paid, I won't give it a second thought."

Heart still racing, she fled the kitchen for the adjoining mudroom to move the laundry forward. Tears burned the back of her eyes and she was breathing hard and she didn't even know why she was so upset, only that she was.

She was furious.

Stupid meathead of a man, thinking he was immortal, invincible, that nothing bad could happen...

Swallowing the curses she wouldn't let herself utter aloud, Harley shoved the tangle of heavy, wet jeans and cords from the washer into the dryer.

But testosterone didn't make a man immortal.

Just daring. Risky.

Foolish.

Her chest ached, the pressure on her heart horrendous. If

David hadn't been so confident. If David hadn't been such a proud man. If David….

"What's the matter with you?" Brock demanded, filling the laundry room doorway as if it were a sliver of space instead of forty inches wide by eight feet tall. "You're acting like a crazy lady."

Harley jammed the wet clothes into the dryer so hard she slammed her wrist bone on the round barrel opening, sending pain shooting up her arm.

Tears started to her eyes. Worry and regret flooded her. Worry for Brock, and regret that she'd said too much. She wasn't here to talk. She was here to work. She knew that. "I'm not crazy," she retorted huskily, rubbing the tender spot on her wrist. "Don't call me crazy."

"You're behaving in a completely irrational—"

"It's a blizzard outside, Mr. Sheenan. And I was merely asking you to take precautions when you headed back out, and if that makes me crazy, then so be it. I am crazy. Make that a lunatic."

His black eyebrows flattened and he looked at her so long it crossed her mind that she'd said far too much, pushed too hard, perhaps even lost her job.

And then his dark eyes glimmered and the corner of his mouth lifted faintly. "A lunatic?"

There was something in the way he repeated his words that made her want to smile.

Or maybe it was the shadow in his eyes that looked almost like amusement.

Or that very slight lift of his firm lips.

He seemed to be fighting a smile. Could it be?

If so, it was the closest she'd ever come to seeing him smile. Brock was a serious man. The agency said the death of his wife had changed him.

She understood. It'd been three years since the accident, and she still grieved for David and her children.

Her desire to smile faded. Her heart burned. She opened her mouth to speak but no words came out.

But then, there were no words.

The pain had been unspeakable.

She closed her eyes, held her breath, holding the agony

in, and then she found her strength, and exhaled, and met her employer's shuttered gaze.

"Let me fill your thermos," she said unsteadily. "I've got some snacks for your saddlebag, too. Obviously you don't have to take them. It's entirely up to you."

He leaned against the doorframe, blocking her exit. "You're even more bossy than my last housekeeper, and yet you're just half her age. I don't want to know you in twenty years."

And just like that he brought her back to reality. Who they were. Why she was here. His temporary housekeeper.

Harley managed a tight smile. "Good. You won't have to know me in twenty years, because I'm only here until January thirteenth." She looked up at him, expression blank. "And if you don't return tonight, then I suppose I'm free tomorrow." She motioned for him to move, with an impatient gesture of her finger. "Now if you'd please move, I have work to do."

Brock didn't know if he should throttle his bossy, imperious housekeeper or fire her.

He ought to fire her. Right here, right now. She wasn't the right woman for the job. Wasn't the right woman for him.

He swallowed hard, biting back the sharp retort as he stared down into his housekeeper's startling green eyes.

What the hell was he doing with a beautiful woman for a housekeeper?

Harley Diekerhoff was not supposed to be attractive.

The name wasn't attractive. The name conjured visions of a stout, strong woman with massive forearms and a sprinkling of dark hair above a thin pale lip.

Or so he'd imagined when the temp employment agency had given him her file as the best possible candidate for the six-week position as housekeeper and cook for his ranch.

He'd wanted a stout woman with massive forearms and a hairy upper lip. He'd been confident he'd hired one.

Instead Harley Diekerhoff was beautiful, and young, and probably the best housekeeper he'd ever had.

It pissed him off.

He didn't want a stunning thirty-four-year-old with hauntingly high cheekbones and eyebrows that arched and turned into wings, making him want to look into her cool green eyes again and again.

He didn't want a housekeeper with a wide full-lipped mouth, creamy skin, and thick hair the color of rich, decadent caramel.

And he most certainly didn't want a housekeeper with curves, endless curves, curves that did nothing but tease his control and inflame his imagination.

His jaw tightened. He battled his temper. "Don't get too carried away," he said curtly. "I'll be back tonight. You'll still have a job to do in the morning."

Her tawny eyebrows arched even higher. Her long ponytail slipped over her shoulder. "Good, because I like the job. It's just—" she broke off, lips compressing, swallowing the words.

"What?" he demanded.

She shook her head, white teeth pinching her plump lower lip.

He tried not to focus on the way her teeth squeezed the soft lip. He didn't want to focus on her at all. "What?" he repeated.

She sighed and glanced down at her hands. "Nothing," she said quietly.

He said nothing.

She sighed again, twisted her hands. "I like it here," she added. "And I like you. So just be careful. That's all."

He stared at her, perplexed.

She was nothing like Maxine, his housekeeper of the past nine years. Maxine didn't laugh or smile or cry. She arrived every morning, did her work, and then left every night when her husband came to pick her up.

Maxine was silent and sober and moved through the house as if invisible.

Harley moved through the house as if a beacon shone on her. She practically glowed, bathed with light.

He didn't understand how she did it, or what she did, only that from the moment she'd arrived seven days ago nothing in this house had been the same.

Suddenly aware that they were standing so close he could smell the scent of her shampoo—something sweet and floral, freesia or orange blossom and entirely foreign in his masculine house—he abruptly stepped back, letting her pass.

His gaze followed her as she crossed the kitchen, hating himself for noticing how the apron around her waist emphasized how small it was as well as the gentle swell of hips. "Just leave my dinner in the oven," he said.

"If that's what you want," she said, reaching for the coffee pot to fill his thermos.

"That's what I want," he growled, looking away, unable to watch her a moment longer because just having her in his house made him feel things he didn't want to feel.

Like desire.

And hunger.

Lust.

He didn't lust. Not anymore. Maybe when he was a kid, young and randy with testosterone, he battled with control, but he didn't battle for control, not at thirty-nine.

At least, he hadn't battled for control in years.

But he was struggling now, inexplicably drawn to this temporary housekeeper who looked so fresh and wholesome in her olive green apron with its sprigs of holly berries that he wanted to touch her. Kiss her. Taste her.

And that was just plain wrong.

He ground his teeth together, held his breath, and cursed the employment agency for sending him a sexy housekeeper.

She walked toward him, held out the filled thermos and foil-wrapped packets of cheese sausage and coffee cake. "Be careful."

He glanced down at her, seeing but not wanting to see how her apron outlined her shape. Hips, full breasts, and a tiny waist he could circle with two hands. Even with her hideous apron strings wrapped twice around her waist.

Aprons were supposed to hide the body. Her apron just emphasized her curves. And olive was such a drab color but somehow it made her eyes look mysterious and cool and green and her lips dark pink and her skin—

"I'm always careful," he ground out, taking the thermos and foil packages from her, annoyed all over again.

He was a man about to turn forty and he'd spent the past eleven years raising two kids on his own, and he might not be a perfect father or a perfect man but he tried his best. He did.

And while he appreciated his new housekeeper's concern, he didn't have time to be babied, and he certainly wasn't about to explain himself. Not to his brothers, his dad, and especially not to a staggeringly pretty woman from California who was now living in his house, under his roof, bending and leaning and doing all sorts of things with her incredibly appealing body, all the while humming as she went about her work as if she were Snow White or Mary Poppins.

Most annoying to have a beautiful housekeeper. He would never have hired her if he'd realized she was so damn pretty. He didn't want pretty in his house. He didn't want to be tempted. He had a ranch to manage and two children who would be home from boarding school for their holidays in another week and he couldn't afford to get distracted by a pretty face or a shapely body.

His gaze narrowed as it swept Harley Diekerhoff's long, lean legs and gently rounded hips before skimming her small waist, then lifting to her face. "Always careful," he repeated, and stalked out through the kitchen door to the back porch.

Harley Diekerhoff might be a perfect cook and housekeeper, but she was also a temptation, and that was a problem he didn't need.

Chapter Two

Harley rang the bell at six o'clock to let the ranch hands know dinner was ready. Brock had trained his hands to come to the main kitchen to help carry their dinner to the bunkhouse. One by one she handed off the various dishes—the platter of sliced flank steak, a substantial casserole of cheesy potato gratin, two loaves of warm buttered French bread, a bowl of green beans with almonds and bacon, a hefty green salad, and an enormous chocolate sheet cake with a gallon of milk for dessert.

Bundled in her winter coat and mittens, she followed the parade of ranch hands through the swirling snow, careful not to drop the oversized sheet cake with its thick chocolate icing. Brock said the hands didn't need dessert every night. She disagreed. A man always needed something sweet before bed. Made a man feel cared for.

At least that's how she'd been raised.

Young Lewis Dilford, one of the newer hands, held the bunk house's front door open for her. She stomped her fleece-lined all-weather boots on the mat, knocking off snow before stepping into the bunkhouse. A fire burned hotly in the cast iron stove in the corner.

The bunk house was actually the original log cabin on the property, and on her first day at Copper Mountain Ranch, JB, Brock's ranch foreman, gave Harley a tour of the outbuildings, including a walk through the bunk house.

JB told her that when Brock had bought the ranch thirteen years ago his plan had been to tear the old log cabin down and salvage the logs for a future project, but when he discovered that the walls and flooring were still sound, and all the cabin really needed was a new roof and some modernizing, he gutted the one-bedroom cabin, adding electricity and plumbing, a small indoor bathroom, and a working kitchen.

With the exception of some of the electrical work, Brock had done all the remodeling himself. It'd taken him a year to complete the bunk house, but he liked being busy, and it gave him something to do during the summers with the longer days of sunlight.

She glanced around the main room which was both sitting room and dining room. Chairs were pushed back against the wall and the pine dining table was already set.

"It looks nice," she said, complimenting their efforts to make the table look nice with the tablecloth she'd given them.

Her first two nights here they'd ignored the table cloth she'd brought them. Apparently Maxine didn't care if they used a tablecloth or placemats.

Some of the men weren't sure they needed to use fancy stuff like table cloths, either. But Harley said it just might make dinner a little nicer, and while she couldn't make them use a table cloth, it was their dinner, after all, and they ought to enjoy themselves. Feel good about themselves.

The next night she entered the bunkhouse and found the table covered with the cloth and five place settings of silverware and plates.

She didn't say anything. She didn't have to. They were watching her face and her quick surprised smile told them everything they needed to know. Since then they used the table cloth every night, and lately, they all washed up and combed their hair, too.

The lost boys of Copper Mountain, she thought, smiling a little as she looked at them now.

"I hope you are hungry," she said, placing the cake and the milk on the table next to all the other dishes filling the center of the table. Maxine used to leave all the food on the buffet, but Harley put everything on the table so the men could stay seated and serve themselves family style. "I think I made too much."

Lewis smiled shyly as he took a seat on one of the benches. "Can never have too much, Miss Harley."

She smiled back, aware that he was the youngest in a family of seven, and from what she'd gathered, there hadn't always been enough to eat by the time it was his turn. "Don't worry about bringing the dishes back tonight. Leave them in your sink and I'll get them in the morning."

"That's not the deal, Miss Harley, and you know it," thin,

dark bearded Al Mancetti said, boots thudding as he sat down opposite Lewis. He'd been here on the ranch for about five years now and tended to be on the quiet side, but apparently he was one of the hardest workers. "We'll bring everything back. You done enough. And we're grateful. You take care of us real well."

"It's my pleasure," she answered with a smile. She liked these men. She enjoyed taking care of them. They appreciated her and that felt good, too. Normally she left after they had everything but tonight she lingered, mustering the courage to bring up her concerns about their boss. "It's bad outside," she said after a moment.

"Yes, ma'am," JB answered, from his spot at the head of the table. "Biggest storm of the year so far. Four feet in the last couple hours alone."

That wasn't reassuring at all, she thought. "Mr. Sheenan's out there."

"Yes, ma'am," JB agreed.

She glanced out the window at the dark night with the luminous snow reflecting ghostly white beyond the window. "He shouldn't have gone alone."

"He shouldn't have gone at all," JB agreed, "but you don't tell him that."

Her brows knit. "Shouldn't someone go look for him?"

JB grimaced. "He'd have our heads for that, and I like my head where it is, on my shoulders."

A guffaw of masculine laughter sounded around the table, and even Harley smiled faintly before her smile faded. "He could be in trouble," she said hesitantly.

"Sheenan can take of himself," Paul, the youngest hand said. He was close friends with Lewis and when they weren't on the ranch, they competed on the rodeo circuit, traveling together whenever possible. Neither of them made good money on the circuit though, so they needed their jobs here on Copper Mountain Ranch to pay bills. "Nobody would mess with him. At least nobody in his right mind."

Heads nodded and Harley glanced at the faces of the ranch hands.

"What about bears?" she asked.

"What about them?" Paul retorted, leaning across the

table to stab his fork into the sliced steak. "It's winter. They're hibernating."

"And wolves?"

"Sheenan has a gun."

Harley's lips pursed, even more alarmed.

Paul and Lewis laughed.

"Don't you worry, Miss Harley," JB said, using the nickname the hands had given her as Miss Diekerhoff was apparently too much of a mouthful, requiring too much effort. "The boss grew up in this part of Montana. He knows what he's doing, and he'll be back before bedtime. Nine or ten and he'll be safe in his bed. Mark my words."

Harley returned to the house and ate her dinner at the oversized island counter that filled the center of the kitchen, the fire warming her back, somewhat soothed by JB's assurance that their boss would be back by nine or ten.

But nine came and went, with no sign of Brock.

And then ten came, and still no sign of him.

Harley dimmed the downstairs lights before heading up to her room, which would be a third floor room if there was a real floor. Instead it was a room carved out from beneath the massive wood beams of the steeply sloping roof. The walls were all lined with planks of weathered, recycled wood—boards taken from old Montana barns—and her bed sat between two low antique chests with matching antique brass lamps. The bed linens were a neutral taupe on cream stripe, which added the rustic feel. The only real color was the deep crimson wool carpet on the hardwood floor. The pop of red made Harley smile, but tonight as she climbed into bed, she didn't feel much like smiling.

It was hard to relax and fall asleep with knots in her stomach. She knew too well that accidents happened, and even smart, strong people could be overly confident of their skills. How could she sleep, picturing Brock lying buried in the snow, slowly freezing to death?

As her bedside clock showed eleven, Harley wondered if she should call the police, or maybe someone in Brock's family.

His father wasn't that far, another ranch twenty minutes south in Paradise Valley, and he had four brothers, although none lived in the area at the moment. But surely one of them would want to know that Brock was missing.

Surely something should be done.

She left bed to pace her room, a long black oversized cashmere sweater around her shoulders for warmth, with the antique wool carpet soft beneath her bare feet.

She was still pacing when she heard an engine outside. A truck was approaching the house. As she headed for the window, bright headlight beams pierced the crack in her curtains, sending an arc of white light across her dark bedroom.

Someone was here.

She pushed aside the curtain, and peered down. A big four-by-four truck with snow tires pulled into the circular drive in front of the house. The truck parked, headlights turned off.

She watched as the driver's door opened, and then the passenger door, too. A man with fair hair wearing a heavy sheepskin coat stepped down from the driver's side of the truck and two children climbed more slowly from the passenger side. All three tramped through the thick snow that had piled up since she shoveled the walkway late in the afternoon.

It was after eleven at night. Who would be arriving now? And with kids?

Harley was at the top of the second floor landing when the doorbell rang.

Downstairs, she opened the door, and blinked at the bite of cold wind. It'd stopped snowing hours ago but tiny flakes swirled and trembled around them as the frigid gust of air sent the powdery snow tumbling from the trees to the ground.

"Can I help you?" she asked, pulling her sweater closer to her body as she glanced from the blond man to the two children at his side. The children, dressed in school uniforms, looked half-frozen without proper winter coats, their navy wool blazers with the red and gold school insignia on the chest, inadequate for the low Montana temperature.

"I'm Sheriff O'Dell," the man said, introducing himself, before pointing to the kids. "These two look familiar?"

Harley glanced down at the two pre-adolescents, the boy with dark hair, the girl's a light reddish brown. Both of their pale faces were lightly freckled. "No," she said, confused. "Should they?"

The sheriff frowned. "They say they belong here."

The girl rolled her eyes. "We *live* here." She pushed past Harley to enter the house, her back pack knocking the door wide open. "Where's Dad?"

"Dad?" Harley repeated, hugging the wall, watching the boy follow the girl in.

"Yes, Dad," the girl replied, glaring at Harley. "Brock Sheenan. Heard of him?"

Harley blinked, taken aback. "Uh, yes. Of course. I'm his housekeeper—"

"Where's Maxine?" the girl interrupted. "Don't tell me Dad got rid of Maxine?"

"No," Harley answered, bundling her arms across her chest, shocked, chilled, unable to process that Brock had kids. He'd never once mentioned kids to her. "She took a personal leave but will be back in January."

"Good." The girl's narrowed gaze swept Harley. "'Cause for a minute there I thought Dad had a girlfriend."

Harley stared at the girl, absolutely blindsided. "And you are...?"

"Molly," the girl said promptly. "And that's Mack."

"We're twins," Mack said, giving Harley a shy smile as he set his back pack down in the hall. "Don't mind Molly. She was just born this way."

"Shut up, Lady Gaga," Molly retorted, punching the boy's shoulder, but it wasn't very hard. "And I got us home. You didn't think I could."

"Well, actually Sheriff O'Dell got us home—"

"From Marietta. But I got us to Marietta from New York," she flashed, nose lifting. "And that was the hard part."

"Just glad we're here." Mack glanced around. "Where is Dad? Is he here?"

"No," Harley said shivering. She honestly didn't know what to make of any of this. "He should be back anytime though. I'd actually expected him before now." She gestured for the sheriff to enter the house so she could close the door.

"Is he out of town?" The sheriff asked, taking off his hat as he entered the house.

"No. He's... out on the property." Harley grimaced. "On horseback."

The sheriff frowned but the kids didn't look perturbed. Mack actually nodded. "He's probably looking for a cow," he said.

Harley glanced at the boy. "Yes."

"That's Dad. He can't sleep if he thinks one of them might be in trouble."

The sheriff looked from the kids to Harley. "So I can leave them here with you? I've got a little girl of my own at home with a sitter, and I ought to get back... if you're okay here."

Harley looked at the pale, wan faces of Brock's twins. They were obviously exhausted. And cold. "Yes," she said, wondering just what the story was here. Surely Brock should have mentioned that he had kids arriving tonight...

Surely he should have mentioned he had kids...

Surely at some point in the hiring process *someone* should have mentioned that he had kids...

The Sheriff reached into his pocket and gave her his card. "If there's a problem, you've got my number, and the office number. Call me."

Harley thanked him for his time and assistance, and then he was off and the front door closed again behind him, leaving her alone with the two kids in the hall.

For a moment they all just stood there and then Harley drew a deep breath, not at all sure what to say, but something needed to be said. "This is a surprise. Your... dad... didn't mention you were coming."

The twins exchanged glances. For a moment there was just silence. Then Mack spoke. "Dad didn't know we were coming... now. He's uh... going to be... surprised."

Brock was going to be surprised?

Things were getting even more interesting. "So he didn't expect you?" Harley asked,

Mack shook his head.

"Why not?"

The kids glanced at each other again. Molly made a face. "School doesn't get out for the Christmas for another week."

"Ten days, actually," Mack muttered.

Harley's eyebrows lifted. "And you go to school where?"

"New York." Mack looked up at her from beneath his lashes. He had a mop of thick, dark hair and his dark brown eyes were exactly the same shade as his father's. Definitely Brock's boy. "It's a boarding school."

"Which we *hate*," Molly said fiercely, shortly, shivering. She had dark shadows beneath her blue-gray eyes that made her freckles stand out even more. "So we're home."

Harley gazed down at the children, thinking they couldn't be much older than ten or eleven. "And you got to Marietta from New York on your own?"

They nodded in unison.

"We took a train and then a bus." Molly sounded proud, even though she was still shivering. "But now we're broke."

Harley still had a dozen more questions but realized they weren't important now. The kids were freezing and had to be hungry and tired. "Grab your back packs. Show me your rooms," she said, unable to imagine the kids in the two guest rooms on the second floor, rooms she kept clean and pristine with daily dusting but it was impossible to picture the kids in those rooms. They were handsome enough rooms, but totally impersonal.

Upstairs, Harley's heart fell as Mack opened the first door on the right. "My room," he said, swinging his back pack onto the full size bed with rustic headboard. The walls were recycled barn planks, just like her room and a red, taupe, and green Native American blanket covered the duvet. A framed antique flag hung on the wall and some old iron brands hung on another wall and those were the only decorative elements.

Harley had been in this room daily and it had never once crossed her mind that it belonged to a child. Where were the toys and posters and framed pictures? Where were the bright colors and fun pillows and stuffed animals?

"This looks so adult," she said, trying to sound complimentary, even as she remembered the murals she'd painted in her own children's rooms, and the colorful matching duvet covers and shams she'd sewn to match the

31

murals. Each of her three had picked out his or her own theme: Ariel and Under the Sea, Peter Pan and Never-Never Land, The Cheshire Cat from Alice and Wonderland.

Molly smothered a yawn. "Dad doesn't do baby-stuff." She gestured toward the door. "Let me show you my room."

Mack followed them down the hall, and the three entered the second bedroom.

Molly switched on the light. "This is my room," she said. Her back pack fell to the floor with a dull thud.

Harley could see it was a slightly more feminine room. The headboard was an old European piece from the 1800s. Harley imagined the tall, austere headboard had come over with a German or Scandinavian immigrant family. The linens were pale and a deep red velvet tapestry blanket was folded across the foot of the bed. An antique oval mirror hung on one wall. A small framed quilt hung on another wall.

"Very pretty," Harley said, heart falling a little more, because the rooms were comfortable and the furniture was solid and the linens were attractive. But the bedrooms lacked life and warmth. They needed photos and knick knacks and posters to make the space personal. The twins were pre-teens. Shouldn't their bedrooms reflect their style?

She turned to look at the kids. They were drooping with cold and exhaustion. She hadn't planned on children being here, but now that they were here, she couldn't ignore them. Not when they looked so pitiful. She drew a quick breath, mustered a smile. "Why don't you two shower and change and get warm, and I'll go make you something to eat?"

Mack nodded eagerly. "Yes, please. I'm *starving*."

"Haven't had dinner," Molly said.

"Or lunch," Mack added.

The kids exchanged quick glances.

"Or much of anything since we left the school yesterday," Molly said wrinkling her nose.

Harley felt her insides tighten, churn. These kids had been through a lot and it troubled her but right now the most important thing was getting them warm and fed. "Grilled cheese sound all right?" she asked.

Both kids nodded.

"Good. I'll bring dinner trays up to your rooms, okay?"

"Okay," Molly said.

Mack shook his head. "We can't." He looked at Molly, and shook his head again. "You know we can't eat in our rooms. It's one of Dad's rules." He glanced to Harley, his expression apologetic. "We're only allowed to eat at the dining room table."

"Not in the kitchen at the counter?' Harley asked, trying to figure out the rules, because there seemed to be quite a few of them.

"No." Mack shrugged. "But it's okay. Some people never eat at the dining room table together. We're lucky we do."

For a moment Harley didn't know if she should laugh or cry. Her lips eventually curved into a reluctant smile. "You're right. I'll see you downstairs."

It was close to one when Harley heard heavy footsteps on the back porch. She'd curled up in the rocking chair next to the kitchen fire and had dozed while waiting for Brock's return.

The stomp of his feet outside the kitchen door woke her. She was on her feet in a flash, opening the door to greet him.

"You're back," she said low, indignantly. She couldn't help it. It's been a long, worrying night. And it was all his fault.

He knocked the snow off his hat and looked at her where she stood in the doorway. "Yes." His lips curved grimly. "Disappointed?"

She wrapped her arms around her to stay warm, her breath clouding in little white puffs. "No. Relieved." She drew her arms even more tightly across her chest. "You have kids." The words tumbled from her. "Two. A boy and a girl."

His eyes narrowed. He frowned, creases in his broad brow. "Yes."

"They're eleven."

His frown deepened. "They're twins."

"Mack and Molly."

His black brows flattened as he shrugged off his snow crusted coat and hung it up on the peg outside the kitchen door. "And this is important... why?"

Her jaw tightened. Of course he'd say that. Tonight as she'd sat in the rocking chair she'd thought about everything that had happened today and it struck her that Brock wasn't reserved. He was rude. "It's important because they're *here*."

His dark gaze shot past her to the dimly lit house. "Here?"

"Yes, Mr. Sheenan. They arrived this evening around eleven, while you were out."

"At the house?"

"Yes. They're upstairs sleeping now. I fed them dinner and put them to bed."

"Huh," he grunted, stepping around her to enter the house. Make that, *push* his way into the house.

Just as Molly had when she'd arrived.

Harley bit her lip, thinking that Mack might have inherited his dad's dark good looks, but Molly had his personality and temper. She followed him into the kitchen where he dropped his damp felt hat on the counter and tugged off his leather work gloves. Melting snow dripped from the hem of his chaps.

His gaze was fixed on the hall with the view of the staircase. "Sleeping, you said?"

She battled her temper, closing the kitchen door and locking it with the dead bolt. "I hope they're sleeping. It's almost one in the morning."

He said nothing to this, crossing to the fireplace to sit down in the rocking chair she'd just vacated. He worked one wet boot off, and then another. The kitchen's lights were turned low and the kitchen was shadowy, save for the red glow of the fire which still burned with a good-sized log. "You kept the fire burning," he said.

"You weren't home," she answered, standing next to the counter, watching him, thinking that everything had changed. Her feelings about being here had changed. She didn't want to be here anymore.

For a moment there was just silence and she curled her fingers into the edge of her fuzzy sleeve, making fists out of her curled fingers.

She should just go to bed right now, before anything else was said.

She should just go to bed before she said something she'd regret.

But she couldn't make herself walk out. Couldn't leave. She was still too upset. Too shocked. Too worried.

Brock Sheenan was a widower, with kids, and his kids were good kids but they were lonely and homesick and being raised with a lot of tough love. Harley came from a strict Dutch family. She understood rules and order but she'd also been raised with plenty of affection, and laughter, and fun.

After sitting with Mack and Molly while they wolfed down their grilled cheese sandwiches and tomato soup, Harley wasn't sure the twins had known a lot of hugs and kisses and laughter.

And that ate at her.

It ate at her after they'd gone to sleep. It ate at her as she sat in the rocking chair. It ate at her now.

Brock leaned back in the rocking chair, his big shoulders filling the entire space, his chest so broad it made the oversized rocking chair look small. "Spit it out," he said.

Harley's fists squeezed tighter. "Spit it out?"

His dark head inclined. "You're obviously dying to say something. So say it. I'm tired. Hungry. I want to eat and go to bed."

She drew a breath and fought for calm. She had to be calm. Men didn't like hysterical women. "You didn't mention them, Mr. Sheenan."

The rocking chair tipped back. He looked at her from under very dark lashes, his dark gaze almost black in the shadowy kitchen. "I didn't know they were coming."

"But you never mentioned them."

"So?"

"So? I'd think you'd mention it when applying for a housekeeper. The agency never mentioned kids. You never mentioned kids. But you have kids, two of them, and they're here for the holidays."

His brow lowered. "They shouldn't be here yet." He paused, thought. "What is the date?"

"December 8th. It's a Sunday."

He said nothing.

She swallowed her impatience. "I arrived a week ago

35

today, on the first. I've been here a week."

Frowning, he gazed at the fire. "They weren't supposed to be here until the nineteenth. That's when school gets out for the holidays," he added, half under his breath.

"Does it not... worry... you that they're here?" she asked. She waited for him to say something. He seemed in no hurry to speak, so she pressed on. "Does it not trouble you that two eleven-year-olds, who go to school in *New York*, are on your doorstep in *Montana* at eleven at night?"

"It most definitely concerns me," he said finally, looking at her. He rubbed a hand slowly across his bristled jaw. "But you said they were asleep. What do you want me do? Go haul them out of bed and interrogate them in the middle of the night?"

Her eyes burned and she looked away, staring into the glowing embers of the fire. She couldn't do this. Couldn't be part of this. She didn't want children or Christmas or a pirate for a boss.

"No, of course not," she said, her voice dropping, deepening. "I just... don't understand. How you could not know the kids were missing from school. Shouldn't the school have called you? Shouldn't you have been on a plane the moment you heard that no one could find your twins?"

He closed his eyes, grimaced. "The school probably did call. I'm sure if I checked my phone there would be messages. But I rarely keep it on me as it doesn't work in the back country so no, I don't pay much attention to it."

Or your kids, she wanted to add.

She didn't.

Her fingers twisted, tugging on the fuzzy sweater sleeve. "But why would you never mention them to me? Why would you never once mention that those two guest rooms were actually your children's rooms and you expected your kids home on the nineteenth for their school holiday?"

He shrugged. "I didn't think it mattered."

She bundled her arms across her chest, cold, so cold. "How could they not matter?"

He leaned forward, his dark gaze skewering her. "I did not say *they* didn't matter. I said I didn't think it mattered if *you* knew." His jaw hardened and a small muscle popped in his square jaw, near his ear. "And don't do that again. Put words in my mouth. I may not be president of the PTA, but I love my kids."

"Then why don't you have any pictures of them? Why don't you have any of their artwork framed? Where are their books and toys—"

"I don't like clutter."

"What about them? What about what they like?"

"Pardon me?" He was on his feet, towering over her.

Her heart raced, blood roaring in her ears. He didn't just look like a savage with the fire's flickering flames casting a glow over his hard features, he sounded like a savage, too. But she wasn't intimidated. She'd been through far too much in life to be intimidated by an eccentric mountain man. "You never once mentioned them to me in a week of working here. I had no idea that those two bedrooms I was dusting every day were your children's rooms. I had no idea that two eleven-year-olds would be showing up here on the nineteenth for their Christmas holidays."

"Clearly their arrival has upset you."

Harley's lips tightened. Her heart thudded uncomfortably hard. "No. They haven't upset me. You have upset me."

"Me?"

"Yes, *you*. You are painfully out of touch as a father, more worried about a young cow than your eleven-year-olds, who arrived in Marietta after an all-night Greyhound bus ride after a train ride, as well a lift from a local sheriff who found them at the bus station in downtown Marietta. He thought they were runaways, and then they told him they were yours."

"Your point?"

"You should have known they'd left the school. You should have known they were missing and you should have been out there looking for them the way you were searching for that damn cow." Her chin jerked up, her eyes stinging as she fought emotion she didn't want to feel. "I don't know why they came home early, only that they did, and they were desperate and determined to come home." She blinked hard, trying to clear her eyes before tears welled. "And you should have been here, to greet them. You should have been the one at the door. Not another housekeeper."

His gaze narrowed. He studied her for a long moment, dark lashes lowered over penetrating eyes. "Quite the expert, aren't you?"

His scathing tone wounded. She winced, but wasn't surprised he was angry. He was a man, a thirty-nine year old man, and of course he wouldn't like being criticized.

"I don't belong here," she said, by way of an answer. It wouldn't serve to get into an argument. She'd leave, find another position. It was the only way. She couldn't be here, with the kids, not like this. It'd tear her apart. Break her heart which was only starting to heal. "I'll call the agency in the morning—"

"You dislike kids that much?" he interrupted harshly.

She flinched. "I don't dislike kids."

"Then why leave? You told me just this afternoon you liked it here, you were happy here."

"That was before."

"Before what?"

"Before I knew about..." Her voice faded, she swallowed hard. "The twins."

"If you'd known about them... what? You wouldn't have taken the job here?"

She hesitated, knowing that the truth would damn her.

But the job was no longer the same position she'd accepted. She'd thought she'd left California and her family and their big Christmas to spend the holidays in the middle of nowhere Montana with a dour rancher and five surly ranch hands. That was the job she'd accepted, and wanted.

And she had loved being here this past week. She loved the granite face of the mountain, the towering pine trees, the pastures tucked into the valleys, as well as the silence and freedom from everything she knew in Central California.

Harley drew a deep breath, aware that she hadn't yet answered Brock Sheenan's question. "Probably not," she whispered.

"*Seriously?*"

The harsh, incredulous note in his voice put a lump in her throat. She bit her tongue to keep from saying more. She'd already said too much.

"You hate kids that much?" he demanded.

She looked away, pain rippling through her even as tension crackled in the kitchen. He didn't understand and she wasn't sure she could make him understand, not tonight. Not when she was so tired and barely keeping it together. But the austerity of life here on frigid Copper Mountain Ranch with its gusts of icy wind and blizzard-like storms had been good for her. It allowed her to work and not feel.

It was good not to feel.

It was even better not to want, or need.

"Miss Diekerhoff?"

She turned her head, looked at him. "I don't hate them at all," she said lowly. "I like children very much."

"Then what are you saying?"

She stared at him, stomach churning, heart thudding, aching. "I'm saying that I don't belong here, and that I didn't understand the situation here—" she broke off, gulping air for courage, before pressing on, "—but now that I do, it's better if I leave."

"*What*?"

"I'm sorry."

"I'm shocked. I can't believe this. I can't believe *you*."

Harley couldn't hold his gaze any longer. The censure was too much. "I'll call the agency first thing in the morning and they should be able to send out a temporary replacement that should get you through the weekend—"

He laughed, a dark low bitter laugh that silenced her. "I see. I'll get a temp for my temp? That's great. That's wonderful. Thank you, Miss Diekerhoff, for a fantastic week but maybe I shouldn't be surprised you're walking out on us. Deep down I knew you were too good to be true."

Chapter Three

I knew you were too good to be true.

The words echoed in Harley's head all night, making her heart hurt and sleep impossible. How could she sleep when every time she closed her eyes, she saw the censure in his dark eyes? Heard the disappointment in his deep voice?

She didn't like disappointing people. And she really didn't like disappointing him.

It's not as if she needed Brock's good opinion. When she left here, she'd never see him again, never have any contact. It shouldn't matter what he thought, or how he said things...

But it did.

She didn't know why. She didn't understand it, but there was something about him that resonated with her. She identified with his silence and rough edges, as well as the deep grief that had made him retreat from the world.

She'd wanted to die after the plane crash that took her family, but her parents and brothers and sisters wouldn't let her quit.

They urged her to cling to her faith.

They told her she still had them.

They reminded her that she was still young with a whole future ahead of her.

She'd weathered the worst of the grief and now she was trying to move forward, putting one foot in front of the other, but it didn't mean she was whole and strong yet.

She still found certain things heartbreakingly painful. Like holidays. And children.

Put the two together and it made her sick with grief.

She wanted her children back. Wanted Emma, Ana, and Davi, nestled close, sitting pressed to her side as they used to when they'd watch a favorite holiday program like Rudolph the Red-Nosed Reindeer or The Grinch that Stole Christmas.

Her kids had loved Christmas and she'd loved giving them the most magical Christmas possible...

Her eyes burned and pain splintered inside her heart, making her want to cry aloud.

She pressed her fists to her eyes to keep the tears from falling. She wouldn't cry. She wouldn't. Tears changed nothing and she had to keep it together. Keep it together and move on.

One step at a time.

One day at a time.

She'd get there. She would.

Harley woke early despite not falling to sleep until after three. Downstairs in the kitchen she made coffee and a cinnamon bread her kids had loved called Monkey Bread, hoping the warm gooey cinnamon bread would be a peace offering.

It wasn't.

Brock didn't speak to her when he came downstairs at six. He filled his coffee cup and stalked out.

Her sticky sweet pull-apart cinnamon bread went uneaten.

Late morning Harley stood on the front porch of the ranch house, cell phone pressed to her ear, as she spoke with the manager of the Marietta employment agency for the third time in the past two hours.

The manager had finally found someone to replace Harley, but the new temp couldn't start until Saturday.

"Saturday?" Harley cried, listening to the manager even as she kept an eye on the barn door, as the twins had disappeared inside, swaddled in puffy winter coats, scarves, hats and boots. "That's six days from now."

"Five, if you don't count today," the manager answered.

Harley was most certainly counting today "You can't get anyone sooner?"

"It took us weeks to find you, Miss Diekerhoff. You don't just pull good temps out of a hat."

Harley suppressed a sigh, acknowledging that was probably true. And she wouldn't want the agency to send just anyone here to the ranch. You couldn't put just anyone in a

41

house with two pre-teens. The agency would have to do thorough criminal background checks.

Speaking of two pre-teens, Harley glanced at the barn again, wondering what the twins were doing.

The kids hadn't spoken to her this morning, avoiding her since Brock had woken up and talked to them in their rooms. Then all three came downstairs and he'd made eggs and bacon for the kids, and sat with them in the dining room, but there hadn't been much conversation at breakfast, and when Brock did speak to his kids, his tone was quite severe. He was clearly upset with them.

When the twins finished their tense breakfast, they'd carried their dishes in, washed them at the sink and then quietly slipped out, avoiding her.

Upstairs, twenty minutes later, Harley discovered the twins had made their beds and already disappeared outside. Again avoiding her.

She knew then that Brock had said something to the twins, telling them to stay out of her way. She ought to be glad she didn't have them underfoot, but their distance and silence made her unaccountably sad.

Harley forced her attention to the phone call. "So Saturday for sure," she said.

"Yes. We have someone finishing a job elsewhere Friday, so Saturday she'll start at Copper Mountain Ranch."

"Okay," Harley said quietly.

"Can you survive that long?"

Harley ignored the sarcasm in the manager's voice. "Things are pretty... tense... here."

"I'm sure they are. Mr. Sheenan is very unhappy, as we are, too. You've put us all in quite a bind, and we've lost a great deal of credibility with Mr. Sheenan."

"I understand," she said, spotting Mack and Molly who'd just emerged from the barn with an old sled and were dragging it off toward a break in the pine trees. There must be a sledding hill somewhere back behind the trees.

"If we should find someone sooner, I will of course let you know."

"Thank you." Harley drew a quick breath. "And will you be able to find me another job in Marietta, or...?"

"No. I don't think so. Forgive me for being blunt, but we've lost face, and I don't think we can recommend you with confidence to any of our clients or accounts here. Now, if you could turn the situation around and find a way to make the job work, then maybe we will all feel differently."

Back inside the house, Harley took off her coat, hanging it up on a peg in the laundry room and then went to the kitchen to figure out what she'd make for dinner.

For long moments she stared blindly into the refrigerator, trying to come up with a plan, but she couldn't focus on anything, too much in a daze.

Everything had gotten so messed up, so fast.

"I thought you'd be packing," Brock said shortly, entering the kitchen to refill his coffee cup.

Harley straightened, shut the refrigerator door, and faced him. "The agency can't replace me until Saturday." She drew a quick breath, tried to smile, but failed. "Looks like you're stuck with me until the weekend."

"You must be devastated," he said, his expression hard.

His sarcasm stung. She struggled to keep her composure.

"Trapped here with children," he added bitingly.

This time she couldn't hide the hurt, her lips trembling, her eyes gritty and hot. "You're making this something it's not," she whispered. "I don't hate kids. I don't dislike them."

His fierce dark gaze met hers and held. "But the moment you found out I had kids you wanted to bolt. True?"

Her lips parted but no sound came out. How to tell him that she'd loved her children so much that when they died it'd killed her?

How to explain that even now, three years without her children, she still woke up in a cold sweat missing them? Needing them?

She gave her head the smallest of shakes. "It's not what you think." Her voice was all but inaudible. "It's a... a... personal... thing."

"Obviously."

She struggled to add. "It's more of a... grief... thing."

He grew still. His dense black lashes lifted. He stared at her hard, searchingly. "You don't have kids."

"No."

His gaze continued to hold hers. "You wanted them?"

She reached for a damp dishtowel by the sink. "Yes."

He said nothing, just looked at her. But it was enough.

Terrified she'd cry or fall apart, she forced herself to action, swiping the dishtowel across the counter, mopping up the glisten of water on the counter. She dragged the dishtowel over another area, this one clean and dry, but activity was good. Activity would distract both of them. Or so she prayed.

But the silence in the kitchen was intolerable. It seemed to stretch on forever.

Finally he spoke. "So you're here for the rest of the week."

"Yes."

"You can handle that?"

"Yes," she said lowly.

"You're sure?"

"*Yes.*"

He turned to leave but stopped in the doorway. "Not that it makes a difference, but they won't require much from you. Just meals, laundry, that sort of thing. I'll keep them out of your way. That should help."

She couldn't look at him. She turned away, feeling naked, and bereft. Harley didn't even know this family and yet she liked them... cared for them. How could she not?

Two freckle-faced eleven-year-olds who'd grown up without a mom.

A darkly handsome rancher who'd become Marietta's recluse.

This big, handsome log cabin house that lacked the tenderness that would make it a home.

"You don't have to tell them to stay out of my way," she said hoarsely, keeping her face averted. "They're fine. It'll be fine. I promise."

Brock nodded shortly and walked out, allowing the kitchen door to slam behind him, glad to escape the kitchen and the grief he'd seen in Harley's face before she'd turned away from him.

He wished he hadn't seen it. He didn't like it, uncomfortable with sorrow and emotions, and already overwhelmed by the twins' sudden arrival home.

The twins weren't supposed to be here, and he was furious with the school and his kids and Harley Diekerhoff for stating the obvious last night—he was not paying his kids enough attention.

But his kids wanted the wrong kind of attention and he wasn't about to reward them for bad behavior.

He grabbed his heavy coat from the hook outside the door, and his dogs came bounding through the snow, the Australian shepherds having deserted him earlier to trail after the kids.

The kids.

Brock's jaw jutted, furious and frustrated. His kids were in so much trouble. Not only had they cut out of school a week early before the school holiday had officially begun, they'd taken two different Amtrak trains and a Greyhound bus to get back to Marietta.

He couldn't even fathom the risks they'd taken, getting home.

He'd taught them to be smart and self-reliant so he wasn't surprised that they could find their way home from New York—after all, they'd all traveled together to the school by train last August, taking the train from Malta to Chicago and then connecting to the Lake Shore Limited, with its daily service between Chicago and New York—but running away from school wasn't smart, or self-reliant. It was stupid. Foolish. Dangerous.

Heading toward the barn, dogs at his heels, Brock shied away from thinking about all the different things that could have gone wrong. There were bad people in this world, people Mack and Molly had never been exposed to, and for all the twins' confidence, they were hopelessly naïve.

Pushing open the barn door, Brock heard the scrape of shovel and rake. Good. The twins were working. He'd told them they couldn't play until they'd mucked out the stalls, a job that would take a couple of hours, and when he'd checked on them twenty minutes ago, he'd discovered they'd cut out to go sledding.

Now they had to muck the stalls and clean and oil the leather bridles… and there were a lot of bridles.

Mack glanced up glumly as Brock came around the corner.

Molly didn't even look at her dad.

"Looks good," Brock said, inspecting the completed stalls. "Just the bridles and you'll be free for the day."

"We really have to take all the bridles, all apart?" Mack asked, groaning. "We just can't wipe them down with leather cleaner?"

"We already talked about this," Brock answered. "I want every buckle undone, all leather pieces shiny with oil and then rubbed down so you get the old wax and dirt off. With a clean cloth, polish the leather up, use an old toothbrush on the bit, cleaning that too, and then put it back together… the right way. If you have to draw a sketch, or take a picture to help you remember how each bridle goes together, then do it, because the job's not finished until the bridles are back hanging in the tack room."

Molly glared at him. "That's going to take all day."

"You're not on vacation, Molly. You were supposed to be in school."

"I *hate* the Academy."

"Then you should enjoy helping out around here. You'll be working all week."

Harley didn't see the kids again until just an hour before dinner. It was dark outside when they opened the back door to troop dispiritedly through the kitchen. They'd forgotten to take their boots off and they left icy, mucky footprints across the hardwood floor before disappearing upstairs.

Harley paused from mashing the potatoes to run a mop across the floor. She was just finishing by the back door when it opened again and Brock stood there.

"Careful," she said. "It's wet. You don't want to slip."

"Why are you mopping now?" he asked, easing off his boots and leaving them outside.

"It'd gotten dirty and I didn't want everyone walking through it, tracking mud through the rest of the house."

He stepped inside and closed the door behind him. "The kids?"

"It's fine."

"It's not fine. They know to take their boots off. That's one of Maxine's big rules. She'd throw them out if they tramped mud and snow through the house." He walked into the laundry, flipping on the light. "Where are their dirty clothes?"

Harley straightened. "I don't know."

"They haven't brought them down yet?"

"I haven't seen them, no."

"They're testing you, Miss Diekerhoff. They know the rules."

"I don't know the rules, Mr. Sheenan."

"Then maybe you need to ask."

Harley lifted her chin, refusing to be cowed. "What are the house rules, Mr. Sheenan?"

"I'll send the twins down. They'll fill you in."

Chapter Four

Harley went to bed Monday night, exhausted and frazzled.

She'd gone from relishing each day at Copper Mountain Ranch to counting down the days until she could leave. The twins didn't like her much. And Brock Sheenan seemed to like her even less.

It was one thing to feed and clothe people. It was another thing to feed and clothe unhappy people. And the twins were certainly unhappy.

Fortunately, Tuesday passed without incident. Brock gave the twins chores, and the kids did their chores, and stayed out of her way.

Tuesday night Brock and his hands didn't come in for dinner as limbs on a massive tree, weighted by snow and ice, snapped, taking down a long section of fence, allowing cattle to wander.

While Brock and the hands repaired the fence and tracked down the missing cattle, Harley fed the twins dinner, serving them at the kitchen counter.

"We're not supposed to eat here," Mack reminded her. "Dad's rules."

Harley filled their glasses with milk. "I asked your dad about that. He said it was Maxine's rule, not his, and since Maxine isn't here, I'm feeding you where I want to feed you."

The twins looked at each other.

"Dad might get mad," Mack added.

Harley placed the milks in front of the kids. "I'm not afraid of your dad, or Maxine. And besides, its nicer eating in here. It's warm and cheerful. The dining room depresses me."

The kids looked at each other again.

"Why does it depress you?" Molly asked, intrigued.

"It's not very cozy."

"Dad doesn't do cozy," Molly said. "Or holidays, or anything festive." She sighed, and stabbed her fork in her chicken. "He used to like Christmas. But not anymore."

Harley turned down the oven to make sure she didn't dry the chicken out. "What do you do for Christmas? How do you celebrate? I noticed you don't have any Advent Calendars out."

"What are Advent Calendars?" Mack asked.

Harley drew a stool out and sat down. "They're a calendar to help you count down to Christmas. Some of them have chocolates, others have little toys. They're just fun."

"Oh, then we definitely wouldn't have them," Molly said. She took a bite and chewed for a long time. After she swallowed, she shrugged. "We don't even decorate anymore."

Harley couldn't believe this. "Nothing?"

"Nope."

"What about a tree?"

"Nope."

"Not even a wreath or garland or candles?"

Molly shook her head. "Dad stopped a couple of years ago with all that stuff. He said it was a waste of time, and expensive."

Harley struggled to hide her horror. "What about presents? Stockings?"

"We get a few presents, mostly practical stuff. But we didn't have stockings last year. Dad said we're too old. Santa doesn't exist." Mack made a face. "And I know Santa isn't real. We figured that out a long time ago, but he didn't have to say it like that. It kind of made us feel bad."

Harley could believe it. Just listening to the twins talk made her feel bad. "Well, maybe we could do something fun while I'm here."

The twins looked skeptical. "Like what?" Molly asked.

"Bake cookies or make a gingerbread house."

Mack frowned. "I've never made a gingerbread house."

"I don't know that I'd want to make a gingerbread house," Molly retorted.

Harley shrugged and rose from the stool. "You're right. Why frost cookies or decorate a gingerbread house and drink hot spiced apple cider, when you can shovel manure and stack hay bales?"

Wednesday morning after starting the laundry and tidying all the bathrooms and giving the hardwood floor a good sweep, Harley put on her snow boots and heavy jacket and gloves and headed outside to cut some fragrant pine boughs.

JB, who was on the smaller snowplow, clearing the path between the house and barn, and barn and bunk house, turned off the engine to ask Harley if she needed help.

"I think I've got it," Harley said, shaking the armful of branches to remove excess snow. "But thank you."

"What are you doing, Miss Harley?"

"Just adding a few festive touches to the house. Give it a little holiday spirit."

JB adjusted his leather work glove. "Have you asked the boss? He's not real big on holidays."

"The kids told me he used to have more holiday spirit."

"It's been a few years."

"What happened?"

"He's just been a bachelor a long time. Hard to do everything and be happy about it."

Harley glanced down at the green fragrant branches in her arms. "You really think Mr. Sheenan will be upset that I've spruced things up for Christmas? I'm just making some garland, adding some candles on the mantels."

He thought for a moment. "If that's all, Mr. Sheenan might be okay. But I wouldn't push him. He's not a man that likes to be bossed around."

Brock entered the house through the kitchen door, which was how he always entered in his work clothes, but he was stopped short this afternoon by the sight of the twins hunched over the island counter carefully frosting sugar cookies that had been cut into stars and stockings, ornaments, candy canes and Christmas trees.

The kids looked up at him and smiled. Mack had flour on

his cheek and Molly was licking icing from her thumb.

"Hey Dad, look what we made," Molly said. "Roll-out sugar cookies."

Brock approached the island to examine the platter filled with fanciful colors and shapes. "Nice," he said.

"Want one?" Mack asked, offering him a candy cane.

Brock shook his head. "Maybe after dinner," he answered, before looking at Harley who was drying the last of the cookie sheets. "Where did you get the cookie cutters from?" he asked her.

"Just made a paper pattern," she said.

Mack nodded. "Miss Harley made the patterns out of cardboard and we cut them all out. It took a while but it was really cool."

"You have to be careful not to roll the dough too thin," Molly explained, "and you also have to watch how much flour you use. You can't use too much or too little."

Brock's eyebrows lifted. "You got them baking today."

She blushed, her cheeks turning pink. She looked nervous as she reached for the next cookie tray. "I thought it'd be a good activity for a cold afternoon."

"Must have been a lot of work."

"It was fun."

Brock glanced back to the counter with the platter of cookies. The shapes weren't perfect and there was more frosting than cookie in some cases, but Mack and Molly looked happy. Happier than he'd seen them since returning from New York. "Maxine wouldn't let you two mess up her kitchen like this, would she?"

"But it shouldn't be Maxine's kitchen," Harley said. "It's yours, and the kids'. This is your house."

Brock frowned. "Well, let's not get too comfortable in here. She'll be back in a month and she'll want her kitchen back." He tapped each of the kids on the head. "Mack, Molly, make sure you help Miss Diekerhoff clean up. You're not to leave her with all the work."

He started for the hall, but stopped at the fireplace. A generous swag of pine covered the mantel, the green branches held in place by fat white candles.

They hadn't just been baking. They'd been decorating,

too.

He slowly turned and looked back to the island counter. Mack and Molly were staring at him, waiting for his reaction.

"It smells good, doesn't it, Dad?" Mack said hopefully.

Mack glanced past the kids to Harley who appeared utterly engrossed in the glass mixing bowl she was drying so very vigorously.

He knew right away who'd been behind the green garland and candles.

"It's fine," Brock said flatly. "But let's not get carried away."

After lunch Thursday, Harley prepped for dinner, creating a mustard beer bath for the two big roasts that would be tonight's dinner, and then peeled the mound of apples for tonight's apple pie.

The kids had been dashing in and out most of the day, doing chores for their dad and then entertaining themselves with various outdoor adventures.

She liked how well Mack and Molly played together. They were extremely close. Not just brother and sister, but best friends.

As Harley rolled out the pie crust and then filled each of the pie shells with the spicy apple cinnamon and sugar mixture, she thought about her daughters. They'd loved baking with her, and despite the two-and-a-half-year age difference between them, Emma and Ana had always been each other's best friend.

After carefully sliding both pies into the oven, Harley moved laundry forward, carrying folded towels upstairs and stacking the clean clothes for the ranch hands in the plastic basket that they'd come and retrieve after work tonight.

Thirty minutes later, she opened the oven door and checked on the apple pies, making sure the crusts on the pies weren't burning. The pies were browning beautifully, the flaky edges turning light gold with juice bubbling through the slits in the sugar-dusted crust.

The kitchen door flung open. "I need a Band-Aid," Mack

said breathlessly. "Maybe a bunch."

Harley straightened and turned. "Everything okay?" she asked, seeing how the shoulder of his coat was powdered with snow, and something... else.... something... red

"I think so," he said, not sounding convincing at all.

"Is that something… red on your coat?" she asked.

He looked down at his sleeve and tried to rub the red splatter off, streaking it instead.

"Where are you hurt?" she asked.

"Not me. Molly."

"Badly?"

"I don't know. She won't let me see."

Harley quickly went into the little bathroom off the kitchen, grabbed a washcloth, and then rifled through the medicine cabinet for rubbing alcohol, gauze pads, and Band-Aids. "Where is she?"

"Behind the house."

"Show me," Harley said, ignoring her coat to rush out the door.

Mack ran through the snow, with Harley close on his heels, snow crunching beneath their shoes, leading her around the side of the corral, to the back gate, where Molly was leaning against a post, her hand shielding her face as blood stained the snow around her feet.

"Dad's going to ground me for life," Mack whispered.

Harley ignored this, and bent over the girl. "Honey, it's Harley. Where are you hurt?"

"My face."

"Where on your face?"

"By my eye."

Harley's heart jumped, fell. "Let me see."

"Can't," came the muffled reply.

"Why?"

"It's bleeding too much and I don't want to get stitches."

"You might not need stitches. Faces and heads bleed a lot when they're cut. You might just need some ice. Let me see. Okay?"

Eventually, with a lot of coaxing, Harley was able to get Molly to look up and uncover her face. Blood crusted Molly's hairline and coated her temple, but as Harley gently dabbed at the gash between the girl's eyebrow and hairline, she could see that the bleeding was slowing, and the wound, maybe an inch, inch and a half, was deep but at least not to the bone.

"How did a snowball do this?" Harley asked, using her thumb to wipe away some of the blood to get a better look at the cut.

Mack didn't immediately answer.

Harley saw Molly's gaze dart to her brother.

"Um, it was a snowball fight," Mack said. "She was standing on top of the corral when I threw the snowball."

Harley glanced at the boy over her shoulder. "So she got cut when she fell?"

The kids looked at each other again. Both were making a strange face. Something was up. Harley shrugged. "You don't need to tell me. But I'm sure your dad will want to know."

"He'll kill me," Mack muttered.

"But it's my fault, too," Molly said, wincing as she touched the cut and checked her fingers for blood. "I... wanted... to play." She dabbed her head again. "And see? It's not that bad. I'm not bleeding that much now. Dad might not even notice."

"Well, let's go into the house and get you cleaned up properly," Harley said, not wanting to think about Brock's reaction, or Brock himself.

They tramped back through the snow and stomped their feet on the porch, knocking off excess snow. The back door suddenly opened and Brock was there. "Where have you been?" he demanded. "Your pies were burning."

It was only then that he noticed Molly's blood-streaked face. "Hell and damnation," he swore. "What happened?"

Brock walked Molly into the kitchen and lifted her onto one of the kitchen stools to get a look a proper look at her face. "What happened?" he repeated.

"Snowball fight," Mack said in a small voice as Miss Diekerhoff went to the sink to wash the blood off her hands and then wet a clean cloth with warm water so he could clean Molly' face.

Brock took the warm wet cloth from the housekeeper with a gruff thanks and gently began to wipe away the blood streaks. "This cut isn't from a snowball fight," he said, shooting Mack a sharp look. "Perhaps you'd like to tell me how it happened."

The kids didn't answer and Miss Diekerhoff went to the stove to study the pies he'd pulled from the oven when he smelled the crust burning.

Her lips pursed as she prodded the blackened crust with a fork, her thick honey ponytail sliding over her shoulder, her cheeks still pink from the cold but she didn't look terribly upset. He was grateful for that. He knew the only reason the pies had burned was because she'd gone to Molly's aid.

He was grateful she had.

But he was also in need of answers. How had Molly gotten a big gash so close to her eye?

He glanced down at his daughter's face, which was still so pale the freckles popped across the bridge of her small straight nose. "So are you going to tell me what happened?" he asked, glancing from Molly to Mack, and fighting to hang on to his patience. "And how Molly got cut in a snowball fight?"

The kids just hung their heads, definitely a sign that something else had taken place. But they also weren't talking. Of course not. These two were masters of collusion. Usually Molly had the big, bright ideas and then applied pressure to her brother until he caved in, agreeing to her bold schemes. Interesting that Molly was the one hurt now. "Molly's usually the better shot," Brock added.

Mack flushed and Molly wiggled uncomfortably on the stool. "I'm out of practice," she muttered.

"Mmmm," Brock answered, pressing against the cut. It was deeper than he'd like but the edges were clean and something that could be fixed with a good butterfly bandage. No need to drive her into Marietta to the hospital. "But something tells me this wasn't an ordinary snowball fight. So what did happen?"

Neither Mack nor Molly spoke.

The housekeeper discreetly disappeared into the laundry room.

Brock waited a good minute, determined that the twins would explain what had happened.

They didn't. They kept their silence and Brock battled his temper. He'd had enough of the twins colluding. This was why they'd been sent away to boarding school. They didn't try last year in sixth grade at their Marietta middle school. They sat in the back of the class, daydreaming and inattentive, rarely participating, and even more rarely turning in completed work. At the end of the year, the principal met with him, and recommended that Mack and Molly attend summer school to catch up on what they'd missed this year, and recommended that the twins have more structure come Fall. The twins, the principal added, were extremely bright, but highly unmotivated, more interested in their own private world than learning and applying themselves.

The twins went to summer school, kicking and screaming every day for the two intensive sessions, and then in late August, he took them by train to New York, again kicking and screaming, where he'd enrolled them at the prestigious Academy for the new school year.

The twins were upset that he left them there, but it was for their own good. They needed to be challenged, they needed to learn discipline, and they needed the study skills and good grades required for college.

But now here they were, home early, and getting into trouble. What was he going to do with them?

He surveyed their blank faces and realized they weren't going to come clean, and it just made him even angrier. Why wouldn't they listen? Why couldn't they cooperate? What was wrong with them? "So no one knows anything," he said curtly. "Fine. Don't know anything, and don't tell me. In fact, I don't think I even want to know now. I just want you two to go to bed."

"Bed?" Mack said.

"But it's not even four, Dad!" Molly cried, staring up at him in horror.

"—without dinner," Brock concluded, unmoved. "Mack, head on up. Put on your pajamas and get into bed. Molly will be up as soon as I get her bandaged up. Goodbye, and goodnight."

Mack walked out, looking beaten, and Molly was silent as Brock cleaned the wound and then used a butterfly bandage from the medicine cabinet to tightly close the cut. It should heal without a scar, but even if it did scar a bit, it wouldn't be Molly's first. Molly was definitely his wild one, while Mack was gentler and quiet, like his mom.

Brock felt a pang as he thought of Amy. His wife had only the pregnancy and then six months with the babies before she died. She never knew them, not the way he did. He wondered if she'd be disappointed in him, as a father. He wasn't a perfect father, not by any means, but he loved his kids. He loved them so much he'd sent them across the country to ensure they had the best education. He hated it when they were gone. The house was too empty. He was too empty. Life wasn't the same without them. But he had to put the kids' needs first. The prep school would get them into the best universities in the country and that's what Amy had always wanted for their children. A loving foundation, a great education, and rewarding careers. Brock was trying hard to honor Amy's dreams, but it wasn't easy.

He'd missed the kids when they were gone, and selfishly, he was glad they were back. But they weren't back for good. He'd drag them back to New York, kicking and screaming if he had to. This was for them.

And Amy.

Amy hadn't had a future. He needed to make sure her children did.

Once Molly was patched up and gone, Brock washed his hands at the sink and then dried them on a hand towel, glancing in Harley Diekerhoff's direction.

Earlier she'd lifted off the burned pastry crust from the top of the pies, throwing it away, before scooping the warn apple pie filling from inside the pie shell, transferring the golden gleaming filling into a dozen ceramic ramekins.

Now she mixed brown sugar and cinnamon and some chopped nuts with a little flour and a lot of butter, creating a crumbly brown sugar mixture.

"Making a crumble," he said, surprised, but pleased. He'd been disappointed that the pies burned. He loved apple pie. He'd wondered if one of the kids had told her it was his favorite dessert.

She nodded, and shot him a quick, shy smile. "What's the old expression? When you burn the apple pie, get rid of the crust and make a crumble?"

He lifted a brow. "I've never heard that before."

"That's strange," she said, lips twitching. "Maybe it's not an expression you use in Montana."

"Or maybe it's an expression that you just made up."

She laughed, once, and her green eyes gleamed as she suppressed the husky laugh. "Maybe I did," she admitted, beginning to sprinkle the brown sugar mixture over the first of the ramekins. "It seemed fitting, though."

He leaned against the counter and watched her work. It was strangely relaxing, watching her bake. She moved with confidence around the kitchen. She obviously liked cooking and baking, and was certainly comfortable feeding a big group. His ranch hands claimed they'd never eaten better in their lives, and it wasn't just the quantity, but the quality. Harley Diekerhoff's food actually tasted good, too.

She continued to heap topping on the ramekins and he stayed where he was, leaning against the counter, enjoying the smells of apple and cinnamon along with the roast in the oven, as well as the sight of an attractive woman moving around the kitchen.

Knowing that she'd be gone day after tomorrow made him feel less guilty for lingering.

He wasn't attached to her. Wasn't going to let his attraction interfere.

And yet she did look appealing in his kitchen, in her yellow apron with cherries and lace trim. She looked fresh and wholesome and beautiful as only a country girl could.

"You're a farm girl," he said, breaking the silence.

She paused, glanced at him. "I grew up on a dairy, and then married a dairyman."

Surprised, he said nothing for a moment, too caught off guard to know what to say. He wasn't good at conversation. It'd been too many years since he'd chatted for the hell of it. "You're divorced," he said flatly.

She sprinkled the last of the topping over the ramekins, making sure each was generously covered with brown sugar and butter before rinsing her hands. "Widowed."

He felt another strange jolt.

"I'm sorry," he said, wishing now he'd never said anything.

She dried her hands, looked at him, her features composed. "It'll be three years in February."

He shouldn't ask anything, shouldn't say anything, shouldn't continue this conversation a moment longer, not when he could see the shadows in her beautiful green eyes. But he knew loss, and what it was to lose your soul mate, and he was still moved by what she'd told him this morning, about how she'd never been able to have children, and how it'd hurt her. "How long were you married?"

"Almost twelve years."

He couldn't hide his surprise. "You must have married in high school."

"No, but I was young. I'd just turned twenty. Still had one more year of college, but Davi had graduated and we married the same weekend of his graduation ceremonies."

"A June wedding?"

"A huge, June wedding." She tried to smile. It wasn't very steady. "I think I had something like seven bridesmaids and my maid of honor."

"You met in college?"

"Yes." She turned away and began placing the ramekins on a cookie sheet. "We were both ag business majors, both from dairy families, and we grew up just eleven miles from each other."

"Your families must have been happy." He was prying now, and he knew it.

She shot him a quick glance, before sliding the cookie sheet into the hot second oven. "They weren't that happy. He was Portuguese, not Dutch. They predicted problems. They were right."

Her voice was calm, her expression serene, and yet he sensed there was so much she wasn't saying.

And yet he stopped himself from asking more. He'd already prodded Harley the way he'd prodded Molly's wound. It was time leave her alone.

"Thank you for taking care of Molly today," he said,

gathering the medical supplies he'd used. "I appreciate it."

"It was nothing."

"Nothing? You lost two perfectly good pies."

She laughed. "And ended up with almost a dozen ramekins. So I think we're okay."

Brock stared at her a moment, dazzled. Her laugh was low and husky and perfectly beautiful.

She was absolutely beautiful.

Maybe too beautiful.

"Well, thanks again," he said flatly, walking out, thinking that perhaps it was a good thing that Harley was leaving the day after tomorrow.

Harley was not an easy woman to have in his house.

She made him feel things and wish for things, and he wasn't comfortable feeling and wishing. He wasn't a man who hoped for things, either. Life was hard, and the only way to survive it was to be harder. Which is why he was raising his children to be smart, tough, and honest.

He'd never coddled Mack and Molly. He'd never read them fairy tales or indulged them at Christmas with holiday fuss, impossible wish lists, or trips to see a department store Santa.

And so, yes, it was an inconvenience to change housekeepers yet again, but better to change now, before Harley Diekerhoff had them all hoping and wishing for things that couldn't be.

Chapter Five

The ranch hands devoured their beef roast and gravy, roasted potatoes, and braised root vegetables, before practically licking the little apple crisp ramekins clean, too.

Harley took the empty dishes and platters from Paul and Lewis, who brought the dishes back most nights, since they were the youngest hands, and low on the seniority totem pole.

"Everybody doing okay over there?" Harley asked, glad to see the youngsters on the doorstep, their scruffy faces ruddy from the cold. Paul and Lewis were nineteen and twenty respectively, still boys, and yet she'd discovered in her eleven days here, that these Montana boys knew how to work, and here on the ranch they certainly worked hard.

"Yes, ma'am," Lewis answered with a shy grin, pushing up the brim of his hat. "We were all just saying that you take care of us like nobody's business."

"It's my pleasure," she answered, meaning it. She'd grown fond of these shy, tough cowboys, and she'd miss them when she left Saturday. It was on the tip of her tongue to mention that she was going but then she thought better of it. It wasn't her place to break the news. Better let Brock tell them when he was ready.

"We made you something as a thank-you," Paul said, reaching behind him and lifting a large hand-tied wreath made from fragrant pine. The green wreath had been wrapped with some barbed wire and decorated with five hammered metal stars, burlap bows, and miniature pine cones.

"It's not fancy," Paul added, "not like one of those expensive ones you'd buy in Bozeman at a designer store, but we all contributed to it. See? We each made a star and signed our name to it." He pointed to a copper brown metal star in the upper left. "That's mine. Paul. And there's Lewis's, just below mine, and JB's, and the rest."

"Hope you like it," Lewis said. "And we hope you know how much we like having you here. We were also saying, if

Maxine can't come back in January, maybe you could just... stay."

Both boys nodded their heads.

Harley smiled around the lump forming in her throat. "That's so lovely," she said taking the wreath and studying it in the light. "It's beautiful. Thank you. Thank all the guys, will you? I'm really touched, and pleased."

Paul blushed and dipped his head. "Glad you like it." He hesitated. "There is one other thing..." Paul hesitated again. "Everything okay with Mr. Sheenan's kids?"

"Why do you ask?" Harley asked.

"Earlier today Lew and me caught the twins trying to cut down a tree with an ax they found in the barn. The little girl was holding the branches back so the boy could chop the trunk. We were worried something would happen, he was swinging right over her head, and told them we'd help them if they wanted to cut the tree down. They said they didn't need help so we left. But later the tree was still there, and the ax was on the ground, and we saw blood in the snow. We got worried they'd cut off their fingers or something."

Harley's stomach rose. Her heart fell. So that's how Molly got hurt. She got hit by the ax.

Brock would flip.

The kids would be in so much trouble.

She struggled to smile. "The twins are fine, but thank you so much for checking on them. If you'll tell me where they left the ax, I can go pick it up."

"No need, we already did it," Paul said. "And we finished cutting the tree down, too. We'd rather do it than see them get hurt. They're just little kids still."

Harley shut the kitchen door, wondering if she should tell Brock about the ax episode or not. He should know, but it should also be the twins who told him.

She glanced down at the beautiful rustic wreath the ranch hands had made her. It was wonderful, thoughtful, and charming and it'd actually look perfect in the kitchen, hanging on the big river rock fireplace above the mantel.

She carried the wreath toward the mantel, and was standing on tiptoe, trying to decide where the wreath would look best, when Brock entered the kitchen.

He'd changed into black plaid flannel pajama pants and a gray knit long-sleeved shirt that clung to his muscular chest and torso, before tapering to a narrow waist. "Thought I heard some of the boys," he said, glancing around.

She nodded, trying to ignore how his flannel pajamas hung from his lean hipbones, revealing several inches of bare skin and taut, toned abs between the pajama waistband and the hem of his shirt.

Her mouth dried. He had quite a hot body. Goodness knows what else all those layers of clothes hid...

She licked her upper lip, moistening it. "Lewis and Paul just left. They brought back the dishes, and this." She lifted the wreath. "The boys made it for me."

"They made you a wreath?"

She nodded, remembering how he wasn't one who liked Christmas fuss. "It's a thank-you for taking care of them."

One of his black brows lifted. "They know you're leaving then?"

She carefully placed the wreath on the seat of the rocking chair. "No."

"They just made you a wreath for the hell of it?"

"I think they like my cooking."

He made a rough sound deep in his chest. "I think they like *you*."

"I'm not encouraging them—"

"Didn't say you were. I meant it as a compliment. They do like you, and I don't blame them for being appreciative. Maxine kept their bellies full but she didn't care too much about making them comfortable, or trying to make anyone happy. That wasn't her job." His lips curved ruefully. "Or so she'd say when the boys complained."

"I can't imagine those boys complaining about anything," she said, filling the tea kettle with water and putting it on the stove.

"They certainly didn't complain about her cooking ever again after she poured a cup of salt in their stew, and overcooked their biscuits by an hour or two, so that when the biscuits reached their table, they were hard as bricks."

Harley laughed. "She didn't!"

"She did. You don't mess with Maxine." The corners of

his mouth lifted. "You eat what she cooks, you stay out of her way when she's cleaning, and you wear your clothes however you find them... wet, dry, stinking of moth balls, or smellin' of bleach."

"That sounds horrible."

"She definitely runs a tight ship. JB calls her Warden behind her back."

Harley spluttered. "As in a prison warden?"

"That's the one."

"No wonder they're hoping Maxine won't return," she said, glancing at the kettle, waiting for it to come to a boil.

"They said that?"

She shrugged. "More or less. But it was probably just a joke—"

"It probably wasn't." He sighed, and rubbed a hand over his jaw. "I will have to do something eventually. Just not ready yet. She's known the kids since they were toddlers, and she knows her way around the place."

"So Maxine is like family to the twins."

He grimaced. "I wouldn't say that. She doesn't remember their birthday or talk much to them, but she's familiar and I trust her. She won't spoil the kids, but she won't hurt them, and she's honest to a fault. So I've put off making changes." Brock looked at her, shrugging wearily. "As you can tell, I'm not a fan of change."

No, it didn't sound like it, Harley thought.

For a moment there was just silence and then she drew a quick breath. "Speaking of the kids... have you checked on them?"

"No. Why?"

"They've been in their rooms for hours."

"They're supposed to be. I sent them to bed."

"I know, but they didn't have much lunch as they were too eager to get back outside to play—"

"If they're hungry, that's their problem, not mine."

Harley bit the inside of her lip.

But he saw her face, could read her worry. "They're in trouble. There have to be consequences for their actions," he said.

"I know, and I agree that there must be consequences, but

I don't think it'd hurt to talk to them, hear what they have to say. They've been gone for months and they only just got home."

"Then they should have made different decisions. They didn't have to go to bed without dinner. They could have told me what they were doing when Molly got hurt, because I know they were up to something. Molly didn't get hurt from a snowball fight. That was a cut next to her eye, a clean cut, with clean edges. Something made that cut and I want to know how it happened, and the kids know. But they're not talking, so they're in their room. End of story."

She nodded, wondering if now was when she should tell him what Paul and Lewis had told her, about the ax and the tree, but she didn't want to get the kids in more trouble.

"What's wrong?" Brock asked. "You think I'm too hard on them?"

The kettle whistled, saving her from immediately answering.

She grabbed a pot holder and moved the shrieking kettle to a back burner. The kettle fell silent. "Would you like a cup?" she asked, motioning to the kettle.

He shook his head. "But I am interested in your opinion. You've been here a few days with them now. Do you think I'm too hard on them?"

She squeezed the pot holder. "I'm not the best person to ask."

"Because you don't know kids?"

"Because they're your kids. I think you have to raise them according to your values."

"My brothers say I'm too hard on the twins, but they're bachelors. They don't know what it's like to have a child, to be the only one responsible for a child, never mind suddenly becoming the only person responsible for two infants still just breastfeeding when their mom is killed."

Harley couldn't imagine what it'd been like for him to bury his wife even as he had to become both mother and father to two babies. "Must have been awful," she said quietly.

"It was hell." His brow furrowed and he stared blindly across the kitchen, grief etched across his features. "Amy was such a good mom, too. She was such a natural... calm, and patient. Nothing flustered her."

"Good thing, considering you had twins."

"That was a surprise, but not a huge shock. Twins run in the Sheenan family, I have brothers who are twins—Troy and Trey—and my dad had brothers who were twins, but Amy and I were a little overwhelmed when Mack and Molly were born. They were small and needed round-the-clock feeding, and Molly had colic. She was so fussy." He smiled ruefully. "She still is."

"But Mack was easy?"

"Mack was born easy. He'd just sit there in his infant seat and chill while his sister wailed." Brock shook his head. "Thank God Mack was so good-natured. I don't think I could have handled two fussy babies on my own."

"You're a good dad," Harley said quietly, meaning it.

"I make mistakes."

"Everybody makes mistakes."

"I guess we are managing, the three of us, but I thought the hard years would be the baby years. Instead, it's getting tougher as they get older. They've got ideas and opinions and they're starting to test me—"

"They're becoming teenagers."

"They're only eleven."

"And a half." She smiled. "They told me they were born in early May. Apparently they are hoping to do something fun with you for their twelfth birthday... something about going to Orlando?"

"I have not agreed to Orlando. I would never agree to Orlando. Flathead Lake, yes. Florida, no."

"Why not Orlando?" she asked.

"Too many people. Don't like crowds. Not a big fan of amusement parks."

"Have you ever been to an amusement park?"

"No."

"You can't blame them for being curious."

"They're Montana kids. They're just as happy camping and fishing. So if they really want to go somewhere for their birthday, I'll take them to Flathead Lake. Amy's parents have a cabin there and we can fish and hike."

"Molly fishes?"

"For their tenth birthday I gave each of them new poles and tackle."

Harley squashed her smile. She couldn't imagine her Emma or Ana ever being excited about a fishing pole and tackle, but her girls were good athletes and had loved skiing and snowboarding and having adventures with their dad. That's how they'd died, too. Setting off on an adventure with their dad.

David should have never taken off in that bad weather. Never, never, ever.

But he never did listen to her. He was always so sure he knew what was best.

Her smile faded.

She realized Brock had stopped talking and was looking at her. "What are you thinking about?" he asked.

She shook her head, unable to talk about the kids, or how they died, or how selfish their father had been, piloting his own plane when there had been severe weather warnings.

"Nothing," she whispered, pushing back the flood of memories, heartsick all over again. Emma and Ana and Davi, her little boy. Gone. All gone.

She turned to the cabinet, stared blindly at the boxes of tea, waiting for her vision to clear.

"I'm sorry," Brock said, after a moment. "I forgot that this is a difficult subject for you."

"It's okay," she said thickly. She turned to face him a few moments later. "I'm sure you know it, but you're lucky. You have such sweet, smart kids. You should be proud."

"I'd be prouder if they didn't run away from school and if they'd tell me the truth when one of them gets hurt."

"Maybe they're scared that if they tell you the truth they'll get in trouble."

"I've never hit them. There's no reason for them to be afraid of me."

Harley regarded him a moment, still feeling the ache of grief that accompanied thoughts of her children. "Maybe they just need you to talk to them more. Reassure them that they can trust you—"

"Of course they can trust me. I'm their father."

"You can be a little intimidating," she said gently,

thinking that right now he looked about as soft and receptive as the granite counter slabs in the kitchen. "Maybe just try to talk to them as a friend."

His big arms crossed over his chest, drawing the knit shirt tight at his shoulders, revealing those hard carved abs again. "I'm not here to be their friend."

Suddenly JB's words came to Harley's mind. *Mr. Sheenan's been a bachelor too long.* Is that what this was?

She dropped her voice, softening her tone. "Don't you want to know who they are? Don't you want to know about their ideas... their feelings... their dreams?"

His upper lip curled. His expression was openly mocking. "For a woman who never had kids, you certainly seem to have a lot of opinions on how to raise them."

She flinched, caught off guard.

She shouldn't have been caught off guard, though. She'd pushed, wanting to help, but her attempt had backfired, and he'd lashed out at her instead.

It was a good lesson. Not just because he'd hurt her feelings, but because she wasn't a counselor, a family member, or a friend. She was his employee and day after tomorrow she'd be gone.

Dropping the teabag in her mug, Harley vowed to mind her own business until then.

She counted to ten as she filled her mug with hot water, and then counted to ten again.

When she was confident she could speak calmly, she faced Brock. "I never said I'd never had kids. I said I don't have children *now*." She looked Brock in the eye, held his gaze. "My children died with their father in a small plane crash three years ago February. And maybe you don't need to be friends with your kids, but I loved being friends with mine."

Blinking back tears, she grabbed her mug and headed to her room to sip tea and read in bed and think of anything and everything besides her children who were angels now.

Brock cursed under his breath as Harley disappeared.

He'd hurt her again and he hadn't meant to hurt her as

much as get her to stop, back off. He wasn't accustomed to being lectured, and she'd given him an earful and he'd had enough of her dispensing advice.

He didn't need advice, not when it came to parenting his children. Mack and Molly were his kids and he was raising them the way he thought best.

But with Harley gone from the kitchen, he could still feel her surprise and hurt. He could still see the bruised look in her eyes when she'd turned away.

Shit.

This is exactly why he didn't date and avoided polite society. He didn't fit in polite society. He was better away from people, better on his own.

Angry with himself, he went to the barn to do his nightly check before bed. As he entered the barn, his dogs were immediately at his heels and followed him from stall to stall as he greeted each horse, stroking noses, giving treats, trying not to think about Harley or what she'd told him.

She'd been a mother. She'd had kids. Her children had died.

He cringed all over again, disgusted with himself, not just for his put-down, but for his need to put her in her place.

What was wrong with him?

Why did he have to shame a woman?

If his mom were alive she'd be horrified. She'd raised her boys to be gentlemen. She'd taught her five sons that women were equals and deserving of protection and respect.

He certainly hadn't been respectful to Harley tonight.

Heart heavy, he returned to the house, locked up the doors, and turned off unnecessary lights but he couldn't settle down in front of the TV, not when his conscience smacked him for being a heel.

Brock climbed the stairs two by two, and then the narrow staircase to the third floor bedroom he'd carved from the attic.

He knocked on the closed door with a firm rap of his knuckles.

She opened the door after a long moment, peeking out from behind the door. Her long hair was loose, a thick golden brown curtain about her face, and from behind the door he glimpsed a bare shoulder, her skin creamy and smooth.

She must have been changing when he'd knocked.

Just like that, his body hardened, pulse quickening.

He wanted her and he couldn't remember when he'd lasted wanted anyone.

"I didn't know," he said shortly, glaring down at her, now unhappy with himself for being unable to manage the way he responded to her. In the eleven years since Amy died he'd never had an issue with lusting or physical desire, but something about Harley annihilated his famous self-control. "And I'm sorry. I'm sorry for being rough with you and not being more... sensitive. As you might have noticed, I'm not a very sensitive guy."

"I share the blame," she said. "I shouldn't have been offering advice. I won't do it again."

They were the right words but somehow they didn't make him feel better.

"Why didn't you tell me you had kids?"

"It's not something I talk about anymore." She tugged her robe up, over her shoulder, concealing her delectable skin. "I've discovered that people treat you differently if they know. *She's the lady who lost her husband and three children...* I could hear people whisper that, or look at me with pity, and I've found that it's just better for people not to know. That way there's no awkwardness." She made another little adjustment before stepping from behind the door, firmly tying her sash at her waist. "Which is why I didn't want you to know I had children. I liked coming here to work knowing that my past didn't matter, that my grief was my grief alone, and that this Christmas I'd get through the holidays with a minimum of fuss."

"And then my kids came home," he said quietly.

"Your eleven-year-olds." Her lips curved but her expression was haunted. "My oldest was eleven when she died." She drew a slow breath. "Eleven is such a great age, too."

Brock could see how hard she was trying to keep it together, trying to be calm and strong, and her strength and courage moved him far more than tears ever could.

He'd wanted her moments ago because she was beautiful and desirable and now he just wanted to hold her to comfort

70

her.

But he couldn't.

There was no way he could make a move, not even to comfort. She was his employee. He was responsible for her.

"Tell me about your kids," he said.

Her head dipped. Her voice dropped. "It's hard to talk about them. Hurts."

He heard her voice crack and his chest grew tight. It was all he could do to not reach out and caress her cheek. "It doesn't help to talk about them?"

Her head shook and she lifted her head, looked up at him, eyes bright. "I'm still mad they're gone. I don't know why they're gone."

It was the tear trembling on her lower lashes that did him in.

He reached out to wipe the tear from her lashes and then the tear from the other side and when he couldn't catch the tears because they were falling too fast he did the only thing he could think of. He drew her toward him and kissed her.

The kiss wasn't meant to be sexual, and her lips were cool and they trembled beneath his. Brock was afraid he'd scared her, but then she slowly kissed him back, the coolness of her mouth giving away to a simmering heat.

He liked the way she kissed him back, her lips opening to him, and he took her mouth, craving her warmth. She tasted both sexy and sweet and he drank her in, feeling more than he wanted to feel, feeling more than he ever expected to feel and he leaned into her, backing her against the doorframe, his big body pressed to hers, needing to get as close as he could.

Harley didn't understand the kiss, only that it was fierce and real, and it opened something inside of her, something blistering, and dangerous, because it silenced her brain and muted all thought.

Suddenly there was nothing but this moment, this man, this kiss.

There was no past, no future.

Nothing but this wild need burning inside her.

The wild need was unlike anything she'd ever felt, maybe because it wasn't about a particular sensation, but all sensation. She needed to feel and feel and feel because it'd been forever since she felt anything but cold, and anger, and pain.

The rational Harley would have stopped him at a kiss, but the rational Harley was gone. This other Harley was in her place, wanting the kiss, wanting his hands, wanting his knee pressing up where she was so very warm.

She arched against him and kissed him back, craving everything he could give her. She'd felt nothing for so long and now this... this inferno, need so great she didn't think she'd ever get enough.

He devoured her mouth, his tongue plunging in, stroking, teasing. Her hands rose to his chest and she clung to him, legs weak, heart pounding. His hand tugged at her robe, pulling it open, exposing her breasts. He lifted his head briefly to gaze down at her, and his dark hot gaze so carnal hungry that she felt as though she were melting.

"You're beautiful," he groaned, head dropping to kiss her again, as he cupped one of her breasts, fingers playing her taut nipple as if he'd known her body forever.

In a strange way she felt as if she'd known him forever, too, and she would have given him everything, and all of her, but a shout came from below.

"Dad! *Dad!* Where are you?"

Brock reluctantly lifted his head. Harley felt a pang as he shifted back.

"Molly," he said, as the girl continued to shout his name.

"Dad, if we promise never ever to be stupid again, can we please have some dinner?"

Molly's wail was both funny and quirky and sweet, just like the girl herself and just like that, reality returned, practically slapping Harley across the face.

What in God's name was she doing?

Brock took a reluctant step back and dragged a hand through his black hair. "Bad timing," he muttered.

"Maybe it's good timing," Harley answered, legs trembling. She'd come so close to losing her head. She'd come so close to losing control...

Shocked and more than a little mortified, Harley dragged the edges of her robe closed. Face hot, cheeks flaming she moved inside her room. "Go to her," she said. "I'll see you tomorrow." And then before he could say a word, she closed the door as fast as she could.

Chapter Six

Brock stood in the middle of Molly's room, grimly listening to the twins recount their tree-chopping adventure, grinding his jaw to keep from expressing horror when he realized just how close his daughter had come to losing an eye... or worse.

"That was as stupid as you could get," he said bluntly, giving his children a severe look as they sat side by side on Molly's bed. "And so damn dangerous—"

"I know," Mack agreed. "I can't believe I let Molly talk me into it."

Brock made a rough sound of disapproval. "Don't blame your sister. That's pathetic, Mack. It is. You have a brain. Use it."

The boy nodded, gaze dropping but Molly stared back at her father. "We wouldn't have to do it if you'd get us a tree," she said, expressing little of the remorse she'd shown when he'd first entered her room fifteen minutes ago.

"That's absurd," Brock snorted "You can't blame me for nearly losing your eye... or your head."

"Why won't you let us have a tree?" she persisted indignantly.

"We have real live trees growing outside. We don't need to cut one and bring it inside."

"Why not? They're pretty," Molly flashed. "And everybody has one. We want one, too."

"Well, sneaking off with an ax into the woods isn't the way to get one."

"Then how do we get one if you won't chop one down for us?" Molly demanded.

Brock was losing his temper. "I'm not discussing Christmas trees now."

"But you never do. You never discuss anything we want to talk about. You just make up all these rules and expect us to follow them—"

"Yes," he interrupted. "That's right. I do. You're the kids. I'm the adult. I make the rules. You obey. See how that works?"

"But your rules don't make sense," she protested under her breath.

"Of course they do," he snapped.

"Maybe to you, but not to us. Some of your rules are just... mean."

"Mean?"

Her head nodded, her lips pressing flat. "It's like you're the Grinch and you hate Christmas—"

"The *Grinch*?"

She nodded again. "You can't stand for anyone to play or have fun. You hate it when we want to do something fun. Sometimes I think you don't even love us!"

Brock's jaw dropped. "*What*?"

"Maybe you even hate us!" she flung at him, scrambling off the bed and running to the adjoining bathroom where she slammed the door closed.

Brock stared at the bathroom door in disbelief before turning to Mack, who sat very still on the edge of his sister's bed.

Mack glanced up at his dad and then looked down again at his hands which were knotting unhappily in his lap.

Brock's heart pounded as if he'd just run through very deep snow. "Is she being dramatic or does she really feel this way?"

Mack's head hung lower.

Brock suppressed the queasy sensation in his gut. Did his kids really think he hated them? "Tell me the truth, Mack."

"I don't want to speak for her."

Brock studied his son's thin slumped shoulders and the curve of his neck. Mack had never been a big, sturdy kid, but he looked downright skinny at the moment. "Then don't speak for her, speak for yourself. How do you feel? Do you really think I don't love you?"

"I know you love us," Mack said in a low voice. He hesitated a long moment. "But... " His voice faded away. He didn't finish the sentence.

"But what?"

"But sometimes you seem so... annoyed...by us. Like we're a pain and always in your way—"

"*No.*"

Mack shrugged. "Okay."

His son's half-hearted response made Brock want to hit something, throw something, which wasn't probably the right response. Brock drew a breath, and then another, trying to be patient, trying to understand when he couldn't understand at all. He'd never dated anyone after their mother in order to protect and preserve Amy's memory. He'd refused to spoil them so his kids would be raised with solid family values. And he'd only sent his kids away to school recently when it became clear that they needed to be pushed, socially, academically, if they were to succeed.

Brock crossed his arms, hiding his hard fists. "Don't say okay just to placate me, Mack. You can speak up, have an opinion."

The boy slumped even more unhappily. "I don't want to make you mad. I don't like making you mad."

"You don't have to be scared of me," Brock retorted.

Mack looked up at him, worry in his dark eyes. "But you are kind of scary when you're mad."

Brock couldn't believe what he was hearing. Dumbfounded, he stared at his boots, unable to think or speak. Were his kids really afraid of him? His gut churned. "Mack, I've never hit you. Never even spanked you. How can you be afraid of me?"

Mack's shoulders lifted and fell. "You don't smile or laugh or do fun stuff with us. You just get mad at us. A lot."

Brock closed his eyes at the rush of words. It was a lot to take in. Hard to process it all. He exhaled slowly. "So I don't do fun stuff, and just get mad. Is that it?"

Mack nodded.

Brock felt like punching something. Instead he drew a deep breath, trying hard to sort out everything he was hearing. "Can you explain the *stuff*? What stuff are you missing out on?"

"Everything. Going to the movies and having friends over and taking trips together somewhere fun. The only time you've ever taken us anywhere was when you took us to boarding school."

Molly opened the bathroom door to shout. "And Christmas! We don't ever have Christmas or Valentine's Day or Easter or Fourth of July. We don't do holidays or anything fun because you don't believe in fun. It's against your religion apparently."

Brock clapped a hand on his head thinking his brain was going to explode. "That's ridiculous. You are both being ridiculous. Knock it off and grow up. You're eleven, almost twelve—" he stopped midsentence, hearing himself.

Grow up.

He'd just told his eleven-year-olds to grow up. It's what his dad always used to say to him and look how close he and his dad were today....

Brock exhaled slowly. If Amy were here, she'd be disgusted with him. If Amy were here...

... none of this would be happening.

The kids would have Christmas and Valentine's Day and all the other days. They'd laugh and play because Amy believed in laughing and playing.

That's why he'd fallen in love with Amy. She made him want to laugh and play and without her....

Without her, life was just hard. He missed her. He needed her. Not just for her laughter, but for her support.

Raising two kids was hard.

Brock had been doing it a long time on his own but God help him, he was tired and lonely and alone.

He swallowed with difficulty, aware that the twins were staring at him, anxious and worrying about what would happen next.

His eyes burned. His chest ached. He loved his children, he did, but he was beginning to realize his love might just not be enough.

"Go down and get a snack if you're hungry," he said quietly. "I'll see you in the morning."

In bed, in her room, Harley heard almost every word.

She didn't want to hear but her room was just above

Molly's and the voices carried far too easily in the air duct. She couldn't remember when she last felt so conflicted.

The kiss... shouldn't have happened. But oh, the kiss, it'd been amazing. And she shouldn't be thinking about Brock, or feeling sorry for him, or the kids. She shouldn't be involved and she shouldn't care.

But she did.

She didn't want to worry about them, but she felt so terribly protective.

It was a mistake coming here. It was a mistake getting attached. She was so very attached.

Leaving would hurt so much.

And she was leaving the day after tomorrow.

Harley closed her eyes, drew a deep breath, trying to block out her thoughts, her feelings about returning to her family.

She couldn't. She wasn't ready to return to California.

A knock sounded on her door.

Harley left her bed, slipped her robe on over her nightgown and opened the door.

Mack stood in the hall with a plate of yesterday's sugar cookies and a glass of milk. "We brought you a snack." He smiled at her and yet his dark eyes looked anxious. "We hope you didn't get in trouble with Dad."

Harley took the cookies and milk. "Thank you for thinking of me, and no, I didn't get in trouble with your dad."

"He's not really as scary as he seems," Mack said under his breath.

"I don't think he is scary at all."

"You don't?"

She shook her head, smiling. "No. I think he's just tired and a little bit lonely. I have a feeling he still misses your mom."

"She died when we were babies. We didn't even know her."

"But your dad loved your mom, and every time he looks at you, he thinks of her." Harley set the cookies and milk on her nightstand. "He loved her a lot."

Mack shrugged. "That's what he says."

"You don't believe him?"

"Oh I believe him. But I kind of wish he didn't love her so much."

Harley blinked. "Why?"

"Because maybe then Dad would have married someone else and we would have had a mom."

Oh.

Oh, baby boy.

Harley's heart ached. Here he was, eleven years old and wondering what it would have been like to have a mom.

She reached for Mack and gave him a swift hug. These kids were stealing her heart, bit by bit, piece by piece. "Don't give up hope," she whispered in his ear before releasing him.

His eyes watered as he looked up at her. "I won't."

Harley went downstairs the next morning at five-thirty. It was the time she started her day but when she reached the kitchen the lights were already on, the coffee made, and the fire burning brightly in the big fireplace, which meant that Brock was up already. She wondered if one of the cows had been calving, or if he was just taking care of paperwork.

At six he walked through the kitchen to refill his coffee. She was making a breakfast casserole and she kept chopping the ham and Swiss cheese, trying to appear nonchalant but her pulse was racing in her veins and she wanted him to say something to help her make sense of what happened last night. That kiss had been so hot and intense... and so damn confusing, too.

She hadn't slept well, tossing and turning, playing the kiss over and over in her head, all the while wondering what he'd say or do this morning. Now it was morning and she just needed to know if he was angry, disappointed, or maybe just regretful.

She dumped the cheese and meat into a bowl and started dicing the green onion.

"Harley."

She looked up to see Brock at the island, hands on the counter.

She set the knife down on the cutting board. "Yes?"

"Did you in any way encourage the kids to go chop down their own Christmas tree?"

Harley wiped her hands on the skirt of her apron. "No."

"You didn't know they were tree hunting?"

"No."

"And if I told you I didn't approve of all this Christmas fuss, and didn't want them to get caught up in any more fuss, what would you say?"

"I'd ask you to let us have one more fun day of fuss before I leave tomorrow."

"But you wouldn't go behind my back? You wouldn't do something I wouldn't approve of?"

"No." Harley reached for the knife and the loaf of French bread. "I wouldn't do that. I couldn't do that." She turned the bread and began slicing. "I don't believe in breaking up families, and it would devastate me if I came between you and your kids."

Brock stared at her a long moment. "You were married twelve years."

"Almost twelve years."

"Did you like being married?"

She paused slicing, her knife suspended in mid-air. She didn't know how to answer that. She'd liked parts of marriage. Parts of it had been so hard. She hadn't expected all the arguing. They'd fought over everything. Mainly money, and then family, sex, control. But always about money. He didn't like budgets and saving. She'd been raised to be frugal, raised to bank your money, not spend it.

And then the discovery that David wanted out. He'd fallen in love with someone else.

"We were separated at the time my husband and kids died," Harley said quietly, turning the loose bread slices sideways to cut them into strips. "No one knew that we were struggling. At least, I'd never told anyone in my family that David wanted a divorce. I couldn't." She looked up at Brock. "I didn't want a divorce. Maybe it wasn't a perfect marriage, but it was my marriage, and David was my husband, and we had three beautiful children. And I lost it all because he went behind my back, ignored me." She gave her head a small shake and returned to cubing the bread. "So no, I would never defy you. Not unless it was life and death."

Brock's dark head inclined. "Thank you," he said quietly.

Harley worked hard to stay busy all day, and worked even harder to stay out of Brock's way, so when the kids were at loose ends in the early afternoon, and Harley had caught up on her chores, she bundled up in layers and headed outside to find the kids, her pockets full of carrots and charcoal briquettes and an extra scarf to help them build a snowman.

At first the twins laughed at her, claiming they were too old to make snowmen, but when Harley started rolling snow around to make a big snow ball, they suddenly joined in, competing to see who could make the biggest ball and before she knew it, they were throwing snow and pushing each other into snow and chasing each other around the yard.

Harley screamed with laughter as Molly shoved a glove full of snow down the back of her coat, and inside her shirt. "That's cold," she shrieked, dancing from foot to foot as she swiped at the snow, trying to get it out.

The snow wasn't going to come out. It was already melting and making her wet and cold, which meant the only thing left to do was give Molly a taste of her own medicine.

Harley made a big snow ball, ducked behind one of the pine trees and waited until Molly was whizzing snow balls at Mack and then dropped her snow ball right on top of Molly's head.

But instead of laughing, Molly fell apart and stormed off, marching into the house.

Harley felt bad when Molly left. "I shouldn't have done that," she said, brushing snow from her gloves.

"You were just playing."

"She didn't like it."

"Molly likes to make the rules and be in charge. If she's not, she has a hissy fit."

Harley shot him a quick side glance. "Does that bother you?"

"Most of the time, no. Every now and then, yeah. She doesn't realize that she wins because I let her win. I just don't care enough to always fight."

"That's very mature of you."

He shrugged. "It's just a survival thing. Uncle Troy always said you got to pick your fights or you'll be like Uncle Trey, serving time for fighting the wrong folks." Mack saw her shocked expression and grimaced. "Yeah. I know. It's bad."

"This is your dad's brother?"

"Yeah, and Uncle Trey was our favorite uncle, too. He used to live in Marietta so we'd see him a lot. But he's been in jail a long time now." Mack added a note of warning. "But don't mention it to my dad. It makes him really upset. Uncle Trey was like Dad's best friend."

The wind swept through the trees, blowing snow from the limbs as they started walking back to the house.

Mack peeled off his gloves wet and tugged off his hat. "I get mad at Molly sometimes," he said, "but she is my best friend."

Harley smiled. "You're lucky you have each other."

He nodded. "Yeah. But it's going to be weird in January."

Harley glanced at the boy. "Weird, why?"

"Because I don't know what's going to happen with the Academy." They'd reached the back porch and took turns scraping snow off the soles of their boots. "I don't want to go back, not without her."

"But Molly's going back—" Harley broke off, seeing Mack's brow furrow and his eyes darken. "Isn't she?"

"They kicked her out." Mack's lips compressed. "Permanently, this time."

"What did she do?"

He sighed. "Everything."

Harley shivered inside her coat. "She's been in trouble before?"

"Yes. They warned her that next time they'd expel her, but that's what Molly wanted. She doesn't like being away from Dad. She thinks Dad needs us here, home, so she... acts out. Does stupid stuff." His dark head lifted, his hair shaggy and thick like his father, his dark eyes his father's too. "She's not bad, though. She just gets so homesick." His shoulders twisted. "I do, too."

Harley heard the dogs bark in the distance. Brock must be

heading toward the house. "Your dad doesn't know, does he?" she asked.

"No."

"He needs to know."

"Yeah. But I don't know how to tell him. He'll just get mad." Mack sighed, expression troubled. "Seems like he's always so mad."

"I think your dad doesn't know how to handle the fact that you and Molly are growing up. I also think he's worried that he's going to make a mistake as a dad, and do the wrong thing."

"The mistake was sending us to the Academy."

"It won't get any easier by not telling him. Better to break the news and get it over with. You'll feel better when you tell him."

He grimaced. "I don't think so."

She laughed and ruffled his hair which was icy cold. "He loves you, both you and Molly, so much. You have to believe that. You have to give him a chance. Now let's go in and get into dry clothes, then you find Molly, make sure she's okay, and I'll start making some hot cocoa. Sound like a plan?"

She was at the stove, monitoring the milk in the saucepan when footsteps sounded on the back porch and Brock entered the kitchen.

"I'm making the kids hot chocolate," she said, skin prickling as Brock approached the stove, glanced down into the pan. "Would you like some?"

"Hot chocolate?" he repeated.

"Yes, with marshmallows and whipped cream and chocolate shavings." She smiled at him, feeling nervous and shy. She'd shared an awful lot this morning and now she wished she hadn't. Only thing to do now was keep it professional. "Or I can keep it simple. Just cocoa if you prefer."

"I'll take some whipped cream," he said, adding a log to the fire before dropping onto one of the stools at the counter. "If it's not too much trouble."

She felt her cheeks warm. "It's not too much trouble." She

checked the milk to make sure it hadn't started to boil and then retrieved another mug. After burning the pies yesterday she didn't want to scald the milk today. But it would be a lot easier to concentrate if Brock were somewhere else.

"Want to call the kids?" she asked, staring down at the simmering milk, gauging the tiny bubbles.

"No."

She glanced at him over her shoulder. He practically filled the island, his big arms resting on the counter, his shoulders squared. "The cocoa is going to be ready soon."

"But it's not ready yet," he said mildly.

"It will be *soon*."

"Soon, but not yet."

She glared at him. "You're being difficult."

"According to my kids I'm always difficult. And mean. And determined to make them unhappy for the rest of their lives."

She hadn't meant to laugh. She hadn't even known she was going to laugh but the gurgle of laughter slipped from her and she clapped a hand over her mouth to stifle the sound.

"It's not funny," he said, and yet his eyes were smiling at her.

"No, it's not." Her lips twitched as she took in his big strong body, his black gleaming hair and his dark eyes in that ruggedly handsome face. "I'm sorry."

"You don't sound sorry at all."

Her lips twitched again. "I'm trying to sound sympathetic."

"You're not trying very hard."

"I'm also trying not to tell you I told-you-so."

"Again, not trying very hard."

She bit down into her lip to check her smile, and yet he was smiling a little, a small sexy smile that made her heart turn over and her insides melt.

He was too good-looking when he smiled. Much, much too good-looking.

"Don't do that," she said, trying to sound severe.

"Do what?"

"Be all friendly and sexy—"

"Sexy?" he pounced on the word, black eyebrows rising.

"Because from now on we are keeping things professional."

"Professional," he repeated.

Her tummy flipped and her pulse quickened. "Platonic."

He said nothing just looked at her from beneath his dark lashes, his expression lazy, sultry, knowing.

He remembered how she'd kissed him last night. He remembered how she responded.

Harley flushed. "I'm here to do a job and that's the only reason I'm here—"

"Harley—"

"I'm serious. I'm the housekeeper and cook—"

He was up off the stool and at her side, yanking the sauce pan with the boiling milk from the hot burner even as the milk bubbled up and over the edge of the pan all over the stove.

"Damn," Harley cried. She could tell from the scorched smell that she hadn't just wasted the milk, she'd burned the pan. She looked up at Brock and jabbed a finger in his chest as he was standing far too close. "This is your fault. None of this would have happened if you'd just gotten the kids like I told you."

Brock stared down into Harley's bright green eyes, seeing the sparkle of anger that made her eyes light up and her cheeks flush. He liked this side of her, feisty and fierce, her finger pressed to his chest as she took him to task.

He'd always admired intelligent women, and Amy had been one of the smartest girls at Marietta High School, testing off the charts, and earning several full-ride scholarships to prestigious universities. But Amy hadn't wanted to leave Montana. She loved Montana and Brock too much to leave either, so Brock and Amy both attended school in Bozeman, earning degrees together, graduating together and settling down on their new ranch, with Brock to work the ranch and Amy to work in Marietta in the commercial banking division for Copper Mountain Savings & Loan. She'd been on her way to work when her car was broadsided.

One of the neighbors, a fellow rancher, was first on the

scene and the neighbor called Brock. Brock made it to Amy before the paramedics, and he was with her at the scene when she died. There hadn't been time to transport her anywhere, and so Brock was always grateful he'd reached her quickly, grateful he'd been able to kiss her and promise to always take care of the babies, and raise them properly.

He didn't know if she'd heard him. He didn't know if she'd understood what he was saying, but in the eleven years since she'd died, he'd kept his promise to her. He'd always put the kids first, which meant he didn't date or go out with friends, or screw around with his brothers.

No, he'd stayed here, on the ranch, focusing on work and the kids.

At times it'd been damn lonely. But Amy was the love of his life and impossible to replace. He hadn't wanted to replace her, either.

But being alone for so long had made him a harder man. He knew he was tougher, colder, less affectionate than he'd been when Amy was alive. Amy had been good for him. She'd been his laughter, his best friend, his sunshine.

Staring down now into Harley's face Brock keenly felt the loss of laughter and sunshine.

It'd been eleven years since he'd had a partner. He could use a best friend again.

Brock reached out and captured Harley's finger, gently bending the finger, shaping her hand into a fist, covering her fist with his own.

Her hand was warm and small, her skin soft.

He liked touching her. Hell, he'd like to touch all of her. Celibacy had lost its appeal a long time ago. "We need to talk about last night, what happened upstairs," he said.

He saw a flicker in her eyes before she dropped her gaze. "No, we don't," she whispered.

"We do," he answered, wanting to kiss her again, needing to kiss her again, but not comfortable bedding her as long as she worked for him. But at the same time, once she left here tomorrow he didn't know where she was going to go or what she planned on doing. "Tomorrow your replacement comes."

"Yes."

"Are you flying back to California, or staying in

Marietta?"

"I haven't thought that far."

"Do you even know where you're going tomorrow?"

"No."

The twins suddenly raced into the kitchen, pushing each other as they rounded the corner. They skidded to a halt as they spotted him holding Harley's hand.

Harley saw the kids' expression as they saw their dad holding her hand and she broke free, moving quickly to the sink. "Just a little burn," she said briskly, turning the faucet on and running her hand beneath the water. "It'll be fine."

Brock lounged against the counter. "You're sure you don't want ice?"

She shot him a swift glance. "It's fine," she said flatly. "But I do need to get a new pan and start fresh milk if we want that hot chocolate anytime soon."

"Or maybe we just forget the hot chocolate," Brock said casually, "and go into town for dinner and a movie."

The twins looked at him, wide eyed. "But you *hate* movies," Molly said.

"And eating in town," Mack added.

Brock frowned. "I don't *hate* movies or dinner out. We just don't ever have a lot of time so we don't go into Marietta much, but I thought it'd be fun to go tonight—"

"Fun?" Molly screwed her face up in horror. "Did you just say fun? Who are you? And where did my dad go?"

"Never mind," Brock said, shrugging. "We can just stay here. Have a quiet night at home—"

"No!" Mack said.

Molly ran to Brock and flung her arms around his waist, squeezing him tight. "Just teasing, Dad. Come on, laugh. Take a joke. We want to go. We do!"

Brock's lips curved in a crooked smile as he glanced from his daughter to his son and back. "I have a very good sense of humor. I have to, with you two for children." Then he stroked Molly's hair, smoothing the reddish-brown strands. "And of course I love you. I've loved you from the moment your mom and I found out we had a baby on the way. Now get your coats and I'll see what's playing at The Palace tonight."

The kids went to get their coats, leaving Brock and Harley alone in the kitchen. "I'm glad you're taking them out," Harley said, happy with Brock for making an effort to do something the kids would enjoy. She was also proud of him for putting his feelings into words. Kids needed to hear that they were loved. Actions were important, but words were essential, too. "You will have fun."

"So will you," he answered, looking up from his cell phone, as he'd immediately gone online to check for movie times. "Do you care what movie we see? Or are you up for anything?"

Harley's mouth opened, closed. A lump filled her throat. "I can't go," she said quietly, going to the stove to retrieve the burnt pan. "This is a Dad and kids thing."

"But the kids like you and I know they'd enjoy having you along—"

"No." Harley's voice was firm. "They might like me, but they *need* you. They need time alone with you, being your primary focus, getting your undivided attention."

"But they've always been my focus. They've never had competition. It's always been the three of us."

"Good." She smiled at him, liking him even more for wanting to include her, but she wasn't part of the family. She was the temporary housekeeper and cook and leaving in the morning. "You go. I'll manage things here and I'm happy managing things here. I love that you're taking the kids out and doing fun things. It's not just your kids who need to play. You need to play, too, Brock Sheenan. You're a good man. You deserve a good life."

He was quiet a moment, staring out the window. "Don't leave tomorrow."

Her heart turned over. "I have to."

"Why?"

"You know why."

"Because it's hard to be around kids," he said.

"Being around kids makes me miss being a mom." She swallowed hard. "Makes me... envious... of what I don't have." She looked at him, wanting him to understand. "If your kids were awful or hateful it'd be easier here. I could cook and clean and leave in January without a second thought. But your kids remind me of m—" she broke off, pressed a hand to her mouth to keep the word in.

Mine.

The twins needed a mother, too, and she knew how to mother. She'd been a good mother and if she weren't careful, she'd want to stay here. She'd want to take care of the kids, spoiling them, hugging them. They were good kids. Lovely kids. They needed to be cherished. Adored.

I could love them, she thought, looking at Brock. *I could love them, and you...*

Harley turned back to the sink, and turned the hot water on, filling the scalded pan. "Go," she said hoarsely. "*Please.*"

Chapter Seven

Harley was in bed reading when Brock and the kids returned from their dinner and movie night in Marietta. It was late, past ten, which meant they had made quite a night of it. She hoped they'd had dinner, seen the movie, and then gone somewhere for ice cream or dessert after. It's what she would have done with her kids.

She listened as voices and footsteps sounded on the stairs. The kids sounded giddy, silly, their voices were louder than usual and animated. She smiled to herself, listening, catching only bits and pieces of their conversation, warmed by their laughter, happy that they were happy.

Book pressed to her chest, she listened to Brock's heavier footsteps echo in the stairwell below. It sounded as if he was in hallway outside the kids rooms talking to them. One of the twins must have said something funny because suddenly she heard his laugh, deep and rich and so incredibly sexy she felt a fizz of pleasure.

He didn't laugh often but when he did it was so damn appealing. He was so appealing. She was falling for him.

That's why she wasn't cold and frozen anymore.

That's why her heart tingled and her body felt so sensitive.

She was coming to life again. She was waking up, feeling, and it scared her. But she couldn't stop the prickling, tingling sensation creeping through her, sensation in her fingers and toes, sensation surging into her arms and legs, into her torso, where she'd been so cold for so long, and she wasn't cold anymore.

Her heart still hurt, but it wasn't the icy pain of old, but a new flutter of emotion, a strange bewildering flutter that was fear and yet excitement.

Exhilaration.

As well as dread.

She was feeling and needing and wanting and yet she

didn't want to be hurt again, wasn't ready to be hurt again.

Harley took a quick breath, and left the bed and began to pack. It wouldn't take long to pack, she hadn't brought that much with her from California, but at least emptying the closet and the dresser drawers would give her something to do.

Activity would keep her from thinking too much. She didn't want to think too much, not tonight, not when she was battling her heart, trying to keep it under control.

She had to be smart. Had to be practical. She didn't belong here, not long term, and she couldn't forget herself and invest in a family that wasn't her own, and risk having her heart broken all over again.

A hesitant knock sounded on the bedroom door. The door opened and Molly stuck her head around the edge of the door. "Miss Diekerhoff?"

Harley closed the suitcase. "Yes, Molly?"

"I wanted to apologize... for earlier. I was kind of bratty outside, when we had the snowball fight. I'm sorry."

"You were fine."

But Molly shook her head. "No. I was rude. I know I was rude and you've done so many nice things for Mack and me and I want you to know I appreciate it."

"I haven't done anything."

"Well, compared to Maxine you've been amazing."

Harley smiled and sat down on the foot of the bed. "Maxine sounds very... interesting."

"Oh, she is. She's... interesting... all right." The girl smiled and glanced past Harley to the suitcase on the floor. "You're packing."

It was a statement, not a question, and Harley felt a pang. "Yes."

"When are you leaving?"

Harley hesitated. "In the morning."

"*What*?" Molly's voice rose.

"I'm only a temporary fill in—"

"Yes, until Maxine comes back, but she's not back for another month." Molly stared at Harley hard. "Did you and Dad have a fight?"

"No."

"So you are upset about me being bratty."

"*No.*"

"Then why go?"

Harley didn't know how to explain any of this to Molly, not when it was so complicated. "I'm not the best fit for the ranch—"

"That's not true. Daddy's happy with you here. We're happy with you here. Everybody likes having you here. Even JB. He says you're the best thing that's happened to Copper Mountain Ranch, and he's been here almost ten years." Molly approached Harley where she sat on the bed, and put her hands together, in a little prayer. "Don't go," she pleaded. "You have to stay. We need you."

"Oh, Molly—"

"*I* need you," she interrupted. "'Specially since they're not going to let me go back to school in New York."

Harley reached out to tug on a strand of Molly's warm brown hair. "I'm sure your dad will figure something out."

"But I don't want to go away. I want to be here with Dad. I want to live at home. And I like being here with you here, too. It feels... better." Molly's eyes filled with tears. "You make it better. You make it feel... good. 'Cause you're not like a housekeeper. You're like a... mom. Or at least, like what I think a mom would be."

For a moment Harley couldn't speak. She swallowed hard, and then again, fighting the awful lump in her throat making it hard to breathe. "Thank you," she said huskily. "That's probably the nicest thing anyone could say to me."

Molly sat down next to Harley on the bed, and looked at her, her small pale brow furrowing. "Don't you want kids, Miss Harley?"

Harley nodded slowly, aching for all that was and all that wasn't and all that could never be.

"But you want your own kids," Molly persisted softly.

Harley bit down into her lip as tears filled her eyes. Her hand shook as she reached up to wipe beneath her eyes, needing to dry the tears before they fell. "I don't know how to answer that."

"Oh, I made you sad!" Molly leaned forward, her eyes searching Harley's. "Don't cry," she crooned, wiping away a tear that had slipped free. "Don't cry. I'm sorry. I always say the wrong thing. Mack says I always talk too much—"

"No, you don't." Harley reached out to cup the girl's cheek. She held Molly's gaze, her own expression fierce. "You're perfect. Absolutely perfect in every way. Don't let anyone tell you otherwise."

Molly nodded and hugged Harley, her small arms squeezing fiercely and Harley hugged the girl back.

"So stay with us," Molly whispered. "I think you're supposed to be with us, Miss Harley."

"And how do you know that?"

"I can't explain it. I just know so."

There were no words.

There was nothing Harley could say. She kissed Molly's forehead and gave the girl a last, fierce hug.

Harley couldn't sleep after Molly left. She was too stirred up, too full of ambivalent emotion.

She didn't want to leave.

She had to leave.

She was already too attached to this family...

It wasn't her family...

As the clock downstairs chimed midnight, Harley gave up on sleep and went down to the kitchen to make tea.

While the water boiled, she added a small log to the burning embers in the fireplace and then remained crouching in front of the fire, letting the red and gold flames warm her.

She felt positively sick about leaving, but that's exactly what worried her. It's why she couldn't let herself stay another day. She'd come here for a job, come here to work, and instead she'd fallen in love with the family.

In nine short days this house, and this family, felt like home.

"I thought I heard you," Brock said, yawning from the shadows of the kitchen doorway.

She rose quickly. "I didn't mean to wake you."

"You didn't. I was thinking about you."

"You look like you were asleep."

He shrugged as he entered the kitchen, dropping into the

rocking chair near her. "I guess I was dreaming about you then."

She moved back a couple steps, needing distance. "You shouldn't do that."

"Do what?"

"Dream about me. Think about me. Any of that."

He tipped his head back. "Why not?"

"Because." She sighed, looked away, running a hand across her forehead, aware that it wasn't a very articulate response but her emotions were so raw. She felt so raw even now. Molly's questions had undone her.

"Molly told me she begged you to stay," Brock said quietly.

Harley looked at him sharply.

"She also said she made you cry," he added.

Harley closed her eyes, holding her breath.

"I'm sorry she upset you." Brock's husky voice seemed to burrow deep inside of her. "She means well—"

"I cried because she made me happy," Harley blurted, opening her eyes, tears falling again, already. "She paid me the nicest compliment and I just wish... " Her voice faded and she shook her head. There were no words...no words at all...

"What do you wish?" he asked.

She shook her head. "It doesn't matter. It won't change anything—"

"You never know. Some wishes do come true."

The tea kettle whistled and Brock got to his feet. "I'll make the tea," he said, motioning for Harley to take the rocking chair. "You, sit. Relax. I've got this."

"Why?"

"You've taken care of my ranch hands, my kids, me. Can't I do something for you, just once?"

Harley slowly sat down in the still-warm rocking chair and curled her legs up under her, watching Brock cross the dark kitchen lit by only the firelight. He was so big and powerfully built, the kind of man who looked right in firelight with all those thick muscles and rippling biceps.

She watched him turn off the burner and set out mugs and search for the right tea. It was a pleasure watching him move, so rugged and beautiful in sweat pants and a white T-shirt that hugged him in all the right places.

Looking at him only made her want him more. He'd felt so good last night, pressed up against her. Warm, hard, strong. He'd kissed her with fire, kissed her with need, kissed her as if she were infinitely desirable.

It felt good to be desirable.

It'd made her hope. And wish. Longing for things she didn't have, and might never have again.

A man who loved her deeply.

A man who loved her and would always love her.

A man who wouldn't tire of her even though she'd given him three beautiful children.

A man who would fight to the end to keep his family together...

Her eyes burned and she blinked, clearing her vision to watch Brock walk back across the kitchen, two mugs of tea hooked by the fingers of one hand and a plate of Harley's gingersnap cookies in the other.

"My lady," he said, bowing as he handed her a mug.

She smiled unsteadily as she looked up at him. He looked so lovely in the firelight, his dark hair rumpled and his jaw shadowed, his black lashes lifting, revealing brown, gleaming eyes.

She liked him, a lot.

It was strange and disorienting and bittersweet to feel so much.

Until a few days ago, he hadn't said more than eight words to her at any one time and she had to admit, it had been better when he'd ignored her. She'd been able to maintain her distance when he was detached.

"Thank you, sir," she said, as he set the cookies on the side table next to the rocking chair and retrieved one of the stools from the island and carried it back to the fire, placing it in front of Harley.

He sat down on the stool facing her, and leaned back against the dark wood, long legs extended, looking very relaxed as he sipped his tea.

Harley sipped her tea, too, but felt far from relaxed.

They might look all cozy and domestic sipping herbal tea in front of the fire, but there was nothing cozy about the tension coiling inside her.

Brock was not soothing company. He didn't calm her down. He wound her up, and ever since he'd entered the kitchen, he'd lit the room up, even though it was still dark.

She didn't know how he did it, either. Wind her up. Turn her on. But last night she literally fell into his arms, and then fell apart for him, and she didn't do that. Harley didn't go through life wanting and desiring. She was far too practical for that.

But Brock was making her want the most impractical things.

Like right now. She was baffled by his energy, a potent male energy that made her aware of things she never thought about, like her body, her lips, her skin.

He was doing it to her again, right now. The tension was incredible. The kitchen was practically crackling and humming.

She was crackling and humming, too, which was baffling, since she hadn't ever hummed for anyone before.

Flushing, she lifted her head, met his gaze. He let her look, too, his dark gaze holding hers, challenging her.

He wanted her.

He wanted to finish what they'd started last night.

Harley's pulse quickened and the silence stretched, wrapping around them, making the spacious kitchen feel very small and private. Intimate.

It wasn't. This was the kitchen, the heart of the house, and even though the kids were asleep, they could come downstairs at any time.

The kids...

She had to remember the twins. Had to remember facts, reality. "Maybe I should go back to bed," she said, shifting uneasily.

"Why?"

"You know why." She licked her upper lip, her mouth suddenly too dry. "Last night."

"What about last night?"

She could feel him across from her, feel him as surely as if he was touching her, just the way he'd touched her last night, his hands beneath her robe, hands cupping, stroking, making her forget everything...

She couldn't afford to forget everything. It was too dangerous. She exhaled in a little rush. "Last night was a mistake."

His dark gaze met hers, held. For a long moment he said nothing, and then his powerful shoulders shrugged. "I've been thinking the same thing."

Her eyes widened. It was the last thing she'd expected him to say. "You were?"

He nodded. "It's good you're going," he added quietly. "It'll be a relief to have you gone."

She stiffened, startled. "Oh."

"Yes, oh," he echoed, setting his mug down. "Because when you're gone, I won't be tempted to do this." He leaned forward, took her tea from her, placing it on the side table before taking her hand and dragging her to her feet.

"Or this," he said, drawing her toward him, pulling her against him until he had her wedged firmly between his thighs.

"Or this." His hands clasped her face, his thumbs brushing her cheekbones, making her skin tingle and burn. "Such a beautiful woman," he murmured, angling her head to cover her mouth with his.

The kiss was slow and hot and unbearably sexy. His fingers slid into her hair, tangling in the thick weight framing her face as he took his time kissing her, savoring her mouth, exploring the shape of her lips with his lips and tongue.

Last night had been good, but oh, this was better. This kiss was intoxicating, so wickedly good but also so sweet that she felt as if she was melting into a puddle of need, just as if she were dark chocolate or marshmallow crème...

Sighing, she wrapped her arms around Brock's neck, luxuriating in the feel of his warm body, holding him tighter, holding him closer, leaning against him as she no longer trusted her legs to support her. But leaning against him just made her more aware of his desire for her, his erection pressing against her through the soft fabric of his sweatpants.

It would be so easy to touch him, stroke him, and feeling strangely empowered, she slid one hand down his chest, over the bunched bicep in his arm before trailing lower to his side, his hip, his thigh.

She felt him straining against her and it made her even bolder. Curious about him, she caressed the length of him, and there was quite a bit of him to explore.

His breath hitched, and he covered her hand with his, his fingers curving around hers. "I don't know how much more self-control I've got left," he said hoarsely. "This might be a good time to talk about the weather or animal husbandry or crop rotation."

Harley laughed softly. "That's awesome." She laughed again, and leaned back to better see his face. "You know I could discuss all three," she said, trailing her fingers over his cheek and jaw, liking the bristle and bite of his beard beneath her fingertips. "I'm especially well versed in animal husbandry. That was my minor at Cal Poly."

He turned his face into her hand, kissing her palm. "I forget you're a farm girl."

"I'm good with cows."

"You're the perfect girl."

"Ha!" And yet her heart turned over, aching a little, wishing. Wishing.

Like a child, all those impossible Christmas wishes...

"What would the perfect girl do now, Brock Sheenan?"

"Not go tomorrow."

Oh. She drew a little hiccup of a breath. "But if she did have to go tomorrow, what would she do tonight?"

"Love me all night long."

Oh God.

Overwhelmed by the intensity of emotion rushing through her, rushing through her, Harley leaned forward and kissed Brock, deeply, fiercely, needing him, wanting to feel him and touch him, and yes, love him.

Because she did love him. As impossible and improbable as it was.

But Christmas was the time for miracles. If anything could happen, it could happen now...

"Yes," she murmured against his mouth. "Yes. I want to."

His hand tangled her hair. "You're my perfect girl even if you don't sleep with me, Harley."

"But I want to," she answered, licking her bottom lip,

heart thudding. "Where would we go? My room?"

"I don't think your door locks." He hesitated. "But mine does."

"What about the kids?"

"They're asleep."

She stared into his eyes, nervous, excited, and scared, but even more scared of this moment going and never having it again. "We'd have to be *so* quiet."

"Baby, I'm *always* quiet."

She laughed, a real belly aching laugh that made her chest and tummy hurt, and it felt so good to laugh a real laugh, felt so good to be warm and fizzy and excited.

Excited.

And that was the moment she knew. She'd fallen for him, head over heels. There was no playing it safe now. No easy, painless way out.

The log in the fire broke, and the fire crackled and popped, sending a river of sparks into the air.

Harley watched the red hot sparks fly and then disappear.

She felt like one of those sparks now, burning so hot and bright. She wanted her Christmas wish now.

"Let's go," she whispered.

He carried her up the stairs and set her on the bed before silently locking his door. His bed was huge, a big wood four poster, and he stripped off his T-shirt and sweatpants, leaving him naked.

The curtains were open and outside the moon shone high in the sky, reflecting brightly off the thick white drifts of snow, casting a silvery white glow across the bedroom.

She could see Brock, all of him. It was amazing—he was amazing—but this was also intimidating because she had to undress next.

Heart pounding she shrugged off her robe, and then tugged off her pajama top and then finally peeled off the matching bottoms, aware that Brock was just standing, watching.

"What are you thinking?" she whispered, suddenly nervous and painfully shy.

"That you look like an angel on my bed."

Her eyes stung but with the good kind of tears. "You say the nicest things."

"I don't like talking, so I only say what I mean."

She put a hand out, reaching for him. "Come here, before I lose my courage."

"There's no reason to be afraid." He opened the nightstand next to the bed and removed a foil wrapped package from the drawer. "And we can stop at any time. I've waited a long time for you. I can wait another night or two."

Brock stretched out on the bed next to her, covering them with the folded blanket from the foot of the bed.

"Kiss me," she whispered, drawing his head down to hers.

"Absolutely," he answered, rolling her onto her back and settling between her thighs.

The sex was so good. The sex was *unbelievably* good.

"Wow," she murmured, cheek resting on his chest, her pulse still racing, her body warm and languid. "You do that like a rock star."

He laughed and stroked her hair. "You've been with a lot of rock stars?"

She smiled, enjoying the husky vibration of his laughter and the steady thud of his heart beneath her cheek. She liked it when he laughed, and loved it when he teased her.

And now this intense physical connection...

If she wasn't careful she'd get completely swept away by the intensity and passion, but she had to remember that the sex—although very good and very hot—wasn't love. It was just pleasure. Physical gratification. And the physical couldn't replace love, friendship, respect.

All she had to do was remember David to know why a relationship couldn't be based on chemistry and passion. Chemistry and passion would fade, and then what?

Harley didn't want to fall in love just for the thrill of it. She wanted what she'd thought she'd had when she married David. A family. A future.

Brock's hand slipped from her hair, to trace down her

spine, his calloused palm so warm against her bare skin. "You're thinking," he said.

"I am," she agreed, regrets creeping in.

"Tell me."

She drew a deep breath, hating how quickly her emotions were changing, hating how all the good feelings were fading, leaving her scared, sad.

It was hard to feel so much, and want so much.

It was hard to care so much when she was leaving in the morning.

"Come on," he insisted, shifting her onto her back, and rising on his elbow to look down at her. "Talk to me."

"I don't want tomorrow to be weird," she said roughly.

He lifted a strand of hair from her cheek, smoothing it from her face. "Why would it be weird?"

"You know. Saying goodbye. And then leaving the kids." Her throat ached. "It's going to be hard to leave... them."

The corner of his mouth lifted. Deep grooves bracketed his lips. "Just them?" he teased, dipping his head to kiss her brow, her nose, her lips.

A tingle shot through her and her tummy flipped at the trio of tender kisses. "And you." She struggled to smile. "I kind of like you, tough guy."

"So stay," he said, kissing her cheek, her jaw, her chin. "Why go? Where do you have to go?"

His kisses were making her pulse race, and his words were making her want things but her head balked. Her head was practical and real. She was practical and real. She'd been swept away by passion once before and she couldn't afford to get carried away again. "It sounds like a horribly depressing romance novel. *The Housekeeper & The Cowboy*."

"Perhaps it'd sound better if you called it, *The Housekeeper's Cowboy*."

"That's even worse."

He kissed the corner of her mouth, and then just beneath her lower lip, making it quiver. "Maybe we just need some adjectives, fancy it up."

"You have suggestions?" she asked.

He kissed the other corner of her mouth, lightly, so lightly that her breath caught in her throat. "How about...*The Hot*

Housekeeper's Lonely Cowboy."

"Too pathetic," she whispered, toes curling with pleasure. The man could *kiss*.

He nuzzled below her ear, and then kissed his way down her neck. "Your turn," he said. "Make it good. Make me want to buy that story."

She giggled then sighed, as his mouth traced her collarbone making her shiver and need. She pressed her knees together, closed her eyes, her body tingling everywhere. "*The Hot Housekeeper's Sexy Cowboy*."

"Now there's a story I want to read," he murmured, moving over her, his big body shifting between her thighs, his erection pressing against her inner thigh. He kissed down, his lips capturing one pebbled nipple. He sucked and she arched up, her hips rocking against his.

Brock's fingers twined with hers. He slid her hands up the mattress, over her head, trapping her.

She liked it. Liked the tension in her arms, the tension in their bodies, it felt hot and raw.

It'd be so easy to open to him. To just take him. She wanted to take him, loved the weight of him, and the feel of him. Loved the way they felt together. But couldn't make love again without protection. "Have another condom?" she whispered.

"More where that one came from... in the bunk house."

"We don't need *The Sexy Cowboy's Pregnant Housekeeper*."

"Not unless she wanted to be *The Sexy Cowboy's Hot Wife*," he answered, shifting so that the tip of his shaft stroked her, making nerves dance.

"Ha."

"We'd make a beautiful baby."

She no longer felt like laughing. Her eyes burned. It hurt to swallow. "That's not funny."

He released her hands, cupped her face, kissing her slowly. "It wasn't meant to be funny." His dark head lifted, he gazed down at her, dark eyes somber, expression grave. "I never thought I'd ever marry again. But I can see you here, with us. You fit with us. I think I'd like being married to you."

She didn't even know how to respond to that. She couldn't wrap her head around any of it. Stay here. Marry him. Be a surrogate mom to his kids.

She'd have a family. It'd be his family.

And that was the problem.

It'd be *his* family. She'd be the surrogate. The fill-in. He could replace her, too. She couldn't bear being replaced, not again.

"It's too soon," she said. "Too fast. You don't even know me. A month from now you might feel differently—"

"I won't."

"You don't know that."

"I do. I'm not reckless. I don't make promises and break them. If I make a promise, I keep it. And if I promise to love you and cherish you all the days of my life, I will."

Just like he still loved Amy...

And perhaps that should have scared her, that he still loved Amy, but it didn't. It reassured her. He had loved his wife. He had been faithful to her memory all these years. His steadfast love gave Harley hope that Brock could be faithful to her.

She closed her eyes, held her breath. It'd be so easy to capitulate. To just give in to the miracle of it all.

Christmas wishes, Christmas dreams...

But what would happen after the holidays were over and it was a new year? How would this work...?

Maxine.

The ranch.

The twins.

The twins.

She exhaled in a small painful puff of air. "Mack and Molly."

"Yes?"

"They've never had to share you with anyone before. They could grow to resent me."

"They won't."

"They could."

He kissed her again. "Then we deal with it."

"You make it all sound too easy."

"Because I think it is easy, after everything we've both been through."

She reached up to touch his cheek. His skin was so warm

and his beard rasped her fingertips. Lightly she scraped her nails across his rough jaw. "My family will say I've lost my mind."

"And mine will say the same thing, until they meet you, and then they'll know what I know."

"And what is that?"

"That you being here wasn't an accident. You were meant to be here. You were sent to be here."

Her chest burned, hot and tender. "Who knew you were so good with words?"

"Not selling you. I'm telling you what I know, what I believe. God brought you here to Marietta for a reason. He knew we needed you, and He knew you needed us, and He put his angels to work and produced a Christmas miracle."

"Stop," she whispered, tears filling her eyes.

"Never. Not if it means letting you go. Can't lose you, Harley. I've waited too long for you. Have prayed too long for you." The corner of his mouth lifted, but there were shadows in his dark eyes, and a hint of his old grief. "Don't break my heart now, baby. Not when I have hope again."

Hope.

Hope.

The hot tears blinded her, falling fast, too fast. She'd lived so long without hope. She'd looked so long with pain. "I can't fall in love with you all and then be sent away."

He dipped his head, kissing her cheeks where they were wet. "Won't ever send you away. We are yours. You are home."

Chapter Eight

She couldn't say yes.

She didn't say yes.

It had all sounded so perfect, but that's what scared her. It was too perfect to be true.

The great sex, the laughter, the beautiful words in Brock's cozy moonlit bedroom.

It was a Christmas Hallmark movie and God knows, she didn't watch those. They were so sweet and hopeful they just made her sad.

So she told him no, telling him as kindly as she could, that as wonderful as his offer sounded, she couldn't accept. It was all happening too fast. But if it was meant to be, they'd find each other later, and try again when the timing was better.

He'd listened in silence. "Better timing? What does that mean?"

"It means..." her voice faded. Her stomach hurt, so full of short sharp pains that it felt as if she'd been eating barbed wire. "It means... I've known you not quite two weeks, and your kids just six days, and we can't risk hurting them, or each other, by being impulsive, no matter how romantic it seems."

He'd said nothing for a long time and then he rolled away and sat up on the edge of the bed, his big muscular back to her, his powerful legs on the floor. "Yeah, Mr. Romantic, that's me." And then he'd rose and walked to his bathroom, closed the door and took a long shower.

Harley had returned to her bed on the third floor, her room frigid, her sheets icy cold.

She'd cried into her pillow.

Cried because she'd hurt him and cried because she'd hurt herself. It was brutal telling him no, brutal telling her heart no. But she had to keep focused on facts and the big picture.

They hadn't known each other long.

He had two children who were so vulnerable right now. His children didn't need drama. They'd been through so much. They should be protected. Surrounded by stability, security.

She was doing the right thing, saying no. Her head was sure of it.

But that didn't stop her from crying.

In the morning she was up at five. It was dark outside. It'd be dark for at least another hour and a half.

She took a quick shower and then dressed, tucking her pajamas and vanity bag into her suitcase. She was totally packed now. When the new housekeeper arrived, Harley would just grab her suitcase and go.

They'd keep the goodbyes brief. No big emotional scene. Nothing drawn out. She was Dutch. She could do this. Quick, crisp, clean.

That's the way goodbyes were meant to be.

Her kids came to mind, their bright eyes and big smiles as they'd left her that last morning, smiling, waving, saying they loved her. Saying they'd see her soon.

Talk about a quick goodbye. They'd walked out the door and she'd never seen them again.

Life was brutal that way. Life was capricious and hard and harsh. Harley couldn't rush into hard and harsh, she couldn't go there again...

Or could she?

She thought of Mack and Molly and how they'd spent their entire life wondering what it'd be like to have a mom. They were just babies themselves and still in need of so much love and TLC.

Could she face her fear for them?

Could she face her fear to love their dad?

Harley wished, hoped, but didn't know. And yet she had to know. She had to believe.

But the confidence wasn't there inside of her. She wasn't sure of anything right now, too caught up in the emotions sweeping through her.

Hope, wish, dream, need.

Heartbreak, loss, pain, grief.

Which was bigger, which was stronger?

Love was stronger, but was there enough love here? Was there enough love to mend their hearts and make them work?

How would she know? How could she know?

Leaving her suitcase by her bedroom door, she turned off her bedroom light and headed downstairs.

In the kitchen, the fire was already crackling and burning.

Dark, rich coffee brewed on the counter.

Brock was up.

And knowing that made her want him, but she couldn't waffle and send mixed signals.

Taking her time, taking things slow was right. Being careful and thoughtful was best.

And yet... and yet... part of her yearned to just run to him. Run and say, *forgive me. Keep me. Love me.*

He would, too. She knew it. Knew that he might not be a perfect man but he was honest and tough and strong and real.

She'd watched him here on this ranch, and he did nothing halfway. When he was worried one of the young calves was missing, he'd gone back out in the dark, in a snowstorm, to track it down. And he hadn't come home until he'd found him.

A man of his word.

A man of the word. He'd waited for her. Prayed for her.

She poured herself a cup of coffee and went to the window above the sink to look out. Stars still shone brightly overhead. She searched the dark sky for a sign... her own North Star.

And then something amazing happened.

The sky lit up in a thousand colored lights. Red, blue, green, yellow, gold, white. Light after light glowing brightly, revealing the white landscape glittering in a fresh clean layer of newly fallen slow.

Leaning toward the window, she realized that it wasn't the sky filled with lights but the big tree in the corner of the yard.

The huge pine tree—twenty-something feet tall—was covered in brilliant glowing colorful light.

The huge pine tree was a Christmas tree.

Oh, God.

The biggest most beautiful Christmas tree she'd ever seen. Here. Here. And she knew who'd done it and she knew why he'd done it and she didn't think she could bear it.

It would have taken hours.

It would have taken all night.

She put her head down on the counter, and cried.

Crying because it was too much. It was. There weren't words for things like this. Weren't words for things so beautiful and magical. Life-changing. Momentous. Life-changing. Healing. Life changing.

Hope.

Faith.

Grace.

God.

And Harley just cried.

How could she leave them? How could she go? How could she leave when there was nowhere else she'd rather be?

"We think you're supposed to be here," Molly said, her voice soft and hushed on the far side of the kitchen.

Harley straightened, turning abruptly, wiping her cheeks dry. It was impossible. The tears kept falling.

Molly and Mack were in their pajamas and yet beneath their pajamas were snow boots and snowflakes glittered on their hair and dusted their pink cheeks.

"We know you're supposed to be here," Mack corrected. "It's the plan."

"The plan?" Harley whispered.

Molly walked to Harley and took her hand. "We figured it out last night after Dad told us about your kids, how you lost your kids, like we lost our mom."

Mack nodded. "We couldn't sleep 'cause we knew why you were here. Mom sent you here. She knew you missed your kids and she knew we missed her..." His voice faded.

For a moment there was only silence.

Molly squeezed Harley's hand. "We think our mom is in

heaven taking care of your kids," Molly said quietly. "Because I bet even in heaven, kids need a mom, and I bet my mom would be a good one. Dad said she was a good mom. Dad said she loved us."

"I'm sure she was the best mom ever," Harley whispered, the lump so big in her throat that she was afraid she'd cry all over again.

"We bet you were a really good mom, too," Molly added. "A really, really good mom. Because you're not even our mom and you're really, really nice to us."

Harley held her breath, praying for control. But when tears fell, Molly's cool fingers were there, on Harley's cheeks, carefully wiping them away.

"We like you," Molly whispered in a low voice. "We like you a lot, Harley, so please don't go."

Mack nodded. "I think, we think, we *know*, Mom sent you to us. That's why Dad put the lights on Mom's tree."

"Come on," Molly said, tugging on her hand. "Let's go outside. Let's go see Mom's tree."

"Why do you call it Mom's tree?" Harley asked, as they pulled her though the hall, past the stairs, and out the front door where the massive cedar tree lit with endless strands of colored light.

"Because Mom planted the tree for Dad," Mack said, drawing Harley down the front steps, into the thick powdered snow. "It was her wedding present to him. She planted it near the house so he'd always remember how much she loved him."

They moved around the side of the enormous glowing tree and there was Brock, waiting for her.

"Amy said the tree would always be here, protecting me, and the house, and our family with love," Brock said, moving toward her, taking her hands in his. "And she has. She's done her part. But she knows we need more. We need you."

Brock dug out of his pocket a ring case, and snapped it open, revealing a sparkling diamond ring. An engagement ring. "I'm not giving up, Harley. Won't give up. I'm a fighter, and I'm fighting for you, and I'll fight for you as long as I have to."

Harley stared at Brock and then at the ring,

understanding, but not understanding. "When did you buy the ring?"

"Yesterday with the kids in Marietta."

The twins nodded. "We helped pick it out," Mack said, shyly. "We wanted you to have a really big diamond, too."

"Girls like big diamonds," Molly said.

"You're serious?" Harley whispered, looking at Brock. "You mean this?"

"Oh, I absolutely mean this, Harley. I've been up all night trying to show you somehow that we need you here, that we want you here. Just have faith. We do."

Have faith.

But she did. It's all that had gotten her through. And now she was here, and was it her faith that had brought her here?

"I do, too," she answered huskily.

"Good." He leaned forward kissed her. And then he got down on one knee in the snow and took her hand, holding it firmly in his. "Harley Diekerhoff, will you marry me?"

"Yes," she whispered.

"Yes?" he asked, making sure.

For a moment there was just silence. It was a perfect silence, accompanied by a sense of peace. A perfect peace.

"Yes," she answered, as he rose and swept her up in his arms. "Yes," she repeated, laughing through happy tears. "Yes, yes, yes."

"I love you," he whispered against her mouth, kissing her.

"I love you, too."

He kept kissing her and the twins cheered. And then there was even more cheering, loud raucous cheering and whistling and Harley realized that all the boys from the bunk house were here, too, watching.

But it was good.

All was right in the world.

Faith had brought her here.

Miracles were possible.

And love would keep them together.

The End

About the Author

Bestselling author Jane Porter has been a finalist for the prestigious RITA award four times and has over 12 million copies in print. Jane's novel, Flirting With Forty, picked by Redbook as its Red Hot Summer Read, went back for seven printings in six weeks before being made into a Lifetime movie starring Heather Locklear. A mother of three sons, Jane holds an MA in Writing from the University of San Francisco and makes her home in sunny San Clemente, CA with her surfer husband.

A Cowboy For Christmas
a copper mountain christmas novella

Katherine Garbera

Dedication

I can't write a Christmas story and not thank my good friend Barbara Padlo who is always asking me to write another one. We both share a love of Christmas, family, and good books.

Acknowledgment

Thank you to Jane Porter who offered me a chance to do something I loved and helped me remember why I started writing.

Dear Reader,

I love Christmas and the entire Christmas season. I put a themed tree up in every room in my house. I start using my special Santa mugs and every night I make hot cocoa with whipped cream and red and green sprinkles on top. I make my three Wise Men journey around the house, hide clues for my kids to find their advent gifts, and dress in sweaters that probably should never be seen outside my house. Why am I telling you all this? To explain how excited I was to be included in the Copper Mountain Christmas Anthology.

Annie Prudhomme left Marietta and Carson Scott fifteen years ago with the intention of never returning. Now that's she lost it all she has nowhere else to go and she returns to town hoping to quietly regroup and figure out her next move. For her, staying isn't an option. But seeing Carson on her first night back gives her a glimpse of how much she's changed since she was eighteen.

Carson Scott moved on after Annie left town. He met and married a nice girl and had a son with her, and when his wife died his brothers circled the wagons and helped him get through it. For three Christmases he's been getting by and telling himself that he was content with his life... until he walks into the Main Street Diner and sees Annie and knows he's been lying to himself.

He also realizes there is only one thing he wants for Christmas and she's not exactly the kind of woman who's been known to stick around, or make his dreams come true.

Happy reading!

Katherine

KATHERINE GARBERA

Contents

Chapter One   119
Chapter Two   129
Chapter Three   140
Chapter Four   146
Chapter Five   159
Chapter Six   169
Chapter Seven   179
Chapter Eight   190
Chapter Nine   201

117

Chapter One

Marietta, Montana did Christmas in a big way with all the storefronts on Main Street draped in garland and twinkle lights. The Main Street Diner wasn't any different with its rustic wreath made with layers of old ropes and decked with red poinsettia leaves and Rocking Around the Christmas Tree playing merrily on the jukebox as Carson Scott opened the door.

No one was exactly sure how the Wednesday night tradition had started, not even Carson, but he knew that his brothers had done it for him. It had been in the dark time right after Rainey had been killed in a head-on collision out on highway 89 on her way back from Livingston. He'd sat at home every night with baby Evan drinking too much Red Bull. His oldest brother Alec had insisted that they all meet in Marietta at the diner for dinner.

Alec had thick blond hair like their momma and piercing blue-gray eyes that Carson had heard more than one girl describe as colder than the glaciers in Glacier Park. But Sienna, Alec's wife, had said that she knew how to warm him up. Which had led to a lot of ribbing by Carson and his other brothers. Alec needed to be taken down a peg or two at times.

But not on Wednesday nights. Carson showed up here after he dropped Evan off at his maternal grandparents' house and ate chili and cornbread with his brothers. There were five of them all together and sometimes Flo, who ran the grill, gave them a hard time about being carbon copies of their dad, but that didn't bother any of them. Their old man cast a long shadow and had a reputation for being honest and hard-working. There were worse things a man could be known for.

There were only five weeks left until Christmas and Evan was being cagey about what he wanted from Santa this year. He'd hinted he wanted a mommy that wasn't in heaven. And the last thing that Carson was interested in was dating any woman, much less one to become Evan's new mommy.

"Isn't that Annie waiting tables?" Alec said as they entered the diner. The walls were heavy red brick and the floor solid wood. There was a counter with red leather-covered stools bolted to the floor in front of it, and for as long as Carson could remember beehive-haired Flo was standing at the grill cooking delicious food, trading gossip, and flirting with any man who entered.

"Annie who?" he asked. He was holding the door open for his younger brother Hudson who had a shopping bag from The Mercantile in one hand and his Stetson in the other.

"Prudhomme. Is there another Annie you'd care about?" Alec asked.

"I thought she'd left town for good," Hudson said.

Annie. Here. Wow.

Why?

How?

When?

It didn't make sense. He ate here every Wednesday with his brothers. She hadn't been here last week. Why was she here now?

Carson craned his neck around his brothers' shoulders to look at the waitress. Goddamn it. She hadn't changed. She was still the same slim pretty girl he remembered. She wasn't tall but had long legs and dark brown hair that hung to her shoulders and curled slightly at the ends. He stared at her until she turned and he met those pretty gray eyes that he had thought he'd never see again.

He hardened his heart. If there was one thing he knew without even talking to her it was that this was a temporary move. He doubted she was back to stay. That wasn't her style and Marietta wasn't her town.

At eighteen it had felt like he'd never love again when she'd left Marietta – and him – all in the same cloud of dust. But at thirty-three he knew that was a lie. He had loved again and married and had a chance for real happiness. But now he wondered –was that another lie he'd told himself to make Annie's leaving him okay?

"Yup," he said, answering his brothers as he turned back to the laminated menu, trying to be blasé when inside he wanted to go and talk to her. Go and find out why she was back and what it meant. Had life turned that ballsy, sassy girl he'd loved into a bitch or tamed her?

But he kept his head down studying the laminated menu like his sanity depended on it. It wasn't as if he didn't know what he was going to order. He always got the same thing when he and his brothers came into town to eat on Wednesday nights. His son was visiting his maternal grandparents at their home on the modest section of Bramble Lane. Rhett and Lily had moved out to Marietta after Rainey had died to be closer to Evan and they said having Carson around made it hard for them to bond with Evan.

The thing Carson was proudest of was his son and how well he and the six-year-old had grown up together after Rainey died.

"Yup?" Alec asked.

"That girl—" Hudson said.

"I know. I'm surprised she's here too," Carson said trying to play it cool. But the thing with brothers was they always knew when he was bullshitting them. "But let's face it... everyone ends up back here eventually. You said Pop wanted some help with something?"

Alec's brother nodded. "He's determined we need to get that old red barn renovation finished by the New Year. I could use some extra help to finish the work."

"I'll send my hands over tomorrow. Is he still planning to sell it?"

"You know Pop, if you can't ranch it then it's a bad investment. And he bought it for Trey to live on with his wife but they aren't interested in settling down here."

"What's his hurry then?"

"Lane has a friend who is looking for a place out this way."

"You do?" Carson asked Lane. "I thought all your buddies were career military."

"He's retired," Lane said. "Like me."

"Is he like you?" Carson asked. Lane had lost the bottom half of his left leg in an IED explosion in Iraq and now had prosthetic leg.

"Why?" Lane asked.

"Just wanted to know if we should make the halls and

bath a little bigger in the house," Carson said. "Maybe we should anyway"

"Nah, he's still got both his legs," Lane said.

"How old is he?" Alec asked.

"Barely thirty but all that fighting has taken it out of him," Lane said..

"We were lucky to get you back when we did," Carson said.

"Thanks, boys. Good to know you care," Lane said.

"Ah, they all care about youngest Scott boy," Annie said coming over to their table.

She walked toward them wearing the traditional Main Street Diner white apron over her own clothing. There was something almost defiant in her manner. It had to stick in her craw that she'd left here to make it big and now she was waiting on all of Marietta.

Her brown hair swung around her high cheekbones with each step she took. A pair of faded denim jeans hugged her legs and the tips of her worn brown boots were scuffed. Her smile didn't reach her eyes and she'd managed to chew off most of her lipstick.

Hellfire. It had been fifteen years and one look at Annie was all it took to get him hot and bothered. It wasn't that she was the most beautiful woman he'd ever seen. She had an attitude bigger than the Montana sky, but she'd always just had something that made him stand at attention.

"We care about all the Scott boys," Alec said pointedly. "Even Carson here when he was dumb enough to fall in love with a girl intent on leaving."

"Sorry," she said.

There was something her eyes that made her seem... more than sorry, almost sad and he cautioned himself about feeling anything for her, even pity.

"Really?" Carson asked.

"More than you can know," she admitted. "But you boys didn't come here to hear about my mistakes. You want dinner, right?"

"We sure do. Did Flo make her jalapeno cornbread today?" Hudson asked.

"Yes she did," Annie said, taking a pen from the pocket of

her apron and holding up her notepad.

"Chili and cornbread for me and root beer," Alec said.

"Same," Hudson said.

"Same again," Lane said.

She looked at Carson and for a moment he remembered the last time he'd held her in his arms, but he'd known then she was leaving. She was always on her way out of Marietta.

"I'll have a Sprite instead, but otherwise the same," Carson said.

"Still don't like caffeine?" she asked.

"Nope," he said.

She nodded and walked away and all he could do was watch her. And admire the way those faded jeans hugged her butt. Maybe it was just physical... his reaction to her had always been strong. He realized his brothers were watching him watch her and he cursed under his breath. The last thing he needed was Annie back in Marietta this close to Christmas. Christmas always made him wish for things that couldn't be.

Annie Prudhomme was definitely something that wasn't meant to be. She'd proven that the day she drove out of town and left him the dust.

"Wednesday dinners just got a little more interesting," Hudson said.

He punched his brother in the arm, but he felt it as well. There was something about that woman that always made the world seem a little brighter when she'd been in the vicinity. And he knew he couldn't be stupid again. Couldn't let himself get involved with a woman who clearly wasn't long for Montana.

The front door opened, bringing a burst of cold air and the jingling of the sleigh bell wreath on the door. They all smiled and waved as Paige Joffe walked in with her two little ones, six-year-old Addison and five-year-old Lewis. For a while the town matchmakers had tried pairing the two of them up but both Paige and Carson had resisted. She was nice enough and pretty, but just not the woman for him.

He didn't know her story except she'd come to Marietta from somewhere in California and had the misfortune to move in during a bad snow storm last February. But she seemed to be adjusting to it. Addison was in the same class as Evan at school.

"Evening Scotts," she said with a friendly wave. Her shoulder-length straight dark blonde hair was pulled back in a low ponytail. She had a strong chin and dimples when she smiled, which she didn't do that often. He'd really only seen her smile when her kids made her laugh.

"Ma'am."

"How's my new waitress treating you?" she asked.

"She'll do," Carson said, but he didn't want to talk about Annie. And it was obvious she didn't want to talk to him either. She'd pretty much avoided their table after she'd dropped off their food. "Don't forget to come out to my place this weekend to pick out your tree. The best ones are going fast."

"Can I come by Saturday morning, first thing?"

"Yes, ma'am," he said. "We're going to have sleigh rides for the little ones too."

"I spoke to Nate. He's got his foreman's sister staying with him for the holidays. She's trying to get a baking operation off the ground. I hate to stick my nose in where it doesn't belong, but I wondered if she might come out to the tree lot. Maybe sell some gingerbread house kits?"

Carson was all for helping out a neighbor and he knew Ty Murphy and respected him. "Sure. Give her my number and we'll get it all set up. I've asked Sage to send Rose Linn out to sell hot chocolate."

"You just didn't want to have to drive to town to get some for yourself," Hudson said.

"You got me," Carson said with a grin.

Paige's phone vibrated and she glanced at it before smiling at their table. "Sounds delightful."

Paige waved goodbye and moved toward her office at the back of the diner. The evening dinner crowd was thick but not too bad and a few times Carson glanced at Annie as she carried dishes to the tables. When she caught him looking she stood straight and gave him a cheery smile. But when she didn't notice, he saw fatigue in her every move. Whatever she'd come to Marietta for, she hadn't planned on waiting tables.

"Hard to believe Mama's little tree farm has grown so

big," Hudson said, pulling his attention from Annie. "Remember when she used to make us water them?"

"Yes. She loved her trees," Carson said. Their mother had been Montana born and bred but instead of ranching she'd always had her mind set on growing trees and preserving wildlife. Their father had given her all of his support and turned fifty acres into a forest where she started her no-cut Christmas tree program in the nineteen-seventies and it was still thriving forty years later. They had to move some of the trees by pallet truck and forklift now, but the families that owned them wouldn't have it any other way.

Carson did a traditional cut-tree service for the town as well and he was happy to be the caretaker of his mother's trees.

After they ate their dinner and his brothers left, Carson sat there nursing his Sprite and pretending he was waiting until it was time to pick up Evan. A smart man would be on his feet and down at Grey's Saloon instead of sitting in a corner booth watching the one who got away.

Of all the ways Annie had thought she'd return to Marietta, this wasn't it. The diner was busy, her feet ached, and she was trying hard to keep her smile from slipping, but it was challenging. She wasn't eighteen and this job was exhausting. Plus everyone kept asking why she was back.

She wanted to do something stupid like climb on top of the counter and shout that she'd screwed up and everyone had been right. Except she knew it was fatigue and nerves bothering her. And that damned Carson Scott.

Rockin' Around the Christmas Tree played merrily in the background but she felt it should be something more manic like the Divertissement from The Nutcracker Suite.

What she didn't get was why he still looked so good. He could have lost a little of his thick hair or maybe developed a beer belly, but no. If anything he was hotter than he'd been in high school. He kept his long legs stretched out the side of the booth and she could see that his boots were worn and his jeans faded. And his eyes were weary as they watched her.

It wasn't as if she'd quietly sneaked back into town and was safely hiding out at La Terre De Reves, her family's old ranch. No – she was waitressing at the busiest restaurant in town just before the holidays. Over the next week, the town of Marietta would be getting ready for the Christmas Stroll. Once Flo had mentioned that Annie could draw, Paige had asked her to help decorate the windows.

Annie had put away her sketch pads during her divorce, but when she'd stopped outside Amarillo for gas, she'd been unable to resist buying a plain drawing pad. And tonight she knew what she wanted to draw. She wanted to capture the lines of Carson's face. The subtle changes that age had brought to his rough-hewn features.

"Order up," Flo called, and Annie ran back to the chicken nugget basket and steak sandwich platter for the dad and eight-year-old sitting in the corner booth.

"Thanks, Flo."

"You're welcome, hon. You doing okay?"

"Ask me that later. I don't have time to even think right now," Annie said with a smile. Finally she thought of the silver lining to all of this. She couldn't think. She couldn't dwell on the past and what she'd lost while she was working this hard.

She served her table and then checked on the drinks for her diners and noticed her hands started to shake when she glanced over at Carson's table. His brothers had left and he was just sitting there by himself nursing his Sprite.

Her boss Paige was in her office in the back with her kiddos. Normally she wasn't in at night—according to Flo, but on Wednesdays one of the kids had some kind of class in town.

She'd met the kids and smiled at them but kept her distance. Annie had never been good with children. To be honest, she didn't see that changing any time soon. She'd been married for ten years to a con man and remained childless through choice. Once Davis had been arrested for fraud and convicted of running a Ponzi scheme on elderly investors, she'd divorced him and tried to get on with her life.

But her high-society friends had avoided her and she couldn't blame them, not really. She'd have done the same thing if she'd been in their shoes. She'd had nowhere else to go and only one place to call her own. La Terre De Reves ranch in Marietta, Montana. The one place she swore she'd never return to.

He glanced over at her again. She straightened up and filled a glass with Sprite and headed over to his table.

"Need a refill?"

"Not as much as I'd like some answers," he said.

"To what questions?" she asked.

"Why is the girl who swore she'd never return giving me a Sprite in the Main Street Diner?" he asked.

She shook her head. She should have anticipated having conversations like this, but she'd been so focused on just getting away from Manhattan and starting over that she hadn't though this through.

"Maybe it's a Christmas miracle. You know, one of those sappy stories where someone comes home and all their dreams come true."

"I don't think coming home has to be sappy," he said. "But then I guess we see the world differently."

"We sure do," she agreed. She turned to go back to the kitchen area, but he stopped her with his hand on her wrist.

"Sit down with me," he said.

She couldn't think beyond the fact that he was touching her. His hand was big, calloused, and warm against her wrist. It had been so long since anyone had touched her... that had to be why a tingle shot up her arm from where he held her.

"I... I don't want to do this, Carson. This is my first night working here and I can't afford to make a bad impression."

"You're not busy, and if someone new comes in you can jump up and get their order," he said. "Besides – I think maybe you owe me a few answers."

"Do I?" she asked tipping her head to one side so that her brown hair slid forward over the right side of her face. She absently reached up and tucked it behind her ear.

"Yes, you do," he said, keeping his gaze steady. He didn't often ask for things but it was a well-known fact that when he did ask, he got what he wanted.

Really? Was she still giving in to Carson Scott? As she lowered herself onto the bench across from him, she acknowledged that it made her feel good to have someone actually want to talk to her. Her sister Marilyn wouldn't return her calls, and aside from Flo and Paige she hadn't spoken to anyone other than her dog in over a week.

"Okay I will," she said.

"Why are you back in Marietta?" he asked bluntly.

"It's my home." No matter how much she'd once wished otherwise. Carson watched her with his steady blue eyes, his gaze serious and intent. It sort of made her want to be better than she was. She almost wished she could say she came back because she was ready to be here. But she knew that would be a lie.

"Are you back to stay?" he asked.

"Who wants to know?" she asked, trying for a convincing smile. Of course he'd ask the one thing she had no idea how to answer. She didn't want to admit it to him or anyone else, but she was a mess.

"Don't play with me, Annie. This might be a game to you but I'm no one's pawn," he said.

"I'm sorry. It's easier to pretend that we don't have a past."

"But we do," he pointed out. "And I could do with a little honesty."

"I know. I just didn't expect to see you again today."

Or that I would feel this way when I did.

Chapter Two

Coffee with Carson was the last thing she expected. But then it was becoming very clear that she hadn't planned this out very well. The homey comfort of the diner made her feel nostalgic and long for something she wasn't sure she really wanted.

I'm Dreaming of a White Christmas played on the juke box and she smiled ironically at Carson. "Don't dream about it, come to Montana."

He gave her one of his half-smiles. "No place prettier for Christmas than Marietta."

She couldn't make herself agree. There was still too much unresolved about this place for her to just say, yes it was pretty. Marietta always made her feel a million and one different things. Just like Carson did.

It was tense, but she had a feeling that all the tension was on her side. Carson looked like the laconic cowboy he was. Not a man for small talk or wasted gestures, so if she had to guess, there was a reason why he'd asked her to join him.

Christmas music played on the jukebox and through the decorated glass window she watched the snow falling on Main Street. But in her mind the blues riff from Look at Little Sister rolled around. She felt embarrassed, she admitted to herself.

She didn't look her best and she wanted to if she was going to be sitting across from Carson. "What'd you want to talk about?"

"You," he said, the glass tumbler looked too small in his big work-roughened hands. He took a sip and put it back on the table in front of him. "Why'd you come back?"

She reached up to mess with her hair, a bad habit, and felt the shorter length and winced. She'd always had long hair. But not anymore. She didn't care how trendy ombre was, she couldn't stand seeing her dark roots coming in and her highlighted hair still there. It had been one more reminder of how things used to be. "It's the holiday season, Car. Everyone wants to be at home, right?"

"Yeah, I might believe that if I hadn't spent long summer days with you in the mountains talking about what we wanted. And not one time did you call Marietta home."

"Oh, I like Marietta. It was La Terra de Reves ranch that I couldn't call home," she said, but that was cutting a little too close to things she didn't want to discuss with this cowboy.

"But that's old news. Catch me up on Carson Scott. The years have been good to you. You're still looking good. Must be the air out there in Paradise Valley."

"I heard they have a lot of pollution in New York City, but it didn't hurt you. You're looking good too," he said.

She tipped her head to the side and batted her eyelashes at him. "Why thank you very much."

He smiled like she wanted him to, but she noticed it didn't reach his blue eyes. He had big-sky-Montana blue eyes. Even when she'd been away from him there had been days when she'd looked up at the sky and had been reminded of those eyes.

"What have you been up to in the last fifteen years?" she asked a bit awkwardly. She had that odd feeling that she still knew everything about him but it had been a long time and they were strangers now. "I haven't been in town to know all the gossip."

"Let's see...I got married about ten years ago," he said.

She glanced at his left hand but there was no ring there. Not even the sun line of a ring recently worn. But then some ranchers didn't wear rings. Married. It shouldn't affect her as strongly as it did. He belonged to another woman.

"Still married?" she asked, admitting to herself she was jealous of his wife even though she had no right to be. It wasn't as if she was still in love with Carson Scott, it was just... he'd sort of been hers and he wasn't anymore.

"She's dead, Annie. Died almost four years ago," he said. His voice flat and low and she felt like an ass.

She'd been jealous. To be fair, she couldn't have known the circumstances, but still. "I'm so sorry. What happened?"

"Car accident out on Highway 89. She was coming back from Billings," he said. His voice was low and rough like sandpaper on her soul, and she ached for his loss. And if she was completely honest, she was envious that he'd found another person he had cared for that deeply.

She reached over and put her hand on his and squeezed it. He turned his hand in her grip and squeezed back and she felt the sudden surge of tears as she realized this was the first comforting human touch she'd felt in the last year. She swallowed hard.

"So you're widowed now."

"And I'm a single dad. I have a six-year-old son. Evan. He's got Rainey's eyes, my hair with that stubborn cowlick, and the Scott attitude that he can do anything."

"Rainey—she was your wife?" Annie asked. She heard the love for her in his voice and the love he had for his son. And she wished just one time that her father had spoken of her or her sisters with that much love.

"Yes. She moved here from Temecula—that's California. She'd seen pictures of dude ranches and wanted the romanticized cowboy experience."

Annie would be willing to bet she got it too. One thing the Scott men knew how to do was cowboy. And they were all the things a cowboy should be—hard-working, honorable, sexy. Where had that come from?

She was here to start over, not relive the past. Lust had been her downfall more than once. Only with Davis it had been lust for wealth and material things. With Carson lust was different--something very earthy and raw. And she thought she was probably old enough to know better. "And she found you."

"She did. What about you? Didn't you marry someone back east?" he asked.

She took a deep breath. That was a loaded question now wasn't it? "I was married but I'm divorced now."

"What happened?"

"It didn't work out," she said. The last thing she wanted to do was talk about that. She'd forgotten something about Marietta that she shouldn't have. Everyone knew everyone's business in town, but the outer world was kept out unless it involved rodeos or ranching. People didn't watch CNN twenty-four-seven like they did in Manhattan.

For the first time she took a deep breath and exhaled all

the negativity she'd been carrying with her since she'd come back to town. There was a pretty good chance that most people here didn't know what a scumbag Davis was or how he'd cheated everyone, including her.

"Tell me about your son," she said. "Evan, you said his name was. How'd you pick that name? I figured you'd pick a traditional Scott name."

"Evan was Rainey's dad's name. And God knows old Jeb didn't need another grandson named after him. You know Alec has J.T."

"I didn't know that. So Alec is married now?" she asked. Letting the conversation drift to his family. She sensed he was doing it because he didn't want to talk about anything too personal... and that suited her just fine.

"Yes – to Sienna. You'd like her. She's feisty and doesn't like ranch living either."

That sounded like a can of worms she didn't need to open. "Ranches can be lonely places if you don't have the right person by your side."

"I guess if you can't recognize the right person, that might be true," he said.

We're both entitled to keep our opinions – after all, we aren't friends anymore. We're just strangers.

"What are you thinking?" he asked. "The Annie I used to know never looked that serious unless she was talking about the future."

"Just realizing we're strangers and I have no one to blame but myself."

He told her about his brothers and his dad, stuff that didn't mean anything because he hated to admit it, but there was a part of him that already was intrigued by Annie again.

He wondered if that made him the stupidest man in Montana because he knew that, despite the fact that Annie was back in Marietta, she wasn't back to stay. She'd never be happy here until she was happy with herself. And that was one thing he guessed hadn't changed.

She looked restless and if he was being honest, more than

a little lost, which meant she wasn't long for Marietta. Only a fool would fall for the same woman twice. And he wasn't lost—the jury was still out on the fool part.

He knew who he was and where he belonged and he didn't think she was looking for a man like him. He rubbed the back of his neck. She hadn't even asked to sit down, he'd invited her and now he was judging her.

"Why are you back here?" he asked. "Not some sentiment like it's Christmas and I had to come home."

"What if that's the truth?" she asked.

"I never knew you to be a liar, Annie. And we both know that you haven't been home for the last fifteen Christmases. Not even the year your daddy died. So I'm curious about why you're here now."

She took a deep breath, turned to check the tables in the diner, and then nibbled at her lower lip as she stared at him with those gray eyes of hers. "I wish I were lying, but to be honest, I had nowhere else to go. And coming home seemed like a good place to start."

"What do you mean? I thought you were a big-deal decorator in New York City," he said.

"Who told you that?" she asked.

He'd seen her sister at the Copper Mountain Rodeo this summer. He'd never been the kind of guy to want to ride bulls or be a roper, but he enjoyed watching his friends participate. Plus Evan loved it. His son had an eye for the ladies and there was a pretty little six-year-old barrel racer by the name of Maisy that he had his eye on, which was how he'd met up with Marilyn.

"Marilyn. I saw her at the rodeo this summer. She's got a girl who's a barrel racer."

Annie's expression grew distant and she looked down at the table, drawing a shape in the ring of water left by the condensation on his glass. "That would be Josie, she's like a mini-Marilyn except she's not mad at me all the time," Annie said.

"Do you see them often?" he asked. Her family had a bit of tragedy—something that Carson realized everyone's did as he got older. But it had torn the fabric of who Annie had been apart. He'd been close enough to see it first-hand.

"Not really. Marilyn and I don't get along. She thought when I bought the old ranch from her I'd move back, but…"

"You didn't," he said. "Why buy it at all? Pops is interested in the land – at least for grazing rights if you want to make some money from it. Or are you planning to stay?"

"I don't know. I'll think about the grazing rights."

"You do that," he said. "I get the feeling you're not telling me everything."

"Let's just say I didn't fall in love with someone as lovely as your Rainey and I don't have any kids. Just another hard city woman."

"There's nothing hard about it," he said. "You seem—"

"Beaten down? Damn, I knew that drugstore makeup wasn't going to cover up the lines."

"Tired," he said. "When did you get back to town?"

"Today. I've been driving for three days."

"By yourself?" he asked, thinking that was a very long trip to do alone. Even though he knew it was the twenty-first century and women could take care of themselves, he didn't like the thought of her on her own.

"No. I had my bulldog with me."

"A bulldog? We have a bloodhound, Puddles, that Evan keeps in the house,"

It was an odd feeling to be looking at someone he used to know so well and realize that he knew nothing about her now. She'd been wise enough to say what he'd been thinking—they were strangers now. There was a calmness to the wild child he'd known so long ago.

"Well Rumple is pretty loyal to me. I've had him for six years now," she said, smiling, and for the first time tonight the expression reached her eyes.

He wondered if that was why she'd come home for Christmas. There was something about the holiday season that kind of made forgiveness and making up for past mistakes easier to do. He knew life was hard, God knows he understood that better than most. But Annie had always lived in his mind as that sunshine girl with the long hair and winsome smile. The one who got away to a better life and he was okay with that.

But seeing her now made him realize that it was, what?

That maybe he'd been fooling himself when he'd thought he'd moved on with Rainey. That he'd lived to love again?

"Dogs are like that," he said.

She arched one eyebrow at her. "That's lame."

"Yes it was, but you don't want to talk about anything real," he said.

"I didn't choose wisely like you," she said. "And I can't stand whining."

"You've never been a whiner," he said. "But maybe we're not ready to talk too much about our lives. You can be my favorite waitress and I'll be—"

"Favorite? I like that, I've been serving you chili and cornbread for almost two years now every week and she's here one night and she's your favorite?" Flo asked from behind the counter.

He turned, winked at Flo and said, "No one could ever replace you, Flo."

"Sweet-talking Scott boy, but I know you boys are sweet on everyone and no one."

"That's not true," Carson said. "We're just not lucky in love."

"That's all right, boy, you're very lucky in other areas, wouldn't be fair if you had it all," Flo said.

Carson knew she was right but a part of him had always wanted more, wanted it all. He didn't understand why he couldn't have a big successful ranch, a happy, healthy son, and a woman who loved him. He didn't think that was too much to ask for.

"You okay?" Annie asked.

"Yeah," he said, standing and tossing some bills down on the table. "It's time for me to go and get Evan. I guess I'll be seeing you around."

"Be hard to avoid me if you come in here once a week," she said.

She stood as well and he couldn't help but let his gaze slide down her slim body, lingering on the curve of her hips. "It's good to see you again. I hope you finally find a place you can stay."

He walked out before she could respond, so that he could pretend he didn't care that she was back in town. Or that he

135

might still want her.

She'd learned early on there was no sense in trying to hold onto things once they'd changed. She wanted more and wanted it all but she'd always found the more she reached for things the faster they slipped through her fingers. And she was certain as she watched Carson walk away that she was saying goodbye to those silly teenaged dreams that had lingered in the back of her heart.

He'd grown and changed and she was still a mess. Always a hot mess searching for something – anything – that would bring back that family she lost when Gilly had been diagnosed with cancer. Since she was thirteen, she'd been searching, and every choice she ever made took her further into the mist and away from this place.

She counted the money from her tips... just sixteen dollars. When she added that to the twenty she had left in her wallet, she realized she might be able to make it to payday. And she had enough money to buy a can of paint from the Mercantile.

Winter Wonderland started to play on the jukebox and she felt the sting of tears as she remembered Christmases past when she'd danced to this song with Davis. She might never have been in love with him, but at least she had someone by her side.

"You're looking gloomy there, girl," Flo said.

"I'm just tired," Annie said. And the words were partly true. She'd been running on nerves and adrenaline since the FBI had seized all her belongings and put Davis in jail. Now she'd stopped and all those emotions were catching up with her.

"Paige!" Flo yelled from the grill. "Annie needs a hot chocolate break. Those kiddos of yours want some?"

"What are you doing?" she asked Flo. She didn't know Paige well enough to know if she was going to be okay with her taking a break especially on her first night.

"Getting you out of your own head," Flo said.

"I'm fine," Annie said as Paige came out of her office.

136

"Well I'm not. I could use some hot chocolate too. You think you can hold down the fort, Flo?"

"Do porcupines like pine nuts?"

Paige laughed and called to her kids. Tyler was ready first with his new blue coat buttoned and zipped up. He came over to Annie as his mom got his sister ready and Annie realized she hadn't talked to a kid in a long time.

He held a toy in one hand and looked up at her. Kids. She never knew what to say to them.

"I'm Annie," she said, holding her hand out to him.

"Tyler," he said, shaking it. "This is my favorite Bionicle, Huki."

"What does it do?" The toy looked like some sort of Martian-alien that was made from Lego blocks. It had a huge orange head with reptilian teeth and a beige-brown body. He held it up to her.

"I also have some other Legos that I make him fight. Like Stormer. He's part of the evil brain. They are bad guys."

As Paige and her daughter joined them, Tyler moved next to his mom to take her hand and as Annie followed the three of them she felt a mixture of relief that she didn't have to try to make conversation with the six-year-old and a pang inside for something she'd never realized she wanted until this moment. Watching those two little kids holding onto Paige stirred some old dreams. Montana dreams that she'd buried a long time ago.

Main Street was decked out for Christmas.

She followed them into the Copper Mountain Chocolates shop. The shop was small and homey and warm after the bitter chill of November. It smelled of chocolate and was lit up with garlands and twinkle lights. If this place had been here when she'd been a kid, her entire Christmas wish list would have been treats from Copper Mountain Chocolates.

There was a short line at the counter. The shop walls were lined with chocolate bars of all sizes and sweetness levels. Including a wall that had A-Z lettered chocolates. It smelled good and she thought of the money she had in her pocket. She could blow it on one chocolate bar or spend her money on groceries and fixing up her house.

And she couldn't do it. "I'll wait outside for you, Paige."

"You sure? I thought you wanted some chocolate," Paige said as her children went to chat with some other kids.

"That was Flo bossing me around," Annie said.

"I've never known anyone to say no to chocolate unless they didn't like it," Paige said.

Annie felt that sinking in her stomach. She hated being poor. It felt like what she'd thought she'd left behind when she had headed out of Marietta, but she was back and nothing had changed. Not one damned thing.

"You've talked me into it," she said. She'd sell the grazing rights to her property if she had to, but she was going to fix up her home and make her life into what she'd always wanted it to be. Especially for Christmas. She didn't want to feel like teenaged Annie Prudhomme again. Ever again.

"Great. So you grew up here?" Paige asked as they waited.

"I did," Annie said as Otis Redding sang Merry Christmas Baby. This was probably her dumbest idea ever. Paige was nice and Marietta had a simple sophistication and a lot of charm, but she still didn't fit in here. "A lot has changed. I really like the new train station. I never thought it could look so charming."

"Speaking of charming," Paige said as a gust of air brushed Annie's back, "here comes Carson Scott. I noticed you two chatting earlier."

"I hope that was okay—"

"Relax. I don't have a lot of rules. I didn't notice any of my customers complaining," Paige said.

"Mommy!" Addison called and Paige walked over to her daughter, leaving Annie to hold her place in line.

"Well hello, Annie," Carson said, coming up behind her. And he wasn't alone. A little boy with Carson's hair and some very big brown eyes trailed along behind him. He had a toy in one hand and his mittens dangled from his cuffs. Carson was holding a knit ski cap with some kind of cartoon character on it.

"Hello Carson—what are you doing here?'

"Same as you. Having some of Sage's famous hot chocolate."

"It's our *tadition*," said the little boy with a slight lisp.

"After we leave Nana's house we come here."

She didn't have to be Nancy Drew to know that it was his son Evan. His eyes were surely his mother's as Carson had said, but his face reminded her very much of Carson when he'd been younger. "That's a great tradition."

"It is," Carson said.

Paige and her kids got their drinks and then hesitated. There were no tables and her kids were obviously ready to walk back.

"I'll be back in a few minutes," Annie said to Paige.

"Take your time," Paige said. "See you back at the diner."

Annie ordered her chocolate and handed over her precious dollars. She took her Styrofoam cup from Sage. Sage had been the year behind her in high school so they hadn't really known each other. But Sage made friendly small talk about her engagement to Dawson O'Dell until Annie stepped aside.

"Wait up, Annie, and we'll escort you back to the diner," Carson said.

She almost said yes but she realized that being here was making her want things she wasn't even sure she wanted. Did she just want them because everyone else had them? Or was it that she had no idea what she wanted anymore?

She shook her head. She was feeling nostalgic because of the Christmas music and that feeling of not wanting to be alone. But that didn't make it real. And it didn't mean that she was any more suited for Marietta or Carson. "Not tonight, Carson."

"Good night then."

"Night," Evan said.

She waved goodbye to him and stepped outside the shop, tipping her head back as the snow fell on her face. She walked a few feet until she was in front of the dark windows of a closed shop and she stood there in the shadow holding onto the hot chocolate, wishing for a miracle. A real Christmas miracle. But she had an idea... you have to know what you want the miracle to be – before it can come true.

And the only thing that entered her mind was Carson Scott.

Chapter Three

Annie still couldn't get used to the fact that the ranch was now her home. She had to drive past the Scott Ranch to get to hers and she stopped on the side of the road and looked at the cowhands coming over the ridge. It was lightly snowing and they were riding back toward the ranch house. One of the riders broke away from the pack and came toward her.

She recognized Carson. She reached up to remove the knit cap she wore to cover her hair, but then regretted it as her ears stung with the cold and she realized her hair was probably flat. She started to put it back on but then decided she was being ridiculous.

"Hello, neighbor," she said as he rode closer to her.

"Hello. What are you doing out here?"

"I live up the road, remember?"

"That doesn't mean you had to stop here."

"I was just enjoying the scenery," she said.

"Want to go for a ride?" he asked.

She'd been back in town for almost a week and had seen him in the diner with his brothers, but otherwise she'd avoided him. It had seemed the wisest course of action since she'd been having hot, steamy, disturbing dreams about him and she was still no closer to having figured out who she was.

"I'd love to but I'm in the middle of a project... actually I might need a favor."

"What kind of favor?"

"Do you have a long-handled paint roller?" she asked. They had one at the Mercantile but it had cost more than she wanted to spend.

"I might. What do you need it for?" he asked.

She tipped her head to the side. "Painting my living room. What did you think I'd use it for?"

"Why are you fixing up your house?"

"It makes me happy," she said.

"That's a good thing," he remarked. "I'll look for the

paint roller and brushes and bring them by your place."

"You don't mind?" It was more than she'd hoped for.

"I wouldn't have offered if I did."

"But why? You said we're strangers now."

"We're still neighbors," he said.

And that meant a lot in Montana. Or really any rural area. "Thank you, Carson. You've treated me better than I deserve after the way I left."

"You were young. Hell, I was too."

He turned his horse and cantered away from her. She watched him go, realizing that being back in Montana had one big plus that she'd never considered—Carson. But she also knew that she couldn't stay for a man. She'd left for herself, and she really needed to be back for herself as well.

She got back into her car and drove to La Terra De Reves. She'd gone shopping in town and bought a couple of cans of paint and a wreath for her front door. Her sister Marilyn had yet to return one of Annie's phone calls but that hadn't stopped Annie from calling.

Being back home made her miss her sister and Annie knew it was past time to mend fences. Neither of them had recovered from losing their mom and sister. Last night she'd felt so mired in the past, but today she focused on the future.

She was still a little scared and very unsure of what, exactly, she was going to do next. She'd had a sense of purpose that had been eroded by time and the years she'd spent away from this quiet valley. Looking at the weathered cedar post and rail fencing that lined the gravel drive leading up to the wooden ranch house didn't inspire her, but the thought of seeing Carson again did.

La Terre De Reves, the optimistic name her father had given the ranch. *The land of dreams*, so named because her mother was an immigrant from France. Annie remembered her early childhood and the happy memories she had. But everything changed when she'd turned thirteen and it was impossible, standing here twenty years later, to forget the intervening years and the experiences she'd had.

A cold nose nudged the middle of her hand and she looked down at Rumple her English bulldog. He was sprawled out next to her, his stubby legs flat so that he could rest his belly on the leather seat. His coat was short and wiry, a brindle mixture of white and red. His face had the normal bulldog folds and he looked up at her with big, wide-set eyes. Running errands in town had worn him out. She scratched behind his ears. He responded with a sloppy kiss on her hand.

"This is it, baby," she said. "We're back home"

Marietta, Montana was a far cry from her apartment on the Upper East Side in Manhattan but the FBI had taken everything that she'd had there. She was literally holding everything she owned. This old rust-bucket of a car, Rumple, and a small duffel bag they'd provided for her to gather clothing and makeup in before the rest of it was seized to be sold. Sold to repay the people her ex-husband had bilked out of their savings.

She groaned and put her head on the steering wheel. She wished she felt like Fantine in *Les Miserables*, but instead she was pissed off that she'd put her faith and her fortune in a man like Davis and now she was back where she started. Older, but she sure wasn't wiser.

She and Davis had been married for ten years, childless by choice, and she'd sort of been his arm candy – and as it turned out, his distraction for potential investors. Davis had been a con man and a fraud... everything her father had warned her about as she'd left the ranch behind.

She put her car in gear and drove up the snow-covered winding road to the main house, which was now hers, thanks to Davis buying her sister out after their father died. She owned a hundred acres of land and this ramshackle single-story ranch house. There was a bunkhouse behind it that looked as rundown as the house, and the pastures had grown over.

The front yard was full of brown batches of dead grass, mounds of unmelted snow, and some ice. The old barn looked as if it had seen better days and needed to be re-stained. One of the doors hung off its hinges.

Looking at the house gave her a sort of tingling in the bottom of her stomach. Not excitement, but just a project that needed her. La Terre De Reves was in worse shape than she was and she wanted to fix the old homestead. She also knew that with enough time, which to be honest she had plenty of now, she could make it a home.

She got out of the car and watched Rumple climb down and head to the weed-ridden flowerbed to relieve himself as she grabbed her large leather Coach bag, which she'd had the good sense to leave with a friend when she went to collect the rest of her belongings.

When her husband had been arrested and indicted for fraud eighteen months earlier, she'd lost everything. She'd divorced Davis and done her best to survive. But there was nothing left for her in Manhattan as even her so-called friends had cut ties to avoid being tainted by the scandal.

It was so quiet here in the valley, no honking horns or rumbling subways. Instead just the quiet of the valley and the magic of the distant snow-capped Copper Mountain. She remembered how this valley had nurtured her as a child and realized that was why she'd come back. She needed to find her center again and hoped that this place could work its magic once again.

As she walked up the stone path, she remembered watching her father lay the river stones. She unlocked the door to the house, and Rumple ambled up beside her and flopped down at her feet as if he'd exerted all his energy just to make it to the door.

"I'm feeling ya, buddy," she said, as she stepped over the threshold and held the door open until the dog followed her inside. A waft of stale air and the oddly sweet smell of her father's cigars surrounded her. She reached into the bag and got out the apple cinnamon plug-ins she'd purchased in town, popping one into the outlet near the front door.

Already it was starting to smell more homey. She went back out to the car and slowly brought in all her purchases. She hung the wreath on the front door and then decided to call her sister again. The call went to voicemail.

"It's just Annie again. Please call me back. I'd love to get together and catch up. I'm sorry I let so much time go by."

She hung up and looked around the house. She had big plans to start redoing it but now it seemed overwhelming. She piled all her supplies, the two cans of paint, and some drop cloths in the dining room. She remembered there were paint brushes and rollers in the garage and went out to find them.

Rumple wandered off and she glanced around the house with its worn furnishings and layer of dust. She wished now that she'd let Davis buy new furniture for the place, but her intent in buying it from her sisters was to get them to stop bugging her to come home.

The sound of her boots on the tile floor echoed as she walked through the house to the garage. It was dark and cold and she fumbled for the light switch, knocking over a box in the process.

The light came on and she glanced at the floor where the box she'd knocked off had fallen on its side. She bent to pick it all up and froze as she noticed what was there. Christmas past stared her in the face. An ornament she had made at Brownies. A family portrait stuck in the middle of a green and red bread-dough wreath.

She held it loosely as her heart caught in her throat. She traced the wreath, feeling the rough texture of the dough where she hadn't kneaded it enough to get it smooth. They had been such a happy family back then. Her dad wore his Sunday shirt and "good" Stetson, her mom smiling over at him and her sisters all healthy and whole. She wanted that again.

But all she had was this empty house. She pushed the other items into the box and closed the lid, setting it aside. She shoved the ornament into the pocket of her jacket and went to gather paint supplies. Back in the house, Rumple was waiting for her.

She scratched him behind the ears, found an old bowl in the kitchen, and filled it with water for him. Placing the ornament on the counter where she could see it, she got to work fixing up the house.

For the first time she wished she had someone to lean on. Someone she could talk to, not so they could solve her problems or fix her, but just so she didn't have to carry this all inside. She'd screwed up and she was back at the one place she never wanted to return to.

She'd had just enough time to make a plan. She hadn't been able to keep her leather-bound planner, but the FBI had let her take all of her notes out of it and she'd used binder clips to keep it together. She sat at the kitchen table and made a list of everything she'd need to make the house livable. It was habitable. A roof over her head and she knew she should be grateful to have it.

Chapter Four

La Terre De Reves was looking a little sad, and as he drove up to the front of the house he noticed signs that Annie was living there now. The wreath on the front door, the cobwebs cleaned from the windows, and a box marked Christmas on the porch.

He knocked on the door and heard a loud bark, and then the sound of dog's nails on the hardwood floor.

"Good boy, Rumple," he heard Annie say a second before the door opened. "You're the best guard dog in the world."

The English Bulldog stopped and barked one last time as he looked up at Carson. He'd always loved dogs and bent over to pet him. The 'guard dog' licked his hand. "Nice to meet you."

Rumple gave him one last lick and then turned around to waddle back down the hall. Carson stood up slowly and noticed that Annie had been staring at his butt. He arched one eyebrow at her and she shrugged.

"You've got a great ass. It'd be a sin not to stare."

He laughed. He figured it was pretty run-of-the-mill but he was glad she liked it. "I had an extra-long paint roller and two free hours if you want some help."

"I'd love your help," she said. "The house is pretty run-down."

"Years of neglect will do that to a place."

"To a person too," she added.

"Have you been neglected?" he asked. "You never did tell me what happened to your marriage."

"That's old news and not very interesting," she said. "I'd rather live in the now."

He didn't like that she kept deflecting any topic that got too close to the real woman. And even though he was attracted to her, he wasn't interested in being just another diversion in the Annie show.

"Forget it," he said. "You can keep the roller – we've got a bunch back at the ranch."

He turned on his heel to walk back to his big Chevy F150, wishing this felt more like a narrow escape than genuine disappointment. Considering he'd spent the last two nights lying his bed and wondering if he might have a shot at the one woman he'd never been able to forget—he knew that was a lie.

"Carson."

He stopped and glanced over his shoulder at her. He wore a cowboy hat, his thick shearling jacket and heavy boots, and he knew that when she looked at him she saw an image. It was the image that had initially drawn Rainey to him.

He saw a woman in a flannel shirt and a pair of skintight leggings. In his mind she looked like home but he knew that was an illusion. For a woman to be home she'd have to want to stay some place and not always be moving on. Annie wasn't home.

"I'm… I don't want to talk about New York or my marriage. It's embarrassing and painful," she said. "But I really don't want you to go either."

"I'm not asking you strip your soul naked. I just need to know that you're not toying with me."

"Why would I be?"

"Because you're a leaver, Annie." He wanted to know if that had changed. He wasn't about to risk falling for her again if it was just an odd breeze that blew her back into his life.

She wrapped one arm around her waist, her gray eyes frosty as the snow covered ground, but lonely too. "I guess I am. What would it take for you to stay?"

Honestly if she asked him he'd stay. And that made him feel sad because he had hoped after all the years he'd be stronger where she was concerned. He was still sort of mad at her and a part of him wished—really wished—he could use her, make her feel something for him and walk away. Because then maybe she'd know what she'd done to him.

But there was a better chance of it reaching eighty degrees on Christmas day than that ever happening. Because he couldn't be around her and not fall a little under her spell.

"Ask me," he said at last.

"Please stay."

He nodded, turned around, and walked back into her

house, picking up the paint roller he'd left by the door on his way. He was damned glad his brothers weren't here to witness this because they'd call him a stupid fool.

Her house smelled like Christmas and he attributed it to the pine garland she had draped over the table in the hallway and on her mantel in the living room. But he knew it was more than that.

It was December and he was dreaming like he always did of a holiday miracle. The kind that his mom used to read to them about when they were little. She'd covered the furniture with drop cloths.

"Looks like you've been busy."

"I needed it," she said. "I've had too much on my mind."

"Like?" he asked, inviting her to be real with him but assuming she wouldn't be.

"You. This place," she said. "I don't get why I can't ever manage to be happy."

He leaned the paint roller against the wall and took off his hat and jacket, placing them over the back of the arm chair in the middle of the room. Her dog lay on a big blanket next to the empty fireplace.

"Only you can answer that," he said. "But I'll tell you what I learned when Rainey died. You can't keep looking back and wishing for things to change."

She nodded. "I guess that was hard for you."

"You have no idea," he said. He knew she figured he was talking about losing his wife and that had been hard. But lately he'd been wondering what might-have-been if he'd been willing to leave with Annie.

And that had bad idea written all over it. "I'll get this room done if you want to work on something else."

"Need me out of your hair?" she asked.

"Something like that," he said, knowing he didn't need the distraction of Annie and the dreams she made him think might come true.

She had that wild out-of-control feeling that she got just before she did something stupid and she couldn't help herself.

But she walked over to Carson and leaned up to kiss him. He was a good guy. He always had been and she'd always felt just a little bit broken.

He sighed opening his mouth and she wrapped her arms around him and hugged him close. She stood there as the warmth of the embrace engulfed her. He pulled his head from hers and cursed under his breath before bringing his mouth back down on hers. The embrace wasn't gentle. His anger was palpable and so was his desire. He put his hands on her hips, drawing her closer.

She opened her eyes and looked up at him. Her heart beat faster and deep inside where she'd been cold for so long, a spark was ignited as she saw the flush on his face and his half-closed eyes.

With Carson there were no games and she knew if she wanted a chance at kissing him again she had to be honest. But her old instincts were kicking into gear. She started to moan because Davis had liked it when she made noise when they kissed and almost as soon as she did it, she knew she'd screwed up.

He pulled back and looked down at her.

"What the hell was that?"

"I was…I'm sorry."

"You can't even be honest when you kiss me?" he asked. "What are you hiding?"

She shrugged and pulled back. "I just didn't want to disappoint you."

"You can't as long as you're yourself. I don't want you to try to be what you think I want. We'll both lose if you do that."

"I don't—

She stopped herself before she could say what she knew was the truth, but she suspected he'd already figured it out for himself. She didn't know who she was.

"Tell me."

She shook her head. When she looked at Carson she saw so much of what she wanted to have for herself. His confidence in his place in the world, his family and those ties to Marietta and the Paradise Valley. But more than, she saw a man she wanted to be able to claim as her own. But she couldn't.

She couldn't because she wasn't really sure what she wanted.

"I don't know who I am."

He nodded. "That's the first honest thing you've said to me since you've been back."

"I'm scared," she admitted

"Of what?" he asked, pushing a strand of hair behind her ear.

For the first time he made her realize that she wasn't alone.

"Marilyn won't talk to me," she said. "I… I didn't come back for dad's funeral because my life was falling apart but I didn't want to admit it and now she thinks I'm just a super-bitch."

He hugged her close. And then pulled back. "One step at a time. She's coming to the tree farm on Saturday to collect her tree. Why don't you show up early and wait for her?"

That frightened her too but she was done laying her soul bare for this afternoon. "Thanks for the suggestion. I will."

"Good. Now about this painting…"

They worked together in the living room with Carson painting the walls and Annie doing the trim. She felt the first tingle of something that she wasn't sure she could define as they worked together, but she liked it. She learned that he loved being a dad and that scared her because Annie and kids didn't mix. But then she reminded herself of Carson's advice…one step at a time. That was all she had to do. Slowly work through the holidays and into her new life.

"Looks good," she said, when he was finished. "Thank you for your help. I don't think I could have hired a better painter in Manhattan."

"Did you do that a lot?" he asked.

"Yes. When I first got married I completely gutted our apartment and re-did the entire thing. It took me eighteen months to get it finished."

"Why did you leave it behind?" he asked. "Why not stay there? I'm guessing it was your divorce that drove you back here."

She shook her head and took a deep breath. "It was and it wasn't. My ex-husband was indicted for fraud and I lost everything."

"What kind of fraud?" Carson asked.

"A Ponzi scheme that involved a lot of really nice senior citizens. Everything was sold to reimburse them and Davis is in jail now."

"How did that affect you?"

She didn't really want to tell him how stupid she'd felt when she realized what Davis had been doing. She'd trusted him and defended him and the entire time he'd been lying and using her to help further his schemes.

"I lost everything too. Everything except this," she said gesturing at the living room. "And I must thank you again for your help. Now the living room looks cheery."

He seemed like he might want to ask her more questions but she was raw and didn't want to expose anything else right now. "I hate to rush you along but I'm working the dinner shift tonight and I was planning to stop at the bank and cash my paycheck. I should have done it earlier."

But she hadn't wanted to risk having too much cash in her purse when she went to the Mercantile. Everyone had their weaknesses when it came to spending and hers was home decoration. She knew she'd have bought all kinds of picture frames and ornaments to decorate the house and she had budgeted to buy gifts for her sister and her family.

"I'll get out of your hair then," he said, picking up his jacket and his Stetson and walking to the door after giving Rumple a rub behind the ears. "See you Saturday?"

"Yes. Thanks for the heads up about Marilyn."

He nodded at her. "Want to have dinner one night?"

"Like a date?"

"Maybe."

"Maybe."

She felt foolish staking out the parking lot at the Scott Christmas Tree lot but there was Marilyn with her two oldest kids, Josie who was thirteen and a barrel racer, and Jake who was eleven. The kids had her sister's deep auburn hair and but Joe's stocky build. Josie and Jake hugged their mom and then went off with a group of kids their age.

Marilyn stood by her Jeep Cherokee looking over at Annie where she still sat in her car. She turned away from her sister to button up the old jacket she'd found in a closet at the ranch house and put on her gloves.

Annie put the leash on Rumple and leaned down for a wet doggy kiss. Then she opened her door and got out. Marilyn walked over to her.

"I can't believe my eyes," she said not a welcoming note in her tone or body language. Her sister wore a black duster over a pair of faded blue jeans and a pair of mountain boots. "What the hell are you doing here?"

"I moved back," she said trying not to sound defensive. Why was it she always was acutely aware that Marilyn was her older sister? She always sounded like she was defending herself.

"I guess you had no choice once Davis took everyone's money," Marilyn said sarcastically.

Her older sister had always been the pretty one with her big green eyes like Momma's and her thick reddish brown hair. Life hadn't been unkind to her and she still looked pretty and young for her age. She was thirty-five and had four kids.

"You're right about that," Annie said. "I... I've done my best to make up for everything."

"You can't make it right with me," Marilyn said. "Or with dad. It's too late for that."

"I know that," she said, then stop herself from saying any more. She wanted to defend herself, but really what could she say?

"I was hoping we could get together for the holidays.

"I can't."

"Oh, why not. I'd like to see the kids. I think they sort of like me," Annie said.

"They do, but we're going to Joe's family for the holidays. We will be at the Christmas Stroll next week. You going to be there?"

"I'll be working in the diner," Annie said.

Marilyn shook her head. "Dad was right about you after all."

"He wasn't right about me," Annie said. Her father had

said she was running away to nothing but Annie had always had her eye on where she'd wanted to be. "I didn't fall on my face, I trusted the wrong man with my fortune. But I made a fortune. And I'm not running home with my tail between my legs. I'm back because when you lose everything it kind of makes you realize what's important. And a fifteen-year-old grudge isn't."

Marilyn just looked at her for a long minute and Rumple tugged on his lead. Moving forward to nudge her sister's legs.

"You're right. I'm sorry. Let's go grab some hot chocolate and chat," Marilyn said, reaching down to pet Rumple.

"Okay," Annie said. She'd missed her sister more than she'd ever admit to Marilyn. Being two years older than Annie, Marilyn often thought she knew best and it still irritated Annie that most times her sister did.

"The kids are here to meet up with friends and ride on that sleigh the Scotts have. Do you remember it from when we were young?"

"I do. Carson and I kissed for the first time on the Halloween hay ride in it," Annie admitted.

"I never could figure out why you dated him. You knew you were leaving," Marilyn said.

"He was hard to say no to," she admitted. "Even harder once he kissed me."

Marilyn laughed and led the way to some pinewood picnic tables that were set up next to a small stand selling hot chocolate. Annie recognized the banner over head as the Copper Mountain Chocolates owned by Sage.

"I think Sage made some sort of deal with the devil because her hot chocolate tastes like sin."

"It does. I have to limit myself to only one a week or I'd be the size of Mrs. Claus before Christmas," Marilyn said. "Why don't you grab us a seat and I'll get the drinks."

Annie led Rumple to the tables and sat down waiting for her sister. As she watched the crowds of familiar looking families she realized how much she missed this. The faces were all a little older and there were some new ones but these were her people. She'd lived in Manhattan for almost fifteen years and she'd never once been in a place that felt like this... like home.

The sun was shining over the valley today and a thin dusting of snow covered the ground and she sat there feeling like she'd found something she hadn't known was missing. Marilyn came back with the drinks in Styrofoam cups and sat down next to her.

"Where are you staying?" Marilyn asked. "Did you get an apartment in town?"

"No. I'm staying at our old ranch," Annie said.

"I wasn't aware you got to keep it."

"Davis had put in my name and we used the money I'd made from selling my business to buy it so the FBI figured it was pretty much mine. They took everything else," Annie said.

"What do you mean?"

"The authorities wouldn't let me back into our apartment. I only had the clothes on my back and the cash in my wallet. I got to keep Rumple here and one bag of clothing I packed. It was a complete nightmare. Maybe you were right earlier when you said Dad knew I'd fail," Annie said.

Marilyn put her arm around Annie's shoulders and hugged her close. "I'm sorry, sissy. I never wanted that for you and I'm pretty sure dad didn't either. We were both just hurt you didn't want to stay."

She hugged her sister back and put her head on Marilyn's shoulder and realized how long it had been since they'd hugged each other. She had missed her older sister more than she wanted to admit to anyone, even herself. She soaked up the comfort her sister offered.

Saturdays in December were busy for Carson, especially the middle of the month as everyone was ready to get their trees up. A storm threatened and a light snow fell, but the lot was festive and everyone wore a smile. Since the tree farm was on his parcel of the Scott property, he had all the families from the neighboring towns coming to get a fresh-cut tree or to pick up their potted ones. He enjoyed it since he got a chance to stay busy and to see so many people.

The tents they'd set up for selling hot chocolate and

cookies had been decorated by his sister-in-law Sienna. She and Alec were having a rough patch but she said that didn't mean she wasn't still a part of the family. He thought that maybe Annie could learn something from the way Sienna had stayed. Sage had sent Rose Linn out to run the hot cocoa booth and he'd hung a Copper Mountain Chocolates banner across her section of the tent. He'd ordered one that said Cookies for Rachel's section.

The entire lot felt like Christmas and as he watched his son walking around with his little Santa hat on, he felt a sense of longevity. He'd done the same thing when he'd been six. They were connected here to the land and to their ancestors.

Liz Anderson, who owned the acting school in town, was running around trying to drum up participants for her nativity play. Evan had already auditioned and would be playing one of the three wise men. Something that the six-year-old took seriously. Just as seriously as his job passing out candy canes to everyone who got off the sleigh that his Uncle Lane was driving.

They used two big draft horses for the sleigh. They'd painted it a few weeks ago, a nice bright red like the barn on the Scott property that they were all helping renovate.

"Nice operation you've got here," Annie said as she walked up to him. She wore a knitted hat on her head and an old shearling jacket over skintight jeans and those same cowboy boots she'd had on the other day. Her makeup was flawless and he couldn't help noticing that she truly was a beautiful woman.

Her English Bulldog looked funny with his tongue hanging out and his little legs moving quickly to keep up with her. As soon as Annie stopped, the dog plopped down on the ground. The poor little thing looked as if the walk from the parking area to the tree area, a mere three hundred feet, had worn him out.

They'd been friends since they first met back in elementary school, so he always just thought of her as Annie. But sometimes – like right now – he was surprised to remember that she was beautiful , especially when she was smiling. He thought that Montana was working its magic on her and hoped that he had a little to do with it.

"It keeps me busy," he said, bending down to pet her dog. "You never did tell me why you call him Rumple."

"It's short for Rumpelstiltskin."

"Truly? The old guy who spun gold?" Carson asked looking up at her.

She nibbled on her lower lip, a habit of hers that was slowly driving him out of his mind.

"Yes. I got him as a gift from Davis right when he started making an insane amount of money."

"Well at least he gave you something," Carson said. "How did the meeting with Marilyn go?"

"It went okay. She was mad and I didn't blame her for that. We're going to meet next week for the Christmas Stroll," she said.

"Come for dinner tonight and tell me all about it," he offered.

She hesitated for a moment and tipped her head to the side, studying him with those searching gray eyes. "I... okay. What time?"

"Six, we eat early. Evan has a strict seven-thirty bedtime."

"Where is he?" she asked.

"Helping pass out candy canes with my brother Lane. Now that you've talked to Marilyn, what can I help you with?"

"A tree," she said. "I was going through my dad's bills and found that he had a potted tree."

"He did. I guess it's yours now. I've been keeping it up every year. Do you want to see it?"

"I'd love to," she said. "And then I need to arrange for it to be delivered to my house. How much is that?"

"Nothing. It's included in your yearly tree bill, which you have paid up for the next five years," Carson said.

"I do like to pay ahead if I can," she said, which is why she'd been able to move back to Marietta. The house was paid off, with the utilities covered for a year. She wondered if she'd had a premonition not to trust that Davis, that the prosperity wouldn't last.

"Good plan. Pop raised us like that as well. He saw too many friends lose everything when they didn't. I'll let the guys know I'm taking you to your tree."

He found Duke, his ranch foreman, and told him he'd be in the back of the tree lot. They had loud speakers booming out the soundtrack from A Charlie Brown Christmas.

When he walked back over to Annie he found Evan standing there telling her some story. He stopped in his tracks as Annie bent down so she was on eye level with his son, leaning in and listening intently. His heart clenched and he saw another way that she'd changed. It wasn't that she'd been uncaring when she'd lived in Marietta... it was just that she'd always been thinking about herself. He was starting to see signs that she had changed.

"He's a silly dog who just eats ice cubes and drools all day," she said to Evan.

"Puddles is silly too. Daddy made me leave him in the house since there would be too many people here today and he might get scared or run off," Evan said to Annie.

"There are a lot of people. It's just Rumple and me and I needed some company today."

"Why'd you need company?" Evan asked.

"Promise not to tell?" she asked.

"I promise," Evan said looking very solemn.

"I get a little scared when I'm meeting people so I like having a friend with me."

Evan smiled and nodded. "Me too. I wish I could take Puddles to school with me."

"I think Miss Abrahams wouldn't like that," Carson said joining them. "Puddles would definitely disrupt the lesson."

"Yes, he would," Evan said

"Everything set?" Annie asked as she straightened up.

"Yes, I'm going to use the Mule to take her out to the trees, you stay with Duke," Carson said to Evan.

"I should keep Rumple too," Evan said.

"Great idea," Annie said, handing the leash over to Evan who tugged the dog to his feet.

The Kawasaki Mule was an ATV that was great for traveling all over the ranch, since there weren't many places it couldn't go. Carson didn't like the thought of Evan wandering around by himself. He ruffled his son's hair and Evan smiled up at him. He was reminded of how much he loved his son.

"I will. I hope you like your tree, Miss Annie."

"I'm sure I will, Evan. Did you take care of it for me?"

"I helped. Daddy did most of the work," Evan said. Then he turned to run over toward Duke.

Carson heard Annie sigh and he looked at her with one eyebrow raised.

"I just never knew kids could be like that."

"Like what?"

"Never mind… I'll sound like a moron if I say it out loud. Where's this mule? Please tell me it's some kind of vehicle and not an actual mule."

"Woman, I'm a cowboy. We only ride horses and ATVs."

Chapter Five

"This has always been one of my favorite parts of the holiday," she said as they zipped through the trees on the ATV. Snow fell all around them and she was tucked next to Carson. The wind was cold as it rushed around her but she didn't mind. It was impossible to dwell on her uncertain future while they raced along. She felt so *in the moment*. There was no time to dwell on the mistakes of the past or worry about her uncertain future as the vehicle bounced along the ground. She just held on and let herself breathe. Something she realized she hadn't experienced in a long time. It had been too easy to just exist.

"Yeah, the first year after Rainey died I think it saved me. I just wanted to hibernate until the season passed, but I couldn't. I got out here and saw the joy everyone has when they are picking out their trees. They all have the sparkle in their eyes as they picture the tree in their own homes. It didn't make the first Christmas without her better, but it did make it easier to cope with."

She wanted to reach over and squeeze his hand but didn't want to distract him. "I don't know how you did it. I can't imagine losing someone I loved like that."

"Well losing your husband must have had an impact on you. Separating is always hard," he said.

"Davis and I weren't exactly a love match. We just liked doing the same things and our lives fit, you know?" she asked.

He stopped the Mule. "We have to walk from here. I don't really know what you mean... why marry someone if you don't love them?"

He started walking toward a copse of trees in the distance and she fell into an easy pace with him. The snow was higher here than it had been in the tree lot, but not impossible to walk on. "I chose a different path than love."

"I guess you did. I'm not judging – just asking, you know," he said.

"I didn't think you were," she said. It was just that she hadn't put too much stock in love. She'd seen it tear her father apart when her mom and sister Gilly had left and she knew she'd never wanted to let an emotion do that to her.

Her family had been taken from her and she'd decided at an early age to never risk losing anyone like that again. And she'd thought she'd done a good job of it until she found herself back in Marietta at Christmas time.

"You seem different now from when you were younger," he said. "I know – what a dumb thing to say, cowboy. Right?"

"I am different, just not the way I thought it would be," she said, stopping and turning toward him. "You never were a dumb cowboy."

"You're just saying that because I used to let you cheat off me in Algebra."

"I let you think that. Oooh! Math is so hard," she said with a laugh. Realizing how free she felt, for the first time losing everything seemed it might have been a blessing.

"Why'd I leave you behind?" she asked wistfully.

"I wouldn't come with you," he said. "I knew that my life was in Marietta."

"I wonder if mine was too," she said under her breath.

"Nah, you were too big for us even back then. I wanted to live out here, you needed a city."

"I did," she said. "And I wanted to design big pretty interiors. Something that there wasn't much of a market for around here."

"How'd that work out for you?" he asked.

"Good. Made me a rich woman," she said. She left it at that.

He led them down a path between two rows of huge fir trees in massive pots. She walked slowly behind him, closing her eyes to breathe in the scent of pine. She let it wrap around her senses and fill her with that joy of the holiday season. "I don't think this is going to fit in my house," she said.

"Yours isn't this big. Those trees are for the mansions on Bramble Lane."

"I can believe it," she said. "They must look so pretty in the window of those old Victorians."

"They do. They'll all be installed and decorated in time

for the Christmas Stroll next week. Evan loves the houses all decorated with lights."

"I do too," she said.

He stopped in front of a seven-foot tree and tipped his head toward it. "This one is yours."

"Mine," she said. It was odd, the things she owned post-Davis. A rundown house, a drooling dog, a beat-up Mustang and a seven-foot Douglas fir. She started laughing at how ridiculous that was, compared to what she used to own. Suddenly her laughter turned to tears. She didn't know why she was crying or how to stop it now that it had started.

Carson started to ask her something but she shook her head and turned and ran away. Just had to get away from everything. Her breath sawed in and out and the cold air burned as she inhaled but she didn't stop... just kept running as fast as she could.

Life was too much. Being with this sweet cowboy who could have been hers if she'd chosen a different path. Being alone in the midst of this fragrant Christmas forest and knowing that she'd continue being lonely. And it was no one's fault but her own that she'd wanted to get away.

She ran into a tree, a spray of snow rained down on her, and the snow stopped her tears. Surrounded by the beauty of this moment and the cold of the snow, she couldn't help being forced into this moment. She reached a fence and stood there staring out at the Copper Mountain, wishing... just wishing life had been different. Her breath huffed out of her in visible puffs, the tears dried on her cheeks making them cold, and she brought her gloves up to wipe them away.

Carson walked up behind her and put his hand on her shoulder. When she didn't run, he drew her back against him and then turned her in his arms. He didn't say anything – just took her face in his hands. They were warm and big as he held her.

He brought his mouth down on hers and rubbed his lips back and forth slowly and gently. She opened her lips under his and his kiss pushed away the sadness that she'd been carrying for too long.

That melancholy that had been her blanket far too long was disappearing under his kiss. It was a kiss she hadn't realized she'd missed until this moment. She stopped dissecting it and just let herself enjoy the minty taste of his breath, the smooth feel of his tongue against hers.

And the way he held her was as if he never intended to let her go. She wrapped her arms around his shoulders and kissed him back with all the pent-up desire she hadn't realized she'd bottled up until now. Until Carson. Carson Scott had always been something different to her.

He tunneled his fingers through her hair, rubbing the back of her neck. She tipped her head to the side to deepen the kiss and stretched up on her toes so she could taste more of him. She hadn't realized how much she'd missed physical closeness. She thought she was sort of sexless or one those women with a low sex drive... but Carson sparked something inside of her.

And now she realized that he was exactly what she wanted. What she'd always wanted, but she'd been afraid to give up on her dreams of something bigger – something more. It wasn't his fault that she'd gone searching some ephemeral thing, only to find it wasn't there.

She hoped that what she really wanted was right here in Montana, but this kiss made her anxious inside, a bit on edge.

She tasted like hot chocolate and peppermint. He held her face in his bare hands, her skin was soft and the trail of her tears damp but he didn't think about anything other than her mouth. It was full and luscious and as his moved hers, he wondered why he'd waited so long to kiss her. She tasted of memories and yet at the same time this was a totally new experience.

The last time he'd kissed her he'd been a boy... eager to cop a feel of her breasts or coax her into the back of his beat-up pickup truck. Now he was a man. While he was still eager, he knew how to savor things, especially – Annie.

He slid his fingers into her hair, beneath the knitted cap she wore. Her hair was silky and smooth. He deepened their kiss, hungry for so much more of her. Her taste was addicting and he knew he'd never get enough of it.

Her hands slid along his sides to his waist and she tugged him closer to her. He canted his hips forward and she rocked hers against him. Damn, she felt good. The bulge in his pants was hard and all he could think of was how to get them both naked.

But a chill breeze blew through the thick fir trees, stirring the scent of the evergreens and bringing a light dusting of snow down on them. He pulled back, but her eyes were closed and her lips full, swollen from his kisses. So he couldn't resist bending down and taking one last taste of her.

He lifted his head the second time, every instinct urging him to scoop her into his arms and find someplace sheltered so he could make love to her. But he knew that now wasn't the time.

She'd been crying. He didn't like seeing her sad. It was one of the reasons he'd contemplated leaving Marietta with her all those years ago, but in the end he knew he couldn't make her happy.

He hoped to God that was not still the truth.

She stood so still and quiet next to him that he took a step away and looked out to the distance where Copper Mountain rose up to meet the sky. He saw the thick clouds that meant another snowstorm was headed their way. He had work to do, needed to get back to the ranch, and make sure his hands had gotten enough hay distributed to the cattle before it snowed.

But he didn't want to leave this quiet area or this woman. He wanted Annie to be back for good, partly for her but mainly for himself. He was tired of sleeping alone in a cold bed and he wanted something he couldn't really identify. Something hard to define, but that seemed to be centered on Annie. He didn't know that Annie was the right woman, but he wasn't talking about forever. He just wanted…

"Sorry about that," she said at last. Her voice was low-pitched and a little raw.

"About what?" he asked, feeling a bit raw himself. "That kiss might have been the highlight of my day."

"Really?" she asked.

"Yes. It's been a while since I've kissed anyone."

"Me too," she admitted. "I guess we both needed to let off a little steam."

"Don't make this into something physical. I wasn't just kissing a woman, I was kissing you, Annie."

She looked down and away from him, and he wondered if he'd read her wrong.

"Me too. I wanted to kiss you, Carson. You kiss like a man now," she said.

"I should hope so," he said.

"I didn't mean to freak out like that. I don't know why I was crying," she said at last and he stepped back and let frigid air and the distance cool his body. Of course she knew why she was crying but she didn't want to admit it and not to him.

"Probably being back home and not having any of your friends and family around you," he said.

"Thanks Dr. Phil."

"Just calling it like I see it. You've always been a bit of a rebel and I think being back here has reminded you of all that. Was it talking to your sister?"

"Probably. I hate how, even though I'm thirty-three and an adult, I still feel like I'm six around her. Why is it I'm still Marilyn's little sister?" she asked. And now it was just the two of them. They were the only ones alive who remembered the joy of their little family and the sadness when it ended. This Christmas she wanted to make some new memories with her sister and her sister's family. There was no reason why she had to be alone.

"It's the same with me and Alec. He's always bossing me around and sometimes I just do what he says before I remember that I don't have to. It's habit for him and for me."

"Yes, I guess so."

"I'll tell you one thing," he said. "When Rainey died, having Alec there made a huge difference to me. He just stepped in and refused to let me retreat the way I wanted to."

"I really am sorry you lost your wife."

"I know," he said, glancing out toward the mountains again. He missed Rainey always would, but he wasn't pining for her. "She would have liked you."

"You think so?"

"Yes, she didn't take any sass off me either," he said.

She laughed like he hoped she would, but the sound was forced and he realized she was still fragile inside. In fact...

KATHERINE GARBERA

kissing her might have been a mistake. Maybe he'd just made her feel even more vulnerable.

But now that her guard was down, maybe he could get a few answers from her. "What are you running from? And don't say you aren't running. You have that look in your eyes."

She shook her head and wrapped her arms around her waist, looking over at him as if to gauge whether she could trust him or not.

"I thought if nothing else we'd once been friends," he said at last.

"We were," she admitted. "But you asked me to dinner to tell you that story and I can't do it right now without crying again. "

"Fair enough," he said. "We should be getting back anyway. I'm not sure how long Evan will be good with Rumple before he tries to ride him or put a pair of Rudolph antlers on him."

"Truly?"

"He did it to Puddles last year. The poor dog looked miserable but he tolerated it. He just loves Evan," Carson said, leading the way back to her tree. "I'll get the tree trimmed up and delivered to your place this afternoon."

"Why don't you bring it by tonight and I'll fix you dinner," she said. "Seems the least I can do since you're delivering my tree."

He'd have to find a sitter for Evan but he suspected his dad might want to have his grandson sleep over. "Sounds good to me."

Annie had gone carefully over her budget and then decided she could just splurge on the fixings of a nice Italian dinner. It was the one meal she was really good at cooking and she admitted to herself she wanted to impress Carson.

An open bottle of Chianti sat on the counter and a hearty lasagna in the oven as she waited for Carson to arrive. She'd put on her favorite Christmas CD by Diana Krall. She had purchased some cookies from Rachel at the Christmas tree lot

165

and looked forward to eating them. But for right now, she was sitting in her living room looking out the big bay window for him.

Rumple sat at her feet, every once in a while looking up at her as if to ask where he was. She knew she was being stupid. This wasn't the way she normally acted. But to be fair, she hadn't had a first date with anyone in over ten years and she was a little out of practice.

One thing a settled relationship did was take the nerves out of things like dinner. Her house smelled of garlic and tomatoes, she'd made her own sauce from her mother's recipe which had been her grandmother's, and there had been something soothing about making it.

She'd felt the same way when she'd been in New York and made it. The food and the recipes of the women in her family linked her to them. It was the closest thing she had to home until now.

She looked at the boxes of Christmas decorations she'd found in the attic, but had been afraid to open. She had no idea what memories lurked in the boxes and she wasn't sure she was ready to face them. But she knew once she had a tree she was going to want to decorate it.

She'd found the box labeled Lights. She should go through them instead of standing at the window like... like a woman who couldn't wait for her man, she scolded herself, and forced herself to turn away. Carson wasn't her man. He couldn't be unless she let herself be honest with him about her emotions. And she'd have to start thinking about staying here. Something she didn't want to do tonight.

She opened the box with the string lights in it and groaned. Last year she'd hired a service to do this. Really, it had been so much easier but then again she'd had the entire interior of her apartment decorated by the service. The doorbell rang and she started at the sound.

"Stop being silly," she warned herself. But she couldn't help the jolt of excitement that went through her. He was here.

She took her time walking to the front door and unlocked the deadbolt before opening the door. Diana Krall had started singing Sleigh Ride and it felt like a sign to her. Carson stood there with his Stetson in one hand and his leather jacket open.

"You look pretty," he said.

"Thanks. You look good too."

"I've got your tree but seeing this door, it's going to be hard to get it in."

Rumple ambled forward and nudged Carson's legs with his nose and he bent down to scratch her dog behind his ears. And she just noticed how well the jeans fit him and when he straightened and looked over at her, one eyebrow lifted in question she sort of blushed and wanted to kick herself for that.

"How'd you do it the last time you delivered it for dad?" she asked as Rumple ambled back to his large doggie bed in the kitchen.

"He never had the tree delivered. Just left it there on the lot said maybe someday he would if his girls came home," Carson said.

Those words made her heart ache. She hadn't been close to her dad. They hadn't gotten along, but if he'd asked her one time to come home she would have. She'd just always felt so unwanted, so in the way. And now she heard from someone else that maybe she had been needed here.

"Oh. I never knew that," she said, feeling it was one more way she and her father had never understood each other. Would it have killed him to call her and ask her to come back?

"That was thoughtless," he said, he ran his hand over his thick hair. "I didn't mean it the way it came out."

"It's fine. I never wanted to come home. I never knew he wanted me to," she said. "Want to come in and see if there is a better way to get the tree in?"

"I think I'd better. I have it on a hand truck, so... don't you have double-sided French doors on the back?" he asked.

"Yes. You want to come in there?"

"I think it'll work. I brought a couple of guys with me. Where do you want it set up?" Carson asked.

"I'm debating. Either next to the fireplace..." she said, leading him into the living room and pointing to the left side of the hearth. She'd already started decorating with a few boughs she'd picked up at the Christmas tree lot earlier. She'd placed them on the mantel with a string of twinkle lights that she'd found in her old bedroom. "... or over there in the middle of the bay window."

Carson looked at both areas then back at her. "It's up to you, I think I'd put it in the window if you want my opinion."

"Why?"

"It's dark in that corner– plus the tree will spill over in front of the fireplace and if you put a blanket on the floor and sit there it'll be crowded."

"I think it might be cozy with a fire on one side, the tree in the front and you on the other," she said. Giving voice to what she wanted. She hadn't been shy before her downfall and she hated that she'd lost that part of herself.

But today out the in the snow, kissing Carson had reminded her of herself. The woman she was searching for. She still didn't really know who she was, but she was remembering a few things about herself that she'd forgotten. And one of them was if she was home for Christmas she was wanted to spend it with this cowboy.

"You sure about that?" he asked.

She pulled him close and kissed him long and hard and deep – and when she took a step back she noticed his cheeks were flushed and his lips swollen and wet.

"What do you think?

Chapter Six

"I think I better get that tree inside and send my boys home so we can be alone," he said, turning toward her front door. He wasn't ready to play games with her and this had the feeling of a game. She'd kissed him and then thrown down a dare.

"Now who's running?" she taunted.

He didn't like being called a coward and in essence that was what she was doing. "I'm not the one who ran away fifteen years ago or even this afternoon. Make sure those doors are unlocked – and you might want to keep your dog out of the way. The guys won't be able to watch the tree and your pet."

"I guess I need to apologize for that," she said.

"Only if you mean it," he said, unable to stem the anger he felt as he watched her and wanted her. It was one thing to let her leave him when they'd been eighteen but to open his heart up to her again... ? And there was no denying that's what he wanted.

"I do. I'm sorry for running away."

"Are you done running?"

She just stood there with the light from the house surrounding her and the pretty Christmas garland all around her. She looked like an angel and he wanted to believe she could be his miracle, but she wasn't.

He turned on his heel and walked at a fast clip to the door. He was debating skipping dinner with her and just going home. He'd forgotten how easily his heart could be bruised but leave it to Annie to show him how simple it was.

"Car?" she called.

He hated that he liked the sound of his nickname on her lips. He wished he could think of her the way he viewed all the other women in town. Paige and Flo and Sage—though Sage was engaged to be married now – but he had never lusted after any of them. And he didn't want to lust after

Annie either. But dammit, she'd always been different.

"Yeah?" He glanced over his shoulder and she stood there in the middle of her living room with the logs burning in the fireplace behind her. She wore a pair of slim-fitting jeans and a long-sleeved red thermal top with the top buttons left open. She looked too damned tempting. He knew he wasn't leaving because this was the one place he truly wanted to be.

"I'm sorry. I was trying to prove something to myself, not hurt you."

He wanted her to be strong and sassy the way she'd always been and there was no way that could happen as long as she was still running. And even if a person stayed in one spot, she could still be hiding out. Like his brother Lane who was back home because as he'd so eloquently put it, he needed to learn how to walk again.

"We can talk after I get your tree sorted," he said. "Dinner smells good."

"Thanks. I made lasagna. Everyone likes it," she said.

"I don't know about everyone," he said as he walked to the door stopping to look back at her as he donned his cowboy hat. "But I certainly do."

"I'm glad," she said.

He stepped over the threshold and closed the door behind him. The old house looked worn down, not at all like it had the last time he'd been inside it more than fifteen years ago. Could she stay in a place like that? It was nothing like he remembered her wanting for her life.

But then she'd admitted that she wasn't the same woman she used to be.

"We've got to take the tree around the back through a couple of French doors," he said as he approached his ranch hands. Carl and Jimmy had been working for him for the last five years and were solid guys.

"When don't we have to do some sort of odd wriggling to get a tree in the house? At least this place isn't built like those Victorian mansions in town," Carl said.

"Stop bitching," Jimmy said. "Let's get it done. I've got a date tonight."

"You do? I didn't realize there were any blind women in town," Carl said.

"Maybe it's the charity of the Christmas season motivating her," Carson added.

"She likes me," Jimmy said. "Said so herself."

They worked quickly to get the tree down from the flat bed and soon had it set up in her living room next to the fireplace where she'd said she wanted it. She had mugs of hot cocoa and cookies waiting when they were done. Jimmy looked like he wanted to decline but Carl was having none of it. They all sat at her kitchen table and talked about the weather. Soon the boys were on their way and he was alone with her.

"Those two are funny," she said. "I don't remember them."

"They're from Colorado. Cousins I think. Definitely good friends. They came to town for the rodeo one year and decided to stay and change their luck."

"Working for you?" she asked. She liked getting to know the details of Carson's life. She realized that he was still a stranger and she had no one but herself to blame for that. But tonight she vowed she'd change that.

"Yeah, I'm a pretty fair boss."

"I'm not surprised," she said. "You're a fair man even when someone's not too nice to you."

He arched one eyebrow at her. It was an arrogant gesture and one she noticed he did often.

"Me. Sorry again about earlier."

"It's already forgotten... well, almost."

"Almost?"

"How the hell am I supposed to forget that kiss?" he asked his voice was low and husky. Seductive.

"You're not," she said. "I don't suppose you want to help me with the lights. We've got another thirty minutes until dinner will be ready."

"Sure, I'd love to. This old house is looking really cheery."

"I'm glad," she said. "I hadn't realized it was in such bad shape but I'm glad for it."

"Why?"

She thought about the sketchpad she'd filled with images for the rooms in the house. She used her paycheck from the diner to slowly buy a few new pieces for the living room and it was shaping up to be what she had envisioned. It was hard to start from scratch but it was what she'd needed. "It gives me something to do," she said, leading the way back into the living room.

She picked up a box and put it on the coffee table. He glanced down and groaned. "Tangled?"

"Sorry," she said, wrinkling her nose. She really didn't want to waste the money on buying new ones. "I guess I should have picked up some new ones—"

"Why do that when these are perfectly fine? It's not my favorite job to do but I can definitely untangle lights."

They both started working together through the box and finally reached the bottom and the last one. He realized that the silence filled only with the sounds of music from her Christmas CD was masking the one thing that he couldn't stop thinking about.

He tugged on the strand of lights and she glanced up at him from where she held the other end and he slowly drew her toward him by coiling the lights in his hand the way he would a lasso.

"Now about that kiss," he said when she was standing not an inch from him.

"What about it?"

"I'd like another chance at it," he said, pulling her into his arms and taking the kiss that he'd been wanting since he'd held her in the pine tree forest and he'd tasted her tears and her passion.

Caution had been her touchstone since Davis had been arrested and her life had fallen apart and for once she wanted to just jump in and forget that there were such things as might-have-beens and regrets. For once she was just going to take what she wanted and, as she'd been doing for the last nine months, she'd deal with the consequences later.

She wanted this moment. She wanted this man and his kisses. They tasted better than the finest cuisine she'd ever sampled. He felt right when he wrapped those big strong arms around her. He was tall but not so much taller that it was a strain to kiss him. And she really liked that his arms around her and his lips on hers had started to feel like home.

Or something damned close to it. The fire crackled behind them and the piney scent of the tree mingled with the smells of the lasagna and for a minute it felt like home.

Home.

The one place she'd never really found in all her years of searching. But home shouldn't feel like this, shouldn't be a person, should it?

His hands smoothed over her waist and he tugged her off balance until she was pressed breast-to-chest with him. She grabbed his hips and went up on her toes as she thrust her tongue deeper into his mouth.

He moaned deep in his throat and his hands tightened on her waist and then slid them lower to her butt. He cupped her and pulled her closer until she felt the ridge of his erection nudging her center. She melted and clung to him as he lifted her off her feet. She wrapped her legs around his waist and her arms around his shoulders.

She lifted her head and looked down at him. Those big blue Montana sky eyes of his were dilated with passion and she easily read the intent them.

"Dinner will be ready in five minutes," she said, her own voice sounded husky to her ears. "I can turn the oven off and…"

"I can wait," he said, giving her a hungry kiss before setting her on her feet. "Just barely, but I can wait. I want this to be about more than sex. Unless you're just looking for a holiday fling."

"I'm not sure what I'm looking for," she admitted. "I'm not trying to lead you on, but I'm a mess right now."

"Fair enough," he said. "Why don't you go and get dinner ready and I'll put these lights on the tree. Then we can drink wine and talk and see where the night leads. No pressure."

"No pressure," she said, but in her mind there was already a lot of it. He was a single dad. He was a Paradise Valley rancher. He was settled. Everything that she wasn't. She had no idea what she wanted or needed. Only that she really liked Carson.

She walked into her kitchen listen to the Charlie Brown Christmas CD that had switched on after Diana Krall and wondering when life was going to settle down.

She'd thought by the time she was thirty she'd have at least figured out how to not be awkward around a guy. But she hadn't. Part of it she blamed on Davis. Not on him exactly, just on having spent ten years living with him as pleasant roommates and almost strangers.

But she knew that her awkwardness owed more to her own uncertainty in herself. She pulled the lasagna from the oven and set it on the counter to cool while she made the garlic bread. It was her dad's recipe for bread and as she melted the butter and added minced garlic and dried garlic powder to it, she was struck by the memory of her entire family in the kitchen.

Momma and Daddy laughing with each other as she and her sisters had set the table and danced around to the music playing. Daddy had to have missed that closeness once momma and Gilly had gone to Ohio to see the specialist oncologist. It had to have been hard for him. Gilly's death from the cancer and her father's reliance on the bottle had meant that momma hadn't come back.

Only as an adult could she see what he'd lost instead of, through her childish selfishness, only focusing on what she had lost. A different man would have handled the situation in a better way, but her father had done the best he could.

She sliced the French baguette she'd bought in town and slowly dipped the bread in the hot butter and placed it on the tray. As she did it she wrapped herself in the memory of the happier times, questioning if she had left Montana searching for the same kind of happiness she'd missed when her mom and sister were gone and their family had shattered.

She pulled the bread out from under the broiler and wrapped it in a towel in a basket and placed it on the table. It would be so easy to just say yes and let herself fall for Carson. Really fall for him because when she'd been younger she'd been too focused on leaving to ever realize what a great guy he was.

But was she trading her dreams for someone else's again?

That was what she'd done with Davis. Was she so easily led that she never knew what she wanted?

"You okay?" Carson asked from the door.

She turned, taking his long, lean frame. Those long legs encased in faded denim that hugged his body in all the right places. The worn cowboy boots that were functional, not fashionable, and the long sleeved Zac Brown Band t-shirt that clung to the muscles of his arms and chest. She wondered why she was thinking so hard on this – on him.

She wanted Carson and if he made her happy, who cared whose dream it was?

"Yes," she said, deciding to stop trying to make everything fit into her ideal of perfect when it was clear that hadn't worked for her in the past.

"I think I am."

Carson knew he was a taking a risk, but since Rainey's death he'd hadn't been much for playing it safe. Life was short – no one understood that better than he did. And Annie had always been the one woman who'd been able to make him feel wild. When they were younger she'd almost convinced him he was meant to leave Marietta... but in the end he knew he'd been right to stay.

But now that she was back in town... well, only a fool would let the same woman slip away twice.

Dinner was good and the conversation stilted at times but he didn't mind it. It felt right, even the odd bits. They were slowly coming to know each other again. He took another sip of the Chianti she was serving and then leaned back, pushing his chair up on two legs.

"What'd you do then?" she asked.

"Lassoed my son to keep him from running off. You should have seen the looks I got from those soccer moms at the playground."

She laughed. "It worked, didn't it?"

"Yes, but then Connie Miller... she was Connie Perkins when were in school, said that three-year-olds weren't calves and needed to be taught to listen."

"How'd you manage that?"

"I have no idea, but Evan liked playing rodeo which was what we'd always called the game, so we still did it when we were at home. But at the park I'd just yell rodeo and he'd stop running away from me."

Talking about Evan now made their learning curve seem funny but in reality it had been hard and scary. And that night after Connie had talked to him, he'd lain awake in bed praying to a God he wasn't sure existed to help him make sure he didn't screw his son up.

"I'm scared to be a parent. Hell, I was scared talking to Evan earlier today that I'd say the wrong thing," Annie admitted. "I can't even remember the last time I talked to a kid before I moved back here."

"Not a lot of kids in New York City?" he asked.

"Not in my circles. And if anyone did have children they had nannies, so I rarely saw them except in vacation photos," she said.

"Your life sounds weird," he said.

"It was. We didn't even decorate our own homes for the holidays. We had services who come in and do it all for you."

He tipped his head to the side… there was a bit of self-deprecation in the way she was talking. "Did you like that? I thought you were a decorator by trade."

"I am," she said. "I was a pain in the ass as they walked through my home trying to do their jobs. I made sure they put up only things that suited my taste. But that's not the same. Some people would say that was bad karma."

"Evan and I do the tree together every year," he said. "You think you're going to be able to remember how to do yours?"

She tipped her head to the side, studying him with that wintry gray gaze of hers. What was she trying to find inside him when she looked at him like that? He hoped she found it.

"Want to help me?"

"I did already – I strung your lights," he said, with a half-grin. He'd taken a look at her other decorations. There weren't any signs of her life in New York. He'd have thought she'd have boxes piled up in the house but she didn't seem to have brought anything at all from her old life with her, but then he remembered she'd had to get rid of everything to pay back her ex-husband's debts. "I have no problems helping with the rest."

"Good, I could use some muscle. Now that I fed you it's the least you could do," she said, with a sweet smile and some batting eyelashes.

He liked her, he was trying to be cool and go slow but the good food and having his old friend back in town made that hard. He'd eaten two big helpings as well as most of the garlic bread. Annie didn't eat like a bird but she was nowhere near his size and ate a significantly smaller amount. He enjoyed the novelty of just eating his food instead of having to stop and cut up Evan's and telling him to use his fork.

She was looking at him and he noticed she'd finished eating. "I guess I should clean up."

"Why?" she asked. "You're my guest."

"You cooked, I clean, right?" That was the deal he'd always had with Rainey and when he'd been growing up as well." His mom had put all of their names on the calendar when they'd been young and each night one of them had to clean up the kitchen while she supervised. She'd sit at the table drinking a cup of tea and Carson had enjoyed those nights a lot. It was the only time he'd had his mom to himself.

"Is that how it works?" she asked.

"Yes, that is how it works. No one should do it all. I'm a grown man and don't need you to be my servant."

She leaned over and kissed him quick on the lips. "Thank you, Carson. It's been so long since I've been around a real man... just pile the dishes in the sink and then meet me in the living room."

She scooted out of the kitchen and he watched her go, enjoying the sight of those tight jeans and the curve of her ass in them. He made short work of the dishes and looked around the kitchen after wiping down the counter and notice the photo on the refrigerator behind a Johnson's Auto Insurance magnet that had been handed out in the nineties.

The photo was of her dog sitting on a park bench with sunshine all around. He thought of how few people she had in her life. It didn't fit with her personality. She'd always been social – what had happened in New York to change that? Then he saw the small red and green braided dough wreath ornament next to it. Her family had been so close before Gilly's cancer. He knew that had changed all of them, but especially Annie. She'd started running then.

Was she ever going to stop running?

He wanted answers, but as he entered the living room and found her looking at the tree, lost in thought, he knew now wasn't the time for the third degree. She needed a friend... and as much as he wanted to be her lover, he'd learned that being friends first was the best way to have a lasting relationship.

And he wanted that. The more he got to know Annie, the more he wanted to keep her in his life for Christmas and the future.

Chapter Seven

The snow fell outside, getting heavier and heavier as she stood staring at the lights, feeling the mistakes of the past scattered around her like shards from the glass ornament she'd broken. She knew she should pick it up, but instead she just stood there transfixed – caught between the past and the present.

"I think the storm that was threatening is finally here," she said.

"Let me check the news."

"You'll have to do it on the radio, I don't have television service yet."

He pulled out his smartphone and did some quick tapping. "I might get snowed in tonight."

"Do you want to go now? Will Evan be okay?"

"He's spending the night with my dad, he'll be fine."

But the snow outside her door was coating everything in white. Making the overgrown lawn look pretty, pristine. Just like her life could be now. She cleaned up the ornament and tossed it in a box she'd set aside for trash and went back to standing in front of the tree. Otis Redding was singing a Christmas song, and she let everything slip away. She wasn't sure how people lived for the moment.

She had a damned hard time letting go of everything.

"'Tis the season to be joyful," Carson said, quietly as he came up next to her.

"Is it joyful for you?" she asked.

"Most of the time. I miss my mom and Rainey and my grandparents but there are so many new faces too – like Evan and my nephew JT and seeing them discover our family traditions for the first time or look forward to them... well, yeah, it does bring me joy."

"I bet it's like that for Marilyn," Annie said. "I don't have any traditions."

He wrapped his arm around her shoulder. "Then let's

start some."

She wanted to but then she started worrying if he'd be with her next Christmas. "What if—

"No. No questions, we are going to start a tradition and that's it."

"Okay, so what is the tradition going to be?"

"Well it starts with me delivering your tree and you fixing me lasagna for dinner... see how I've guaranteed you'll make dinner for me again?"

"In a year? Don't you want dinner before then?" she asked, worried. She realized that she was afraid because she wanted this to be real. She wanted everything she felt for Carson to be perfect and if it wasn't she had no idea what she'd do. She was out of places to run to. Maybe that would be enough. Maybe it'd be enough to stay this time.

"We'll have dinner again before next Christmas, but this is about our tradition."

"Okay," she said. Stop worrying, she warned herself. "What's next?"

"Well, we decorate your tree," he said.

"You're just saying the things we're doing," she said. "Does that count?"

"That's how traditions get started," he said. He took a box of hand-wrapped ornaments that had been her mom's and handed them to her.

She took them and unwrapped them slowly. "This one was my paternal grandmother's."

"Tell the stories behind it. How did you end up with it?" he asked.

"She gave it to us the year that Gilly got diagnosed with cancer—the first time. This little angel was meant to watch over us and make sure that Gilly got healthy again. Grandma P came for Christmas that year and she helped us make a chain for the tree that was made of wishes. We each wrote them on a scraps of paper and then she made them into rings and we draped our wishes around the tree and the house," Annie said. She'd forgotten how special that Christmas had been. So full of both fear and hope much the same as she felt this year.

"What a wonderful memory," Carson said.

"It is. I'd forgotten. I remember how bitter I was toward the ranch. I called it hell on earth. That wasn't fair," she said.

He came over to her, standing way too close and looking way too good for her peace of mind. "You were young. At least now you can appreciate it."

"I definitely can," she said.

They finished up the tree with her telling him a few more stories and Carson sharing how the Scott men always strung a lot of feet of popcorn and decorated the banisters in the big old ranch house that had been in their family for generations.

"How long does that take?" she asked.

"An entire day. We eat almost as much as we string. Mom always used to make us say something we were grateful for."

"How's that work?" she asked. "You did seem to be fighting a lot with your brothers when you were younger."

"Well, when mom was in the room we'd say things *like I'm grateful Alec passed his old saddle on to me.* But when she left I might say, *I'm grateful Lane is such a wuss so I can beat him up.*"

She laughed and he shook his head.

"Now I'm grateful Lane is home."

"I bet. I heard he was wounded in Iraq," she said. Flo had mentioned it at the diner after the Scotts had left last Wednesday night.

"Yes, he lost the lower half of his left leg. He wears a prosthetic now so you wouldn't know, but for a while it was touch and go. We're all just glad he's home."

She hung the last ornament on the tree and stepped back as she did so. Carson stepped back too.

"What do you think?"

"Beautiful."

"You're not looking at the tree."

"No, I'm not. I'm looking at you, Annie Prudhomme and thinking."

"What are you thinking?"

"That I'm glad you're home," he said.

She was glad too, especially when he snagged the thick wool blanket off the back of the couch and spread it out in front of the fire. He sat down, maneuvering until his back rested against the couch and he was facing the tree. Then he patted the blanket next to him. "Come sit with me. Let's stare at the lights and pretend that Christmas miracles do happen and that this is the beginning of some very sweet traditions for both of us."

She hesitated as fear nipped at her again but then she looked into those big-sky-blue eyes of his and realized that there was nowhere she'd rather be than in his arms. She sank down next to him and he put his arm around her shoulder and drew her close, resting his head on top of hers. Slowly the fear she felt in herself melted away, leaving nothing but the fact that she was being held by her very own Christmas cowboy.

Carson tipped Annie's head back and she closed her eyes. He suspected she was trying to hide whatever she felt from him and he was okay with that. Holding her had convinced him that whatever happened later tonight, he wanted Annie and he wasn't walking away from her.

He touched her gently. One finger tracing the planes of her face, they'd dated and he'd been hot and horny back then but she'd been determined to not sleep with him. It was heady to have her in his arms now. The high cheekbones, that narrow nose of hers, and then that stubborn chin. Her neck was long and slender and he leaned down brushing his lips over hers, seducing her with slow, soft kisses. Because after waiting so long to have this one woman in his arms, the last thing he wanted to do was rush.

Yet his body seemed to have other ideas. His fingers tingled where he touched her and a fire seemed to start deep inside him, spreading quickly through his entire body. He reached the small buttons at the top of her Henley shirt and slowly undid them, one by one. Three little buttons that ended in the heart of her cleavage.

Her eyes opened and she looked over at him. That sexy-sweet look in her eyes, and he wondered if he'd ever be able to really know what she was thinking. He knew she had no idea what she did to him. She shifted to her knees and pulled her shirt up and over her head, then moved to straddle his lap. He groaned as a bolt of pure lust shot through him making his blood flow heavier in his veins.

God, he wanted this woman. He'd been hungry for her for too long. His hands went from her waist up her midriff, touching her ribs. She giggled as he ran his fingers over her skin.

"Ticklish?"

"You know I am," she said. She reached for his ribs and danced her fingers over them. But he didn't feel like laughing.

"I like your hands on me."

"I do too," she said.

He found the scar he remembered her getting when they were kids playing in the swimming hole on his family's ranch. It was about three inches long and still rough.

"I remember this," he said, pulling her closer so he could lean down and kiss it. He lapped his tongue over it and realized that all the wounds she was carrying with her right now would one day be scarred over as well.

She put her hands on his shoulders and then in his hair. "You have a great hair, Car. It's so thick and soft, I love touching it."

"I love touching your skin," he said, skimming his fingers up her back to the clasp of her bra. It was a very pretty lace and silk model that covered her breasts. He didn't pull the fabric from her but instead used his mouth to trace the outline of the fabric around her and then leaned his head back to look up at her.

She straddled him and stared down at him with a hot glance that made him glad he was a man and that she was his woman. She shifted so that her center rubbed against his thickening manhood. He put his hands on her hips and rocked her back and forth at a slow pace to just tease them both because it felt so damned good.

She tossed her bra off on the floor behind them. He palmed her breasts as she leaned forward and whispered in his ear, hot sexy words that made him almost explode. He'd waited for her for years and now all that time apart seemed almost worth it. "You're mine, now."

He grabbed her waist in both of his hands and rolled her over so she was underneath him. His control was falling away with each brush of their bodies together, but he wasn't willing to give in to her. Grinding his hips against hers he took her hands in one hand, stretching them up over her head. "Who's in control now?"

She rocked her hips, twisting them a little and then leaned up to bite the lower lobe of his ear before sucking it into her mouth. He was so hard he thought he'd explode in his pants. "I think I am."

"Are you sure?" he asked, dropping teasing kisses all over body and watching her react. Her skin was glowing and soft and her hips undulated as he continued touching her. He craned his neck and captured her nipple in his mouth, she tasted warm and sweet. She arched underneath him, driving him out of his mind with her movements.

He fondled her other breast slowly exploring every inch of her torso and enjoying the fact that he had the right to do so. He wanted to go slowly but the demands of his body were eroding his own self-control. He lowered his head and licked at her belly button and then moved lower to open her jeans. He reached inside, skimming his hand lower to trace the line of fabric low on her abdomen between her skin and her panties.

He swept one finger beneath the band and felt her smooth skin. He shifted back on his knees and pulling her jeans down her legs and then shifting around to get them completely off her legs. He stayed where he was next to her on the blanket. She was naked except for a pair of thick red socks.

Centerfolds had nothing on Annie. She was the embodiment of every wet dream he'd had in high school and he couldn't wait to plunge inside her. And at the same time he also sort of wanted the after too. He wanted to hold her all night and thanked God for the storm that would keep him here.

She smiled over at him and raised both eyebrows at him. It was the smile that got him, and later when he could think of something other than how good she looked with her creamy skin, tight pink nipples and that small thin line of hair guarding her secrets, he'd remember it, but right now all he wanted was to explore every inch of her body.

He grabbed her ankles and placed a nuzzling kiss on each one and then slowly tugged her legs apart, then slide up her body, caressing her with his entire body as he slid over her.

His abdomen rubbed over her center and she squirmed underneath him. He wanted to caress every inch of her first with his fingers. God, her skin was soft. He wondered for a moment if his work-hardened hands would be too rough for her. But she captured one of his hands and brought it back to her breast. Holding it over her and making him squeeze gently.

He kissed her upper thighs and then her more intimate flesh. He parted her with two fingers and ran his tongue lightly over her core. She started and her hips jerked up. Her hands came to the back of his head as he rocked his tongue over her and then he slowly sucked that pleasure bud into his mouth. Her thighs came up along the side of his head and she moaned his name in one long drawn-out sigh.

He tightened even more in his jeans and it took all of his control not to spill himself. She tasted good—too good. He couldn't wait much longer to be inside of her. He lifted his head and saw that her skin was flushed her nipples taut, hard berries and her eyes were partially closed. Her head was tipped back and he wanted to remember her like this always. On the cusp of her orgasm she was beautiful. More beautiful than he'd ever seen her before.

He reached between their bodies to open his jeans and free himself, then he crawled up over her body, caressing her with his entire body, rubbing his chest over hers and then settling his hips over hers. He meant to tease them both but his manhood found the opening of her body and slipped inside. Damn, she was so hot and so wet, he pushed himself all the way inside of her.

Drove into her until his entire length was buried inside of her. He stopped and she opened her eyes and looked up him. She didn't say anything but wrapped her legs around his hips, her arms around his back and leaned up to capture his mouth with hers.

The kiss was earthy and raw and touched something untamed in his soul. He stopped thinking and just followed his instincts, which demanded he thrust into her again and again until he felt her tighten around him. Felt the first waves of orgasm against his flesh as she tightened her legs, arched her back and called his name.

He thrust harder and deeper, burying his head against her neck and sucking on the pulse at the base of her neck until everything inside of her clenched and he came. His body emptied itself into her yet he couldn't stop thrusting. He kept moving against her until he was completely drained and then wanted to collapse against her but knew he'd crush her if he did.

He wrapped his arms around her and rolled them to their sides. He buried his head in her neck so that she couldn't see the emotions he knew were on his face. He wanted to pretend this was just a way to assuage his curiosity from the past but he knew it was so much more. He was falling for her again. He hugged her close to his still-racing heart. He rubbed his hand over the back of her head and kept her as close as he could for as long as she'd let him.

In the flickering warmth of the fire, under the pretty lights of the Christmas tree, Carson admitted to himself that he wanted something for Christmas this year. He wanted Annie and he wanted her to stay and be his. And he had a feeling that, even if Santa existed, that wish might be too much for him to deliver.

Annie closed her eyes to hide from Carson but also from herself. She wanted to just cuddle closer to him under the pretty Christmas tree lights in front of the fire and let this fantasy become reality. But that same stupid flood of emotion that had overwhelmed her earlier was back. She wanted to be better than she knew she was. She wanted to be able to stay with him this time, and that scared her more than anything else in the world. She'd have to trust him if she did that and she wasn't sure she could let herself be that vulnerable.

Damned if she was going to start crying now. She had to keep it together. And she was just about doing that until he leaned down and kissed her temple with a gentleness she hadn't experience in a man's embrace before.

She tipped her head back and met his big-sky-blue eyes and inside something in her shifted. And she realized that this man was starting to fall for her. She didn't think she was fooling herself because in his gaze were emotions she'd never thought she'd see on anyone's face. He cared for her and she thought of all the people who'd loved her over her life and how she'd always let them down.

It wasn't that she wanted to hurt him or herself but she had never had a relationship that didn't end in heartbreak. She closed her eyes and rolled away from him. Trying to protect him, but also trying to keep her own heart from breaking wide open. It was awkward – the after-sex moment where they both stared at each other and realized they hadn't used birth control.

"Uh, I'm not on the pill," she said at last.

"Sorry," he said his voice was gruff. "I wasn't thinking."

"Me neither," she admitted. "There's a bathroom off the main hall you can use."

"Seriously?"

"Sorry. I have no idea how to act now. I was married to Davis for ten years," she said.

"You don't have to act any way, Annie. You just have to be yourself. Be honest."

He didn't ask for much. Just everything. And she couldn't give it to him at this moment. She was surrounded by the past and by Christmas and by everything that she'd left behind and never realized she'd thrown away lightly.

"I'm trying," she said at last, gathering her clothes and walking away from him. As soon as she was in her bedroom she sank down on the floor and just sat there clutching her clothes to her chest and feeling lost and alone.

She should have just kept her eyes closed and stayed in his arms. But no, she had to get up and ruin the little bubble they'd been in. But that little bubble wasn't reality as much as she wanted it to be. Carson had a life and family away from her house. And this was it for her. This and her job down at the Diner.

She knew she wanted more or something else. And tonight complicated her plans. She hadn't realized how smart she'd been to never sleep with Carson as a teenager. But now she did. Because that fantasy she'd been having all night, the one he kept feeding by talking about traditions was taking root in her heart. Making her pray she could be a different sort of woman. One who could be part of the fantasy in her head.

She forced herself to her feet and cleaned up. She had the start of a hickey on her neck and she didn't mind it the way she probably should. But she liked the thought of carrying something of Carson around with her.

She put her head in her hands. She didn't cry because she knew tears weren't the answer. But she should never have had sex with him. Carson had been a complication before he'd entered her home and now he was even more of one.

She forced herself to leave the bedroom and heard Carson singing in her kitchen God Rest Ye Merry, Gentlemen with Rascal Flatts. She stood in the doorway watching as he made hot chocolate at her stove. Rumple was at his feet with an ice cube between his paws.

She stood there for a minute, afraid to move forward and claim him and take a chance on him, yet afraid to back away. Afraid to let him go. She knew there was a connection between them. There always had been and it had always been strong.

She wanted this to be real. And she wanted to be woman enough to keep her cowboy.

And stopped herself. This was real. There wasn't anything fake about the evening. Carson wasn't pretending to be a great guy—he was one and she just had to trust it—trust herself.

He turned to her singing, "Each other now embrace... I was afraid I'd scared you off. I'm sorry if I rushed things tonight."

She stepped into the kitchen. "You didn't rush anything. But that doesn't mean I'm not a little bit scared by what happened."

"I'm sorry for that. This has been, well, one of the best nights I've had in a long time."

He turned back to the stove and removed the saucepan from the flames. She went to her pantry cabinet and took the pack of marshmallows she'd splurged on earlier in the week.

When she walked back over, he'd poured the hot liquid into two mugs. She dropped the marshmallows into the cup and then tossed one on the floor for Rumple.

"I'm sorry I'm such a mess," she said, looking up into those blue eyes of his.

"I'm sorry you are too, but it changes nothing. I still want you. I still want to know you better. And unless you tell me otherwise, I'd like a chance to see if we can make something that will last."

His words were a balm for her lonely soul. She'd been on her own since the day she'd left Marietta fifteen long years ago. But at the same time, they scared her. When she was on her own at least the only one affected by her mistakes was her.

Could she take a chance? Could she risk hurting Carson or even his sweet little boy? Because he was asking her to be a part of his life and she knew she still wasn't sure if she wanted to stay in Montana and live this honest, country life.

"Can we take it slow?" she asked at last.

"Considering we kissed for the last time fifteen years ago and just got around to making love, I think it's safe to say we aren't moving too fast," he said.

Chapter Eight

The snow fell heavier and, even though she wished the storm would lighten up so she could push him to leave her place, she knew he was going to have to stay and she was happier than she wanted to admit. She wished sometimes that she was simpler. That she didn't get in her own way and make life so hard. But the truth was that she'd always wanted things to fit a certain mold.

And inevitably life never did. Being with Carson was at once the answer to some secret dream she'd long held inside of herself, and also the scariest thing she'd ever encountered.

She hadn't been kidding herself when she'd acknowledged that it would be way too easy to just change into what he needed. Especially right now when life seemed so damned screwed up. She could just abandon her old self and become a new Annie in the image of whatever Carson needed.

Perhaps be a mother to his young son and some kind of modern nineteen-fifties housewife. It appealed to her because she could just give up on fighting for her dreams while they lay in tatters all around her.

But then she looked over at Carson, where he sat next to her on the couch staring out at the snow and she knew he deserved better. And frankly, so did she.

That left her with nothing but the tough questions and the hard decisions. She could continue on like this, he wouldn't push her for a commitment and she'd have some time with him and his precious son until Christmas.

Or she could be honest with him and with herself and let him know that she couldn't be his fairytale. That she wasn't his princess and he couldn't be her white knight because she didn't know what she was hiding from or even if she needed to be rescued. It seemed that she was both the heroine trapped in the castle and the evil queen who put her there. And there was no easy way out.

Carson seemed like the solution but she knew in her heart

he couldn't be. Because if she let him rescue her and she broke his heart, well, she was pretty sure she'd break her own too.

"I can't believe the storm blew in that quickly," she said as her CD ended and silence echoed around them. "One thing I've always liked about snow is the quiet of it, but with that wind howling not so much."

"I like the storms," he said, hugging her close. "It's the one time there is nothing else for me to do except stay inside and stay warm. Something that is certainly not a burden when I have you in my arms."

She snuggled down next to him, letting him hold her in those big arms of his and she wanted to say something else but for once she couldn't plan this. She didn't want to ruin the moment by talking or thinking. Instead she just enjoyed the comfort that came from Carson.

She knew it wouldn't last and she suspected by the way he held her that he knew it too. She wondered if they were star-crossed lovers. Meant to always fall for each other but never get too keep each other.

"Carson?"

"No," he said.

"I haven't asked you anything yet," she said.

"You have that look. Can we just enjoy the rest of this evening?" he asked. "I know that nothing is settled between us and you're going to want to hash it out."

"How do you know that?"

"Um…you're a woman, aren't you?"

"That's sexist."

"It doesn't make it not true," he said.

He had a point but she didn't have to like it. "I just don't want to ruin anything. I feel like we're friends again."

"We are," he said.

"And—

He pulled her down closer to her, put his mouth on hers, and kissed her until she couldn't think of anything but the way he tasted of milk chocolate and something that was uniquely Carson. She wrapped her arms around his shoulders and he lifted her onto his lap and rubbed his hands up and down her back.

He was a good kisser. Not rushing this embrace but just

taking his time with it. Suddenly all her fears dissipated and there was magic in the air. A sort of Christmas magic that came from the snow and the lights twinkling on her tree.

The scent of the pine log in the fire and Carson's cologne surrounded her and she almost believed that this was meant to be. That she'd been creating a problem that didn't exist.

He stood up, carrying her easily in his arms and started down the hall to her bedroom. He hesitated outside her door. "I'm not going home tonight."

"Good. I want one entire night with you," she said.

"I want more than one," he said.

"I know." She put her head on his shoulder.

He didn't say anything else, just carried her into the bedroom that was lit only by the spill light from the hallway. He set her down next to the bed and slowly removed all of her clothing.

"Take your socks off this time," he said.

She bent over and took them off and then switched on the lamp on her nightstand to watch him slowly undress. He looked better than a body had a right to, she thought. His muscles were heavy and delineated from years of hard ranch work. He had a washboard stomach with a very thin line of hair that led downward ...

She reached out stroked him and he hardened in her hand. She drew him closer and leaned over to take him in her mouth. His hands went to the back of her head and rubbed over her skull while she caressed him with her lips and tongue.

He pulled away after a few moments and pushed her onto her back, coming down over the top of her and entered in one smooth swift motion. He thrust heavily into her again and again until her orgasm rushed over her and at the last minute he pulled out of her and came on her stomach.

She understood why he did, but it just made her a little sad as she thought that even he knew that this wasn't something that could last forever. After they cleaned up, they crawled back in bed together and held each other as it were the last time.

Liz was waiting for Annie when she got off her shift at the diner. Liz had been her best friend in high school they'd both wanted to get out of Marietta. Liz had gone to Hollywood to become a star and had done it. But something had happened and she'd ended up back here in Marietta, teaching drama to school kids.

Annie knew there had to be more to the story, but she had her hands full dealing with her own problems right now and she had a feeling that Liz would talk about it when she needed to.

"You waiting for me?" Annie asked.

"I sure am. Imagine my surprise when my old high school friend moved back to town and didn't even say anything," Liz said.

"We haven't talked in like ten years," Annie said, given that Marilyn had been giving her the cold shoulder and she'd gotten a less that warm welcome from most of the Scott brothers, she hadn't realized anyone was happy she was back other than maybe Carson. "But I'm sorry I didn't tell you I was back in town."

"I know. Why is that?" Liz asked.

"Life," Annie said. "So we're both back here where we swore we'd never be," Annie said.

"Funny the way it is," Liz said with the same grin that Annie remembered from high school. She was still a uniquely beautiful woman with a beautiful face. Not classically elegant, but her features were stunning. "I actually could use your help."

It was a little cold with the snow falling and Annie was on her way to meet Marilyn and her kids at park to start the Christmas Stroll. She and her sister were trying to rebuild their relationship, but Annie was coming to realize that she wasn't the only one with trust issues. "Do you mind walking with me?"

"Not at all. Heading to the park?" Liz asked as she took a sip of the hot chocolate in the Styrofoam cup that said Copper Mountain Chocolates on the side. The town looked magical tonight all decked out for Christmas. At the end of Main Street she noticed a couple of sleds and saw Lane Scott holding the reins to one of them. It was hard to believe he'd lost part of his leg. He seemed so hale and healthy. The fact that he seemed happy and wasn't running away just made her feel like more of a coward since she'd been dodging Carson's calls.

"Yes, you too?" she asked.

"You, me, and everyone else," Liz said, putting her hand on Annie's arm to stop her from walking. "I need your help with the nativity play we are putting on."

"I'm not really that good at acting."

"You had a reality TV show, girl."

"That's different and it was only for one season," Annie said. Not at all surprised that Liz knew about her foray into television. It had ended the day the FBI had interrupted a lunch she was having and brought her in for questioning. "Do you know why it ended?"

Liz stopped and pulled Annie off the sidewalk. "I do. I'm here if you want to talk about it."

Annie nodded. It was odd to have that part of her old life come up now and she realized that it was part of her past. She hardly thought of that any longer. She'd been focused on redoing her house, rebuilding her relationship with her sister, and finding her place in Marietta. "I don't know—"

"It's okay, Annie. I'm just saying I'm here. What I need you for is designing some sets for me. I have all my little actors and a lot of their parents have volunteered to help paint and build things but I need someone with a good artistic eye."

Annie was tempted. Even though she'd promised herself she wasn't going to put down roots here. Not after the way she was busy trying to keep her distance from Carson. But Liz's offer struck a chord deep inside of her... something that she'd been missing for a long time.

"Okay, I'll do it. What exactly do you need?" Annie asked.

Liz whooped and hugged her close. "I knew you'd say yes. Here's the script and I sort of blocked out a storyboard of some ideas. It's rough."

Annie took the script that Liz had pulled from her large Louis Vuitton bag and did a quick flip through the storyboard pages. She was excited about the project. It had been a long time since she'd done anything creative. She'd been sketching on her breaks at the diner but this was different. "I think I know what you want. I'm working at the diner full time, you know. When do you need these?"

"I can work with your schedule – I'm designing the sets over at my studio. Do you know where it is?"

"No," Annie admitted she'd been pretty busy working her shift and going back to La Terre De Reves to spruce it up.

"It's by the ballet studio. Here's my card. Do you think you could have a rough design done tomorrow?"

"No." She'd be embarrassed to let anyone see something rough. She'd been such a prima donna when she'd left Marietta, and it was bad enough she was back in town but to put up a design that wasn't her best—she wasn't going to do it. She might have had to come back, but it wasn't because she couldn't cut it in the outside world.

Liz laughed again. "Okay. I just need something for the parents to start painting and building. How soon?"

"Let me look at this tonight after the Stroll and I'll call you and let you know. It's not that complicated, maybe three or four set changes."

"That's what I was thinking but I'm open to your vision," Liz said walking over to one of the trash bins to toss out her cup. "Thank you."

"I'm sorry I haven't been a better friend," she said.

"I was being silly. We both had lives away from here and each other, but I'm glad you're back. I found Marietta is where I'm meant to be.

"I'm still not sure I'm staying," Annie admitted. Saying it out loud made her regret it. What if Carson heard about it from Liz instead of from her?

"Really? Where else would you go?" Liz asked the same thing that Annie had asked herself a million times.

"I don't know," she said. "It's hard to think of staying here after never wanting to."

"That was a girl's dreams. You're a woman now and you know what life is like outside of Montana."

Liz had a point. Annie didn't say anything else but she thought of the way that Carson had held her the other night and she knew that she didn't want to leave him. She had been so worried about staying for the wrong reasons—for a dream that wasn't truly hers—that she never thought about the fact that she might be leaving for the wrong reasons. Just clinging to her old ideas of what life was and her stubborn idea that she couldn't be happy in Marietta.

Right now that seemed stupid. And as she and Liz parted ways in the park in the center of town where the big tree was being lit, she caught sight of the families and felt a pang that she didn't have one.

"Hey, Annie!"

She turned to see little Evan waving at her and smiling his gap-toothed grin. She waved at him and then looked up at Carson standing right behind his son. Carson tipped his hat her but didn't smile or come over to her and she couldn't blame him.

She'd sort of played fast and loose with his feelings—again. All because she wasn't sure what she wanted. But as the band started to play "We Wish You a Merry Christmas" and everyone around her started singing, she felt someone behind her. She turned hoping it was Carson, but it wasn't. It was only Marilyn and her kids.

She hugged her sister in an awkward embrace that felt a little too long. She reminded herself she couldn't hold it against Carson if he'd taken her at her word when she'd said she needed space. Though a part of her wished that he had pushed her, because she knew she'd give in.

And then the decision would be out of her hands... which was probably why he wasn't doing just that. He knew the same way she did that it had to be her decision to stay in Marietta, and not just for Christmas.

Carson made himself stay away from Annie. She'd made it clear when he'd left her house that she was conflicted about him, Marietta, and her life. And he was damned if he was going to be left by her again.

But hell, it wasn't as easy to shut off his emotions as he wished it was. Evan saw some of his friends from school and they joined up with the group. Carson was glad this was an evening event and that there were dads in the group of parents. There were some times when he was the only dad and the other moms were nice enough, but he didn't want to talk about organizing the car tote or a new planner system.

"You look trapped, bro," Alec said as he came up next to him handing him a cup of hot chocolate.

"God, I wish Rainey was still here. I'm not good with the parents' group, but I don't want Evan to be the only one not hanging out over there."

"I know what you mean," Alec said. "JT, stay where I can see you."

JT ran off to join a group of kids his age. He was a year older than Evan. Alec's wife Sienna was standing with the same parent group that Carson was hesitating to go and join. "I guess you can't just walk over there.'

"Oh, I can. It would piss Sienna off but since one of her mandates to me is that I'm not involved enough she has to fake-smile and pretend she's happy I'm there," Alec said. "I thought I was done with these kind of games once I got married. How did mom and dad make it work?"

"I have no idea," he said. "Our dad must have more game than we have given him credit for."

He thought about Annie and how she'd been practically ignoring him since they'd been snowed in together. He knew that she had issues. And he'd probably rushed her by taking her to bed, but in his mind they'd already wasted enough time. No one lived forever. Time was finite and he hated to squander a second of it.

"I miss my wife," Alec said in a moment of raw honesty.

Carson ached for his brother. He wanted him happy and had no way to help him out of the current situation he was in. So he clapped his hand on his shoulder. "I'm here if you need to talk."

"Screw that. Talking is what got me into this situation. I think it's time I checked up on my wife. Want to come watch the fireworks?"

"Sure," Carson said. Watching Alec and his estranged wife was interesting. Sienna was the only thing that Carson had ever seen rattle his brother. She'd moved back to town three months ago and taken JT with her. But JT didn't want to live in town and it had caused all sorts of interesting problems for Alec and Sienna.

"What are you two going to do about Christmas?" Carson asked.

"We're spending it together at the ranch. JT asked her if she'd come home," Alec said.

Damn that was hard. There was no way a parent could say no to something like that. "What are you going to do?"

"I have no idea," Alec said. "I can't fix this the way I usually do and I'm not sure what to do next."

Carson didn't know the intimate details of his brother's marriage and frankly, didn't want to. He just wished that Alec and Sienna would fix whatever was broken because he liked them both and hated to see them so miserable. "I wish I could help."

"Me too, little bro."

"Daddy, I'm ready to go see Santa," Evan said, coming back over to him.

"Don't you want to go with your friends?" he asked his son. Evan was usually part of a large group of kids who did everything together. But there were times like now when he got a little cagey.

"Some of them already went," Evan said evasively. "Can we go now?"

"Yes, let's get in line. I'll talk to you later, Alec."

Alec nodded and Evan led Carson to the line, which was getting longer by the minute. Evan's little hand in his was steady and sure. They waited patiently for their turn. Evan intently staring at the guy in red.

"What are you going to ask for?" he asked his son.

"A mommy."

"Evan," Carson said on a heavy sigh. He bent down next to his son and hugged the little guy close and tight. "It doesn't work that way."

"I'm asking," Evan said stubbornly. "You said whatever I wanted. I've been good."

This whole Santa thing was going to make him crazy. Evan had been good and he did deserve to be happy and have a mom. But that was complicated. "You have been very good but Santa can't bring you a mommy. He brings toys and stuff like that."

Evan shook his head. "Richie said that he thought Santa

could bring anything you asked for. He said his mom asked for a trip to Hawaii last year and got it."

"That's a bit different. A mommy would have to live with us."

"So," Evan said. "I think it would be nice to have a mommy in the house."

Carson couldn't say anything else. He thought having a woman around would be great too. He hugged his son as their turn was next. "Just don't be disappointed on Christmas morning if she's not there."

"She will be," Evan said.

Carson watched his son approach Santa and stood off to the side. This was something he couldn't control. There was only one woman he was interested in right now and she had no plans to be a mommy. Now or ever. She couldn't have been clearer.

He took his phone out and snapped a photo of Evan with Santa.

"Why are you glaring at Santa?" Annie asked, coming up next to him.

"Evan wants something he can't have," Carson said. "I was hoping my son would be a little older before he had his belief in magic shattered."

"Oh, what does he want? Tyler told me he wants a new Bionicle."

"Not a toy. He wants a mommy."

"Well that's a tall order for Santa," she said.

"Yes it is. Especially since the one woman I'm interested in isn't planning on sticking around."

She blanched and stepped back from him. "I didn't say that."

"You didn't have to," he said. "You've had one foot out the door since you got here."

"I'm sorry. Wouldn't it be worse to say that I could be that person for you and Evan and then find out in six months that I wanted to leave?"

"Yes, it would be," Carson said, but as he looked at her in the lightly falling snow and the glimmer of the Christmas lights, he believed that nothing could be worse than this moment. But inside there was something he wanted. Someone he'd always wanted and had never realized how much so until this moment. He leaned in and kissed her and knew it was goodbye. It had to be. His little boy wanted a mommy and he wanted Annie and both of them weren't going to get the one woman who could answer both of their wishes.

He didn't blame her for being cautious. And a part of him... almost understood where she was coming from. "I guess we're both just different in that way."

"What way?" she asked.

"I'm not one to run away. Even the unknown and the scary things I'm not sure I can handle. I dig in and stand my ground."

"Excuse me, cowboy, we can't all be Scotts and so sure of ourselves that we just know we're right. And I told you from the beginning I'm a mess."

With that she turned on her heel and walked away. Evan slipped up next to him. "I think Annie would make a good mommy. And I really like Rumple."

He groaned and bit back a curse. "Liking her dog wouldn't make her a good mommy. Plus she's not sure she wants to stay in Montana."

And now that he'd goaded her, Carson was almost positive she'd be leaving as soon she could.

Chapter Nine

Annie spent the next week immersed in her job at the diner, putting the finishing touches on the dining room at her house, and designing the sets for the Nativity play. Plus mostly trying very hard not to think about Carson. It should have been easier to forget him but it wasn't. No matter how hard she tried, she kept seeing his Big-Sky-blue eyes in her dreams and felt his arms around her when she slept.

But when she was awake and when she saw him in town he crossed the street to avoid her. Tonight though, there was no escaping for him. Liz had all of her adult volunteers wrangled into one room. She was surprised to see Carson here, but then scolded herself. If there was a more involved father in her circle of friends, she'd yet to meet him.

Evan was a priority for him and she understood that now more than ever. He was on the far side of the room with the other men with power tools. They were in charge of taking her designs and cutting them out of the plywood. She had two moms who were tracing her designs onto canvas, which would then hang on the plywood.

"I love these designs. Why didn't you come to LA with me?" Liz asked, coming up behind her. She had her hair in a low bun at the back of her neck and tendrils of curls hung around her face. Her wide smile was welcoming and soothing after spending so much time by herself.

"I didn't want to follow your dream," Annie said. "Thanks for the compliment on the sets. I'm happy with how they turned out as well."

"The kids are so excited. This is the first production I've done in town. I hope that everyone likes it."

"I'm sure they will. You're really good with the kids," she said. Liz had been carefully coaching the kids along and helping them in their roles. She was firm and direct but also very positive.

"They are good," Alec said coming over to her. "I never cease to be amazed at the talent that our little town has produced."

"Glad you approve," Liz said. "Considering you are the man donating our manger animals, do you think they will fit in our prop stable?"

"They should," Alec said.

Carson's older brother was of the same height and had the same thick dark brown hair, but the similarities ended there. Where Carson had those big friendly eyes, Alec's were cold, steel-gray, and had never looked very approvingly at her.

Liz was called across the room by someone else, leaving Alec and Annie alone. Oh goody, she thought.

"You really are very talented," he said, but it was almost a reluctant compliment.

"Thanks. I have always enjoyed creating things like this. I didn't have much call to do anything similar in the last five years. I didn't realize how much I'd missed it."

"Is that all you missed?" he asked her as he continued to study the sets.

"I'm not sure what you are asking me," she said. Sure that this conversation had two meanings to Alec at least.

"Did you miss my brother?" he said bluntly.

Hell, she missed him right now. Each night she was reluctant to go to bed since her pillow still smelled of his aftershave—though it was starting to fade now. She hugged the pillow close to her and pretended he was there next to her. The thing was she knew if she'd take a chance and call him he'd give her a chance to come back into his life. But she was too afraid to chance it.

Alec leaned in and it was little intimidating to have him standing over her like that. But the part of her that liked Carson was very glad he had his brother. Though she knew he'd be angry if he realized how protective Alec was of him.

"I don't see how that's any of your business," she said at last.

"Listen, Miss Marietta's-Not-Good-Enough-For-Me, Carson deserves a woman who isn't playing games with him," Alec said.

"I'm not playing with him. We know where we stand. I don't think he needs you to fight his battles."

"You're right, he doesn't. But I've seen the way you look at him when you think no one is watching. You want him," Alec said.

"Is that a crime?" she asked, but inside she died a little. She'd thought she was doing a better job of hiding how she felt.

"No," he said, "It's not. What's keeping you from going after him? Is it Evan or is it— "

"It is actually none of your business, Alec," Carson said coming over to them.

Alec put his hands up and backed away. Annie stood there feeling raw and exposed and afraid to move. She thought she'd hidden her feelings about Carson but it was clear she hadn't. And a part of her really didn't want to hide.

"Sorry about that," Carson said. "Alec had no right to bully you like that."

"It's fine. He's right. I do watch you when no one else is looking. I miss you," she said softly. Soaking in every inch of him. He looked tired but still so good. Her arms ached to hug him close and she wanted to make promises she wasn't sure she'd keep if it meant he'd hold her again even for one night.

"Then why are we apart?" he asked, the emotion in voice was raw.

It touched something inside her and she wrapped her arm around her waist to keep from touching him. But she wanted to. He looked tired and his hair was a little too long, in need of a trim. And she remembered the last time she'd pushed her fingers into his thick hair and wanted to do it again.

"Annie?"

She realized she was just staring at him, and for the first time since she'd left Manhattan she knew what she wanted. She wanted Carson Scott. She wanted everything she knew about him to be true and be real. And she really wanted to be worthy of his love.

"Because you already lost one woman you loved, I don't want to be the cause of you losing another one. I'm not saying you love me, but I know you, Car. I always have, and the two of us both sort of always...

"Get each other," he said at last. "Yes we do. But I don't

want you settling for me."

"I don't want that either. That's why I'm trying to stay away but it's hard. Harder than anything I've ever done before."

"Do you think that maybe staying away isn't the answer?" he asked.

"What else could be? I heard Evan ask Santa for mommy, and it's not fair for me to be with you when I don't know if I'm staying or going. But that doesn't mean it's easy for me to just ignore you."

"It's not easy for me either," he said. "What do you think we should do about it?"

"I'm not sure. But I have a few ideas."

"I have to pick Evan up after this, but on Saturday I'm hosting a cast and crew pre-production party out at the Red Barn. My brothers and I just finished fixing it up. Why don't you come by early and we can talk then."

She nodded and watched him walk away and for the first time had an inkling of what it must have been like for him when she'd left and she knew she had to make very sure of what she wanted before she did anything to hurt him again.

Saturday morning dawned bright and sparkly white. As Annie opened the door to let Rumple out, she realized there were only five days left until Christmas. She'd spent the evening before at her sister's house with her family wrapping presents and decorating cookies. It had made her realize how much she'd missed being a part of a family and had opened her eyes to the fact that she wanted one of her own.

The Nativity play was going to be performed on Christmas Eve, four days from now. And her involvement had been extended by Liz to include some backstage management of all the tiny performers.

She had used the last three days since she'd seen Carson at the set-building evening to really figure out some things in her life. She enjoyed indulging her artistic side so much that she'd been working almost non-stop at the old ranch house. At first she thought about fixing it up to sell and then she realized, as she worked her way through the rooms making sketches of them, that she was creating a home for herself.

It was that moment late last night that had made her accept today she was going to tell Carson she'd decided to stay in Marietta. She knew it might be too late for him. But she was also damned sure that once she put her mind to it she could convince him to give her a second chance.

Rumple came back in and she fed him and then tied a pretty red bow around his neck, which he tolerated. She glanced at the clock and realized she had eight hours until she was due over at Carson's but she didn't want to wait another minute. So she gathered Rumple and her coat and headed over to Carson's ranch house.

She drove under the sign, which proclaimed it the C & E, and up to the front of the two-story house. The front porch was decorated with garland and lights and there was a wreath on the front door and a sign by the steps that said *Santa, stop here.*

She wiped her sweaty palms on her thighs and opened her door, letting Rumple go first as she climbed the stairs and knocked on the door. She heard the sound of dog nails on hardwood and running before the door opened.

"Annie!" Evan said. He had chocolate on this face and that big gap-toothed grin that made her want to hug him.

"Hello, Evan. Is your dad home?"

"He's out on the range. I'm making cookies with my Aunt Sienna. Want to come help?"

She had no idea if his Aunt would want her help or not. But Sienna appeared in the hallway wiping her hands on a kitchen towel. "I'm Sienna. You must be Annie."

"I am," she said, holding out her hand. Rumple and Puddles were sniffing each other. "This is awkward. I guess I should have called."

"Nonsense. All this snow has just added to the workload for the men so I volunteered to keep the boys busy today. Come on in."

Annie realized that this was Alec's wife as soon as she stepped into the kitchen and saw JT. He smiled over at her from the table where he was busy decorating a cookie. "We're getting them ready for tonight."

"I can see that."

"Want to help?" Evan asked. "You get to eat the broken ones."

"Oh no," JT said as a cookie broke in his hands and he ate it.

"Scamp," Sienna said. "I know not all those cookies were broken and I need to have some to serve tonight to the cast and crew for the Nativity. Miss Rachel is making one of her special gingerbread houses and I said I'd help out with some Plain Jane cookies, so that's the last one for now."

"Okay, mommy."

She ruffled her son's hair... Annie noticed Evan watching JT and Sienna, and realized how important having a woman in his life was to him. She also had a momentary fear that maybe she wasn't ready for all of this but she didn't let that stop her. She had been afraid when she'd left Marietta, but determined and she'd made her dreams come true.

Just because her dreams had changed didn't mean she couldn't make them come true again. So much power in coming to realize what was important in her life and understanding that it centered on the new life she had made for herself in these last few weeks.

She sat down next to Evan, scared of doing the wrong thing, but even more afraid of not even trying. As she helped him decorate, she found that she enjoyed it. Sienna was funny and easy to talk to and the boys were smart for their age. She had never experienced anything like this. In her mind, she tucked this away as a tradition she hoped she'd be able continue next Christmas.

The back door opened with a blast of cold air and the sound of raised masculine voices. Carson stopped as he saw her sitting at the table – and Alec, and then Lane slammed into his back.

"What the hell's your problem?" Lane asked.

Then he glanced over at her. "Oh, hello. I'm Lane. We weren't really properly introduced that night at the Diner and you were too many years ahead of me at school for us to know each other."

"I'm Annie," she said, shaking Lane's hand. He had a good hard grip and intense green eyes. He wore his hair cut short—military short, and he was an inch or two shorter than Carson and Alec. "Was that a polite way of saying I'm old?"

"No ma'am," he said with a wink.

She turned to Carson. "Sorry I didn't call first. Sienna let me stay."

"Of course I did. I needed some girl time. There's too much testosterone when the Scotts all get together."

"What's test-toast?" Evan asked.

"Man stuff, kiddo," Annie said.

"Annie, can we talk in my office?" Carson asked.

"That would suit me just fine," she said.

"Let me wash up first," he said. He gave Evan a kiss on the head, stole two cookies and walked out of the kitchen followed by his brothers.

"How come Uncle Carson got to eat a cookie that wasn't broken?" JT asked.

"Because it's his house."

"Does that mean I can too?" Evan asked.

"You both can, now that we have enough for tonight. Why don't you go into the living room and play? I'll bring some cookies and milk in for you," Sienna said.

"Yay!"

They both dashed out of the kitchen quickly. Sienna turned to her. "You okay?"

"Why wouldn't I be?" she asked trying to be find the same courage she'd had when she'd driven over here earlier. But it was hard because now she had to put her faith in herself to the test and trust that when she'd realized she was in love with Carson she hadn't been fooling herself.

"Because you're in love with a Scott. And they are difficult," Sienna said.

"I'm the difficult one," Annie said. "I was all ready to talk to him and now that he's here I'm sort of nervous all over again."

"Don't be," Sienna said. "Carson's a good solid man and that's one cowboy you don't want to let slip away."

Carson sat in the big leather chair behind the mahogany

desk that his grandfather had given him the day he'd graduated from college. It was solid and, as his grandfather had said, it was a serious piece of furniture for a solid sort of life. Carson had always known he'd make his life and his living here in Paradise Valley and it didn't bother him in the least that he would never live farther than a few miles from the house he grew up in.

Thinking about the furniture kept him from giving too much meaning to the fact that Annie was here. She was in his kitchen baking cookies with Evan and making like *she wanted to be here.*

Hell, for all he knew she was waiting to say goodbye to him.

Why was she here? He'd had a long, cold morning, added to the fact that he hadn't slept worth a damn since that one night weeks ago when he'd stayed at her place.

He looked around the office that Evan had decorated with chains of popcorn and homemade reindeer antlers that he'd cut out of construction paper. This wasn't a sophisticated life, but it was his.

There was a knock on the door.

"Come in."

The door opened slowly and Annie walked in with two steaming mugs in her hands. Sienna closed the door after Annie. Annie stood there in the doorway for a split second and then took a few steps forward. She put the mugs on his desk.

"Coffee. I remembered you like decaf," she said.

"And I remember you like yours very sweet," he said.

"We both have really good memories," she said awkwardly standing there before sitting down on the padded ottoman that was in front of his desk.

"Yes, we do," he said, wanting her to be here to stay so badly that he had to clench his hands into fists to keep from reaching for her. And that made him mad. He'd never been a man to not reach out and take what he wanted. But with Annie, that kind of gesture would just spook her and make her run.

She reached up and tucked a stand of hair behind her ear and watched him for a moment, then she took a deep breath.

208

"I don't know any other way to say this but to just get it out, and I'm scared because once I say it there's not taking it back," she said, on one long breath.

He almost smiled because in his heart this started to feel like she wasn't coming to say goodbye. And he was afraid to hope that she might have found her way to staying here in his valley with him.

"Just say it."

"I don't want to leave Montana. I was afraid that I wanted to stay because of you, but then I realized that if I was leaving just to prove that I wasn't staying for you, that was wrong too."

Carson leaned forward, resting his elbows on his desk, hoping he appeared nonchalant, but knowing he'd failed miserably. "I want you to stay, Annie. More than anything. But it has to be for you."

"I know. That's what's been tying me up in knots and last night as I was sketching my plans for the redesign of one of the guest rooms, I realized that I wasn't drawing a house that would sell well, but my house. A place I wanted to live in. I knew then that I wanted to stay there.

"The more I drew the clearer it became that just staying here wasn't enough. In my mind I also pictured you and Evan here too. I wanted both of you to be a part of my family."

She stopped talking and looked over at him for the first time since she'd put the coffee on his desk. "I know I haven't done anything to prove that I can be part of your family, but I'm here today to ask you to give me a chance."

"Are you sure?" he asked.

She nibbled her lower lip. "Yes, but that doesn't mean I'm not going to make mistakes or have moments of doubt. It's just that I do know that I want to be here and I need to be with you."

"I need that too," he said. He walked over to her but stopped before he touched her. "But I need to be sure you're not just feeling lonely."

"I am lonely and scared and all the things you probably wish I weren't, but there is one thing I know for sure and that is that I'm staying here. And if it takes me the rest of our lives to prove it to you then that's what I'll do."

He pulled her into a bear hug and held her tightly to him so she wouldn't see the emotion in his eyes. The words he was longing to say to her slipped out. "Thank God, woman. I love you."

"I love you too, Carson. I think I've been a little in love with you since the day I saw you at the Diner but I was so afraid to trust it."

He kissed her hard and then set her back on her feet. "I can't rush into anything."

"Me neither. In fact, I'd like to just take it slow until we both feel more comfortable. And I really want to get to know Evan a lot better. I want us to become a family if that's what you want."

"Well that is all I wanted for Christmas," he admitted.

"Truly?"

He nodded. "I think you were the one who got away and I never let myself let go of you."

"Maybe that's because I was meant to come back to you," she said.

"I think you were. My family is all probably waiting right outside that door," Carson said, realizing how quiet the house seemed.

"Probably. Sienna said she'd try to keep them away but that Scott men are stubborn."

"Yes we are. And we're loyal too. I'm yours now and that means I'm never letting you go."

"Good because I've discovered I'm pretty stubborn too and I'm not letting you go either."

He kissed her again and kept her hand in his as he opened the door and found his brothers lounging in the hallway trying to look nonchalant.

"Good news?" Lane asked.

"Like you don't already know," Carson said.

"We couldn't hear everything through the door," Alec admitted.

"But we did hear that she's back to stay with you."

"Really?" Evan asked.

"Yes."

"Maybe Santa does still have magic, Daddy," Evan said. "I'm a lot closer to having a mom now than I was before I asked him for one."

Everyone laughed and Carson kept a tight hold on Annie but realized she wasn't going anywhere. That rambling look was gone from her eyes and she had found what she'd been looking for, right here, in the Paradise Valley, Montana.

The End

A Cowboy For Christmas

About the Author

USA Today bestselling author Katherine Garbera is a two-time Maggie winner who has written more than 60 books. A Florida native who grew up to travel the globe, Katherine now makes her home in the Midlands of the UK with her husband, two children and a very spoiled miniature dachshund.

Home For Christmas

a copper mountain christmas novella

Melissa McClone

Dedication

To Katherine Garbera and Jane Porter.
Thanks for inviting me to Copper Mountain this Christmas!

Acknowledgments

Special thanks to Lisa Hayden, Teresa Morgan and Terri Reed
for their input and my family for their love and support.

Dear Reader,

I'm so excited to be a part of the Copper Mountain Christmas novellas. Nothing beats a holiday romance novel, especially one set in Montana with snow, pine trees, and cowboys!

As I brainstormed the story, I looked at how my family celebrates Christmas. Tradition is big around here. We light candles on the Advent wreath each night, count down the days in December with a chocolate-filled calendar, read Christmas stories aloud, place a Nativity scene underneath the tree, decorate a gingerbread house, bake goodies, and watch lots of Christmas movies.

After typing the end, I realized this story contains many of our Christmas traditions. Two in particular—gingerbread and Charles Dickens' *A Christmas Carol*—play big roles in the romance between baker Rachel Murphy and cowboy Nate Vaughn.

I hope you enjoy spending Christmas with Rachel and Nate at the Bar V5 ranch and in Marietta, Montana!

Melissa

Contents

Chapter One

"You didn't tell me the Bar V5 held the Guinness World Record for the longest driveway." Rachel Murphy stared out the windshield of her brother Tyler's 4x4 pickup. Against Montana's big sky—a gorgeous, cloudless, cornflower blue this December morning—the snow covering tree branches and mountaintops looked white enough to eat, like whipped cream or better yet meringue. "Guess you need to make sure guests can't run away from the ranch and hitch a ride back to town."

Ty tapped his thumb against the leather-steering wheel in time with the Christmas carol playing. "People come to the Bar V5 to escape the daily grind. But some folks can't survive without being connected 24x7 and are gone by the second day."

Rachel checked her mobile phone. Zero bars. Plenty of snow, but no cellular service. She couldn't decide who was crazier—her brother for choosing to live year round in the middle-of-nowhere or her for agreeing to spend December with him.

"Truth is, most guests hate to leave the Bar V5." Ty's satisfied smile and pride in his voice reaffirmed how much he loved his job at the working dude ranch, his life as a cowboy.

She couldn't be happier for him, even if she missed him. After their parents' deaths when she was ten, he'd put his life on hold, staying in Arizona and raising her. He'd waited until she was settled into culinary school before moving to Marietta, Montana seven years ago.

"We have repeat visitors each summer," he added.

"Summer being the operative word. I should have come then."

"It's not that bad."

"You're oblivious to the elements." She wiggled her freezing gloved fingers in front of the heater vent. The warm air helped a little. She hadn't been warm since she flew into Bozeman four days ago. Boy, did she miss Phoenix. She'd never complain about the heat again. "Montana's lovely, don't get me wrong, but I don't think there's been a temperature in the double digits since I arrived. I finally understand why people flock to Arizona in the winter. This is brutal."

"You get used to the cold and snow."

"I suppose, but this is nothing like home." Rachel needed this breather, a winter adventure in the northwest with her brother, but she'd been born in Arizona and lived there her entire life. Her mom and dad were buried there. She had no plans to move away from the desert. Ever. "Sunny and dry. Saguaros and Sun-Devils."

"Home is wherever the people you love are."

The affection in his voice chased away the cold. Tyler Murphy was over-protective and treated Rachel like she was twelve, not twenty-six, but she couldn't imagine Christmas—or life—without him. "Guess I'm home for the next three weeks."

"Damn straight. We'll make the most of the time and the holidays like we do every year."

"Except we'll be having our first white Christmas."

"It's going to be special."

Rachel nodded, but she couldn't get too excited. She kept thinking about the Phoenix bakery that no longer belonged to her. Last December, she'd worked crazy hours at two jobs to save money and loved every minute. This year felt... different. She swallowed a sigh.

Her brother reached across the bench seat and squeezed her hand. "Thanks for coming to Montana, kiddo."

Ty had always come to her for the holidays. Some years when he had extra money he flew, other times when he was low on cash he drove, but they had a great Christmas no matter the balance in their checking accounts. Decorating her tree, hanging lights on her apartment's balcony, counting down the days to December twenty-fifth with a chocolate-filled Advent calendar, hiking South Mountain on Christmas day...

But Ty had asked her to visit him in Montana this year. After her life fell apart—okay, exploded in an icky mess of sugar, spice and everything-not-so-nice, she'd jumped at the chance to escape and try to forget about being played a fool by so-called friends.

A hundred-pound ball of regret and hurt crushed her chest. Rachel forced a breath, then pasted on a smile. "How could I turn down an invitation to spend Christmas in a winter wonderland with my favorite brother?"

"I'm your only brother."

Ty followed up the old joke between them with a silly face, one that used to make her laugh when she felt like crying. So far during her stay, she'd cried only twice. Progress. "Then it's good thing I didn't go to Wyoming."

He stuck out his tongue.

She did the same.

Getting away from Arizona and spending time with Ty was helping. She enjoyed seeing his life in Montana, rather than imagining it from phone calls, texts, and Skype chats. He had a room at the Bar V5 and also leased an apartment in the small town of Marietta. A refuge for times he wanted to get away from the ranch, he claimed. More likely, knowing her brother, when he wanted to get drunk at Grey's Saloon and not drive. Getting a ride to the ranch late at night must be impossible.

The truck's studded tires crunched against the snow. "All I Want For Christmas" played in the background, the jolly melody a counterpoint to her *meh* mood.

All Rachel wanted for Christmas was to get a do-over for the last six months ago. Not even Santa could manage that.

She'd been on her own, dealing with the betrayal and loss of her dream these past weeks, wishing there'd been someone special in her life, someone who lived closer than Montana, who she could have leaned on for support and who would have made her smile when all she wanted to do was cry. She hadn't dated much, but in hindsight none of those guys had treated her better than the Darbys. She'd picked the same kind of boyfriends as she did business partners. Sad, but true.

Up ahead, the road curved toward a two-story log house decorated with white Christmas lights. Garland tied with red ribbon hung from the railing of a wide porch. Light glowed from inside wood pane windows, reminding her of a painting she'd seen on display in a Scottsdale gallery. She leaned forward, the seatbelt strap pressing into her shoulder. "Wow."

Ty parked. "That's what I said my first time here."

She'd visited the Bar V5's website to check out where her brother worked, but the photographs didn't capture the beauty and grand scale of the ranch house. The architecture made her think of a mountain lodge—high-end, luxurious accommodations—not a place where cowboys and guests in hats and spurs drank beer and ate at plank tables after a long day on the trail. "I get the appeal. Christmas card perfect."

"Wait until you see the inside. You'll love the kitchen."

She'd been struggling for three days trying to bake and construct gingerbread houses in Ty's tiny kitchen with a narrow oven and less than three feet of counter space. "Thanks for asking your boss if I could use his."

"Nate's a good guy. Knew he wouldn't mind."

Nate Vaughn owned the dude ranch. She'd never met him, but Ty had only good words to say about his boss. "I'll bake him something special as a thank you."

"He'll appreciate that."

Rachel opened the truck's door; eager to get to work and rid herself of the restlessness she'd felt being unemployed. The cold hit hard and fast, seeping into her bones in spite of her heavy parka, jeans, boots and wool beanie. With a shiver, she grabbed the box full of baking supplies from behind the seat. "Brrrr. It's colder than yesterday."

"This is nothing. Wait until February."

By then, she'd be back home, enjoying the nice weather and, if things worked out as planned this time, baking in her own shop. Maybe she would find a guy to date, a nice guy with manners who treated her well and met with her brother's approval.

Ty carried two bags full of groceries. "I can't believe you're working during your vacation. I wanted you to relax."

"Baking relaxes me."

"Starting a brand new business less than forty-eight hours after you arrived is not relaxing. It's insanity."

Rachel's boots sank into the snow, but her feet remained dry. The sales person at the sporting goods store had been honest when he'd sold her cold weather gear. That surprised her. Few people told the truth these days. "Maybe, but the gingerbread houses are selling faster than I can make them, thanks to your friends."

"You're working as much as I am."

"I might as well do something productive. If I can earn some money…"

"I've got money you can have."

"Thanks, but I'm capable of earning my own." She didn't need or want anyone's help, not even her brother's. She wanted Ty to treat her like an adult. If she took more of his money, whether a gift or a loan, he would keep thinking of her as his kid sister. "If I sell enough gingerbread to cover a lease deposit, I'll be one step closer to opening a bakery."

Of course she needed to revise her business plan and create new products, ones she wouldn't share with a soul this time.

"There are vacancies on Main Street. Front Avenue, too." Ty bypassed the porch, walking to the right side of the house toward a Dutch door with a window on top. A hanging electric lantern illuminated the area. "Forget about Phoenix. Open a place in Marietta."

"There are guest ranches in Arizona." They'd had this discussion for the past seven years, but seeing this place, she didn't blame him for staying in Montana. But still she played her part. "You should move back. Better weather. Longer tourist season."

Ty unlocked then opened the door. "Get inside where it's warm and see your new kitchen."

Rachel entered a small room. Benches with cubbies underneath, some empty, some filled with shoes, lined the wall on each side of her. Tall cabinets covered the wall behind her. A few cowboy hats, wool beanies, jackets, insulated pants and jeans hung from rows of hooks on the far wall.

She removed her boots and tucked them into a cubby. "Socks okay?"

"Fine." Ty motioned to a basket of lined moccasin-type shoes. "Unless you want slippers."

Rachel shrugged off her coat, thankful for the forced air heating set at a comfy temperature. "I'll stick with socks."

Carrying the box, she followed Ty through a doorway. The tile floor gave way to gorgeous wide-plank hardwood.

She looked up. Stopped. Gasped.

The most beautiful, most clean, most perfect kitchen she'd ever seen was on display in front of her.

Her brother laughed. "Knew you'd like it."

"Ty knows best, except I don't like it. I love it." She'd baked in a variety of commercial workspaces—culinary school, restaurants, cafes, bakeries, and a television studio. None came close to what was now at her disposal. The hickory cabinets, butcher-block counter, wood floors and log walls and high ceiling gave the space a homey feel in spite of the top-of-the-line professional appliances and industrial stainless steel countertops. Her heart danced a jig. "I'm practically drooling."

He removed items from the grocery sacks. "As opposed to the crying in my kitchen."

"That crying wasn't about your apartment, and this will definitely cheer me up." Rachel set her box on the island's stainless steel top. Not one, but two professional ranges with so many burners she might have to try out a few fudge recipes. Maybe play with sugar. Warming drawers, two dishwashers, a wall-sized refrigerator, more than enough counter space to assemble the gingerbread houses and make do-it-yourself kits. She spun, giddy with excitement like a kid on Christmas morning. "This is a dream kitchen."

Ty's lopsided grin transported her back to sunny days of tubing on the Salt River, spring training baseball games, and late night swims in the apartment complex pool with the temperature still over a hundred. "Then you'd better put on your apron and get busy making your dream come true."

Talk about a nightmare. Nate Vaughn cursed under his breath. The brisk morning air cleared his head, but did nothing to soothe his frustrations. He removed his duffel bag and a Christmas wreath from the back of his pickup. Yes, he should be over what happened twelve hours ago.

But he wasn't.

He slammed the shell's hatch against the back gate.

Last night had been a total waste of time. His date, a twenty-nine year old lawyer named Addison from Helena, was pretty, smart, and fit. Her profile seemed ideal, except she'd left off one critical piece of information—her addiction to texting.

Five minutes after being seated at the finest steak house in town, he wanted to toss her mobile phone off the top of Copper Mountain. The date spiraled downhill from there. If he'd wanted to eat dinner by himself, he could have stayed home and saved the money he'd spent on gas and a motel in Helena. If he hadn't drunk one beer too many at a dive bar after saying goodbye to Addison, he would have driven home last night.

No more online dating. No more high-priced matchmaking services. No more blind dates.

He trudged to the front porch.

This cowboy was going back to finding a woman the old-fashioned way. He wasn't talking mail order brides like his great grandfather, either.

Nate would find a date in person.

Somewhere in the state of Montana there had to be a woman he wanted to date more than once. Hell, he might propose on the second date if things ever got that far. All he had to do was find her…

Preferably before New Year's Eve.

He'd like someone special to kiss when the clock struck midnight and start the year off right.

Nate glanced at the house brightly lit. He'd left more lights on than he realized. At least the interior wouldn't be dark when he went inside. Empty and quiet though.

The off-season sucked. He'd take summer anytime, when the Bar V5 was full of staff and guests. No time to be bored… or lonely. He'd thought about staying open in the winter, running the ranch like a B&B, but Ty liked giving the horses time to rest. Maybe once the upgrades and remodeling projects were completed they should reconsider.

Nate set the wreath on the front porch, making a mental note to find the hanger, and headed to the mudroom. A silver pickup with an American flag decal in the back window caught his eye.

Ty Murphy—his best friend and partner, though Ty preferred to call himself the foreman—was here. Not surprising. Ty was the hardest worker Nate knew, the one person he could always count on.

He kicked the snow from his ostrich dress boots and opened the mudroom door.

The smell of ginger, nutmeg, and cinnamon slammed into him like a stampeding steer. Only this didn't hurt.

Well, his stomach did. Hunger pains.

His mouth watered with anticipation. He had no idea what was baking or which of his employees had started the morning off in the kitchen, but he wanted a taste.

The scent of Christmas circled his head, tantalizing his nose and taste buds. If he could bottle and sell the scent, he would make a fortune. He glanced around to make sure he hadn't entered the wrong house.

Nope, this was the Bar V5, the place he'd grown up and, God willing, where he'd die and be buried when his time came.

He hoped that wasn't in the next five minutes, but if the Grim Reaper was on his way, Nate had better get into the kitchen so he could get a bite of whatever was cooking first. He placed the duffel bag strap on his shoulder then stepped through the doorway.

What the…

Silver mixing bowls, spoons and pans stacked haphazardly on top of each other in the sink like a culinary edition of Jenga. Pull one thing out and the entire pile would tumble down.

Cereal bowls, full of different colors of icing, sat in a cluster on the island. Pastry bags twisted like licorice between plastic containers full of sprinkles and candies.

Decorating cookies?

He took a closer look.

Not cookies. Gingerbread.

Like his mom used to make.

That explained the smell.

He rubbed his chin. Stubble pricked his fingers.

Someone had made themselves at home, but who? Ty grilled. He could smoke a mean brisket. But bake? Not likely. The other wranglers usually stuck to the bunkhouse. Maybe elves had decided to pay a visit.

Nate circled the island for a closer look.

White icing held together rectangular and square pieces of gingerbread in various stages of construction. Houses, cottages, even a barn.

On the far counter, miniature white lights illuminated the insides and hung along the eaves of three houses. Christmas trees made from star shaped cookies were strung with lights, too.

Charming and creative.

He wanted a taste.

A small piece of gingerbread, the size of a window cutout, and a few others sat on a paper towel. Scraps to be tossed? No one would miss one. He popped a square into his mouth.

Flavors exploded with just the right mixture of spices and sweetness. Oh, yeah. Whoever baked this knew what they were doing. Wanting more, he reached for another piece. His hand froze. He did a double take.

One of the gingerbread houses looked like the Crawford House. Same Victorian architecture. Similar gables and bay windows. A hint of the whimsical.

Cha-ching.

Mrs. Annabeth Collier, formerly Crawford, one of Marietta's First Families, would pay top dollar for a custom gingerbread house. Rather her daughter Chelsea's billionaire boyfriend Jasper Flint would. And not only them.

Nate wanted one of the Bar V5.

People around here went all out for the holidays. These houses would go over big. He didn't know how much one cost to make or the profit margin, but with the right marketing…

"Hello." The feminine voice wrapped around him, warm and welcoming as the scent of gingerbread baking. "Can I help you?"

He turned toward the sweet-as-molasses sound.

A twenty-something woman stood in the laundry room doorway. Blonde hair piled haphazardly on top of her head. Strands stuck out of the messy bun. A puzzled expression complete with two little creases above her nose made him want to see a smile on her pretty face. Clear complexion, straight nose, full lips and warm hazel eyes.

His pulse rate kicked up a notch, maybe two. Okay, five.

Nate recognized, but he couldn't quite place the color of her eyes. But the way the color changed from light brown to green to a golden hue captivated him.

She wore a simple purple long-sleeved turtleneck, but streaks of white across her chest—flour perhaps?—distracted him, made him want to volunteer for cleanup duty. Faded jeans hugged her hips and thighs until flaring slightly at her calves. Long legs and curvy in all the right places.

Cute candy cane striped sock-covered toes peeked out the bottom. The pattern amused and intrigued him. Part of an elf's costume or holiday attire?

Either way, Christmas had come early.

He'd been good this year and deserved a reward from Santa. Hot gingerbread baked by a hot woman was making him hot. The only improvement to his wonderful gift would be if she was naked and wearing a red ribbon. Though he could live without the ribbon.

His heart raced, as if trying to catch his horse Arrow when the stallion had escaped from the pasture. Sweat dampened the back of his neck. Had someone turned up the heat?

Her mouth twitched. She looked like she was waiting for something.

Oh, yeah. Him. "Hi."

Clever, Vaughn. Impressive show of eloquence with a two-letter word. He would try again. "Thanks for the offer, but I'm good. I don't need any help."

His mouth twisted. He felt tongue-tied like a teenager talking to his first crush.

"Are you a ranch hand?" She studied him. "Or Nate?"

"Nate." She knew his name, but he didn't have a clue who she was or why she was walking around like she owned the place. He should probably care more than he did. But she was pretty and her cooking smelled delicious and most importantly, she wasn't holding a cell phone or pointing a gun or, he double-checked her left hand, wearing a wedding ring. "And you're…"

"I was rinsing out my apron in the laundry room," she said at the same time. A charming pink spread across her face. "Sorry, I'm Rachel."

"Rachel." A lovely name to go with a beautiful woman. A woman he wanted to get to know better. Intimately. Before New Year's Eve. "Nice to meet you."

"You, too." She walked toward him, a subtle sway to her hips he found mesmerizing. "Ty's told me so much about you."

"Ty?"

She nodded. "Thanks for letting me use your kitchen."

Yesterday's forgotten conversation rushed back, bunching Nate's muscles. He rubbed the back of his neck. He knew exactly why her hazel eyes looked familiar.

"You're Ty's sister." So much for an early Christmas present. Nate should have known finding a beautiful blonde cooking in his kitchen was too good to be true. "You're older than I thought you'd be."

The corners of Rachel's mouth curved upward in an almost smile. "Ty thinks I'm still a kid with ponytails crushing on boy bands."

I don't. But Nate couldn't say about his friend's sister when said friend was as protective of her as a new foal's momma. "Ty's a good guy."

"The best."

Nate's gaze held hers a moment too long. He looked away so she wouldn't think he might be interested in her.

Not going to cross that line, even if he were tempted. He was, but Ty meant too much to Nate for him to do something stupid like put a move on Rachel.

He motioned to the gingerbread houses. "Nice work."

She stood on the opposite side of the island. "Thanks."

"Are they gifts?"

The lines above her nose deepened. She picked up a bag full of white icing. "No."

"Planning to sell them?"

"Does it matter?"

A little defensive. He wondered why. "Just curious." About the gingerbread, he reminded himself.

"I made a house for Ty. A friend of his saw it. She ordered one. Then another friend ordered another, and well, here I am."

"Nice way to earn extra cash."

Another nod. "We'll see how many more orders I get."

"I want one."

"Yours is on me. A thank you."

Not only pretty, but sweet. "Thanks."

"I'm the one who should thank you for letting me use this awesome kitchen."

"No worries. You're Ty's sister. That makes you family."

Family didn't date or lust after each other or imagine if she had a beauty mark like the one to the right of her mouth anywhere else on her body.

She adjusted the silver tip on the pastry bag. "That's nice of you to say."

"It's the truth. Your brother is a big reason the Bar V5 has been so successful." Ty's dedication over the years made Nate want to help Rachel. "Do you have a marketing plan yet?"

She held the icing bag in front of her, tip pointed at him like a weapon. "Why do you want to know?"

Her suspicious tone matched her stiff posture. Nate had no idea what was wrong, but time for damage control. "I was a venture capitalist before I came home and took over the ranch. I still invest if I see an opportunity."

She pressed her lips together. "No opportunity here."

"If you decide you want help—"

"I'm good. But thanks again for letting me use your kitchen. I'll be sure to clean up my mess before I leave with Ty this afternoon." She angled her shoulders away from Nate. "I'd better get back to work and leave you to yours."

Rachel didn't want his expertise. Fine. But Nate didn't like being dismissed in his own kitchen when he would rather stay and find out why she acted like he was a villain in a black hat when all he did was offer his help. She was off-limits by virtue of being Ty's sister, but that didn't mean Nate couldn't find out more about her.

Nah.

Sticking around and getting to know her any better would be a bad idea. He didn't want to piss off Ty. Might as well get to work. "Have fun baking."

Though having another taste of her gingerbread couldn't hurt. Not much anyway. Nate wondered if she would be willing to share...

Chapter Two

Rachel leaned against the island counter, watching Nate Vaughn's retreating backside, relieved to see him go. Forget about wanting a nice guy in her life, even flirting was too strenuous for her bruised heart. She only wished she hadn't noticed how nicely Nate's jeans fit or how his leather jacket showed off wide shoulders or how the duffel bag he carried made her wonder where he'd spent last night.

None of those things should matter.

Not to her.

He might be show-off sexy with that razor stubble on his handsome face and an I'd-like-to-get-to-know-you-better smile, but she didn't need his business help or advice. She didn't want anything from him. Well, except the use of his kitchen.

Nate glanced over his shoulder, meeting her gaze straight on.

Busted for staring. Heat rose up her neck. Good thing she was flushed from the heat in the kitchen. Maybe her blush wouldn't give her away.

His lips curved into a wry grin.

Too late. Her face burned hotter. "Forget something?"

"If it's not too much trouble, save a piece of gingerbread for me."

By the time she finished baking, she would have platefuls of ends and cutouts. "No problem, as long as you don't mind the scraps."

"Don't mind at all. My hungry stomach won't know the difference."

She expected him to turn back. Walk away. Let her work.

Nate continued staring. He must want another look at the gingerbread houses. Except... she wet her lips... he was looking at her.

The hunger in his eyes made Rachel's blood simmer. His gaze ran the length of her slowly, appreciatively, like he

234

wanted a taste of her.

Her heart thudded.

Something stirred inside Rachel. Excitement, yes. But also possibility.

He made her feel like an unexpected, but welcomed, guest at a cocktail party. That her flour-stained clothes were as appealing as a little black dress.

Did she dare let herself have some fun? Something missing from her life for a long time.

Self-preservation told her to look away. Run away would be better.

Safer.

She might not have dated many men, but she knew that look from the last cowboy who had broken her heart after Ty had broken his nose. Nate might be a great guy according to her brother, but she needed to keep her distance. She knew better than to think she could handle a man like Nate Vaughn.

Rachel cleared her dry throat. "Is there, um, anything else?"

"No."

He didn't look away. Or move.

She was transfixed herself.

Which made zero sense.

His dark chocolate eyes would not be good for her heart. His interest in her gingerbread would not be good for her peace of mind. His being a cowboy would make Ty go ballistic.

Rachel stared into a plastic container full of gumdrops. Green, red, yellow, purple and white. She imagined using the candies on the Bramble House B&B gingerbread replica she was designing, but Nate's sexy smile kept flashing in her mind, doing odd things to her tummy. Reminding her that people wanting to *help* was the reason her bakery belonged to someone else.

Footsteps sounded.

Rachel listened until the steps faded. She shot a glance at the doorway leading to the living area. Gone. She exhaled.

No one, especially a good-looking cowboy with an investment background, was going to play her for a fool.

Do you have a marketing plan? If you want any help or ideas...

She grimaced. She'd lost years of hard work thanks to America's favorite television baker, Pamela Darby, and her crook of a husband, Grayson. They'd acted like surrogate parents. Rachel had eaten up the attention and praise, never once realizing they were using her for their own gain until it was too late. She would not be taken advantage of again. She would focus on what needed to be done and forget everything else.

Including yummy Nate Vaughn.

After a quick shower and shave, Nate headed to the barn. A small staff worked year round to help with the cattle, horses and maintenance. Men he trusted to do the job whether he was here or not. His female wrangler, Charlie, short for Charlotte, had gone to Colorado for the winter. Ty hadn't said whether she was returning in the spring.

Nate zipped his coat and lowered his hat to shield himself from the cold wind. No snowfall last night meant no shoveling the paths or plowing the driveway this morning, but he'd bet the creek and ponds froze over and would need to be opened. Again.

A dog barked, a sharp sound he knew well.

Dusty, an Australian Cattle dog, ran toward Nate. The dog, who belonged to his late father, rarely left Ty's side.

"Morning." Ty rounded a corner, carrying a pickaxe and wearing heavy, insulated outwear. A thin layer of ice covered his waterproof boots.

"Been busy?"

"Broke through the ice at the creek. There's plenty of water for the herd now. I told Zack to check the creek in a few hours if the temperature doesn't rise."

Zack Harris was a wrangler, who also taught shooting in the summer. He was a veteran with multiple deployments to Iraq and Afghanistan. Nate fell in step with Ty. "You get the work done before I think to ask."

"I'm the foreman. That's my job."

"You do it well. Too bad my father hadn't listen to you."

Ty's ready smile vanished. His serious face, reserved for

sick animals and wayward sisters, appeared. "Your dad was a fine man. Stubborn as a mule, God rest his soul, Ralph Vaughn did what he thought best for the Bar V5. But I'm thankful you've listened to me. Or at least pretended to hear me."

"I hear you." Nate would not repeat his father's mistakes. If not for Ty, his dad would have lost the ranch and Nate would have never known until it was too late. "And I owe you."

"A paycheck, a room, and a place for my animals are all I need."

Ty put the cattle and horses above everything else, including his own comfort. Nate had moved a cot into the office in the barn when he learned Ty would sleep there if an animal were sick or injured. Ty could have his own cabin or a house at the ranch, too, but he chose a room in the bunkhouse with the wranglers instead.

He shot Nate a sideward glance. "How did the date go?"

"Bad. A text-a-holic."

"You weren't home when we got here."

Nate shoved his gloved hands in his pockets. He wasn't about to lie to his friend. "I stayed in a motel. Alone. Too many beers. Slept through my alarm. Got home later than planned."

"Sorry, bud."

"Yeah, but learned my lesson." The barn doors were open and the four-wheel drive tractor gone. "I'm only dating women I meet in person. Even if their pics look hot."

"Sometimes the hotter the woman, the less interested she is in kids. I'll put up with a lot of crap for that combo."

"This one was nothing but trouble." Not that hot, either. Rachel was more attractive. Nate adjusted his hat, as if the action could turn off that part of his brain thinking about Ty's sister. "Not the good kind of trouble."

"There's only one thing to say when this happens."

"What's that?"

"Next."

Nate laughed. Good advice. Except the next woman he would consider dating was the one woman he didn't dare ask out—Rachel. Mixing business with pleasure would not be a good idea. He would keep looking. New Year's Eve was still a few weeks away.

Ty entered the barn with Dusty trotting next to him.

Nate followed. The smell of hay and manure and tradition hung in the air. Gingerbread might smell like Christmas, but these were the scents of his childhood, of home.

An old black cat named Onyx rubbed against his boot.

Nate scratched behind the cat's ear. "Sure hope this cold spell ends."

"Me, too." Ty suspended the pickaxe between two hooks. "The horses are huddled in the pasture like an ice age is coming. But they'll be running through the snow as soon as the temperature warms up."

Cold weather brought challenges to the ranch, especially when feeding and watering animals. Nate checked the barn cats' water bowl. Full and not frozen. "Bet the cattle were hungry this morning."

"Lined up waiting for the hay to hit the ground." Ty tossed a dog treat and Dusty caught it mid-air. "They know exactly when it's feeding time. Just like this old guy."

As if on cue, the dog barked.

Ty's grin widened. "Damn dog's smarter than me."

"You said it, not me."

Ty's eyes, the same color as Rachel's, brightened. He gave the dog a pat on the head. "See, even the boss agrees with me."

Dusty's tail wagged furiously.

Nate observed more similarities between the Murphy siblings. Same chin. Same forehead. Same head tilt. Maybe if Rachel smiled as readily as her brother, Nate would have guessed they were related. "I met your sister."

"She's a great kid."

"Not really a kid." Behind a wheelbarrow, yellow eyes stared at him. One of the newer feral cats he'd received from the rescue shelter in Bozeman. He reached in his jacket pocket and tossed cat treats to Onyx. Then he threw pieces farther away. One by one, cats dashed out to grab one. "The way you talk about Rachel makes her sound so young. Eighteen or nineteen."

"Twenty-six isn't old."

"I hope not, for our sake." Ty was thirty-four. Nate thirty-three. "I had a taste of her gingerbread. Addictive."

"She's got the touch. Just like my mom had. Though

Rachel can cook too. Wait until you taste the stew she's making us for lunch."

"Lunch?"

"I never cook when she's around. "

"Your choice or hers?"

"Laugh it up, funny guy, but you'll see. The entire crew will be throwing bribes her way so she'll take over the kitchen for good."

"Sounds great."

Ty nodded. "Times like these that make my investment in culinary school worthwhile."

"High outlay for the limited benefit you receive."

He shrugged. "Worth every penny. You'll agree after you eat lunch. And I'm not kidding about the bribes. I hate having her so far away. But every time I bring up the idea of her moving north, she reminds me I'm the one who left. Says I should come back to Arizona."

Nate's ribcage tightened like a belt. "You can't be considering leaving."

"I never thought I would, but after what happened last month..." Ty stared at the dirt floor and shook his head. "Rachel needs me. It's damn selfish for me to stay away."

"Hold on." Nate had no idea what had happened, but nothing warranted Ty moving away. "Think about what you'd be giving up. Vaughn might be the name on the ranch's deed, but you're as much an owner of this place as me. Hell, the livestock belongs to you."

"I know, and we would work something out. But I'm the only family Rachel's got." Ty's ready smile was nowhere in sight. Unfamiliar emotion sounded in his voice. "I raised her after our parents died. I was pretty much all she had before that because of the crazy hours my mom and dad worked. I need to live closer to her. If not the same town, the same state. There are ranches in Arizona. Hot ones, but still..." He tipped his hat.

Ty was the heart and soul of the Bar V5. His dad knew it. So did Nate. "Rachel's here for a few weeks. Show her all Montana has to offer. Maybe she'll fall in love with the place."

"I sure hope so." Ty stretched his shoulders. "I keep thinking if her gingerbread business takes off here..."

"She'd want to stay."

Nate needed to change Rachel's mind about accepting his help. If not, he would help without her knowing. "I'll do what I can to make sure her gingerbread business is a big success. Give her confidence, contacts, a good foundation to go off on her own."

"You'd do that?"

"Damn straight. I'll do whatever it takes to keep you at the Bar V5." Ideas exploded like popcorn in Nate's head. "I'm happy to give you a stake in the—"

"You know how I feel about that," Ty interrupted. "This ranch is your family legacy. The land needs to stay with a Vaughn. I'm fine with our arrangement."

"Except for your sister."

He nodded. "My thinking about leaving has nothing to do with you or the Bar V5. It's all about what's best for Rachel."

Fine. Nate understood doing what was best for someone he cared about. He would do what was best for Ty—convince Rachel staying in Montana was the best thing for her and her brother.

The morning flew. Rachel held the tip of the decorator bag over a stacked gingerbread tree. Each layer, made of a star-shaped cookie, needed frosting.

"I hoped you saved me some."

A glob of green icing spurted from the tip and landed, not on one of the points that needed frosting, but all over.

Darn it. Darn…Nate. She blew out a puff of air.

"Sorry if I distracted you," he said, his voice contrite.

She was a guest in his kitchen and her brother's boss. Ignoring him would be rude. She wiped her face with her forearm. "No biggie. It's fixable."

"Looks like you've been busy."

"I have." She glanced his way, felt the tube of icing slip from her fingers.

Howdy, Cowboy.

Nate leaned against the doorway to the mudroom, one

booted foot crossed over the other. The cold reddened his cheeks. His nose, too. The scruff of whiskers had been shaven off. He looked younger. More approachable. Cute. Ways she never would have imagined him looking this morning.

Her tummy tingled.

His hair was shorter than she expected considering her brother's length, but strands stuck up. His casual stance told her he didn't care about his hair or what anybody thought of him.

Rachel didn't know why she found that so appealing.

"Let me fix the tree for you," he offered.

He removed his jacket. His long sleeved Henley shirt accentuated his V-shaped physique and flat abs. He shouldn't look so tasty.

"No worries." She had enough of to think about with her temperature rising and heart racing. "I've got it under control."

Or would, when she dragged her attention from the faded spots on the front of his jeans.

She gulped. Looked away.

Rachel reached for a spatula. She ran the edge across the gingerbread to remove the icing. She missed some so pressed harder this time. A section fell to the island.

"Looks like I arrived just in time," Nate said.

Her lips tasted dry, tingled. "For what?

"To eat the broken pieces. I'm starving."

He sauntered across the kitchen, six feet of male hotness and charm, heading in her direction like a drone missile locked on a target.

She stepped back, away from the island, unsure if his wolfish grin was coming for the gingerbread—or her. Heaven help her, but she hoped it wasn't her cookies.

Her heart pounded in her throat.

Rachel was used to dealing with her brother's testosterone-fueled swagger, but Nate Vaughn was different. Oh, he and Ty were both male and cowboys and around the same age. But the similarities stopped there.

Nate might look cute with his red cheeks and mussed hair, but the man was as dangerous as a Wild West outlaw. Forget needing a six-shooter. His weapons were his smoldering eyes and killer smile.

Downright smokin'.

She'd faced her brother's wrath after dating a cowboy from the guest ranch where he worked in Wickenburg and having her heart broken when she was seventeen. Granted Nate was also a rancher, innkeeper and venture capitalist, but cowboys chose their independence over love and family. Look at Ty.

She swallowed. "Any gingerbread on a plate or paper towel is up for grabs."

Nate snagged a piece before she could blink. Took a bite. "Good stuff."

She could say the same about him. He reminded her of a piece of chocolate decadent cake, rich and indulgent and mouthwateringly delicious. Good thing she preferred cupcakes.

"Too bad you weren't in Bozeman on Saturday for the annual Christmas Stroll," he continued. "There's a gingerbread contest. Yours would do well. Likely win. Maybe next year."

"Ty will be spending Christmas in Phoenix with me. That's what we usually do."

Nate picked up another piece of gingerbread. "Not this year though."

"Extenuating circumstances."

He raised a brow.

His questioning look meant he would either ask a question, one she might not want to answer, or make up his own mind. Neither appealed to her. "I'm between jobs."

"Hard to believe, given the happy dance in my mouth."

"My job situation has nothing to do with my cooking." Except for her being too good at what she did. She wasn't about to brag or open herself up to more questions. But she didn't want to leave him with a bad impression. For Ty's sake, Rachel told herself. Yeah, right. And crème brûlée had zero calories. "I'd hoped to open my own shop after Thanksgiving, but things… fell through. I'd like to give starting a bakery another go when I get home."

If she made enough money here and the stars aligned and the Arizona Cardinals made the Super Bowl. Otherwise, she would end up working for someone else her entire life, just like her parents. God rest their souls.

She pushed the bleak thoughts aside. Thinking negatively would never help her succeed.

"If you change your mind about wanting help or if you need a business partner, I'm in."

"Business partner?" She sounded as incredulous as she felt. Pamela and Grayson Darby had wanted to be Rachel's business partners, too. Or so they said. All they'd wanted was to stay close so they wouldn't have that far to throw the knife into her back. "You don't even know me."

"I know your brother. Family, remember?"

She focused on the tree, taking apart the layers of cookies so she could start over. "Family doesn't always get along."

"We're getting along."

He couldn't be serious. She looked up at him, trying to see if he was joking. "We've been in the same space for what? Five or ten minutes?"

"Sometimes when you see a golden opportunity, you have to leap."

Gingerbread was not golden. Her hinky-meter buzzed big time. The guy was up to something. "I've leaped before. Felt a lot like base jumping without a wingsuit."

He cringed. "Hard landing?"

"Brutal. Never again."

Nate raised a confident brow. "It'll be different this time."

She knew better than to ask, knew she should change the subject, but curiosity got the better of her. "Why?"

"Because I'm involved."

"Humble."

His you-can-trust-me smile slanted. "That's the last adjective anyone would use for me."

"At least you're honest." Her voice rose on the last word, as if she were asking a question.

"I am. Ask your brother." Nate rested palms on the island. Big hands, rough hands scarred from hard work and manual labor. She couldn't imagine him in a suit sitting behind a desk. "I always carry an extra parachute. If you forget your wingsuit, I've got you covered."

He was saying the right words. Someone else might be

swayed. Charmed. Not her. She no longer made emotional decisions. They were too unreliable. Just like people. Well, except for her brother. "Thanks, but my feet are firmly planted on the ground. No more leaping."

"You look more adventurous than that."

"Looks can be deceiving."

He ate another piece. "You have to admit The Montana Gingerbread Factory has a nice ring to it."

Her mouth dropped open. "We just met and you're naming a company?"

"Not *a* company. *Our* company."

Unbelievable. Though she had to give him props for not giving up. "I live in Phoenix. That name wouldn't work."

"Arizona Gingerbread Factory," he said, without missing a beat.

"I bake more than gingerbread."

"Saguaro Sweets. Desert Desserts. I could do this all day."

Maybe she could bore him so he would go away. Most men weren't into baked goods, unless the sweets were going into their stomachs. "Those names are closer to the business model I have in mind."

He straightened. "Business model?"

"I want to do more than sell baked goods. I want a space big enough to hold events and parties."

He leaned toward her, one hip against the island, an elbow on top. "Tell me more."

Not the blank stare she was hoping for, but that would come shortly. "Groups often put on events to raise money or earn service hours. Lots of possibilities to explore. I also want to hold private parties, making and decorating cookies, cupcakes, or gingerbread houses. Baking is fun no matter your age. It's perfect for birthday parties and showers. An activity and take-home gift in one."

Lines creased his forehead. Almost there. Any moment his eyes would dull, and he'd space out.

"Bridal and baby showers," she added.

That should do it.

He grabbed another piece of gingerbread. "You've put thought into this."

Wait a minute. Nate didn't look or sound bored. He

should have tuned out, turned off, not be attentive and interested.

"Um, yes." She had an entire business plan that was useless. "I'm a baker who wants to do more than work for someone else her entire life."

She'd been on her way.

Before falling like a soufflé.

She would rise again. All she needed was time to regroup and replenish her savings account. Two things she could accomplish in Montana.

Ty burst into the kitchen, his eyes widening at the site of houses covering the island and counters. "Check out all that gingerbread. I hope you had time to make lunch, kiddo. The others are on their way."

"The stew's on the stove. Salad's in the fridge. Bread's in the oven."

Nate motioned to the island. "Gingerbread for dessert."

"Brownies, too," she said.

Ty nodded. "Told ya my little sis would take good care of us."

Rachel picked up a dishtowel and snapped it at her brother. "I'm not little."

"Shorter, then." With a wide grin, he headed toward the bathroom. "I'm going to wash my hands."

"I'll get the table set," she said.

"I'll help." Nate removed plates and bowls from the cupboard before she got the chance. "A home-cooked meal beats a cold sandwich."

She put on oven mitts. "Is that what you usually eat?"

He took flatware from a drawer. "It's self-serve in the winter when we don't have a kitchen staff."

Rachel pulled the bread from the oven. "Don't tell me you're one of those guys who only knows how to boil water, heat cans of soup or chili, and use a microwave."

"Okay, I won't tell you."

She poured the stew into a large serving bowl. "This kitchen seems like overkill if that's the limit of your culinary skills."

He moved closer to the oven, to her. "I didn't say anything about my cooking abilities." He picked up a ladle then handed it to Rachel. "You did."

"I assumed…"

"Assumptions can be dangerous." A mischievous, sexy grin spread across his face.

Her pulse accelerated. She took a step away from him before she dropped the stew.

"Well, you know your way around the kitchen." She needed to keep her distance. He made her heart go pitter-patter too much for Rachel to think getting close to him would work out well for her. "You must cook."

"Yes, but if I had my choice I'd grill everything on a barbecue." He grabbed napkins. "In the summer, the chef and cooks make sure these fancy appliances don't go to waste."

"And during the off-season?"

"They're used, but not often. Which is why you're welcome to the kitchen while you're in town."

Bowl of stew in hand, she followed Nate into the breakfast room to the right of the kitchen. Sunlight streamed through windows that provided a gorgeous view of a snow-covered pasture with mountains in the background. "You really don't mind?"

He set the long wood table. "Not if we're going to get a hot meal at noon."

She placed the stew on the table. "That's the least I can do."

"You've got a deal."

"You haven't tasted lunch yet."

"I trust Ty's judgment."

She headed back to the kitchen. "My brother thinks I'm the next Julia Child."

Nate followed. "Maybe, but he knows I like to eat. He wouldn't lie to me."

She removed the salad from the fridge. Took a step back. Bumped into Nate. The scent of him, dirt and animals, made her think of kissing and rolling around in a hay bale.

Not with any random stranger.

With him.

The image appealed to her more than it should, especially with his lips so close to hers.

Hot and bothered, Rachel shoved the salad bowl at him.

"Put this on the table."

He did.

She sliced the bread, hitting the cutting board with the knife. Better not take her frustrations over Nate out on the loaf of French bread. She grabbed the serving utensils, the plate of brownies, and butter dish. "Looks like we're ready."

Nate carried in a pitcher of milk, one of water, and a carafe of coffee. He surveyed the table. "The boys are going to love this. And you."

"Thanks." She knew better than to date any cowboys. But she could cook for them. "Just so you know, I take menu requests."

Nate pulled out her chair. "How are your oatmeal raisin cookies?"

She sat, liking his manners. "Blue ribbon at the Arizona State Fair."

"How can I say no to award winning cookies?"

She wondered what he would say no to. Or yes...

Strike that. Rachel placed her napkin on her lap. None of her business. She only hoped Nate realized that her baking was none of his.

Chapter Three

The next day, morning chores were completed and Arrow exercised, but Nate was restless. The biggest item on his To Do list needed attention. He saluted the wranglers in the snow-covered pasture. "See you at lunch."

He hopped on his snowmobile with one thought on his mind—Rachel.

The prospect of Ty moving back to Arizona had made for a sleepless night. When Nate decided to turn the Bar V5 into a working dude ranch, Ty wanted to leave. Instead, they'd worked out an arrangement—a partnership. Nate owned the land. Ty provided the livestock, ones he'd purchased from Nate's father when his dad decided to sell off everything and additional animals Ty purchased himself. Nate handled the finances, and Ty ran the operation. A great team. Nate didn't want to run the place on his own.

Ty was the true cowboy, the one who made guests return year after year. He could match a horse to a skittish guest so well they'd miss each other until next summer. He belonged here as much as, maybe more than, Nate.

Thanks to an early morning call with Carson Scott, a friend and school classmate, Nate's plans on how to get Rachel to stay in Montana were coming together. Carson's Christmas tree farm would be the perfect place to sell gingerbread.

Time to kick off Operation: Hansel & Gretel.

Back in his venture capital days, Nate used code names to make eavesdropping on his conversations at meetings or a trendy lunch spot in Palo Alto a useless endeavor. Silicon Valley was full of corporate spies and people wanting insider knowledge of the next hot IPOs and anticipated product releases. He wasn't worried about that here in Marietta, but if Rachel kept shutting down his offers of help, Nate didn't want her to know what he was doing. Just a hunch, but if Rachel found out he was going to make her gingerbread business soar so she'd stay in Montana, she would probably catch the next

MELISSA MCCLONE

flight back to Phoenix and take Ty with her.

Not. Going. To. Happen.

A few minutes later, Nate parked outside the main house. He headed to the mudroom, anticipation building over seeing Rachel and telling her about the tree farm.

Opportunity and possibility.

He would focus on those two things when he spoke with her. Two things that helped him when he returned to the Bar V5 four years ago. Two things that kept Ty from bailing when this place became a dude ranch. Two things that made the Bar V5 a success today.

Helping Rachel meant Ty would not only remain at the ranch, but Nate would be able to repay his friend for all he'd done for his dad and for him. A win-win-win situation. The best kind.

Movement caught Nate's attention. He stopped. Something was in the meadow behind the house. Deer?

He took a closer look. Glimpsed a flash of red.

Not a deer.

Rachel.

A gray hat covered her hair and ears. She wore a black parka with a red scarf and matching gloves. Her jeans were tucked into snow boots. She was making a snowman, one nearly as tall as her.

He walked closer and glimpsed her profile.

A nice pink tinged her cheek.

He'd thought she was pretty yesterday. Today, out here in the fresh air with a smile on her face, she looked beautiful.

Nate sucked in a breath. The cold air stung. He didn't care, didn't want to take his gaze off her.

Standing in front of the snowman, she pushed two pebbles into the face for eyes then stuck a carrot in the center for a nose. She stepped back, surveying her work.

"Aren't you a handsome fella? But something's missing." Rachel removed her scarf and tied the bright cloth around the snowman's neck. "That's better. You'll drive all the snowwomen crazy."

The way she talked to the snowman as if he were Frosty come to life was cute. She sniffled, shook her hands, and tugged on her gloves.

249

Knit gloves, the wrong kind for playing in the snow. But someone who wasn't from around here might not know that.

Nate took a step forward, then stopped. Telling her she needed different gloves wasn't the right tactic, given her independent streak. He'd bring her a pair. Let her see the difference herself.

He sprinted to the house, grabbed gloves from a basket in the mudroom then returned to the meadow. "Nice snowman."

She stiffened, glanced his way then looked back at her snow friend.

"A little lopsided." She stuck sticks into the sides for arms. "But not too bad considering it's been ten years since I last made one."

"Not a lot of snow in Phoenix."

She straightened the scarf. "We had a little in February, a mix of snow, rain and hail. I had to work, so missed out on the fun, though driving to and from the bakery was interesting."

"You worked at a bakery?"

"I was on the before-the-sun-rises, also known as the moonset shift. That's what we called it." She adjusted the snowman's nose. "I also worked as a pastry chef at a restaurant in the evening."

"When did you sleep?"

"Whenever I could."

"Not a lot of time for fun."

She rubbed her hands together. "The hours were hard on my social life, but I had no complaints. I made decent money, enough to save some so I could open my own business."

Nate could provide her with all the capital she needed this time. He'd spent a significant amount of money turning the Bar V5 into a working dude ranch, but had his own fund for investment ventures. He preferred investing locally so he wouldn't have to be away from the ranch.

"Your gloves look soaked." He held up the pair he'd brought out. "These are waterproof. They'll work better when you make the next one."

"Thanks, my hands are kind of cold." Little lines formed above her nose. "But how did you know I wanted to make more than one snowman?"

"I saw how much food you make. You don't seem like a

less is more kind of person."

"I'm not." She struggled to remove her gloves. "But Ty is. He always put my needs ahead of his own."

Not this time, if Nate could stop him. A year from now, Rachel would be living in Marietta, unable to remember what she liked about Arizona. "Let me take off your gloves."

He expected Rachel to say no. She held out her hands instead. A good sign? He hoped so.

Nate peeled off the first glove, then the second. He tossed them on the snow. "These are soaking wet."

She wiggled her pale fingers. "It's not so bad."

"That's what they all say before frostbite sets in." His dad used to carry a handkerchief in his back pocket. Nate wished he had one now. "We need to dry off your hands."

"My scarf."

He wiped her hands with the side not touching the snowman. "That's better, but they're still cold."

"I'm fine."

"Yes, you are." He removed his gloves then tucked them under his arm next to her new ones. "But your hands aren't. Let's warm them up."

"O-kay." She sounded hesitant, anything but okay.

He covered her hands with his. So cold he let go for an instant. "You're fingers feel like popsicles."

Rachel tensed, pulled back slightly. "You're exaggerating."

He rubbed his hands over hers, trying to use the friction and his own body heat to help her hands. "This will be quick and painless."

"I wouldn't be so sure about that," she muttered.

"Relax." Rachel didn't have the soft, pampered skin of some women he knew. His fingers brushed over calluses and rough patches. These were the hands of a worker. His thumb ran back and over what felt like a wide scar. "What happened here?"

"A burn."

"From an oven?"

"Campfire. Making s'mores." She sighed. "I'll never get a job as a hand model."

"No hand model could bake as well as you."

Her gaze met his and sent a lightning bolt of heat crackling through him.

"Thanks," she said, her voice quiet.

Nate didn't know if she meant his compliment or warming up her hands. He didn't care. Not with awareness of this woman zinging through him. "You're welcome."

He liked the smaller size of her hand compared to his. Hers were practical hands, clipped nails with no polish. Hands that kneaded dough and worked magic with icing. Hands that belonged at the ranch, able to do long days of hard work without complaint. Hands that fed stomachs and souls.

Her skin wasn't silky smooth, but warm. He massaged each of her thin, tapered fingers.

"Um, Nate." Her lips parted, her cheeks redder than before. "My hands aren't cold anymore. I'm ready for the gloves."

Crap. He let go of her as if he were holding a scalding branding iron barehanded. How long had he been holding her hands?

Nate held open the gloves, trying to convince himself what he'd been doing was nothing but basic first aid to ward off hypothermia and frostbite.

Rachel stuck her hands inside. She adjusted her jacket sleeves while he put on his gloves. "These are better. I'm glad you stopped by."

Then he remembered his reason for being here. Nate had completely forgotten about Operation: Hansel and Gretel once he'd touched Rachel. Not first aid, foreplay. He shook the thought from his head. Time to focus. "I'm here because I want to talk to you about gingerbread."

She released a slow breath, the condensation hung on the air. The only thing missing was the word *SIGH!* floating inside a dialog bubble. "Do we have to now? I want to build another snowman."

"I can multitask."

"Then let's get started." She dropped to her knees and made a ball of snow. "I want to make a bigger one this time."

Her jacket inched up enough, giving him a nice view of her butt. He could stand here and stare all day except he was supposed to be building a snowman and talking with her.

"Okay, but your jeans are getting wet."

Not that he'd mind warming up her calves, knees, thighs...

"I always bring spare clothes." She rolled the ball in the snow, making it bigger. "Cooking mishaps, snowman making. You never know what a day will hold."

That was for certain. He'd better stop slacking off and make the middle section.

"So you wanted to talk about gingerbread?" she prompted.

"Any orders come in last night?"

"One, but getting the word out about a new business can be challenging. It takes time."

Nate didn't know if she was trying to convince him or herself. "Christmas is less than three weeks away. This is the prime time for gingerbread. What do you think about selling your houses and cookies at a tree farm this weekend?"

Rachel froze. She looked up. "Christmas tree farm?"

Nate nodded.

Emotions flashed across her face. Surprise, excitement, caution, wariness. She pressed her lips together. "I don't need your help."

Replacing the *need* with *want* would be closer to the truth. Too bad. He would help her whether she liked it or not. "Just passing along an opportunity."

"Opportunity?"

The disbelief in her voice made Nate feel like a scam artist trying to con senior citizens out of their social security checks. He didn't like the feeling one bit. He was helping Rachel, not hurting her. "An opportunity to sell your gingerbread during one of the tree farm's busiest weekends."

She sat on her heels, crossing her arms over her chest. "Why are you going to so much trouble to help me?"

Nate felt like he was talking Ty into the dude ranch proposition all over again. Nate knew Rachel was wary of his business interest. He assumed she had good reasons to be so suspicious. He would have to be careful.

"Couple of reasons." Nate rolled his ball of snow. "You bake great gingerbread. Your houses are creative and well done. You could make a killing this Christmas with the right marketing approach."

"The second reason?"

"Ty."

The lines above her nose returned. "What does my brother have to do with this?"

"If not for your brother, the Bar V5, what my father always called our Vaughn family legacy, might belong to someone else. I've tried to repay Ty with both money and land, but…"

"He won't accept anything."

Nate nodded.

"So you want to do something nice for Ty by helping me."

"Yes." Not only beautiful, but also sharp and quick. Nate liked the idea of her sticking around town, too. "Except you keep saying no."

She went back to working on her snowman. "I'm not saying no to be difficult."

"Then say yes."

"It's not that easy."

"Three letters aren't difficult so say."

"It's just…" Her shoulders sagged then she straightened. "Something happened recently in Arizona. Something that makes it hard for me to, um…"

He was tempted to back off—she was private, he respected that—but secrets wouldn't regain a business or keep Ty here. "Hard for you to…"

"Believe what people tell me."

This must be what Ty had mentioned. "What happened?"

She focused on the snowman, but her eyes looked miles, if not states, away. Most likely back in Arizona.

He wanted her to share everything, but at her pace. "If you'd rather not…"

"I want you to know this isn't personal."

He worked on the snowman, ignored the urge to move closer, to lend her a comforting hand.

She moistened her lips, took one deep breath, then another. "Two people I considered good friends, people I admired and worked hard for, offered to help me start my own shop a few months ago. We became business partners. Set our Grand Opening for Black Friday."

"That was a week and a half ago."

She nodded. "They fooled me. They didn't want to be partners. They wanted the business for themselves, including the space I'd found, and ended up stealing everything I'd been planning for years."

Nate had a feeling there was more to the story. One day she might feel comfortable enough to share that with him. "Did you speak with an attorney?"

"Yes, but we'd never signed a contract. Everything was verbal. Their word against mine. Even if I had a way of proving what they'd done, they are so wealthy. I couldn't afford the legal fees to take them to court."

"I'm sorry."

Nate was. He understood Ty's concerns better.

"You can see why I'm wary if anyone offers their help, right?"

"You've got to realize some offers are sincere." He noticed her slight shrug. "Mine is."

Her gaze jerked up to meet his. "Because of Ty."

"And you." Nate meant that. Sure, he wanted Ty to stay, but Rachel was a smart woman with a world of talent. Nate liked having her at the ranch.

Not that he was going to start anything or beg, but yesterday's lunch had been the best off-season meal in years, comparable to summer meals that took a kitchen staff to prepare.

Another shrug.

This was going to be a harder sell than he'd imagined. "You were screwed. It's easy to see why you're reluctant. But hear me out about the tree farm."

"I'm listening."

"This morning I spoke with Carson Scott. We grew up together. He owns a Christmas tree farm. This weekend is his biggest of the year. Big crowds. Well, big for Marietta. They'll be offering sleigh rides to customers. Sage Carrigan, who owns Copper Mountain Chocolates, will sell hot cocoa. I told Carson about your gingerbread. He said you could set up a stand. Sell cookies and your houses."

"You talked to him about me?"

Nate couldn't tell from her tone if she was interested or angry. "Your product seemed a good fit."

"A perfect fit, except..." Those adorable worry lines above her nose returned telling him her brain was trying to figure things out. "I'll need tables, a pop-up tent, lots more supplies to make gingerbread."

Smart women with a workable plan had always been a turn-on. "Sounds like a yes."

"If I can figure out the logistics. Where to get all the stuff I need. How much to bake."

"No worries," he said. "We use tables and tents in the summer. Tell Ty what you need and he can pull them out of storage."

"Only if you let me rent them."

Nate wanted to list the reasons she didn't need to pay, but realized she wouldn't use the tables for free. Fine. He could play this her way. "Sure, if you pay me in baked goods."

"Deal." She bit her lip, making him wonder what she tasted like. Sweet or a little spicy? "I'll need to borrow Ty's truck. Baking supplies will be cheaper in a bigger town."

"Bozeman has a Costco. I have a membership."

"Nate—"

"I have things to buy there myself." So what if he'd shopped there two days ago? He could find something to buy in the warehouse, whether he needed it or not. This was for Ty, even if the idea of spending the afternoon with Rachel appealed to Nate on a gut level. "Make a list of what you'll need. I'll drive you after lunch."

That wariness returned to her gaze. "Don't you have work to do?"

"I have five guys who can cover for me. The winter is our slow season. The priorities are keeping the driveway plowed, the paths shoveled, the animals fed and watered, and the utilities working. We fill the time with maintenance and upgrade projects."

"Okay, then." She stood, wiped the snow off her legs. "I'd better get busy."

"What about your snowman?"

"Later. I have work to do if I'll be away this afternoon."

Nate laughed. Same work ethic as Ty, only Rachel was

better looking and smelled nicer. "You're so much like your brother."

"That's the best compliment you could give me." Her bright-as-Christmas-tree-lights smile made Nate feel warm and fuzzy. "Even if he can be a pain in the butt."

Ty had tried Nate's patience a time or two, but agreeing with her didn't seem wise. His loyalty was to his best friend and partner. Even if the woman in front of him heated him up better than a cup of coffee.

"Thank you for talking to your friend," she added. "This could be the break I needed."

"I have another idea if you're interested in hearing it."

She opened her mouth then closed it. "How about on the drive?"

"You've got yourself a deal."

And though she didn't realize it, she had herself a business partner, too. A silent one.

"You were quiet during lunch."

"It's hard to talk over all you cowboys." Rachel put the last plate into the dishwasher then faced her brother. "You boys have two volumes, loud and louder."

"True, but you were talkative yesterday." Ty's eyes darkened to a stormy green. "What's going on?"

She wiped her hands on a dishtowel, glanced out the window at the snow-covered meadow and sparkling river in the distance. "It really is beautiful here."

"Now I know something's wrong. Tell me what's going on, kiddo."

"Nothing."

"Don't say nothing when there's something."

Ty knew her too well. Of course he did. He was all she had. He'd been there when she'd started her period. When she'd nearly failed Pre-calculus. When she'd been dumped three days before the homecoming dance. When she'd gone against his judgment and kept dating one of his cowboy co-workers only to find out the jerk was cheating on her.

But Ty hadn't been there with the others, especially the

Darbys.

Would he have seen through their lies and fake smiles? She toyed with the towel, twisting the fabric.

"Tell me."

"It's Nate." Rachel didn't know where to begin, but she knew what to leave out—that she thought her brother's boss was a tasty piece of eye candy and she'd gone from freezing to feverish in seconds when Nate rubbed her hands. "He talked to Carson Scott about my selling gingerbread at his tree farm this weekend."

"I know Carson. Nice guy."

"Nate said you could get tables and a pop-up tent out of storage for me."

"Sure, but—" Ty scratched his head "—this sounds like a great opportunity. How come you're not bouncing around with a big smile on your face?"

She ran her teeth over her lower lip. "Nate's driving me to Bozeman this afternoon so I can buy baking supplies."

"Still not getting why you look like a barn cat who missed out on the last mouse instead of one with an overflowing food bowl."

Not missed out, had the mouse stolen right from her mouth. "Nate's going out of his way to help me."

"He's that kind of guy."

"You trust him, right?"

"Completely." Ty's gaze softened. "I know you got burned bad in Phoenix, but folks here are different."

"Accepting Nate's help feels… weird. Wrong." She wrapped her arms over her stomach. "I want to do this on my own."

"You've been doing great on your own, but everyone needs help sometimes." Ty placed his hand on her shoulder. "Nate's a good guy. Honest. Smart, too. I thought turning the Bar V5 into a working dude ranch would destroy it, thought about quitting, but turns out Nate was right. He's the one to ask if you have a question about business."

"You sound certain."

"I am. I trust him with my life and with you."

Rachel knew her brother wouldn't lead her astray, but she couldn't help question Nate's motives. He made her feel warm and safe and smile in spite of herself. No one made her feel like that except Ty, but he was her brother. Nate was a businessman. A nice guy, maybe, but she couldn't shake her misgivings. He reminded her of a firecracker, something to ooh and ahh over and watch explode from a safe distance so she didn't get burned again. "I guess I wouldn't have found out about the Christmas tree farm without Nate."

"That's right." Ty pulled her in for one of his bear hugs. "Everything will be fine, kiddo. Let Nate help you. I have a feeling if you do, you'll make enough money for a lease deposit."

Rachel wanted to believe Ty. But people didn't offer help without wanting something in return. Repaying her brother was one thing, but he could invest in more promising ventures than hers. This had to be about more than gratitude and gingerbread.

Not sex.

Someone wealthy and handsome like Nate could get any woman he wanted. A hardworking baker wasn't high on the trophy wife list. He wanted something else. The question was what.

And would whatever Nate Vaughn wanted be more than she was willing to give?

Chapter Four

The next afternoon, Rachel stood outside the Main Street Diner with Nate, a folder full of order forms pressed tightly against her chest. Something was ringing. She looked around toward the jingling sound. Down the street in front of the bank, a woman dressed in red and wearing a Santa's hat shook a bell in front of a charity's collection bucket.

"I'm so out of my element." Rachel didn't mean the winter weather. "I can't believe I let you talk me into this."

"Come on." Nate wore a black wool coat over his button down shirt and slacks. He'd left his cowboy hat in the truck, but the gingerbread creations he held in a box looked out of place. "You thought canvassing businesses was a great idea yesterday."

"I did." On their drive back from Bozeman, he'd shared his idea. Giving businesses gingerbread replicas of their storefronts in return for them displaying her order forms had sounded brilliant at the time. She'd spent the evening baking and this morning perfecting each miniature shop, but now the prospect of rejection made her nerves as taut as wire cutters. She loosened her grip on the folder and wiggled her fingers. "I wasn't thinking straight. I was caught up in a flurry of excitement."

The wicked gleam in his eyes sent a shiver shooting through her. He cocked a brow. "I excited you."

Yes, but Rachel would die before she admitted that. She'd been trying to take Ty's advice to heart and let Nate help her. Yesterday afternoon, that had worked.

Talking during the drive, shopping at the warehouse, every minute she'd spent with him yesterday had been exhilarating. She'd never shopped with a man who wasn't family or a cook. Had no idea that mundane activities like loading bags of flour and sugar onto a cart and chatting in the checkout line could feel so much like a date.

She must have misread his intentions, her chronic

problem tripping her up again. Because Nate's raised eyebrow suggested he was joking around with her, making fun of her or trying to annoy her. Maybe all three. Like a friend of her brother's. She gave him a drop-it-now look. "I'm talking about buying supplies."

He staggered back. "And here I thought I was more than your driver and baggage carrier."

"Don't forget cart pusher," she teased.

"I need to push you right through the diner's door."

His lighthearted tone told Rachel he was kidding, but the courage she'd mustered on the drive from the Bar V5 to Marietta had shriveled like a rotten grape, leaving her insides trembling. Her stomach churned, clenched, and churned again.

"I don't think I can do this." Her voice sounded breathy, barely above a whisper.

"Why not?"

Her feet felt glued to the pavement. The queasiness in her tummy intensified with each passing second.

"I…" She stared inside the diner. Customers sat at tables, eating and drinking and laughing. A waitress dressed in black carried plates full of food. A dark blonde in a long, patterned skirt and black sweater answered the phone. Nothing strange or out of the ordinary as far as restaurants went. But a spider web of apprehension made Rachel feel like the diner's entrance led to the underworld of doom. "I'm a baker. I don't have a head for business. It's one thing to push sweets and treats when I'm standing behind the counter, but to go in and do a hard sell…"

Nate shifted the box to one hand then touched her shoulder, a comforting gestures, something Ty would do. Except this felt different. Not brotherly. More boyfriendly.

Her throat tightened.

Nerves were one thing, but the concern in Nate's eyes did funny things to her tummy. Butterfly things. Things she wasn't used to feeling and didn't want to feel.

Maybe Ty was right when he'd said starting a business was insanity. Maybe she was insane, had lost her mind, somewhere between taking off from Phoenix International Airport and landing in Bozeman.

Nothing else could explain what she was feeling for a guy she'd known three days.

Had to be insanity, right?

"You're a baker, a salesperson, and a businesswoman." Nate squeezed, a gentle pressure that soothed and gave her strength. "You know how to bake. Now you're learning a new way to market your talent. This is a new territory for you. I have no doubt you'll succeed." His words made her feel all gooey inside, like melted chocolate chips. "You need to believe it, too."

"I want to believe, but I keep thinking about the couple in Arizona."

"The couple that screwed you over?"

She nodded. "I wasn't sure if I knew enough about starting a business so that's why I wanted their help. Pamela said my recipes weren't quite there yet and Grayson questioned whether the health department would allow a decorate-your-own-sweet-treat bar in the shop."

"I thought they stole your ideas and recipes."

Rachel nodded.

"They were messing with your head. Making you doubt yourself so you'd think you needed their help. They sound like a pair of master manipulators who have done this before. Put the past behind you and move on. They taught you a lesson: trust wisely and believe in yourself, in your vision."

His words made what happened sound like no big deal, that her confidence hadn't been scrubbed away with a scouring pad.

She fought the urge to lean closer to Nate, as if less distance would allow some of his courage to transfer to her. "I need to believe."

He touched his forehead to hers and sent those butterflies fluttering inside and outside and upside down. "Say it again."

She could barely breathe. "I-I need to believe."

His breath was warm and minty against her face. Her lips.

"Again," he said.

Inches separated his mouth from hers. "I need to, uh, believe."

Breathing would be good. Thinking, too.

"Again."

She pulled away, but he tightened his hold on her shoulders.

"Is this some ninja cowboy mind trick?" Maybe with more distance between him and the guys if he tried this at the ranch.

"Just say it."

"I need to believe."

"Once more."

She took a deep breath. "I believe."

He backed away. "Now we do this."

Rachel hadn't figured out Nate, but so far he was proving himself to be as good a guy as her brother claimed. He could have kissed her, if he'd wanted. She wouldn't have said no, and she had a feeling he knew that. That would have mortified her but she was already on edge. No time for being a sissy about a guy knowing she liked him.

"I'm a fan of your motivational style. I do feel calmer. Does it work with all women?"

He blinked. "It didn't work with my ex-fiancée."

"What happened?"

"Long story." He glanced from Rachel to the diner. "After we've finished, I'll tell you the lowlights."

"Sounds tragic."

"Not really, but if that'll get you inside…"

"Okay, okay."

"You're still not moving."

He pressed his hand against the small of her back. In spite of the layers of clothing and her jacket, she could feel his hand. His touch comforted, but also unsettled her.

Rachel stepped forward, and his arm fell away. "I'm moving now.

She missed his touch. Total insanity.

Nate opened the door. "Inside."

Rachel took a deep breath. She'd lost her dream to the Darbys. There wasn't much left to lose.

She glanced at Nate. At least she hoped not.

An hour and a half later, Nate opened the toy store's door. Rachel breezed past him with a bounce to her step, an empty file folder in hand, and the biggest smile he'd seen all afternoon. He followed Rachel outside, stopping on the sidewalk outside the ice cream shop.

"I'm in shock," Rachel said, her face flushed.

"And you claimed to be nervous. You nailed every sales pitch."

Rachel spun around, the bottom of her beige jacket flaring. "They all said yes. The diner, the kids' clothing store, Café Java, the photo studio—"

"And the flower shop and toy store want to sell your decorate-it-yourself kits." He liked seeing her so happy, expressing her passion, looking to him for encouragement before talking to business owners. "You did it."

She stopped twirling. Gratitude shone in her eyes. "We did it. Without you, none of this would have happened."

"We make a good team."

Rachel nodded once.

Warmth balled at the center of Nate's chest then spread outward. Admitting they worked well together must've been hard for Rachel. Independence was her shield. "This is only the beginning."

Another nod. She chewed on her lip.

He wanted to wrap his arms around her and kiss away her uncertainty. But if he did that she would bolt. So he brushed stray hairs that had fallen out of her ponytail off her face instead. Ignored how soft the strands felt against his fingers. Pretended his pulse wasn't stampeding like a herd of bison on the plain.

Hard to do with her right in front of him, all he would have to do was dip his head and brush his mouth over hers.

He knew all the reasons why he shouldn't…couldn't, but his heart thudded, a booming annoyance. One taste would shut it up. He hoped.

Rachel's gaze locked on his. Her lips parted slightly. Full, pink lips that likely tasted sweeter than the fudge she'd made earlier.

Kiss me.

Hell, he could almost hear her saying the words.

Talk about tempting and the perfect way to celebrate their success today.

Do it.

The devil on his shoulder urged him on. Nate wanted to, oh, how he wanted to kiss Rachel until they needed to come up for air or they passed out.

Kiss her.

He would. Except...

Rachel wasn't leaning in or moving to kiss him. She was beginning to trust him. He didn't want to blow it.

Unless she gave him a clear invitation, something unmistakable, Nate had to back off. He couldn't be caught up in the moment unless he was sure. He'd never once had the urge to kiss any of the start-up founders he'd worked with as a venture capitalist. No matter how good the news or how much money they made.

This was different. She was different.

Still he couldn't kiss her. Forget Rachel giving him a sign. He couldn't kiss her without betraying his friend.

Ty was the reason Nate was helping Rachel. Ty would not want Nate kissing his sister or her kissing anyone. Rachel was a desirable woman, but Nate couldn't jeopardize his friendship and working relationship with her brother.

Not for a kiss.

Nate let go of her hair and lowered her arm. "Don't tell me you're not a salesperson. You had a 100% close rate."

She tapped the toes of her boots as if wanting to dance except they were standing on a sidewalk and the only music was a bell ringing down the street. "I still can't believe it."

"You were impressive, sweetheart."

A honk sounded. He glanced over his shoulder. Driving down Main Street, a pickup truck slowed. Brock Sheenan, a widowed rancher with a large spread in Paradise Valley, waved. Nate acknowledged his friend.

"Do you know everybody in Marietta?"

"It's a small town, and I grew up here. You see a lot of the same faces, though there are new ones." Nate thought he'd feel her out about Montana. "Like yours."

"I'm just here for Christmas."

Too soon. He'd back off. "We're glad to have you here for

Christmas. And your gingerbread."

"You have a one-track mind."

"I know what I want." Operation: Hansel and Gretel was coming together faster than he'd anticipated. She would change her mind about staying in Marietta once she saw how much money she could make with her gingerbread. "Go after it."

"I thought that's what I'd been doing until today. I have a lot to learn."

"You're catching on fast." He motioned across the street to the Main Street Grill. "Hungry?"

"Yes, but Ty—"

"Can fend for himself." No cars were coming so he grabbed Rachel's hand and crossed the road. "You deserve a night off from cooking."

"I do, don't I?"

Nate opened the door to The Main Street Diner, the place where they'd started this afternoon. "After you."

She sashayed into the diner, overflowing with confidence and attitude. Yes, he was attracted, and damn if he hated not doing anything about it. Nate followed her inside.

The smell of basil and rosemary lingered on the air. Two men, realtor Tod Styles and deputy Scott Bliven, stared at Rachel with appreciative glances. She didn't notice the male attention. She seemed more interested in surveying the pictures and knickknacks hung on the brick walls.

That didn't deter the men.

Nate balled his hands. Looking wasn't against the rules. He'd been doing the same thing when he was with her, but the guys needed to stick their tongues back in their mouths and try to be subtle. No wonder Ty got upset if any of the wranglers mentioned Rachel outside the context of her cooking.

Feeling territorial, Nate moved closer to Rachel, so close his leg touched hers.

She stiffened.

"Making room for others." Except no one else was near the hostess stand waiting for a table. Maybe she wouldn't notice. He liked the way she smelled—vanilla and sandalwood.

266

"The décor of this place is interesting," she said. "Welcoming."

Paige Joffe, the diner's new owner, a young widow from California, led them to a table. Her skirt swished around her black leather boots. "Welcome back. Ty's favorite is the Bison Burger with Parmesan fries, if your tastes are anything alike, Rachel. "

Nate pulled out Rachel's chair. "Annie was busy when we were here earlier. I haven't seen her in years. Is she working tonight?"

"She is. I'll send her over." Paige handed them menus then walked toward the kitchen.

"How is not seeing someone possible in a town this size?" Rachel asked.

"Annie's been living on the east coast for the last ten years or so." He sat across from Rachel. "She arrived around Thanksgiving time."

Rachel glanced over the menu before looking up with surprise. "Call me a city girl, but I expected variations on steak and eggs, not cedar-plank salmon with asparagus and couscous."

"I told you about assumptions being dangerous."

A blush spread across her cheeks. "I know."

"Marietta might be a small town, but we've got some real gems, including this place. You can count on great food and service."

"Compliments are always welcome here." Annie Prudhomme greeted them with a big smile. She placed glasses and a carafe of water on the table. "Good to see you, Nate. It's been a long time."

"Too long." Her blond hair had returned to its natural brown, the color he remembered her having in school. "I was talking to Carson about that yesterday."

Annie wrung her hands together. "You talked to Carson?"

Nate nodded. "How's it feel to be back in Marietta?"

"A little strange, but I'm adjusting."

Her troubled gray eyes contradicted her words. But Nate understood. Annie had been the one who couldn't wait to escape this small town. Being back would be difficult after living in New York. "How's the ranch?"

"The same." Her smile wavered slightly. She looked at Rachel. "Who's your friend?"

"Rachel Murphy," Nate introduced them. "She's new in town."

"I'm visiting my brother Ty for the holidays," Rachel clarified. "He works at the Bar V5."

Annie's gaze narrowed. "You're the gingerbread maker."

"How'd you know?" Rachel asked.

"I saw you speaking with Paige earlier, but I must have missed Nate." Annie glanced at the gingerbread house sitting on the hostess stand. "You do a wonderful job. Creative choice of colors and candy. Love the textures and details. The little white lights are the perfect accent. Sorry, I used to be an interior designer."

"Please, don't apologize," Rachel said. "I welcome compliments, too."

You're beautiful, smart and sexy as hell. Probably not what she was looking for, Nate realized.

Annie leaned closer. "A few customers picked up order forms on their way out. I'm taking one. I know a kid named Evan who would have fun with a do-it-yourself kit."

"Thanks." Rachel sat taller in her seat. "Today seems to be my lucky day."

He was the lucky one. Rachel had such a great smile.

"Would you like to orders drinks while you look over the menu?" Annie asked.

With drink orders placed and a few minutes later, dinner ordered, Nate took a sip of his beer.

Rachel leaned forward. The neckline of her sweater gaped, giving him a peek of white lace and creamy skin.

That kind of looking would get him into trouble. He drank more.

"So do I get to hear the lowlights of your love story now?" she asked in a lighthearted tone.

Nate choked, nearly spewed beer all over the table, but managed to force the beer down. He wiped his mouth with his napkin. "I thought you forgot about that."

"Memory like an elephant's." She tapped the side of her head. "So…"

He hated this story as much as he hated living it. But he wanted her confidences. He would have to cough up his own. "Four years ago, I was living in Palo Alto. I had a great job, worked crazy hours and spent any free time with my girlfriend Marissa."

"Sounds like a perfect life."

"I thought so, until I got a call from your brother."

Her nose crinkled. "Ty?"

"Yeah, my dad's health and mind had deteriorated more than I knew. He was making bad decisions, crazy ones no one who knew about ranching would make. Ty was doing all he could, buying livestock and hay with his own money, but then he learned my dad had taken out loans using the ranch as collateral. No one knew where the money went. Ty asked me if he should look for an assisted living apartment for my parents because the debt was too deep. The bank was going to foreclose."

Rachel inhaled sharply. The glass of Pinot Noir her hand wobbled. She steadied it with her other palm. "That's horrible."

"Yeah." Nate stared into his beer, remembering the guilt and frustration he'd felt waiting to board his flight to Bozeman. "I arrived the next morning. By afternoon, I knew I'd have to move back to Montana and take my dad's place, and even that might not be enough to save the Bar V5."

"Here you go." Annie placed a cutting board with slices of bread and a dish of whipped butter in the center of the table. "I'll be back with your salads."

"Thanks." Rachel watched Annie walk away then looked at Nate. "Did Marissa stay in California?"

"No, she came to Montana." An image of a diamond in a platinum setting popped into his mind. "I wanted her to know I was serious about our relationship, so I proposed. She said yes. But the ranch was too remote and rugged for her tastes. She was ready to leave after three days."

"The Bar V5 isn't rugged." Rachel made a face like the thought was ridiculous before she sipped her wine. Adorable. She might call herself a city girl and think she belonged in the desert oasis of Phoenix, but deep inside her was a mountain and plain. Rugged was reserved for a cabin deep in the woods without power and indoor plumbing. The idea of getting her into one and under a pile of quilts…"

Don't go there.

"This was four years ago." He grabbed a slice of bread, bypassing the butter. Adjusted in his seat, his body thinking about being under those quilts with her. Forced himself back to the grim story about Marissa. "I've done significant remodeling. Added guest cabins. The ranch house is almost brand new. All the rooms have private baths. The mini-suites have fireplaces and king-sized beds."

Beds. He shifted again.

This wasn't a date, but he was desperate to touch his dinner companion. Consume. The contrast to Marissa was remarkable. She hadn't asked one question about the ranch beyond, "How much longer do we have to stay?"

"Your fiancée couldn't see the potential?"

"Not really." A new SUV and a credit card he paid for bought him three more weeks. "She broke up with me and flew back to the Bay Area before a month had passed."

"Her loss."

"Nice of you to say."

Rachel set her glass on the table then took a piece of bread. "It's the truth."

"I was sorry to see her go, but there was so much work to do and panic about losing the place, I didn't miss the stress. A month later, she asked me to come back to California, but that was never going to happen. By then I loved the ranch more than her." If he'd even loved her at all. "Sorry if you were expecting sordid and all you got was boring."

Rachel lathered the piece with butter, not seeming to be worried about cholesterol or calories. He liked that.

"Boring is better sometimes."

"What about you?" Nate wanted to know more about her. "Do you have a boyfriend?"

She toyed with the napkin on her lap. "No."

His question made her uncomfortable. That intrigued him. "There's got to be more than to it than no."

Rachel shrugged. "My hours make dating anyone not in the food service industry difficult. Even then it's hard with a brother watching out for you, even from Montana. But I've gone out with a couple guys. The most recent was a sous chef."

"I bet you made beautiful meals together."

She half-laughed. "We did, until he met the restaurant owner's daughter and the two eloped to Laughlin, Nevada. He now has his own café."

"Financed by his father-in-law."

She nodded. "He wasn't stupid. I'm not, either. I turned down a job offer to work for him. But please don't tell Ty. He thinks I'm too young to date let alone have a serious relationship with yet another loser. His words, not mine, though he's been right."

"You're his younger sister. He feels protective."

She ate a bit of her bread then wiped her mouth. "I know, but not talking about dating makes things easier for both of us. He threatened to send me to a convent when I was seventeen."

Nate leaned forward, interested to hear the story behind that. "What'd you do?"

She straightened. Frowned. "What makes you think I did anything?"

"A convent isn't your typical boarding school for problem teens."

"Okay," she relented. "It wasn't that big a deal. I sneaked out on a few dates with a wrangler who worked with Ty at a guest ranch in Wickenburg."

"How old was this cowboy?"

Her cheeks reddened. "Nineteen. Maybe twenty."

Nate whistled. "Is the cowboy still able to walk?"

She nodded. "Ty punched him after he found out we kept dating after he told us to stop. I didn't feel too bad about that after I found out the guy had been cheating on me the entire time."

"Your brother must've had his hands full with you."

"Sometimes." She ran her finger along the stem of her wine glass. "But I was pretty good considering…"

Considering the way she lost her parents so young, she must've been a near angel. Some kids would have fallen apart. But she and Ty had gotten stronger. Another reason Nate admired them.

Another reason not to piss off his friend.

Nate took a sip of beer. He needed to write those words on a napkin or his hand.

She stared into her wine glass. "I tease Ty that he doesn't want me to get serious because he's terrified at having to wear a tuxedo and walk me down the aisle"

"Most cowboys don't like to dress up like a penguin."

She looked up at Nate. "What about you?"

"I don't mind, but I'm more a rancher than a cowboy. I own a tux from my VC days. But Marietta doesn't have many black tie events. A wedding every once in a while."

Rachel leaned forward. "Ever have a wedding at the ranch?"

"No. Someone mentioned it once. Just never happened."

A wistful expression crossed her face. "The Bar V5 would be a perfect location for a wedding. I've seen pictures of it during summer."

"Maybe if we put up a big tent on the lawn."

Her mouth gaped. "Or the great room for a small ceremony in winter. The ranch is beautiful with all the snow. You should stay open all year."

"The horses need a rest after a long summer."

"Do you need to use the horses in the winter? There are lots of other activities in the area. Skiing, snowshoeing, snowmobiling, ice climbing…"

"For someone new to the state, you know a lot about Montana."

"Ty's been playing tour guide."

Doing his part as Nate was doing his. "I've thought about staying open during the winter months. But what we're doing works for now."

"And gives you the time to help strangers make money instead of making it yourself."

An odd mixture of caution and curiosity laced her words, not quite a flashing red light, but she was still wary. He would have to work harder to gain her trust. "You're family. And I like helping others make money. Most people wouldn't consider that a vice."

"I don't," she admitted. "Not when I'm the lucky recipient."

"You worked hard to get all those business owners to say

yes. Luck was not involved today."

"Maybe not, but I do know one thing that was lucky."

"What?" he asked.

"Meeting you." She lifted her glass in the air.

He tapped his against hers. A chime lingered in the air. "I feel the same way about meeting you."

"I know I said I didn't want any help, but thank you." Her gaze met his, making him feel unworthy of such appreciation. "Whether orders pour in or not, I put myself out there and gave it my best shot."

"You did." Something passed between them. A connection, an invisible thread. He should look away, but he didn't, couldn't. "As I said this afternoon, today's only the beginning."

The lines above her nose, ones that had been absent most of the day, returned.

Damn. He didn't want her to go all flashing-yellow-caution on him. "Remember the Christmas tree farm this weekend."

"Oh, right."

But she didn't feel right. He could see it in the lines around her mouth, her cloudy gaze and her rigid posture.

Maybe he could get her to lower her guard. "What we did today was only one idea."

Rachel's chin tilted. "You have more?"

"Lots more." He took a sip of his beer. "If you're game…"

She scooted back in her chair. Pressed her lips together. Shut down. "Let's see how much business I get from the order forms and tree farm first."

"Sure." He had his work cut out breaking through her cautious firewall. "But one of these days, Rachel, you're going to want to leap. I plan on being around to see it."

"Don't hold your breath."

"I won't."

But Nate didn't think he'd have long to wait.

Once Rachel recovered her confidence, he knew she would fly.

Chapter Five

Saturday at the Carson Tree Farm, Rachel watched tiny
snowflakes fall from the sky, the humble beginning of a
massive winter storm forecasted to hit the mountains of
Montana this week. A steady stream of cars, trucks and SUVs
brought those on their annual Christmas tree pilgrimage.
Children ran, laughing and kicking up snow. Carolers sang,
taking requests and encouraging everyone to join in.

Merry Christmas, Copper Mountain.

She stood underneath the pop-tent, hands dry and toasty,
waiting for a customer to decide if they wanted cookies or a
gingerbread house. Garland decorated with candy canes and
gingerbread ornaments hung from the edges of the canopy.
Red tablecloths covered the tables that held her gingerbread
houses and cookies.

Surrounded by pine trees and delicate snowflakes, Rachel
felt more holiday spirit than she ever had in Phoenix. But the
change in scenery didn't explain her happiness. This
Christmas was going to be the best since she was a kid, not
because of her gingerbread's popularity or the beautiful
mountain location or the song-worthy wintry weather, but
because of the people who lived in and around Marietta. The
hellos and hugs from the customers bumping into friends and
family looking at trees touched her heart.

Life in a small town.

Rachel hadn't expected such joy in the air and on faces
today. No matter where she looked, she was surrounded by
Christmas and she loved every single minute.

Back home in Phoenix, houses and apartment balconies
would be decorated with lights and stockings hung. But she
didn't remember the last time she'd talked with a neighbor.
She had friends, the kind to grab a drink after work, but not
the kind who would notice her gloves were soaked.

Or buy her pretty new ones to wear today.

"We'd like a dozen cookies." A twenty-something

woman handed over cash. A sleeping toddler, a girl, based on the pink snowsuit, slept against the woman's shoulder. A little boy in blue tugged at her pants. "Six angels and six men. A do-it-yourself kit, too."

Rachel gave the woman her change. "I'll box the cookies. It'll just take a minute."

"While you do that, we're going to grab a hot chocolate." Scooping up the toddler with impressive grace, the woman walked to the end of the line at Sage Carrigan's hot chocolate booth. The mom would need help juggling the cups and the gingerbread boxes, but Rachel had no doubt someone would help.

The smile on the chocolatier's face matched Rachel's elation. Business was booming, and it was only noon. Brisk morning sales meant she'd covered the cost of supplies two hours ago. Everything else she made today and tomorrow would be profit, money she could put toward a lease deposit. She wiggled her toes with excitement.

Rachel had one person to thank—Nate.

Thoughts of him sent a burst of heat through her veins, warming her insides better than thermal underwear.

Nate had been on her mind a lot lately. Like an undertow, pulling her where she didn't mean to go. She'd fallen asleep thinking about him. Dreamed of him, from the way she'd twisted her sheets. Woke up wondering whether he'd stop by for coffee and a muffin. Slide his cute backside onto the counter. Look at her in the way that turned her knees gooey as bread dough.

He'd been nice and polite at the diner the other night, building her up and treating her like someone who managed her own world, but his words and glances made Rachel wish they had been on a date. That they were...

Together.

That freaked her out.

Enough she hadn't wanted to hear Nate's other ideas about her gingerbread. She liked being the center of his attention and wanted...more.

Stupid, stupid, stupid.

Focusing on opening a bakery these past months had turned her into a swooning female as soon as a handsome guy, who knew how to coax her into doing what he wanted with the skill of a horse whisperer, came near.

Pathetic.

Rachel placed twelve cookies onto tissue paper inside a white bakery box.

She needed balance in her life. Affection. Attachments. Even annoyance, like the way Ty bragged about her cooking to everyone who'd listen when she was just making oatmeal or soup. She wanted friends who would greet her with hugs if she bumped into them at a Christmas tree farm rather than a cool *hey* at a club. Food service employees came and went quickly. A few stayed, but she hadn't formed any deep friendships, the kind she saw here in Marietta. The kind she wanted.

Her fault, she realized with a start. She'd always been working toward the next thing—culinary school, a better job, her bakery. Maybe that was why she'd ended up dating stupid jerks who took advantage of her. Or fell for smooth-talking friends who betrayed her.

She tied a candy-cane-striped bow around the package then set the box on top of a decorate-your-own gingerbread house for the woman who returned with the sleeping child and a cup of hot cocoa. A man with pine needles on his jacket carried the boy, who held his own cocoa.

"I'll take those," the man said.

Just as Rachel expected. Just as she wanted for herself someday.

She handed over the gingerbread. "If you have any questions, my phone number and email address are on the instructions. Have a very Merry Christmas."

Watching the four of them head to the parking area brought a pang to her heart.

They reminded her of her family. The last time they'd been together had been sixteen years ago. She missed her parents and hated that the memories weren't as clear as they used to be. But she made the time to visit them at the cemetery. At least once a week.

But Mom and Dad wouldn't want Rachel to be sad on a day like today. They would want her to smile and enjoy herself.

She would.

Humming along to "Deck the Halls," a favorite Christmas carol, she set out more cookies and added another do-it-yourself kit to the empty spot on the front table.

"So is that how it works?"

The familiar sound of Nate's voice gave Rachel chills, ones that had nothing to do with the cold mountain air or falling snowflakes. She glanced up.

He stood on the opposite side of the table looking way too hot on this cold day. Her gaze ran the length of him, from his wool hat to his jeans hugging muscular thighs, making her want to touch them and see if they were as firm as they looked. "What works?"

"Making a guy purchase a gingerbread house to get your number. Well done. Every single man in Marietta will buy one."

"Very funny."

"You think I'm kidding."

"You are." She straightened one of the decorated gingerbread samples. "I have an older brother. I know when I'm being teased."

The carolers burst into a spirited version of "Jingle Bells." Twin girls, dressed in matching purple parkas, snow pants and boots, jumped up and down while their parents filmed them with smartphones.

"I know a few things, too," he said. "It's time for you to take a break and have lunch."

She'd been standing since arriving at seven o'clock this morning. Her only food had been cookies and Sage's delicious hot cocoa. "I forgot to bring a lunch."

"Of course you did. You were focused on work." Nate raised a cooler. "Lunch patrol to the rescue."

Rachel stared dumbfounded. "You made me lunch?"

"Seems fair, given you make us lunch." He sounded casual, like he didn't have chores to do and half a dozen businesses to check. She'd been watching him closely. He didn't have free time.

Guilt's nasty fingers poked at her. "My making lunch was part of our deal for using your kitchen. This—"

"Is, too."

His smile and bright eyes said he was happy to be here. The guilt crept away, replaced by... wonder. No one ever made her lunch. She'd been making her own lunch for as long as she could remember, before her parents died and after Ty took over. "Th-thanks."

One of the Scott brothers, Hudson, carried a tree to the parking area. Rachel took a closer look. Oops. That was the younger one named Trey. She recognized his Santa hat. Three children followed him like he was Jolly Old St. Nicolas in the flesh.

"Ty and Zack offered to man the booth while you eat. They're checking out a couple of carolers with RJ MacCreadie. They decided that's better than fighting over who gets to ask Harley Diekerhoff out."

The name wasn't familiar, but she'd met so many people today she couldn't keep everyone straight. "Who is that?"

"Brock Sheenan's new housekeeper and cook," Nate said. "She moved here from California. A real looker."

Rachel wondered if Nate wanted to ask her out. The thought made her stomach clench and her curiosity go on high alert.

Don't ask.

Even if she was dying to know. She focused on the ice chest, looking for a distraction.

"You're hungry," Nate said, thankfully misreading her. "I'll grab the boys."

"It's okay. I can wait."

"But...?"

But I'm thinking about you. She pushed the thought aside. "What do you mean by 'but?'"

"Whenever you're thinking about something or worried, little lines form above your nose."

She touched her face. "I don't feel anything."

"The lines are there. What is it?"

The way he could read her so well bothered Rachel. A person should be able to keep her lustful, hopeful, insane thoughts to herself. They'd known each other only a few days. Her discomfort increased tenfold. "You keep going out of your way for me. I get helping me sell gingerbread because of Ty, but lunch..."

"Can't you just say thank you?"

"I said thank you."

"Okay, you did," Nate admitted. "Why does there have to be a reason? Can't a person do something nice? It's Christmas. The season of giving." He studied her. "You don't seem like the bah-humbug type."

"I'm not. I love the holidays, but I'm—"

"Cautious. Skeptical. Suspicious."

Scared. She added two more cookies from the container of extras to the table. "You make me sound paranoid."

He gave her a look.

She raised her hands. "Okay, maybe I am."

"Not that I blame you, except when it comes to me."

"That makes you sound like the fox in the henhouse."

He winked. "You are a chick."

Rachel imagined most breathing females, married or single, would call Nate Vaughn a fox. He qualified, though she preferred the term hottie in spite of the falling snow and below freezing temperature. "I shouldn't encourage you."

"Too late."

"Too late for what?" Ty asked, approaching the booth.

Zach Harris was at her brother's side. "I hope we're not too late for cookies. The ones you left at the ranch are... gone." He threw a nasty look at Ty.

Rachel ignored it, but the flattery these guys heaped on her cooking built her confidence. She'd smiled more this week than in the entire year before. She motioned to the plastic containers on the back table. "Take your pick, Zack. And thank you for—"

"You're going to be selling the cookies and houses that took hours for Rachel to create," Nate addressed Ty and Zach with a firm voice. "Not stuffing your faces. Got it?"

Ty snagged a gingerbread angel, then reached into his pocket and tossed a dollar on the table. "Sure thing, boss. Looks like business is good, sis."

"No complaints," she said.

Zack eyed a cookie. "We'll sell tons of stuff."

She handed him an angel to eat. "The price list is on the back table along with extra stock, supplies, and the cash box. If someone buys cookies, pick them up with the tongs, wrap them in tissue paper and put them into a white box. Tie a ribbon around it."

Zach frowned. "No one mentioned anything about ribbon tying. Only gingerbread. And snow bunnies." He shot another evil look at Ty.

What was it with these two?

Ty rolled his eyes. "I'll tie the ribbons. I've tied enough in Rachel's hair."

"That was years ago," she said.

"Doesn't seem that long ago." Ty moved behind the table. "You must be hungry if those are the only instructions you're giving us."

She placed her hands on her hips. "So one of you thinks I'm paranoid, and the other thinks I'm bossy."

Zach made the timeout sign. "I'm staying out of this one. I had to make my own lunch today. I'm not used to that since Rachel came. I'm mentally and physically exhausted."

"Yes, you're bossy." Ty didn't spare his buddy a glance. "But only when something matters to you. Go eat. Zach and I have everything under control."

"Damn straight we do." The cowboy grinned. "Especially the cookies."

She took a step back toward her booth. "Maybe—"

"Nope." Nate took her arm. "They only need to be told once. You're coming with me."

Rachel found herself being pulled past the tree shaker machine, the twining machine and the long line for a ride in a quaint, horse drawn sleigh driven by Carson. The horse, a pretty chestnut mare named Star, wore bells.

In between a line of trees decorated with multicolored lights, she glimpsed tables. A family sat at one drinking cocoa and eating her cookies. "I didn't know there was a picnic area."

"You haven't had a chance to walk around."

"It's been busy this morning."

"Good thing you've got me to show you." He led her through the trees then placed the cooler on one of the empty tables. "Sit."

Rachel did, because having someone else make her meal was a treat she was determined to savor. "What's on the menu?"

Nate removed a plastic container and spoon. "Chili."

"One of my favorites."

"I know. I asked Ty."

Rachel didn't want to be impressed, but she was. She was also starving and would rather eat than question Nate. She removed the lid and dug in.

"It's not homemade," he said.

"Doesn't matter." The chili heated her from the inside out. "Tastes great. Perfect for a winter day like today."

He handed her a rectangle wrapped in aluminum foil. "Cornbread. I made it with a mix. Added can of jalapenos. Yours is better."

"Don't be so sure of that." Mix or not, cornbread—the entire lunch—took effort.

Thought.

Her chest tightened. A lump burned in her throat. Nate made her feel so special. This whole day—trip, really—had been one gift after another. Rachel unwrapped the cornbread, focusing on the foil to keep herself from crying or gushing over him. She noticed had had no lunch in front of him. "Aren't you eating?"

"I ate at the ranch, but I'll keep you company."

A thrill shot through her. "If you have to be somewhere…"

"I don't."

Good. She liked his company. They'd eaten other meals together. She took a bite of the cornbread. "Yummy, with a little heat from the peppers."

"There's more if you want it." A satisfied smile graced his lips. "Are you going to need more gingerbread for tomorrow?"

"Depends." She wiped her mouth. "If sales keep up this afternoon, I will. If you don't mind."

"Don't mind, but that'll make for a late drive back to town. You and Ty should stay at the ranch. No use driving to town and back when time will be tight and you're tired."

"That would make things easier, but I don't want to be an inconvenience."

"You're not. There's plenty of space at the house for you."

Her brother would be staying in his room at the bunkhouse. That would leave her alone in the big house with Nate.

All. Night. Long.

The idea appealed to her in more ways than it should, ways that had nothing to do with his gourmet kitchen or driving distances.

Rachel ate another bite of cornbread. She followed that with a spoonful of chili. A little spicy.

Like her thoughts.

But starting anything with Nate when her life was such a mess would be a bad idea, a risky one. "Um, sure. I'll talk to Ty. Make sure the logistics work."

"Good idea," Nate agreed. "I know the perfect room for you. Fireplace, private bath, king-sized bed, gorgeous view of the mountains."

"Sounds lovely."

"It's two doors down from mine." His smile crinkled the corners of his eyes.

Rachel's heart skipped two beats, one for each door that would be separating them. Maybe she was mistaking the invitation in Nate's voice, in his eyes. But maybe not. She swallowed. "Great."

Only it wasn't.

Two doors down from mine.

If Ty had any idea where her mind was going right now, he'd think this was a bad idea. Not that she needed his permission to stay...

Two doors down from mine.

Staying at the ranch would be more convenient. Ty wouldn't have any concerns about her being in the house with Nate alone. Her brother trusted her.

Two doors down from mine.

The question was did Rachel trust herself with Nate?

Back at the gingerbread booth with Rachel, Nate adjusted his gloves, waiting to hear what Ty thought about staying at the Bar V5. This was the next step in Operation: Hansel &

Gretel. He'd increased visibility and sales with his first two ideas. Now he wanted to immerse Rachel into the Montana way of life by having her at the ranch 24x7.

"Sounds good to me. I'll be able to drop Rachel off here in the morning and get back to the ranch faster." Ty picked up one of the extra pieces of cornbread. "Dusty will be happy if I'm at the bunkhouse tonight. Damn dog chased my truck nearly to the road yesterday afternoon. He doesn't like when I leave."

Nate made a mental note to buy Dusty an extra special bone. He didn't like when everyone said goodbye, either. The ranch house felt emptier after having Rachel in the kitchen cooking all day and the boys coming in and out for food.

Another idea formed, crystalized. Nate exhaled. "You're welcome to stay more than one night."

Rachel inhaled sharply. Worry flashed across her face. But her forced smile didn't waver.

"If you think that would help Dusty and make things easier," Nate added.

"Sure would save on gas and driving time." Ty looked at Rachel. "What do you think, kiddo?"

"Let's see how tonight goes," she said. "Make sure I'm not intruding on Nate too much."

He wanted her to intrude. That was part of his problem. He wanted her around as much as he wanted Ty.

More, actually. In a different way.

Ty's sister, Nate reminded himself. "It's up to you."

If it were up to him, he would her drive to Marietta after she finished up here and help her pack.

"Right now, I need to sell gingerbread." She shooed them away as if her hands were a horse's tail and they were flies. "Get back to the Bar V5. Do whatever cowboys do."

Nate needed to check the room she'd be using. A housecleaner came twice a week during the off-season, but he would turn on the gas fireplace and set a chocolate on her pillow to make her feel welcome.

"Come on, boss." Ty slapped Nate's shoulder. "The kid has spoken. If we listen to her, we might get a hot breakfast tomorrow morning before she has to be back here."

Zach's grin took ten years off his face. "Chocolate chip

pancakes are my favorite."

The guy acted like a big kid even after all those Middle East deployments and being wounded. When Zack arrived at the ranch looking for work, Ty had hired him on the spot. A very good call, one Nate wasn't sure he would have made. That was why he needed Ty as a partner. "Omelets and hash browns are mine."

Rachel released an exaggerated sigh that hung on the air. "The only reason you want me to spend the night is so you can have breakfast."

Ty snickered. "She's onto you, Nate."

He hoped not. "Breakfast would be an added bonus. It's not required."

"Like lunch," Zack teased. "Though if you're going to be there, dinner would be nice."

She shook her head and hid a smile. "I'll see what I can do. But remember, I'm a baker, not a short order cook. Now go."

Nate fought the urge to glance back at Rachel. Not a good idea with Ty right next to him.

"Looks like that guy could use a hand." Zack ran to help a man get his tree on top of his car.

Ty pulled out a toothpick from his pocket then stuck it in his mouth. "You're going out of your way for Rachel."

"That's the plan. Convince her to stay." So Ty wouldn't move back to Phoenix.

"This is all about Rachel's gingerbread business."

It wasn't a question. Nate rubbed his neck. "And you. You're the one who has to drive her back and forth. If she wasn't here, you'd be staying at the ranch during the week."

"I would, but I want to make sure nothing's changed."

"Nothing has. I told you about Operation: Hansel & Gretel. I've been working on that like we agreed." Except as Nate said the words, he kept seeing Rachel's smiling face, the way she ate as if the chili were haute cuisine, because he'd brought it for her. He felt a few inches taller with Rachel, but smaller with his best friend. This wasn't going to end well. "Anything else?"

"No. Just make sure your goal is to keep Hansel here, not get Gretel."

"Hey—"

Ty raised his hand, cutting him off. "I worry about my little sis."

"Rachel isn't a kid. Someday, she's going to meet a guy and want to get serious. No checking in with big brother first."

"Someday, sure. Until then it's my job to protect her. My sister's been hurt in the past. By those crooks who stole her business and assholes that broke her heart. I don't want to see that happen again."

"Rachel's grown up fast. She seems careful with her heart and her money now. From what I can see."

"But I can help her avoid the wrong kind of guys, ones who don't have the best records when it comes to long term relationships like us cowboys."

Us. The word settled in the bottom of Nate's stomach like a horseshoe. He wasn't a dusty cowboy with wanderlust in his soul and a wandering eye. He owned a ranch and had an investment portfolio. He wanted to settle down and have a family. Ty knew that or should. "Speak for yourself, hotshot. I've been working my ass off to find a woman who'll put up with me for life."

Ty's eyes narrowed. His lips thinned. "You interested in my sister?"

Crap. "I'm interested in her staying in Montana. For you."

"Good, because even though I love you like a brother and you're a great business partner, I've seen you choose your work over women every single time. Not that I haven't agreed with you when it happened, but Rachel deserves better."

His words sliced Nate like a knife, a direct hit at his heart. "That's harsh, man. You know how much the Bar V5 means."

"Damn straight, I do. That doesn't change the facts."

"Falling in love with a woman who would never fit in here makes no sense."

"Exactly." A thoughtful expression crossed Ty's face. "Just because Rachel's enjoying this vacation, don't think she'd want to live on a ranch that's as isolated as the Bar V5. Rachel's lived in Phoenix her entire life. She wants to open a bakery. If she decides to stay in Montana, she'll want to live in town. A place out in the middle of nowhere would drive her crazy."

Nate didn't think Ty knew his sister as well as he thought he did. "You should ask Rachel what she wants, and be prepared to accept what she says. You can't control her like she's ten years old."

"No, but having Rachel closer is to help her, not let her get hurt again. If worse comes to worst, there is something I can do."

Nate didn't like his friend's ominous tone. "What?"

"Tell her it's time for us to get her the hell out of Dodge. She would listen to me then."

He bit the inside of his mouth, afraid Ty was right.

Chapter Six

Two nights later, a winter storm raged. Good thing it wasn't Christmas Eve or Santa would need Rudolph to lead his sleigh through the whiteout conditions.

Inside the Bar V5, Rachel slid hot pans from the oven. She placed the gingerbread on cooling racks then looked over at her brother, who was munching on a cookie. "I filled two thermoses with coffee and there's a container of Chex Mix for the bunk house."

"Thanks, kiddo." Ty looked more like a mountain climber than a cowboy with his winter gear, especially the neck gaiter. "And thanks for staying at the ranch. Makes my life easier with this storm."

"Mine, too." Driving back and forth to town didn't make sense in this weather. Especially when her big concern about staying here—Nate—had been a non-issue. She saw him only at mealtimes with the rest of the guys. A little frustrating. She missed talking with him and hearing his ideas and seeing his smile. Alone. Now she was being silly. He was just a business adviser and friend. That she might happen to have a little crush on.

Ty stared at her strangely.

Shoot. They were talking about...staying at the ranch. "I picked up new orders this morning. Glad I made it back here before the snow got too heavy. I wouldn't want to be stuck baking in your kitchen."

"Haha."

"What's so funny?"

Rachel didn't need to turn around to know Nate had arrived. If she hadn't recognized his voice, her racing pulse would have been a dead giveaway. Yeah, not seeing him much had probably been a good thing.

"My li'l sis is dissing my kitchen." Ty picked up another cookie. "Yours has spoiled her."

"She's spoiling us with her cooking and baking."

Rachel turned to thank him, but the words died on her lips. No man should look that hot in workout clothes. She nearly dropped her oven mitts into the sink.

"That's true." Ty stood right next to her, but he might as well have been talking in the laundry room with the door closed.

Nate stood in the doorway to the living area, his hair damp, the ends curly. A plain white T-shirt stretched across his wide chest and showed off his strong arms, not the muscles of a bodybuilder, but a man who did hard labor. He wore black sweat pants and was barefoot. Even his feet looked sexy. "Guess you're not going back out tonight."

"Nope." He tilted his head toward Ty's direction. "This crazy guy is going to make sure everything's locked down."

"That's right," Ty said. "You need to get off that ankle."

"Ankle?" Rachel noticed the way Nate leaned against the door jamb, his right leg supporting his weight. She took a step toward him. "Did you hurt yourself?"

"Nothing serious." Nate waved off the concern. "Twisted it."

"Trying not to step on a barn kitty," Ty added. "That little beast appeared out of nowhere. We should rename him Lucky."

She stared at Nate. "You hurt yourself because of a cat?"

"I couldn't step on a kitten."

Her heart melted. "That's so sweet."

"I try." His grin crinkled the corners of his eyes. "It's no big deal. I'm going to grab some ice, a beer, and watch TV tonight. I'll be fine tomorrow."

"Grab a spot on the couch and make yourself comfortable." Rachel had taken care of Ty many times when he'd hurt himself working at a guest ranch while raising her. She grabbed a gallon-size plastic bag. "I'll get you ice. Anything else?"

"Popcorn if you don't mind." Nate gave the thumbs up to Ty. "This is turning out better than I expected. Give Lucky a treat for me."

Ty nodded. "Now all you need is something to watch."

"A Christmas Carol," Nate said.

"I love that movie." Standing at the freezer, Rachel put ice into the plastic bag. "Such a great message for everyone."

"Not if you're scared of ghosts," Ty teased.

"Well, I'm not. I love the Ghost of Christmas Past." Rachel wrapped the bag of ice in a clean dishtowel. "Nothing scary about reliving fond memories from long ago."

When Mom and Dad had been alive. She needed to take flowers to the cemetery when she got home.

"I'm a fan of the Ghost of Christmas Yet to Come," Nate said to her surprise. "I'm an optimist, always thinking the best is still on its way, rather than behind me."

"The Ghost of Christmas Present is the realist. That's me." Ty grabbed a beer out of the fridge, removed the cap, then took a pull. "Looking back won't change what happened yesterday. Who knows what will happen tomorrow? The best thing is to concentrate on right now. We're going to have an amazing Christmas together."

"It's going to be great," Rachel agreed.

Ty's eyes turned serious. "Montana starting to grow on you?"

"It's hard not to get caught up in the Christmas spirit," she admitted. "The snow, the people. What's not to like?"

Ty's gaze met Nate's.

Rachel looked at her brother. "What? I thought you wanted me to like it here and would be happy."

Ty's smile lit up his face. "I am very happy."

"Why don't you two watch the movie with me?" Nate asked. "I need someone to make beer runs to the kitchen during commercials."

"No explosions. No hot women. No sex. I'll pass." Ty picked up the thermoses and plastic container. "But Rachel loves the movie. She'll keep you company and be your runner."

Nate looked at her with hope in his eyes. "Will you?"

"You could learn a lesson here, big brother. Nate lets me decide for myself."

Ty shrugged. "Your answer's still going to be a yes."

"True. It's one of my favorite holiday films." The way he kept weight off his foot bothered Rachel. So did the bruise. Someone needed to stay with him and make sure he was okay. That duty fell to her tonight, and she didn't mind one bit. "I'll make the popcorn and be right in."

Nate glanced at the clock on the microwave. "The movie starts in ten minutes."

"Plenty of time." She looked at her brother. "Help Nate into the great room. Make sure his foot is elevated on pillows above his heart."

Nate started to speak.

Ty raised his hand. "Don't say a word. Just go with it. Been here myself. You're in good hands."

Six minutes later, Rachel entered the great room, tray in hand. Wood crackled and flames danced in the stone fireplace. Pine boughs and holly covered the wood mantel. Candles and the word JOY spelled out in silver letters were interspersed among the greenery.

A rope hung across the front of the fireplace and strung through the loops on red stockings with names on the white cuffs, one for each of the ranch employees and one for her. She'd been touched and honored. The only family she had was Ty, but here at the Bar V5, she felt part of something bigger. "I appreciate your hanging a stocking for me."

"I told you the first day we met. You're family."

Family should feel comfortable around each other. Being alone with Nate unnerved Rachel, like she was standing on a cliff, with deep water below, unsure if she should jump or edge back slowly.

She placed the tray with his beer, her mug of steaming tea, and a bowl of popcorn on the coffee table. "Do you need ibuprofen?"

"Took some for the swelling. Any pain will be eased by the company." He sat with his foot on pillows and the makeshift ice pack against his ankle. "This couch has a better view than the other two."

Maybe, but the other leather sofas were empty. She wouldn't be seated right next to him.

"You'll be able to reach your tea from here, too," he added.

True, but he would be within arm's reach. Oh-so-tempting.

"Come on." He patted the cushion next to him. "I haven't seen you much except during meals."

She sat, a cushion away from the spot he'd patted. A safe distance.

Or maybe not.

His soap scent had replaced the dirt and musky male smell she'd gotten used to while eating with a bunch of ranch hands. She wanted another sniff of the fresh aroma. And his skin.

He picked up the beer bottle. "How do you like your room?"

"It's amazing." Sleeping between luxurious high-thread count linens on a soft-as-a-cloud mattress made her feel like royalty. The plush, white towels in the bathroom went to the top spot on her if-I-win-the-lottery-list. Maybe if she limited any *naughty* thoughts about Nate and stayed on the *nice* list, Santa would bring her a set for Christmas. "Nightly turn-down service and a Copper Mountain Chocolate on my pillow are nice touches. You or Ty?"

Nate's cheeks reddened, answering her question. "That's what we do for guests."

"I thought I was family."

"Guests and family." He took a swig of beer.

She glanced around the room until her gaze rested on the fifteen-foot Christmas tree positioned in front of two floor-to-ceiling windows, twinkling with multi-colored lights. A shiny gold star sat at the top. A wooden carved nativity was centered beneath the branches, on a colorful patchwork tree skirt. "

Rachel loved this place. "Staying here's spoiled me. Will make it hard to go back to Ty's apartment."

Or hers in Arizona.

That was a crazy thought. She picked up her mug. The desert was home, not the mountains.

"You're welcome to stay as long as you want."

"Thanks." The russet of her tea reminded her of Nate's eyes. Rachel's heart bumped. "I imagine Christmas must be lovely at the ranch."

"It's quiet." His voice sounded lower, more serious than normal. He shifted positions. "At least until people come over for Christmas dinner. Folks know there's an open invitation so I'm never sure who'll show up 'til they step through the door.

It's a potluck rather than a traditional menu, though I do cook a turkey."

"Sounds fun."

He leaned toward her. "You'll be here?"

She reached for the popcorn to put more distance between them. Avoid crawling onto his lap like the kitten he'd saved. Being careful of his ankle, of course.

What would happen if she did?

That was what she'd been thinking about at night, two doors away, waiting for him to walk past her room. Knock. Just to check on her.

Right.

"Rachel."

"Oh, yeah. Of course we'll be there. I brought my favorite holiday recipes with me. I'll cook a couple of dishes."

"The more the merrier. This place was built for a crowd."

And that's when she realized what Nate Vaughn wanted—company. The guy was lonely with no guests to care for and entertain. Helping her with the gingerbread houses might be for Ty, but also gave Nate something to do, something other than being alone in this big house.

He touched her shoulder. "Hey. You seem miles away. The movie's starting."

Her sweater kept his skin from touching hers. Yet heat emanated from the point of contact, sending chills down her arm. The good kind, ones she hadn't felt since the last time he'd made this happen a few days ago. She swallowed. "Just enjoying the Christmas tree."

And his touch.

All she had to do was scoot a couple inches to her left. She had a feeling he might meet her halfway. Maybe put his arm around her. Except…

Her stomach knotted, like curling ribbon that had fallen off the spool into a jumbled mess.

Rachel didn't want to repeat her past mistakes. They'd cost her so much, too much. What if this turned into another misstep? Her heart didn't want to take the chance.

Reluctantly, she leaned forward, set her mug on the table, and reached for the popcorn bowl.

His hand slipped off her shoulder, the way she'd

expected. He rested his forearm on the cushion between them. Exactly what she'd wanted to happen. But darn it, she missed his touch.

Rachel offered Nate popcorn then forced herself to stare at the television. Concentrate on the opening credits. Focus on the first scene.

Except she couldn't stop thinking about the man seated next to her. For so long, she'd allowed work dreams of a bakery to dominate her fantasies, pushing thoughts of a serious relationship, having her own family and the future out of the way. But here in Montana, those thoughts were becoming stronger, more vivid, and starred Nate. She shivered.

He placed his arm along the back of the couch. "There are blankets on the quilt rack by the Christmas tree if you're cold."

"I'm fine." She remembered his ankle. "Do you need one?"

"Nope." He tipped back his beer. "I'm nice and warm."

Hot, actually. But no one was asking her opinion.

The bowl of popcorn rested between them.

Weird. Nate seemed to have moved closer.

A full cushion no longer separated them. But even stranger, he hadn't been the only one to bridge the gap between the bottom sofa cushions. She'd done the same thing.

Uh-oh.

At this rate, they'd be on top of each other before Marley appeared, dragging his heavy chains. That appealed to her more than hearing Tiny Tim's famous words at the end.

She thought Nate felt the same way, at least by the way he was acting tonight, but what would that mean?

A holiday fling.

Rachel's stomach plunged to her feet. A sign what might happen to her heart. Splat.

Nope. Best to keep things nice and easy between them, like friends. Good, helpful, care-about-each-other friends.

That meant she had make sure she didn't move any closer to him and not eat any popcorn. She didn't dare reach into the bowl and accidentally touch Nate.

Because despite her friends-only intentions, she might not want to let go.

The snow kept falling. Nate didn't mind the white stuff, but he didn't know how many days of the storm he could take being stuck inside. Lying in bed, he punched his pillow, trying to get comfortable. He hadn't slept well.

His ankle, but mostly Rachel.

Last night Nate had been too focused on her to pay attention to the movie. He could have made a move, see if she was interested in him romantically or not, but no, he sneaked peeks and touches like a fourteen-year-old, too afraid of the consequences if he crossed the imaginary boundary line set by her over-protective older brother.

Stupid.

Not to mention that he was the worst friend ever.

But he couldn't help himself.

Nate tried to think of Rachel as an old friend like Annie. He tried to think of her as an employee like Charlie. Even tried to think of her as a sister. Nothing worked. Rachel's baking skills, her creativity, her kindness, her compassion and her nurturing made his desire grow stronger each time he saw her.

If Ty knew, he would never stay at the Bar V5. He'd want to take Rachel with him. And she would likely choose her loyalty to her brother over a man she'd just met.

But Nate wasn't the kind of guy to assume the temperature was too cold for a swim without dipping in his toe into the water. Or in this case, tasting the water.

Besides a few touches and a near kiss, nothing physical had happened between them. These thoughts and feelings about Rachel could all be in his head, a fantasy, a Christmas wish. He needed to find out whether they were real or not. And if real, whether they were reciprocated.

If they were, he was screwed.

A knock sounded at the door. Must be Ty. He checked on employees whenever they were sick or hurt. Nate's ankle throbbed. He hoped Ty came bearing ibuprofen and a fresh ice pack. "Come in."

Rachel entered, carrying a tray. "Good morning."

He bolted upright, his blanket falling off his bare chest. At

least his ankle had been bothering him too much last night to
bother taking off his sweatpants. Otherwise she would have
caught him in the nude. "Hey."

Her eyes widened. Her gaze dropped to his chest.
"How's, um, your ankle?"

"Okay. A little sore." Seeing her made him feel like the
sun had burst through the clouds. She wore a red apron over
her long-sleeved forest green shirt, faded jeans and multi-
colored, polka dotted socks. She walked toward him, her
lopsided ponytail bouncing and a wide smile on her face.
"Nothing that more ice, a couple anti-inflammatories, and
breakfast can't fix."

He wasn't sure how Rachel managed to look beautiful
and adorable at the same time, but she did. "Thanks."

She rested the tray against her hip and handed him an ice
pack. "Put this on your ankle."

He did, never taking his gaze off her.

Forget keeping Hansel at the ranch. Nate wanted Gretel
in a bad way.

"Take it easy today." Her voice slid over him, soft and
sweet. "Stay in bed."

Hell, he wanted her to set the tray on the dresser then
slide in bed and spend the day with him, limbs and tongues
tangled, without the cute clothes. That would give him all the
answers he needed.

She gave him the tray. "I made you a cheesy scramble
with hash browns, molasses toast and a strawberry-banana
smoothie."

Nate didn't know what smelled better—breakfast or her,
a mix of vanilla, something floral, and sugar plums.

He was losing his mind.

Cabin fever must have set in during the last, oh, sixteen
hours. Either that or wanting to have sex with his best friend's
sister had re-wired Nate's brain.

She leaned toward Nate. Touched his forehead. "Are you
okay?"

No. But he could fake it. "Hungry."

"Let me know if there's anything you need."

Nate wanted her, but he knew that wasn't what she
meant. "Company would be nice."

Way to go, Vaughn. Why not light ten sticks of dynamite to see what might happen? Or ask to see her breasts?

She nodded. "I'll be back once I pull the gingerbread out of the oven, okay?"

He nodded, even though none of this was okay. Ty would never be okay with Nate having sex with Rachel.

Crap. He stared at the food on the tray, his appetite completely gone, then up at Rachel. His chest tightened.

If he kept this up, he would destroy his relationship with Ty.

Change the Bar V5 forever.

Nate couldn't do that.

I've seen you choose your work over women every single time.

Ty's words echoed through Nate's head. He'd done that, and he would do the same thing again this time. Put the ranch above his personal needs. Above Rachel.

Nate needed to push all physical attraction and desire for Rachel away. No testing and tasting between friends. Or their sisters.

He might want to, but he couldn't. Wouldn't. Not worth the risk to her, to him, to the Bar V5.

Maybe if Nate told himself that enough times, he might start to believe it.

By the time the storm passed two days later, Rachel knew all about Nate leaving the Bar V5 to go to college, business school, and into venture capital, to his return, falling in love with the ranch and never wanting to leave. The worst part was she wanted more. More talking. More sharing. More Nate.

With a sigh hanging on the chilly morning air, Rachel made her way to the barn along the shoveled path.

Nate's openness to questions surprised her. He didn't act smooth or gloss over his mistakes. His honesty gave her hope about guys, and she appreciated the way he listened to her. Ty only heard a few of her words before suggesting fixes and dismissing concerns. Nate waited until she finished, no matter how long she took to get something out then gave an opinion only if she asked. Talking with him felt different, like shopping with him had felt different. Not so much side-by-side buddies hanging out, but more like they were... together.

But he hadn't made a move or asked her out on a date. She couldn't be sure if he was just being super-friendly, her Christmastime BFF, and was going to let her down slowly from her obvious crush.

At least her crush was obvious to her.

Nate acted oblivious, but she didn't know if that was on purpose or not. She wasn't sure what to hope for, except she didn't like the status quo.

In spite of her cold-weather gear, her teeth chattered. She carried a container of fresh-from-the-oven scones, a jar of jelly, and container of butter. Yesterday, he'd mentioned how his mother used to make scones for him and his dad, so Rachel had decided to surprise him. Cowboys had to take breaks once in a while, right?

She entered the barn. Empty.

"Hello?" A peek into Ty's office showed a desk and chair covered with barn cats, making the most of the heated room. "Where is everyone?"

"Define everyone." Nate walked toward her, no trace of a limp now that his ankle had healed, and a black cat at his feet. He stretched his arms wide. "Will I do?"

A wool cap pulled low hid his hair, but the shoved-down gaiter around his neck showed his smiling, handsome face. With his thick jacket, insulated pants and heavy boots, he looked rugged, a total hottie who'd stepped out of a glossy Carhartt ad.

Staring at him was like plunging herself into a hot tub. The chill disappeared in a flash. "You'll do."

"Something smells good." He eyed the container. "You come bearing gifts."

"Scones."

His smile widened, spreading across his face to his eyes. "You remembered."

Her heart stumbled, head over heels, until dropping at his booted feet. The man had no idea how he twisted her into knots. Rachel smiled tentatively, glancing up at him. "Told ya. Mind like an elephant. They're still warm. I brought jelly and butter. Thought you all might want a break and a snack."

"Thanks, but the guys aren't here."

Rachel had made the scones as an excuse to see Nate, but she'd made plenty for everyone. "Where are they?"

"Down at one of the cabin clusters, clearing snow from rooftops." A more intense smile replaced the sexy Carhartt model grin.

Alone. Just like she wanted.

Until an avalanche of second thoughts buried her with a vengeance.

The way Nate looked at her would melt the snow on those roofs in a flash.

This was not a holiday fling. This was not diving off a cliff into a pool of cool, deep water. This was jumping off the ledge of a burning building, flames licking at her heels, and trusting the guy with his arms out would catch you.

And trust was *so* not her thing. Not anymore.

She stood firmly on her ledge and her fingers clawing into the wall.

"Let's go," Rachel said. "Nothing beats a warm scone."

The intensity in his face ratcheted down. "Sure, I'll take you anywhere you want to go."

His words blanketed her like the goose down duvet on her bed in the ranch house. "It's time I saw some of the Bar V5 beyond the main house, barn and meadow in back. It'll be a nice walk."

"There's no shoveled path."

"I don't mind a little snow."

"There's a lot of snow. You could get lost. Fall. Drop the scones." He met her gaze. "I'll drive you over on the snowmobile."

"Sounds like fun."

He grabbed a backpack off a hook and held it open. "Put your stuff inside."

She did.

He put the pack on her back then handed her a helmet.

"Put this on and follow me." Outside the barn, Nate climbed onto a black snowmobile. "Get on the back."

Excitement buzzed through her. She'd never been on a snowmobile before. Or so close to Nate. She straddled the seat.

"Scoot closer to me," he said.

Rachel did, her thighs pressed against Nate, her arms wrapped around his waist. Her pulse skittered. The thick outerwear they wore provided a layer of cushion between them, but that didn't change the intimacy of the seating arrangement.

The engine roared to life, the snowmobile vibrating beneath her, making her want to clench her legs tight around Nate's hips, to get as close as possible. If only all these clothes weren't in the way… She swallowed.

Maybe this wasn't such a good idea.

"Hold on."

No worries there. She wasn't about to let go.

Rachel had proved she was a chicken, sending them off into the cold when they could have stayed at the barn and kept each other warm, because she was afraid.

Afraid of Nate. Afraid of falling in love. Afraid of being hurt again.

Pathetic.

Chapter Seven

With Rachel on the back of the snowmobile, pressed up against Nate like his shadow, making his body buzz, he decided he had a new favorite way to get around the ranch. Arrow wouldn't be happy.

Thanks to the thoughtful and tasty scones Rachel had baked and given to everyone at the cabins, well, today was the closest to heaven Nate had been in a while. A brief escape from his self-imposed friend purgatory.

Not that Nate minded much.

He enjoyed hanging out with Rachel. He hadn't needed to milk his ankle as an excuse with the storm keeping them inside. She liked to talk, ask questions, talk some more. One more day of snow and he'd thought she would pull out a bottle of sparkly polish and paint their fingernails.

Okay, not really.

But pretty damn close, and he wouldn't have minded painting her toenails. She treated him like a girlfriend, and he was taking her lead, being her friend, supporting her, being a decent guy. Something Ty needed to see him be.

Being Rachel's friend didn't suck.

Sure, Nate wanted to get physical. Wanted it more than his next breath on some days. But talking was underrated.

Still, being her bud wasn't easy. He felt closer to Rachel in two weeks than he had to Marissa in two years. Marissa would talk about work or a call from her mother, a dress she loved, or a friend who was dating a jerk. Nate was expected to listen—and he did, kind of—until she was finished and moved on to the next topic. She never asked him for more than to stop by her place on the way home from work so she could change before dinner.

Not that he'd offered more. He hadn't included her in his Montana past until he'd had to return to the ranch.

Maybe that was why Marissa couldn't understand the importance of the Bar V5, of keeping his family legacy, of making sure his parents could live out their final days in their house, the only home his dad had ever known. And why had Nate been so surprised to tell Rachel how he felt when he lost his first horse and when he learned of his father's dementia.

She'd asked, and he answered. It wasn't hard.

Cue the chick flick.

Nate drove the snowmobile over a slight rise, to take the scenic way back to the house. Rachel would get a mini tour of the Bar V5 and he'd enjoy having her arms around him for a few more minutes before stepping back into friend mode. If not for the riot that would ensue if she didn't cook lunch, he would keep her out here all day, wind on their faces, her body spooning his.

Not exactly friend-like motives.

So sue him.

He might not have this chance again. Ty hadn't seemed to mind. The guy had thanked Nate for bringing Rachel and her scones to the cabin and keeping his sister entertained. Nate would make the most of this opportunity.

Rachel pointed to the herd of horses in the pasture, coats thick from the cold and the breeze in their manes.

He stopped near the fence then turned off the ignition.

She climbed off, removed her helmet and made her way to the fence. The horses ran toward them, kicking up snow. "They look like they're having so much fun out there."

"With no guests at the ranch, winter is their season to play."

"So carefree." She sighed. "They don't worry, do they? Must be nice."

The wistful tone in Rachel's voice didn't surprise him. She'd told him more details about what happened in Phoenix with Pamela Darby and the television cook's husband. Nate wasn't big on using violence to solve problems, but if he ever game across Grayson Darby in person, the crook was going down. "They only worry if we're late bringing dinner. Like we'd forget them with all their clomping and whinnying."

"But they don't worry about their work."

"No, they love it."

She leaned against the fence, resting her arms on the top rail. "The way you love the Bar V5, the animals and the people here. Worries, hard work and all."

It wasn't a question, but he decided to answer anyway. "I love everything about this place, from the twisted iron sign hanging on the gate to the Bar V5 brand on the animals. There's no place like the ranch anywhere. Totally worth every gray hair she's given me."

Rachel peeked under his hat, brushing her fingers through his hair. "I don't see any."

Her touch was light and playful, but a pulsing electric current rippled down his body. "They're…uh…"

"Oh, I see one."

"*Really?*"

She looked up with a gotcha-grin. "No, but I see how vain you are."

He had no comeback, but wanted to kiss the smile off her pretty face. Not fair he couldn't use the weapons in his arsenal to get even.

Two horses chased each other.

Rachel jumped onto the lowest rail of the fence and laughed, a sweet sound that lingered on the air. Dressed in casual clothes, she looked gorgeous splayed over the fence, arms waving at the horses to call them over.

The rapt delight on her face hit Nate like a horse's hoof to the gut.

She loved the outdoors. She could love the ranch.

She could love…

Idiot. He shook his head.

Rachel was on vacation, having a great time. Everyone did at the Bar V5. That was why they returned each year. To visit. Not to fall in love with the guy who couldn't leave the ranch for more than a few days without getting homesick.

If Ty was right, the best Nate could hope for was Rachel settling in Bozeman or Billings or Butte. Cities a hundred miles or so away, plenty close for Ty. He'd probably like having a place to crash in a bigger city.

Not nearly close enough for Nate.

He needed Rachel spooning him on his snowmobile at the Bar V5 every day. For the rest of their lives.

Nate blew out a puff of air. "We should get back to the house."

"You must have work to do."

"You do," he said. "Zack wanted me to make sure I got you back in time so you could make lunch."

She shook her head. "At least my cooking's appreciated here."

"No one wants to see you leave." Nate, especially.

"Their stomachs will miss me."

"I'll miss you."

Crap. Had he really said the words out loud? He rubbed his face.

"You'll miss my oatmeal raisin cookies."

"And a bunch of other stuff." A part of him wanted to cut through the friendship crap. To find out if she really thought baked goods were what mattered to him and if she knew that he was into her, as more than a friend. But he'd rather stay where he was than hear her say she only saw him as a friend. "I have a feeling Zack will cry when it comes time to say goodbye."

"I shouldn't laugh. You may be right. Poor guy. I'd better get busy with lunch so we don't have any former soldiers falling to pieces."

Nate motioned to the snowmobile. "Let's go."

She took a step away from the fence, her foot sank into the snow, causing her to stumble forward.

Nate grabbed onto her, one hand on her arm, the other around her waist. "Careful."

He lifted her so she could pull her leg out of the snow. He set Rachel on the ground, not letting go, and stared into her eyes. "You okay?"

She nodded, her face so close to his he could see her individual eyelashes. Man, she had beautiful eyes. They changed colors again, more green than brown, with shades of gold.

Let her go. Step back. Get on the sled and go home.

The voice of reason shouted. Common sense screamed.

Nate didn't want to do either of those things, even if he knew he should.

Rachel's gaze didn't waver.

Her lips parted, soft and inviting. He wanted to skip the RSVP and join the party now. The tip of her pink tongue darted out, wet her lower lip then disappeared back into her mouth.

His insides clenched, twisted.

Damn, she was making this difficult.

But this was his land. He wouldn't leave the Bar V5 because a woman he liked found it too remote. He needed to find a woman who loved this land as much as he did. Nothing Rachel had told him in all their days of sharing had come close. She'd admitted her heart would always be in Phoenix because of her parents. He removed his hands from around her waist. "Let's go."

Rachel rose up on her tiptoes, her lips coming toward him.

He leaned in closer, meeting her halfway.

She brushed her mouth across his.

Soft, warm, sweet...

And then gone.

Before he could process what was happening, before he could enjoy the kiss.

But his lips tingled, wanting more.

"Now we can go." Rachel didn't look up at him. She walked toward the sled, her steps careful, but quick over the snow.

He took off after her, lengthening his stride to catch up with her. "What was that?"

She shrugged, still not meeting his eyes.

He touched her shoulder. "Why did you want to kiss?"

She shook the snow off her gloves. "I appreciate how much you've done for me. I like spending time with you. I kissed you as a kind of... thanks."

"A thank you kiss."

She glanced up at him. Her big, beautiful hazel eyes sent his pulse sprinting. "To show my gratitude. In case you're getting tired of my baking."

He grinned. "I'm going to have to do more things you'll be grateful for. Though thank you kisses usually come on the cheek, not the lips."

"It was the moment. I was happy. The opportunity presented itself." A satisfied smile curved her lips. "I went for it."

"What? Like a dare with yourself?"

"Kinda, yeah. You're very cute."

Her cheeks burned bright pink.

Okay, she might be grateful, but she *was* into him, too.

Good. Except he didn't know what that meant to her. "And…?"

She looked at the horses. Wet her lips again. "You've been a good friend. Made things easier for me."

She was so nervous. Had her experience with men been so bad a peck was all she could risk?

Sinking back on his heels, he knew the answer.

A kiss was all she was willing to chance. Nate didn't blame her. He'd heard about every guy she'd had a crush on or dated, scumbags one and all. No wonder she didn't trust her judgment or him. He wanted to help her so she could.

If Rachel would give him the chance…

"We should go." She hopped back to the snowmobile like a frightened rabbit, using the footsteps they'd made to speed her movement and prevent needing another rescue.

He had his sign. She wanted him.

But on her terms, if at all.

Damn. He was in deep trouble.

Things hadn't changed now that he knew she was attracted to him. But something inside him had. Forget being her friend or having a fling. He wanted her to be a larger part of his life.

Nate couldn't expect her to feel the same, not this soon, after what she'd been through. If he pushed Rachel, she would claim they were friends. Affectionate, thankful friends. But just friends.

There was Ty to consider, too. He didn't think Nate deserved Rachel, and a part of him agreed. But he couldn't walk away without out at least seeing if there could be something there? Could he?

Three days later, Rachel still couldn't believe she'd kissed Nate. Standing in the church's hall with him at her side and a cast of children dressed in their costumes for the Christmas

Eve Nativity pageant on a makeshift stage, the moment replayed in her mind. Over and over again, in astonishing detail considering the kiss lasted a second, maybe two.

Why did you kiss me?

She hadn't dared tell Nate the truth. That after missing her chance to let him know how she felt when they were in the barn, she'd wanted to take a risk instead of playing it safe. She'd wanted to be brave.

Instead, she'd been stupid.

Rachel cringed inwardly for the hundredth time for risking potential disaster. Up until that moment, she'd decided to play it safe, despite her crush, and keep Nate in the friend zone. He was a charming cowboy, a rancher and venture capitalist, who was acting as her business advisor. Having a fling with her brother's best friend then flying back to Phoenix like nothing happened would not be good for her. That much she knew. So what if her body responded to him or she seemed to be falling for him? Being friends seemed like the best—the only—option.

Until she blew it by kissing him.

The attraction was now out in the open, invisible, but as solid as a wall between them in everything they said to each other. Another kiss would surely start something, but she didn't think that was a good idea, even though all she could think about was kissing Nate again.

She was caught in limbo, frustrated and unsure.

The children sang "Silent Night." A sheep played with her tail. A camel yawned. A shepherd, wearing a blue robe and headpiece and holding a staff, burped. The kids stopped singing and giggled.

On the far side of the room, Annie, Nate's friend from the diner, painted elaborate large scenery panels that looked like they belonged in a Broadway play, not a children's Christmas play. Annie shook her head then returned to painting.

Nate leaned closer, his breath warm against her neck, sending pleasurable sensations up and down her spine. "That boy's dad was the same at his age. Though he was more into farting than burping."

Rachel covered her mouth to keep from laughing. The kids were distracted enough.

306

"Let's try that again," Betty Anderson, the thirty-something play director who also worked at the high school, said. "This time without the sound effects."

"Good luck with that." Nate's mischievous look made her wonder what *he* was he had been like as a kid. She'd bet he was a handful. And cute. Just like his kids would be.

Betty clapped at the end of the song. "Everyone worked so hard tonight. You get a treat. Miss Murphy has a special gingerbread cookie for each of you. Make sure you see her before you head out. And no one leaves this room without a parent."

"Yes, Ms. Anderson," the children said in unison then ran toward Rachel like ants attacking a leftover piece of pie during a picnic.

Too bad she was the pie.

"Slow down." Nate stepped in front of her, his arms out toward the bouncing kids. "If you want a cookie, you'll need to get in line."

The children quieted and did as they were told. Cookies had a magical quality. A little help from a cowboy didn't hurt.

One by one, the kids approached to receive their cookies. Each gingerbread angel was wrapped in a cellophane bag, tied with a ribbon and candy cane. She'd included a label with a line from the play's script.

A little boy approached. Rachel handed him a cookie. "Merry Christmas."

"Nice job up there, Evan." Nate gave the boy a high five. "Tell your dad I said hi."

The kid nodded.

An angel with shimmery wings and a gold halo took a cookie then, rewarded Rachel with a front-teeth-missing grin. "Such great costumes."

"Thank you," a woman with dark brown hair and twinkling brown eyes stepped forward with two children, a boy and a girl, who looked to be the same age. "I had no idea what was involved when I said yes to making costumes but it's been fun. I'm Harley Diekerhoff."

So this was Harley. Pretty. A looker, as Nate had called her. Around his age.

"The costumes are great," Nate said. "This is baker

307

extraordinaire Rachel Murphy."

Rachel shook the woman's hand. "Nice to meet you."

"Same here. Brock bought one of your do-it-yourself kits. Mack, Molly." Harley gestured to the twins. "All of us had fun decorating the gingerbread house."

Both kids nodded, their gazes locked on the bags of cookie in Rachel's hands, like puppies wanting a treat.

"Thanks. Glad you had fun." Rachel handed cookies to the kids. "Merry Christmas, Mack and Molly."

For the next fifteen minutes, a steady stream of kids stopped by, each wanting a cookie and to show off their costumes to new people. Rachel oohed and awed over each one, genuinely impressed with Harley's designs. Nate knew everyone by name, and he introduced her as Ty Murphy's sister or the gingerbread baker.

Exactly what she was. So why did she yearn to be something more to Nate?

They had nothing in common. She wasn't up for a fling. She would be returning to Phoenix after Christmas. Pining over a kiss and wanting more made no sense.

Nate showed her the empty box. "The kids are gone and so are the gingerbread angels. A good thing I got my fill at the Bar V5."

"You're going to have a mouthful of cavities if you keep eating so many sweets."

"You're going to have a ton of more orders after this great marketing idea," he said. "You catch on so fast."

"I'm not doing this to market my gingerbread. I didn't put my name on the tags or anywhere."

"You spent hours making the cookies and packaging them."

She shrugged. "Doesn't matter. When I bumped into Annie, while I was delivering products, she told me about painting sets for the performance. She described how hard the kids have been practicing, trying to memorize their lines and get their parts right. I thought cookies would be a nice treat. Nothing more."

"That's very sweet of you."

"I've been earning a lot of money from people here in town. I don't want to be greedy."

"No one would ever accuse you of that."

She shrugged, feeling greedy for wanting more time with Nate. More kisses.

"You're good with kids," he said.

"Lots of children came into the bakery where I worked. We kept a container of free cookies for the kids."

"You like them."

"Very much. I can't wait to be a mom." The words rushed out. "I mean, I can wait to have babies. But I would like a family. Not today or tomorrow. Someday."

Oh, no. She was rambling, talking about babies and family with a guy. She'd clinch the insanity title for sure.

"Those will be some lucky kids to have you as a mom."

Her heart sighed. He was so sweet. "Thanks. My brother feels like he's already done the kid thing with me and wants no part of it again. Do you want a family?"

"Half a dozen kids sounds about right."

"Six? Whoa. That's an intimidating number." She remembered what he'd said the first night of the storm. "The more the merrier."

"You really do have a good memory."

Nodding, she pictured little kids with light brown hair, hazel or brown eyes, a mix of her and Nate. Emotion clogged her throat. She swallowed. "If you want six kids, you'd better get started."

"The old biological clock hasn't started ticking yet. Plenty of time to find the right woman."

"Good luck." Rachel tried to sound flippant, but she wasn't sure she succeeded. "Or do you not need any?"

One corner of his mouth rose up, in a sexy slanted smile. "A little luck in this case might actually help."

"I have a lucky arrowhead you could borrow."

"Thanks. I'll let you know if I need it, but I'm hopeful I can pull this off on my own."

His words suggested something would be happening, something soon. She didn't know whether to be chock full of anticipation or scared to death.

But she might keep that good luck charm for herself.

Chapter Eight

Later that week, Nate carried a shoebox full of mistletoe into the house. Warm air, a chocolate-y scent, and a song about Christmas greeted him. The tug at his heart made him glanced into the box of greenery tied with red satin ribbon.

Time to figure out exactly what was going on between him and Rachel. Being friends with a serious flirtatious undertone was not working for him. Nate hoped she was in the kitchen. He didn't want her to see his purchase until he was ready.

The other night at the church, he'd seen a different side of Rachel. One he'd glimpsed when he twisted his ankle, one that had now sent his world spinning like a top. Seeing her with the kids, passing out cookies and complimenting them on their costumes, made him picture her as a wife and mother.

His wife and the mother of his kids.

Imagining Rachel as that woman when they'd never dated or kissed for longer than a nanosecond worried him.

He'd never imagined Marissa as a mom. Spit-up wouldn't coordinate with her designer clothes. Not that they'd talked about having kids. Yet he'd proposed.

Unbelievable.

He needed to stop the ghost of relationships past—the ghost of Marissa most of all—from clouding his judgment. Ty, too, with him saying Nate wasn't good enough for Rachel.

He could love a woman, make her happy on the ranch, have children with her, love those children 'til the end of his days and pass on this ranch to them. That was his dream. He had to believe it would come true.

Right now those dreams centered around Rachel. His feelings for her kept growing stronger, until spiraling out of control the other night. For days he'd tried to ignore it. Tried and failed.

Maybe he was inflating how he felt about Rachel because he wanted a family. Maybe not. Today he would find out.

That was where the mistletoe came in.

Nate needed to know not only if his feelings were real but if Rachel's were, too. The last thing he wanted to do was hurt her or scare her. A holiday kiss would be less threatening, more like her *thank you* one out in the snow. All he needed was for her to stand under the mistletoe and agree to a kiss. Once she did, he would turn that kiss into a real one and gauge her reaction.

He entered the main living space.

Empty. Good.

That would make... decorating... easier, quicker.

He set the box on the coffee table then retrieved a ladder and stapler.

If Rachel drew back from his kiss, he would accept that they were not meant to be and find a New Year's Eve date. If she wanted more from his kiss, they would figure out a way to deal with Ty and everything else.

A simple plan that should work.

Nate set up the ladder where he thought people—okay, one particular person—might stand. He'd purchased an extra spool of ribbon so the mistletoe could hang down from the vaulted ceiling. He would also hang sprigs in a couple of doorways to be on the safe side.

Risky? Definitely.

But Nate needed to see if he had any chance with Rachel before these feelings got any worse and made him do something stupid. Something he might regret.

He hoped she agreed to the kiss.

Rachel refusing was a distinct possibility. One he didn't want to happen. If it did, Nate would walk away, head held high. He would try to find the shutoff switch for the happily ever after highlight reel running through his brain.

Yes, his kissing Rachel plan made perfect sense. He climbed the ladder and went to work.

Half an hour later, Nate looked over his handwork from ground level. Mistletoe hung from the ceiling extended on long ribbons, like bait attached to a fishing line. Sprigs graced the tops of three doorways.

"Very festive." Rachel stood in the one place he hadn't hung mistletoe. "Though I don't think I've ever seen so much mistletoe in one room."

"I like green and red."

She moved into the great room. Stopped. A sprig dangled overhead.

Damn. He was brilliant.

Too easy. He could have managed with much less mistletoe than he'd hung.

"I hope no one has mono," she said.

"I don't." Nate moved closer, each step calculated, not quite a jungle cat stalking prey, but he was full purpose. "Good thing, since you're standing under the mistletoe."

Panic flickered across her face. "Do you think this is a good idea?"

Elation soared. Anticipation surged. If she didn't want to kiss him, she would have retreated to the kitchen. But she was still standing here, looking at him, waiting.

Score.

"A kiss under the mistletoe. It's tradition. Nothing's going to happen from a holiday kiss."

She glanced at the doorway to the kitchen. "Make it fast. My timer's about to buzz."

"One quick kiss coming up."

Nate crossed his fingers when he said quick. He pressed his lips against hers, not wanting to give her a chance to change her mind.

Soft and sweet, the way he remembered from before. Totally delicious.

He moved his mouth over hers, soaking up her warmth. He'd always had a fondness for vanilla and cinnamon, not to mention gingerbread. But Rachel was now his favorite flavor, the perfect blend of sugar and spice. Boy, was it nice.

His arms wrapped around her, pulling her closer. The ends of her hair tickled his hand.

She arched against him, her breasts pressing against his chest.

He sifted his fingers through the strands of her hair. His tongue tangled with hers.

Rachel's arms looped around him.

He didn't know how much closer he could get to her, but he wanted to try. He wanted more of her kiss, more of her. He

MELISSA MCCLONE

pressed harder against her lips, his blood simmering.

She brought her hands down, her palms splayed on his chest, breaking the kiss. She backed away from him.

Her lips look swollen. Her neck and face flushed. Her ragged breathing matched his own. "That's wasn't, and I quote, 'one quick kiss.'"

No, it wasn't. But he had his answer. In spades. "Blame the mistletoe."

"Is that what you're going with?"

She didn't sound upset. The telltale worry lines above her nose hadn't appeared. But he was having a hard time thinking straight. "You bet."

Rachel looked up. "Thank you, mistletoe."

"Hey." He used his finger to bring her chin down. "How about thanking the guy who hung the mistletoe and just kissed you?"

Amusement twinkled in her eyes. "You said blame the mistletoe."

"I was wrong." In more ways than he could count. The mistletoe had proved something. Whatever he felt was oh-so-real. One kiss was never going to be enough. "The mistletoe was only the catalyst. Blame me."

"I may have to, since I asked Santa to bring me the wrong thing... towels."

"What do you want now?"

"More kisses." Her words floated in the air, as if gift wrapped and attached to a helium balloon.

"Towels are going to pale in comparison," he said.

"I know." She wet her swollen lips. "And here I had such high hopes for a perfect Christmas."

"How about I give you one of your presents early?"

"I don't see any gifts under the tree for me."

"Trust me, this is exactly what you want."

Oh, wow. Wow. Wow. Wow.

Nate's lips moved over Rachel's. His kiss was going at the top of Rachel's Christmas list from now on. The man knew how to kiss, sending sparkly tingles to places inside she'd forgotten about. Her toes were going to take a while to uncurl. She'd been kissed well before, but Nate's kiss... totally hot and better tasting than ganache.

313

Had she said wow?

Mistletoe was her new favorite holiday decoration. She would have to hang some in the kitchen. All over the house. And keep the green stuff hanging until Easter. Or Thanksgiving.

She heard a moan, a sexy sound.

Was that her?

If so, she wanted more. If not, she wanted him to kiss her until she sounded like that.

Rachel deepened the kiss.

Nate took the not-so-subtle hint. His lips pressed against hers, moving with a skill and precision that must have taken years to perfect. Rachel cared less about the women he'd kissed before. She was the one reaping the benefits now.

His hands held her close, one against her back, the other on her butt. She arched against him with unfamiliar eagerness. She didn't just want more kisses. She wanted all of him.

Slowly, molasses-being-poured-into-batter slow, Nate drew the kiss to an end. Desire gleamed in his eyes. "What do you think of your gift?"

"Best Christmas present ever."

"You think?"

She nodded. "Maybe we should try it again. To make sure."

Rachel took the lead this time. She kissed him, not tentative, like she'd been outside by the horses, but with deep need she didn't understand. She pressed her body against him and let her tongue explore his mouth.

Hunger and heat.

Talk about a turn-on.

Her hands ran up and down his back, feeling the muscles beneath her fingertips and palm. He did the same, touching her with his lips and hands until she felt mushy inside.

"What the hell is going on?" Ty yelled.

No. No. No. The fury in her brother's voice made Rachel jump back.

Nate raised his hands, palms out. "Mistletoe."

Ty's nostril's flared. She knew that look. At least he hadn't punched Nate. Not yet, anyway.

Rachel pointed to the ceiling, wanting to diffuse the

situation. Ty probably couldn't fathom the idea of her making out with a guy, let alone wanting to have sex. "Just a kiss under the mistletoe. A holiday tradition. That's all."

A vein ticked at Ty's jaw. "Looks like more to me."

Rachel shrugged. "I like kissing."

Nate nodded. "No harm intended."

"Where did all the mistletoe come from?" Ty asked.

"Getting ready for having people over on Christmas. Thought the place needed more decorations. Hanging mistletoe is easy plus livens things up a bit."

Ty's watchful gaze slid from Nate to Rachel. "Be careful where you two stand from now on."

"I will."

Her brother sounded worried, but she she didn't think Nate was trying to take advantage of her. Okay, he'd planted mistletoe all over the house. But that was because he wanted more kisses. She couldn't be upset when she'd wanted more, too.

Rachel noticed where her brother was standing. She stood on her tiptoes and kissed his cheek. "You'd better be careful, too."

The timer buzzed.

She'd never been so happy to hear that sound before. "I need to finish up dinner. You two clean up in here."

Part of her felt bad for letting Nate take all the heat, but the two men were friends.

What was the worst thing that could happen?

Nate watched Rachel disappear into the kitchen. Three, two, one…

"What in the hell are you thinking?" Ty picked up the ladder. "Let me guess, your little head was in charge instead of your brain."

"It was the mistletoe."

Ty glared. "You liked kissing her."

"I like kissing in general." Nate picked up the stapler and ribbon, not wanting to upset his friend with the truth. That he planned to keep kissing Rachel.

"So my sister was the only available pair of lips around?"

"Unless you count yours."

Ty shook his head. "You need to find yourself a woman."

Nate had found her. Rachel's smile, her eyes and the sound of her laughter captivated him as much as her hot kisses. "I've been trying."

"Try harder." Nate walked to the front door carrying the ladder. "I don't care if you're standing under twenty pounds of mistletoe, do not kiss Rachel again."

"Not even if it keeps her in Montana?"

Ty stopped. Cursed. "You said you'd do anything to keep me at the ranch, but flirting with my sister, making her like you, was never part of the plan."

"Whoa, cowboy. That's not what I'm doing."

"Sure about that?"

"Yes," Nate said firmly. "Rachel's a wonderful woman. Talented, smart, pretty. A guy would have to be crazy not to want to go out with her."

"A guy like you."

Nate straightened. "She could do worse."

"Look, I get that you love the Bar V5 and want the best for her. Me, too. But at what cost? Your dad told me about the time you brought a horse about to foal to a science fair."

"I won."

Ty's brows furrowed. "Three women fainted."

"Not the judges. Plus the prize money bought me another colt."

"Thank you for illustrating my point."

"Nothing wrong with winning."

"I saw you in action when you turned the Bar V5 around. No one believed you could do it, including me," Ty admitted. "I see what you've done with Rachel's gingerbread business, too."

"So what's the problem?"

"You want to win so badly, you're blind. You might not think kissing Rachel has anything to do with Operation: Hansel & Gretel, but I can't be sure about that. I don't want Rachel's heart to get caught up in your drive to succeed." Ty's jaw tensed. "Touch my sister again and I will hurt you. Bad."

And leave the Bar V5.

The words were unspoken, but implied.

"No one is leaving." Not Ty. Not Rachel. Nate knew his friend was speaking out of genuine concern for his sister, with a heart full of worry. Nate wasn't about to hurt Rachel. All he needed was more time to figure this out. "I've gotten to know your sister this week."

"Sure as hell better not be in the biblical sense."

That wasn't worth a response. "Today I figured out the best way to keep Rachel in Montana."

"How?"

"By giving her what she wants most for Christmas." Nate wasn't talking towels or more kisses, but when she'd talked about presents, he knew what would keep Rachel in Montana. That made the gift perfect for Ty, too. "I'll take care of everything tomorrow. Trust me, you'll be able to pack her stuff up in Phoenix and be back here in time for New Year's."

That way she'd be kissing Nate when the clock struck midnight on New Year's Eve.

Ty led the way to the shed. "Promise me it doesn't have anything to do with kissing or the exchange of bodily fluids."

"Promise."

"Okay, then." Ty looked over at him. "Do you think the Broncos will beat the Seahawks on Sunday?"

After dinner, Rachel retreated to her room. She assumed her brother and Nate had worked things out, given she saw no split lips, bloody noses or black eyes. A big relief.

She put on her pajamas and slid into bed with a cookbook. Staring at ingredients and cooking techniques was better than analyzing every second of kissing Nate earlier.

A knock sounded on her door.

Rachel's heart leaped. She placed her book on the bed. A few kisses could change everything. She wasn't falling for him. She'd fallen. Hard.

Anticipation hummed through her. She brushed her fingers through her hair then pinched her cheeks to give them color. "Come in."

Ty entered.

She ignored the rush of disappointment and kept her smile in place. "Hi."

He sat on the edge of the bed. "New cookbook?"

She nodded. "Like to check out the competition."

A beat passed. And another. "He won't touch you again."

Rachel didn't need Ty to tell her who *he* was. "I'm an adult. You don't have to watch out for me. I can take care of myself."

"What about the Darbys?"

That hurt. But Rachel wasn't about to cower or cry like she'd done in the past. Nate had made her see she was stronger than that. She raised her chin.

"I made a mistake." She'd been playing it safe, but that hadn't kept her from getting hurt. Maybe it was time to try something new and take a chance. "But Nate's not like that. You said so yourself."

"I was talking about getting business advice from him, not having a vacation fling."

"We kissed. That's a far cry from a fling. Though whether I have sex with anyone is none of your business."

A pained expression crossed his face. "Rach..."

"You told me you trusted Nate. You must. You work for him."

"I don't really work for him," Ty said. "We're more like partners. All the Bar V5 livestock, except a couple horses, belong to me."

"I don't understand. I knew you owned some animals, but all of them?"

"Nate's father suffered dementia. Decided to have a barn sale and get rid of the livestock. I tried to stop him. When that didn't work, I called Nate, but couldn't reach him. I drained my bank account, maxed out my credit cards and borrowed money from Brock Sheenan to keep the herd together. The horses, too."

"I can't believe you kept that a secret. Why didn't you tell me?"

"Because you kept asking me to come back to Arizona. I knew if I told you, you wouldn't ask even if you needed me back."

"Ty..."

"It's okay. "He touched her hand. "When Nate took over for his dad, he offered me a half stake in the Bar V5 for half a share of the animals. Land. A house. My name on the deed. But I said no."

"That sounds like more than a fair offer."

"Overly fair, but this land has been in his family for generations. It was an original homestead way back when. Only a Vaughn should be on the deed. We made a deal, a partnership. I keep my animals here and run the entire operation."

"That's wonderful." The reality of his words sank in. Weight pressed down on her chest, making breathing difficult. "You're never coming back to Arizona."

Her words were whisper soft. All she could manage under the circumstances. She knew he loved Montana, but she'd always hoped they could live closer someday.

"Well." He blew out a breath. "I've been thinking about moving back."

Rachel straightened. "But look what you have here at Bar V5. You can't leave and give up all this."

"I'm too far away from you."

And Mom and Dad. She never understood his choosing to live so far away from the place their parents were buried. A place Rachel found solace. Her family. She studied Ty's face. "You'd give up everything for me?"

"You might not be a kid, but you still need your big brother. And I need my li'l sis."

"I do need you. I love you," she said. "But you've sacrificed enough. You put your life on hold once for me. I'm not letting you give up your dream and your animals for me. It's not an option."

"Any chance you'd consider moving this way? Bozeman is a nice town. Butte, Billings and Helena are bigger cities."

"I don't need a city. Marietta or Livingston would be fine, but I hate to leave Mom and Dad."

"Baby, you know they aren't there."

"It's all I have left. I've… forgotten so much."

"Mom and Dad would want us to be together, even if that meant we weren't near their graves."

Rachel nodded, in her heart she knew that was true.

"There's another reason I could see moving here."

"Your business."

"That and… I like Nate."

"I like him, too."

"I really, really like him."

Ty stared at her, confusion written all over his face. His mouth formed a perfect o. "So it wasn't all about the mistletoe."

"Not for me."

His gaze narrowed. "Nate? Really?"

She nodded.

"I thought you'd end up with a chef, someone you had a lot in common with."

"Do you think you'll end up with a cowgirl?"

"No, but—"

"I tried the chef thing. Epic fail."

"Really? I had no—"

"You're not the only one with secrets."

"Guess not."

"We can't plan who we fall in love with."

Ty's mouth gaped. He closed it. "Is that what you think this thing with Nate is? Love? Because I'm not sure—"

"I'm not one hundred percent positive, either." Though Rachel was ninety-nine-point-nine percent sure she was falling in love with Nate Vaughn. She held her brother's hand. "But I want to find out. I need to."

Ty started to speak, then stopped himself. He tried again. "I told Nate not to touch you again or I'd hurt him."

Her shoulder's sagged. "Ty."

"I accused him of using you to keep me at the Bar V5. The guy has put the ranch before a woman every single time. You deserve—"

"To figure this out on my own," she interrupted. "Your business relationship with Nate is separate from mine with him. My choices or crises cannot dictate your decisions. You have to step back. Let me fail again if that's what it takes."

"Rach…"

She squeezed his hand. "One thing life's taught me—Nate's taught me, actually—is I don't have to be afraid of failure. Some ideas, some businesses, some relationships don't work out. That's okay. My failures are what got me here. Made me who I am. They'll lead to my success. I can feel it in my heart."

Ty's lopsided smile appeared. "My baby sister must be grown up if she's teaching me a thing or two."

"Too bad you won't learn to cook," she teased. "I don't know how you guys got along without me."

"Looks like we might not have to."

Rachel felt like she belonged at the ranch. She hoped Nate felt the same way.

"Come here." Ty hugged her, the way he'd done her entire life, but for the first time she let go before he did. "I'll still kick his ass if he hurts you. I'll quit, and he knows it."

"I'm sure he does. Nate's a smart guy."

Smart enough to take a chance on her? Only time would tell, but Rachel was ready to jump. She hoped he would be there to catch her.

Or have his extra parachute handy.

Chapter Nine

Sold out!

Two days before Christmas and no more gingerbread for Rachel to bake, unless the boys at the Bar V5 wanted more. She walked out of the toy store with a spring to her step, an unbelievable balance in her checking account, and her heart full of... intense *like* for the man at her side.

The clear blue Montana sky greeting her was the icing on the this-is-really-happening cake. "We did it! I have enough money for a deposit and fixtures and...I'm going to pull this off. Thanks to you."

Nate's smile made her breath catch in her throat and the sun pale in comparison. "This was all you. I was just the idea guy."

"And the marketing guy and the networking guy."

And her guy?

Tingles tap-danced through her. She sure hoped so.

She was staying, moving here once she packed up her apartment. She'd talked to her landlord last night. They had a waitlist for units, so he was happy to accept her notice to vacate and break her lease. Soon she would be living in Montana.

With her brother.

Maybe with...

No, she didn't want to jinx anything.

Nate had factored into her decision making, but she hadn't wanted the move to be dependent on him or what he thought or...

Tell him, an inner voice urged.

Rachel hadn't told Ty about moving yet. Not officially, and Nate probably didn't have a clue what she was thinking.

She took a deep breath. The cold air stung her lungs, but she inhaled again to muster her courage.

"I have a surprise for you," Nate said before Rachel could open her mouth. "Come with me."

He led her across Main Street towards the diner. She followed excited to find out the surprise. "A celebration lunch?"

"Better."

They crossed First Street heading toward Grey's Saloon. Two customers sat at the bar, though it wasn't lunchtime yet.

"Little early for cocktails, don't you think?" she asked.

"We're not getting drinks, though we may later. To celebrate."

Another kiss? Rachel hoped so. She liked those kinds of surprises.

They passed Marietta Western Wear. "Guess that means coffee at the Java Café is out."

He stopped in front of an empty storefront with a *STYLES REAL ESTATE For Lease* sign in the window. "Look at this place."

"Great location." Rachel peered through the glass windows to see brick walls and wood floors. She imagined where the display cases would go and tables, including a separate party area. And the space was available. Her pulse accelerated, picking up speed until she had to force herself to breathe. "So much character. It's wonderful."

Perfect for a bakery.

Her bakery.

Excitement buzzing down to her toes, she cupped her hands on the glass for a better look. This was the ultimate in window shopping, more of a thrill than anything she could buy. Having Nate think along the same lines was a double thrill.

The lone woman inside looked to be in her fifties or sixties, dressed stylishly in a long, tan wool coat and black boots. She removed the *For Lease* sign out of the window then walked out the front door, a beaming smile on her face. "Hello. Fancy meeting you out here."

Rachel stared at the sign in the woman's hand, her excitement replaced with a heavy disappointment. Someone had leased the shop.

Her shoulders dropped, but she straightened a second later, not about to let anything ruin a wonderful morning. Chances were she couldn't afford the prime retail spot anyway, and seeing this place gave her hope she could find something similar, if not in Marietta then another nearby town.

Nate motioned to the woman. "Rachel, this is Elinor Styles. She runs the Styles Realty Office here in town. Her son Tod is a realtor. Elinor, meet my friend Rachel Murphy."

Friend. But Rachel realized this wasn't a disappointment to pout over, either. Nate *was* her friend, and her business adviser, even her inspiration. If she wanted him to be more, that was a separate story. "Always good to meet another friend of Nate's."

Elinor set the sign at her feet, shook Rachel's hand then handed a set of keys to Nate. "He's off showing a property. I know you wanted the keys right away."

Rachel didn't understand. Her gaze bounced from Elinor to Nate.

"I love my gingerbread house," Elinor continued without missing a beat. "The Copper Mountain Gingerbread and Dessert Factory will be a nice addition to Main Street. Merry Christmas."

Rachel's heart pounded in her throat. She tried to speak. Ask the questions hammering her brain. But she couldn't find her voice.

"Thanks, Elinor," Nate said, as if the woman had handed him a candy cane and not the keys to a dream location for a bakery. "Have a Merry Christmas."

With a wave, Elinor jaywalked across Main Street.

Rachel searched Nate's face for answers, but saw only an oh-so-pleased-with-himself smile. "You leased this shop?"

"For you." With his hand at the small of her back, he escorted her into the building. "This is your surprise. Beats a set of towels."

What about more kisses? Those had replaced the towels on her list, but this... She wasn't sure what was going on.

"Christmas is two days away, but I couldn't wait," he continued. "What do you think?"

A part of her wanted to be excited, to throw her arms around Nate and kiss him. Hard. Except he was acting like a business advisor, not a wanna-be boyfriend. Every public moment they'd shared had been business-related, like she was some kind of project. Beyond the mistletoe kiss Ty witnessed, Nate had never let anyone else think they might be involved.

As if he had an agenda.

"I don't know what to say." That was the truth. "I mean, this is so generous. I'm overwhelmed. But why would you lease this space for me? I live in Phoenix, not here."

Not yet anyway. But he didn't know that.

"I know you talked about going back to Phoenix and opening a shop there, but when I took a closer look at this place, I knew it was perfect for the bakery you told me about. Space for your baked goods and an event area." He reminded her of a salesman warming up to give his pitch. "You've made a name for yourself in Marietta. You have a clientele ready to support your new business. Not to mention Ty's here."

Ty.

I accused him of using you to keep me at the Bar V5. The guy has put the ranch before a woman every single time.

Her brother's words from the other night hit Rachel like a cast iron skillet. The air rushed from her lungs. Her knees wobbled. She reached out to grab hold of something, but only Nate was there.

Rachel jerked her arm back. "You leased this place because of Ty."

"I leased this place for you, as a believer and backer of your products, skill and potential. But if you staying makes Ty happy then it's a win-win."

Nate's words sunk in, swirled around her mind, dropped straight to her feet, landing next to where her heart had just crashed, sans parachute. Destruction complete.

She should feel hurt, anger, some awful, icky emotion over what the man she'd fallen in love with had done, not this odd numbness as if she were an outside observer. "Leasing this place. Helping me with my business. It was all so I'd move to Montana and Ty would stay at the Bar V5."

"I told you I wanted to help you so I could repay Ty."

"What you did, you're doing, is not repaying a favor." Everything was so clear to Rachel now. "It's not about Ty. He says you owe him nothing. It's about you wanting to keep your foreman. Your partner. Livestock."

Nate's forehead creased. His mouth slanted. "That's not

fair."

"Do you think kissing me was fair, making me think there was more there than friendship between us, making me want to stay in Montana to find out?"

He took a step forward, his gaze intent upon hers. "I want you to stay and figure things out. Don't let this change your mind about anything."

"Oh, it won't." She lifted her chin. "I am staying, but that decision has nothing to do with you. Not now anyway."

"Rachel—"

"Did our kisses mean anything to you?"

"Yes," he replied, without hesitation. "Kissing you wasn't part of this."

"Part of what?"

"The plan," he said after a long pause. "To keep you here. Ty knows about it. Operation: Hansel & Gretel."

She half-laughed, more saddened than amused. "Brother, sister, gingerbread. Clever. So what did you call your plan to keep Marissa here? Project: City Mouse or Operation: Tiffany Cut?"

"Don't say that." Nate reached for her, but she backed away, not wanting him to touch her. "I thought you'd be happy, not upset."

"I'm not upset. I probably should be, but I'm not. I'm more...resigned. This isn't the first time someone let me down." She stared at this perfect space, at the man she'd believed was perfect for her. "But I really thought I could trust you. I wanted to believe I could."

"You can."

Rachel looked at Nate, as if seeing him for the first time. "You're as bad as the Darbys."

He frowned. "Come on, that's not true."

"It is." The realization made the numbness disappear. Her heart split into jagged, raw pieces. "You're willing to do whatever it takes to get what you want. The Darbys are the same. They stole my dream, ripped it right out of my hands. But you tried to change my dream, not because it would be better for me, but to benefit you and the Bar V5. And you did this after knowing what I'd been through."

"Rachel, please..."

"I have to go." A lump burned in her throat. Her eyes stung. She struggled to hold herself together. "I can't accept your gift, but no worries. Ty won't be going anywhere. I'm going to ask him to pack up my things. I'd rather not go back to the ranch."

Nate touched her shoulder, holding her back. "Can I convince you to sit down and talk it through over lunch?"

Her gaze locked on his desperate eyes. "No. You've done too much convincing already."

She walked out of the shop with her shoulders squared and a headache about to erupt. Not that anything could be worse than her aching heart.

You have to step back. Let me fail again if that's what it takes.

Ty had done what she asked. And she'd failed.

Even though her heart had led her to believe she would succeed.

She had no idea what to do. All she knew was she hurt and love sucked and she wished Christmas was already over.

Nate downed the rest of his beer at Grey's Saloon. He caught bartender and owner Jason Grey's eye. "Another, please."

Jason refilled the glass with a local microbrew. "You can't drink away your troubles."

"No, but I can forget them for a while."

"Thought I might find you here." Ty slid onto the next stool. "Let me guess, the present you got her didn't go over well."

Nate raised his pint. "I crashed and burned. Disintegrated into a billion particles. Most of which will never be seen again."

"Ouch."

Nate sipped. Two beers weren't going to be enough. Four might give him a proper buzz. Six might do the trick. "Leave me alone. I have some serious drinking to do."

"Looks like I'll have to stick around to drive you home," Ty said.

Nate set his beer on the bar. He looked over at Ty, at his

best friend and his partner. "You'd do that?"

Ty tipped his hat. "That's what friends do for each other."

"Even after I broke Rachel's heart."

Ty's face reddened. His nostrils flared. "You son of a…"

He punched Nate. A right hook that he hadn't seen coming.

Jason grabbed Ty from across the bar. "Take it outside or I call the police."

Ty held up his hands. "No need. I did what I had to do."

Nate rubbed his aching jaw. Nothing felt broken. But man, he hurt. "Feel better?"

Ty flexed his fingers. "Yeah, but my hand doesn't."

"I deserved it."

"Damn straight you did."

"Rachel's staying in Montana."

"I thought she might, but you're certain?"

Nate nodded once. The movement sent a sharp pain through the left side of his face. Maybe he'd spoken too soon about something being broken. "Told me so herself. Right before she walked out of her shop."

"What shop?"

He touched his lips. At least he wasn't bleeding. Good, Jason wouldn't want a mess at the bar. "The one I gave her. Well, tried to give her. I leased the space next to the pharmacy. But she doesn't want it."

Ty shook his head. "You're not only stubborn like your dad, Vaughn, you're as stupid as an ass. And you can't use dementia as an excuse."

"Huh?"

"You can't use bribes to get an easy win."

"I wasn't—"

"You were." Ty grabbed Nate's glass and took a long swig. "You tried it with me and Marissa. Given all that money you spent on degrees from fancy universities, you should have realized that doesn't work and changed your MO."

Nate thought about his offer to Ty four years ago. How he'd proposed to Marissa, purchased a ring, an SUV and given her a credit card with no spending limit. Those things hadn't been for Ty or for Marissa, but for Nate. "Crap. You're right."

Ty motioned to Jason for another round. "The truth

hurts."

"I was focused on the win, getting Rachel to move, but only so that part was out of the way. Then we could move on to more interesting negotiations." Nate put up his hands in surrender. "Don't hit me again. I meant that with due respect to the woman I'm falling in love with."

Beers appeared in front of them. Ty sipped his. "You're such an idiot. Even I know that order would never work. And don't mention love and my sister in the same sentence unless you've fallen and mean it."

"Do you think Rachel would give me a second chance? To switch the order."

"Not if you call it negotiations, buddy. Most women don't appreciate being considered a business transaction. I know my sister. That'll scare her faster than anything."

Fair enough. "I hurt her bad. She said I was no different than the Darbys."

Ty stared over the rim of his beer. "Were you?"

Nate remembered what she'd told him. "Yeah, I was. Worse actually. She'd told me how hurt she'd been, but I didn't let that stop me."

From trying to win.

And now he'd lost.

He was only beginning to realize how much.

Nate pushed his beer aside. "If I were her, I'd never want to see me again."

Ty took a sip from his glass. "So what are you going to do about it?"

"I don't know," Nate admitted. "But I sure as hell don't plan on making the same mistake again."

Would that be enough for Rachel?

On December twenty-fourth, Rachel stood outside the Dutch door at the Bar V5. Her cellphone buzzed. She didn't have to look at the screen to know another text from Nate had arrived. He wanted to see her.

Too bad.

Nate was in town, trying to track her down. Ty had told

her as much when he handed off the keys to his pickup. Her brother had packed up her things, but Rachel wanted to make sure nothing had been forgotten, especially her baking gear. She also had something only she could drop off. This ranch had felt like home. She couldn't leave without a final farewell.

The mudroom door was unlocked, as it usually was during the day. With a tote bag hanging from her shoulder, she carried the boxes containing gingerbread houses and trees inside, walking straight to the dining room.

Rachel dropped the tote on the table then set the boxes next to her bag. She never wanted to see Nate again, so she was planning a move to Butte or Helena. A little far from Ty, but closer than Phoenix and safer for her heart than Marietta. She opened the top box.

The scent of gingerbread greeted her, a bittersweet smell that intensified the squeezing, achy pain in her chest. Even though she wanted to wring Nate's clueless neck, she owed him for the use of his kitchen, letting her stay here in a beautiful room and sharing his business expertise.

Rachel was here to pay in the only currency she had that Nate might appreciate—gingerbread.

Then she could move on, feeling no further obligation to Nate Vaughn. Well, as long as she didn't need her heart back soon. The emotions would take time to heal. The memories would linger, too. Not for too long, she hoped.

She took in the majestic tree's ornament-laden branches, her name on one of the stockings by the fireplace, the cursed sprigs of mistletoe hanging like acrobatic Cupids and the breathtaking mountains outside the windows.

The vise tightening around her heart made breathing difficult. But being here was hard. Only a day ago she thought she might stay here forever with Nate, with the man she'd fallen in love with. Now she was looking at the ranch for the last time.

She wouldn't be returning. Not ever.

The tears she expected pricked her eyes. She was horrible at goodbyes. Maybe because they were never her choice.

Pull yourself together.

With a wipe of her eyes, Rachel set to work on the gingerbread. She had to be finished before Nate returned. That didn't give her much time. Marietta was a small town to search.

Chapter Ten

The ranch was the last place Nate wanted to be on Christmas Eve. Too empty. Too quiet. Too lonely. Just like his life.

Until Rachel had arrived.

If only he hadn't screwed up.

She'd told him exactly how to break her trust, and he'd used her own words, like a map, to do just that. What burned the most was he'd become one of *them*, people she believed had manipulated her for their own gain.

People she never wanted to speak to again.

His talk with Ty yesterday had sparked hope. If Nate could tell Rachel he didn't care whether her brother remained his partner maybe she'd give him another chance. All Nate cared about was getting her back, earning her trust.

Earning, not winning.

But Nate had tried calling, texting, emailing, showing up at Ty's apartment in person and searching through town. There were no more chances.

Worse, he only had himself to blame.

Nate tossed his keys onto a bench in the mudroom. He didn't remove his boots. Who cared if the floors got wet? He didn't care about anything but Rachel.

Maybe he should cancel tomorrow's Christmas potluck dinner. He didn't feel like being a gracious host or cooking a turkey. Getting drunk sounded pretty damn good. There hadn't been time for that yesterday or today.

He walked into the dark kitchen, the only lights the glowing digits on the microwave clock. The Nativity play at the church would be starting in less than an hour. Most everyone he knew would be there, including Rachel. At least that was what Annie had told him this afternoon when he'd stopped by the diner.

An elephant, one with an amazing memory, seemed to sit on his chest. Damn, he could hardly breathe.

He walked past the bare island and counters. No gingerbread or cookies or cakes in sight. No mouthwatering scent of baked goods in the oven or dinner simmering on a burner. No mealtime where he would get to sit next to her and listen to her talk and talk.

Nate missed Rachel so much.

He lengthened his stride to get out of the kitchen faster. The memories of her were too strong, even in the darkness. Maybe by spring he wouldn't mind so much. Until then he'd eat out or cook at the bunkhouse's small kitchen.

In the great room, the Christmas tree lights twinkled. He could build a fire and turn on a few lamps. Or maybe not. Sitting in the darkness fit his mood.

Tiny white lights reflected in the window. Ones he didn't recognize.

Nate took a closer look.

On top of the dining room table sat a huge gingerbread house, a replica of the Bar V5, the barn and three lighted trees.

Air rushed from his lungs.

I want one.

Yours is on me. A thank you.

Rachel had remembered and gone overboard with the lights inside, mimicking the warm glow through the windows. He'd told her about getting lost in a blizzard one February. Frostbitten, he'd found his way home due to that light. She'd made tiny footprints—his footprints—in the snow, depicting the moment he'd reached safety at the ranch. The moment when the warmth of his home had not only enveloped him, but saved his life.

Nate's heart beat like the timpani in Handel's Messiah. He forced his feet to move, turning on the light when he reached the dining room.

A small envelope with his name written in cursive leaned against the tree. He opened the flap and removed a note card. The picture on the front showed two gingerbread men with bowties and a red-plaid heart ornament leaning against a lantern with a lit votive candle inside. Cheery and Christmassy. Very Rachel-like. He opened the card.

Nate,

I appreciate you giving me free rein in your kitchen and house. Being at the Bar V5 was a dream come true this December. My goal was to make enough with my gingerbread to afford a lease deposit. Thanks to you and your business expertise, I have more than enough seed money to start my own bakery. I hope you have a very Merry Christmas and find your heart's desire in the New Year. Thanks again for everything!

Sincerely,

Rachel

She'd drawn a heart on the right side of her name.

He reread the note. Twice. If she were speaking the words, she would sound thankful, appreciative, professional.

All business, but that was okay.

At least she didn't sound upset, angry, hateful.

Every word spoke of her gratitude. She even wanted him to find his heart's desire. Too bad he'd found it, only to screw up and lose the one thing that meant the most.

That elephant returned, stomping on his heart, the pain more intense than before. He plopped onto one of the dining room chairs.

Rachel.

He loved her.

It was as simple and as complicated as that.

He'd screwed up. He'd been a first class jackass. But he couldn't let her go without at least trying to make things right. And apologize.

His gaze zeroed in on the heart next to her name.

She hadn't sounded angry. No attitude or negativity. That had to be a good sign.

The heart could be another sign.

A choir might not be singing Hallelujah, but the hope growing inside him more than made up for the lack of voices.

Nate could be in denial. He would admit being desperate.

But a woman who stormed away from him with tears gleaming in her eyes only to bring him a special gingerbread house and a gracious note was capable of forgiveness.

He pulled out his cellphone to call Ty. This had to work. Otherwise tomorrow really would be a blue Christmas.

At Ty's apartment, Rachel sat on the couch and wrapped her brother's last stocking stuffer. The green and red polka-dotted paper was cheery, but she felt as if Christmas had gone missing and she didn't know where to look for it.

But she couldn't give up—or give in—to the melancholy wanting to bring her down.

Yes, her heart was hurting. Broken. She'd misjudged someone again, and fallen in love with him to make the situation even harder.

But she'd told Ty she was okay if she failed.

Time to suck it up. Put on her big girl panties. Not ruin Christmas for her brother. She'd survived losses and not been broken. She'd survived because Ty had been at her side. When he left Arizona, she'd been disappointed, hurt even, but she understood. He had his own life to live and dreams to follow. Even from far away, he did what he could to make sure she felt loved. Ty deserved to be happy. And so did she. If all they ever had for family was each other, she was still lucky.

This was going to be their first white Christmas. The first of many.

Rachel glanced at the clock hanging on the wall. She had fifteen minutes until the Nativity play started, plenty of time to make the short walk to the church and meet Zack, who was driving out from the Bar V5 where Ty was held up.

But he'd promised he would be back at the apartment when she returned. She hoped so because tonight was one night she couldn't bear to be alone.

"What in the hell are you scheming now?"

The sound of Ty's voice made Nate look up from his computer monitor. "Thanks for staying late."

"You haven't answered my question."

"I'm going to get your sister back. She made me a gingerbread house and a barn. A tree, too."

"As a thank you. That's what Rachel does."

"I've got a chance." Nate couldn't explain why he felt that way when the odds suggested he would fail, but he did. "If I don't at least try... I've got a plan."

Ty rolled his eyes. "Heaven help us, another plan."

"This is a good one."

"You always think so."

"I'm going to present the pros and cons of Rachel making Marietta her home vs. moving to another town in Montana."

Ty stepped closer to the laptop. Scowled. "Aw, bloody hell. Please tell me you're not making her a PowerPoint presentation."

"It'll get the job done."

He closed the laptop. "Stop. Don't treat her like one of your investments. Rachel's not looking for a business partner. She's looking for love."

"I care about your sister. More than I've cared about any other woman."

"Then stop with the venture capital mumbo jumbo crap. This is a decision she needs to make with her heart, not her head. Don't show Rachel slides full of useless statistics and pretty pictures about which place to call home. Show her."

Show her.

Nate let the two words sink in. He was good at telling people things. He'd made a successful career out of telling. Showing, not so much. He wasn't even sure what Ty meant or how to pull it off, but Nate knew in his heart a PowerPoint presentation wasn't going to get the job done.

Rachel needed to understand why staying in Marietta was the best thing for her. Not Ty. Definitely not Nate.

But he wanted her to know what she meant to him. She needed to know that, too, even if her knowing changed nothing.

But how?

How could he show Rachel where she belonged and how he felt and make her understand this was home?

On the morning of December twenty-fifth, Rachel stared out Ty's apartment window. Fluffy snowflakes fell from the sky. "Merry Christmas to me."

Bah humbug would match her mood better. Okay, not really. Her heavy heart wasn't ready to embrace an Ebenezer Scrooge attitude, but she wished...

Don't think about him.

She couldn't think about him. Not today. Not tomorrow. Maybe someday.

Rachel tossed off the covers. No matter how much she felt like crying and moping, she wouldn't. Ty wanted this to be the best Christmas ever. She would make that happen. She'd prepared a Swedish Tea Ring last night. All she needed to do was stick the pan in the oven to bake.

She put on a robe, slipped her bare feet into fuzzy slippers then padded her way into the living room.

Stopped. Gasped.

She blinked then refocused. Still there.

Santa stood next to the tree in a full red suit, a leather belt with shiny gold buckle and boots, polished black boots. A fake beard hid his face and wire-rimmed glasses made seeing his eye color difficult. He tipped his red cowboy hat. "Ho-ho-ho."

The booming low voice didn't sound familiar. He was too far away for her to recognize. But she knew exactly who Santa's partner in crime was this white Christmas morning.

Ty, wearing an elf hat, stood next to the jolly fellow in red. He looked silly, embarrass-via-social-media-silly, but affection for her brother swelled. "Hey."

Not exactly Elvish, but at least understandable and recognizable. Which was more than she could say about the situation.

Rachel moved farther into the room. Each step brought her closer to Santa. She took a closer look. Her heart jammed up into her throat. Not Kris Kringle.

Nate.

She clutched the back of the recliner. Her fingers dug into the leather. "I don't understand."

Ty stepped forward, gave her a big hug, the kind that

always made her feel better. Not this time. "Merry Christmas, kiddo."

"You, too." She searched her brother's face for an explanation. He knew how she felt. She couldn't understand why he'd brought Nate here on Christmas morning. "What's going on?"

"Ask Santa."

She faced Nate, her insides trembling. This was the man she loved, the man who had broken her trust. She wanted to feel indifferent to him and hated that she felt much more than that. "So…"

He removed his hat, and with a flourish, bowed. "I'm the Santa of What Could Be."

Heart racing, mind scrambling to make sense of his words. "Huh?"

"Dickens—A Christmas Carol," Nate said.

So sweet. Her heart jangled like jingle bells.

Nope. Not sweet. Manipulative.

To protect herself, she crossed her arms over her chest. She couldn't let her heart start hoping, wishing. That would be too painful. Her emotions were too fragile. "Those were ghosts."

"Ghosts are dead," Nate explained. "I'm very much alive. Plus I didn't have access to a ghost costume so I thought Santa would do."

"I know this is confusing," Ty said to her. "But just go with it. For me."

Rachel would do anything for Ty. For Nate, not so much. But her brother's pleading gaze convinced her. "Okay. So what kind of ghost…Santa…are you again?"

"I'm the Santa of What Could Be." Nate placed his hat on his head. "I want to show you what your life could be like if you lived in Marietta."

She gave Ty a look. "Did you put him up to this?"

He held up his hands, palms facing her. "I take no credit. This is one hundred percent his idea. I'm just his—"

"Elf," she offered.

"Better an elf than Mrs. Claus." Ty winked. "Hear him out, Rach. Please?"

She nodded. "So Santa, what do you want to show me?"

Nate pointed to the bedroom door. "You need to get dressed first."

"Scrooge got to wear his pajamas," she countered, relieved she'd put on her robe. Not that flannel long sleeved jammies showed anything, but it made her feel self-conscious.

"Hypothermia isn't a concern in novels and movies," he said.

Good point. She'd bought herself a special Christmas outfit, to celebrate her move and look cute for Nate. The last part no longer applied, but why let new clothes go to waste? "I'll go change."

Nate watched Rachel disappear into the bedroom, his heart sinking with each of her steps. "This was a stupid idea."

Ty played with the bell at the end of his hat. "I tried to tell you that."

"Thanks for your support."

"Come on. I'm here, dressed like an idiot, so you can try to get my sister back. I wouldn't be helping if I didn't believe you could make her happy. I realize you must love her if you're willing to go to so much effort."

Nate had been up all night figuring things out. "I love Rachel so much I'd leave the Bar V5 to you and follow her anywhere, even the desert."

"That's all I need to hear. I pray this works. Just don't be an idiot." Ty straightened his stupid-looking elf hat. "While you put on your show, I'll be a good elf and have everything ready at the Bar V5."

"*If* she comes back with me."

"She'll come back to the ranch if she knows I'm there."

He sighed. "That's not the reason I want to use to get her to the ranch."

"Joking." Ty shook his head. The bell at the tip of his hat jingled. "Man, I hope this works out or you are going to be one helluva pain in the ass."

"That's no way to talk to your partner."

"No, but if you actually pull this off and one day become my brother-in-law…"

"I have your permission?"

"Damn straight you do. But if you blow this—"

"I won't." He couldn't. Not now.

Rachel was all Nate wanted for Christmas. He would never ask for anything else. "You know what to do."

"Committed to memory." Ty tapped his forehead. "But I have a backup copy in my pocket in case I forget."

"Don't forget."

"Again. Joking."

"Sorry." Nate had no sense of humor this morning when his future happiness depended on the outcome.

"Let me know when you're on the way home," Ty said.

Nate nodded, feeling anything but confident.

Ty slapped his shoulder. "No worries. This will be the best Christmas ever. I promised Rachel, and I always keep my promises to her."

I want that job.

Nate wanted to be the guy who kept promises to Rachel. To earn her trust. To take care of her. And much, much more.

To do that, he needed to nail the most important, and most unusual presentation he'd ever given. But this wasn't for a job or an investment. This was for something much more important. His future, his life. Not to mention his heart.

Nate adjusted the belt on his Santa suit. "You do your part, and I'll do mine."

That was all he could do.

The rest would be up to Rachel.

Ten minutes later, Rachel walked out of the bedroom. She looked around the apartment. Things were missing, including her brother. "Where's Ty?"

"On his way to the Bar V5."

Yearning struck, a pang at her heart. She ignored the feeling. "Did he take the presents and stockings or did the Grinch stop by and clean us out while you had your head up the chimney?"

"Your brother has everything with him."

"We're spending Christmas here at the apartment, not the

ranch."

Sweat beaded on Nate's forehead. She'd never seen him look so nervous.

"You can bring the presents back when we're finished," he said finally.

"Let's get this over with then." Rachel didn't care about the impatience in her tone. Nate might be dressed up like Santa in a red suit and a fake beard, but he was still capable of unleashing butterflies in her stomach. Getting over a guy like Nate would take a long time, but she couldn't be with a man she didn't trust. Her body would have to deal with it for however long this took.

He led her downstairs to the street. His horse, Arrow, was tied to a bike rack.

That was odd. She knew how much the animal meant to him. "You brought your horse to town."

"I don't have any magical powers or flying reindeer to wow you with, so I figured Arrow would have to do."

He'd gone to a lot of trouble. She didn't want to be touched, but she was. A little excited, too. Anticipation thrummed. She tamped it, not wanting to get carried away. "What are we going to do?"

"You're going to ride." Nate steadied Arrow with one hand and helped her up into the saddle with the other. "I'll lead you to our first stop to show you…"

"What could be," she finished for him, remembering when they'd watched A Christmas Carol together, and how he'd claimed to be optimistic. Did he feel that way about her? About…them?

Not that how he felt mattered. Not much anyway.

He walked west, toward the shops on Main Street. The street was deserted. Everyone was at home with family.

Except for her.

Her stomach clenched. Ty was at the ranch. That might as well be Alaska at the moment.

Nate stopped in front of the space he'd leased for her. Arrow stopped, his eyes intent on his master. But Nate was looking at her with such intensity she couldn't breathe.

"I know you don't want this place, but I signed the lease. I'd rather not sublease it, but will if you don't want the space.

The decision is yours."

"I already decided."

"Yesterday. You made the right decision then. I hope once we're finished here, you'll reconsider."

What did that mean?

He continued walking. "Our next stop is a place you know well, but will know better and love as much as the rest of us living in Marietta...the Main Street Diner. It's the perfect place for dates and special occasions, birthdays and anniversaries. You, Paige, and Annie will become friends. Share recipes and girls' nights out. Start a book club. Be godmothers and honorary aunts for each other's children. You need more friends in town than your brother and Nate. Not that Nate isn't a good boy, but he has ulterior motives, as you know."

His words implied so much more. Her heart beat rapidly, agitating the butterflies. Maybe she should skip the tour and just go home. "Nate..."

"There is no Nate here. Only Santa."

Next came City Hall for any and all her licensing needs, whatever he meant by that.

The church, adorned with a festive wreath on the door and a large Nativity set out front, was their third stop because, as Nate explained it, this was where much of life happened when you lived in a small town. "You'll attend weddings and christenings here."

Rachel didn't know what Nate was up to, but she didn't like it. Especially when she was imagining their wedding taking place inside this church and baptizing their six babies, too. "I know what happens at churches."

"One day you'll walk up these steps in a beautiful white gown with a veil on your head, a bouquet in your hands, and your brother complaining he looks like a penguin at your side. When you walk out, you'll be on the arm of the man who loves you."

The picture he painted with his words was one she'd dreamed about, with him playing a starring role. She swallowed around the lump of longing in her throat. "I see Marietta's appeal, but I'd like to get back to the apartment so Ty can come home and we can celebrate Christmas."

"Only a couple more stops." Arrow's hoofs clomped, all the way to the Graff Hotel. "Some people choose to have their wedding receptions here. Others prefer the casualness of a barn."

The look in his eyes, making her feel like the only woman on this planet, sent her heart hammering. "I, um, I'm not planning to get married anytime soon. I'm not even dating anyone."

And she wouldn't for a while. Her heart needed time to get over him.

"Remember I'm the Santa of What *Could* Be," he said. "Someday you will get married and have a family."

She should have known where they were heading when he led Arrow across the railroad tracks—the Marietta Regional Hospital. "Let me guess, this is where I'll have my babies."

His fake beard didn't hide his satisfied grin. "You're catching on."

Tears threatened. Rachel yearned for the life he talked about, the life that could be if she stayed, but she knew it wasn't possible. He was doing this to keep Ty at the Bar V5, not for her. "Nate—"

"Santa." He led Arrow back over the train tracks and down Front Avenue.

She inhaled then exhaled slowly. "Okay, Santa, this is sweet of you. You've put a lot of thought into this… tour, but—"

"One more stop." His pleading tone matched the look in his eyes.

"Fine."

She wanted to get this over with because knowing he'd gone to so much trouble for her was messing with her resolve to put him behind her. She'd never wanted to see him again, yet here she was spending Christmas morning with him. At this rate she'd be trying on wedding dresses at the shop they were passing before ringing in the New Year. She grimaced.

When would she ever learn?

Nate continued up Fourth Street and stopped at the elementary school. He helped her dismount.

"This is where you'll take your kids on the first day of kindergarten. You'll attend years of choir and band concerts, drama productions, science competitions, and sporting events. And one day, while you're sitting at the promotion ceremony sending the oldest off to middle school, you'll have tears in your eyes and wonder where the years went. But Nate will be right next to you, handing you a tissue. Maybe even a linen handkerchief like his dad used to carry."

Her eyes stung. She looked up. Blinked. Her heart couldn't take much more of this. "Nate…"

"I'm sorry, Rachel. I can apologize a million times and it won't be enough." He held her hand so tenderly she didn't dare pull away. "I can never take back hurting you, but I'll spend the rest of my life making sure it never happens again. I love you."

Love?

The air plunged from her lungs, leaving her gasping for a breath. She'd never hyperventilated before, but thought she might be close. She covered her pounding heart with her hand. His words tilted her world, turned her life upside down.

He loved her.

She opened her mouth then closed it, unable to speak.

"I spoke to Ty," Nate continued. "He's given us his approval, if you'll have me. Can you give me another chance? I don't care if you want to live in Marietta or Maine. I'll go wherever you want to go. The choice is yours. I just want to be with you."

Nothing was standing in their way. Nothing but…

Her.

Rachel didn't know what to say or do. She didn't trust others, but she didn't trust herself, either. That was her real problem, why she relied on her brother so much. Why she had wanted help from Pamela and Grayson in the first place. Why she accepted help from Nate.

Rachel rubbed her face, full of uncertainty and fear.

Nate had shown her what she could do on her own, but could she do this?

"I've always put the Bar V5 ahead of everything." Emotion sounded in his voice. "Not any more. You're first, Rachel. You'll always be first."

The decision was hers to make. Was she willing to trust herself, her heart?

MELISSA MCCLONE

Rachel thought about her brother, who was overprotective to the point of holding her back. He'd punched an ex-boyfriend. He'd done so many other things. Ty wasn't perfect, but he made sure she felt perfectly loved. Why was it easy for her to offer understanding and forgiveness to her brother but not the good man she'd fallen in love with?

Because she did love Nate. Loved him like family and nothing she'd ever known.

Why wouldn't she offer him another chance when the alternative was a life without Nate who believed in her, who made her believe in herself?

Live without him? No way.

Not without one more try.

Rachel heaved in a cold breath, enjoyed the way Santa's gaze flew to the way her parka hugged her chest.

Bad Santa.

Not really, but she found the courage she needed.

She took his hands and used them to steady her. "I love you, but I'm scared. Ty's always been straight with me. When our parents died, he didn't say they were gone or had passed. He told me a tractor-trailer driver who'd fallen asleep killed them. Said they'd died instantly, hadn't suffered, and our lives would never be the same. He was only eighteen at the time, but that kind of honesty gave me peace. Still does. I don't like guessing what you're up to, or if you've got a hidden agenda. That makes me nervous. Afraid to take a chance and jump. Doubt you."

"I get that, sweetheart. I truly do. I've never been in love, I know that now, and I didn't understand how badly the business model applies. Never again. I promise."

She laughed, cupped his face, pulled away the silly white beard. "Okay. That was a good one. I forgive you. And you've set the bar high for future apologies."

He kissed her, a kiss full of hope and love and possibility.

She tingled everywhere. The warmth of his lips set her on fire.

Nate caressed her cheek with his finger. "As long as there's a future for us, I'll make apologies my new best skill."

"Best skill?"

It was his turn to laugh. "Second best, then. After making

you feel happy and loved in every way I can imagine. And I'm an innovative guy."

"Wouldn't that be innovative *cowboy* given the hat you're wearing?"

"Just wait until you see this cowboy in action for real." He kissed her hard. "Ty's waiting for us at the Bar V5. He's got your Swedish Tea Ring ready to go in the oven. We'll save our private celebration for later."

Her spirit's soared. "You thought of everything."

"I want this to be a Christmas you'll remember."

She stared up at him, her heart overflowing with love. "Trust me, I'll never forget."

"Come on." He laced his fingers with hers and held onto the horse's reins. "Let's get Arrow into the trailer and go home."

"Home." She leaned against him, remembering the first time she'd driven down the world's longest driveway only a few weeks ago. "There's no place else I'd rather be."

For Christmas.

Forever.

The End

About the Author

Melissa McClone's degree in mechanical engineering from Stanford University led her to a job with a major airline where she travelled the globe and met her husband. But analyzing jet engine performance couldn't compete with her love of writing happily ever afters. Her first full-time writing endeavor was her first sale when she was pregnant with her first child! Since then, she has published over twenty-five romance novels with Harlequin and been nominated for Romance Writers of America's RITA award. When she isn't writing, she's usually driving her minivan to/from her children's swim and soccer practices, 4-H meetings and dog shows. She also supports deployed service members through Soldiers' Angels and fosters cats through a local non-kill rescue shelter. Melissa lives in the Pacific Northwest with her husband, three school-aged children, two spoiled Norwegian Elkhounds and cats who think they rule the house.

Thank you for reading
A Copper Mountain Christmas!

If you enjoyed this book, you can find more from all our great authors—including out rodeo anthology *Love Me, Cowboy*—at MontanaBornBooks.com, or from your favorite online retailer.

6661406R00188

Made in the USA
San Bernardino, CA
13 December 2013